FOUR SCOTTISH JOURNEYS

By the same author

Crossing the Shadow Line

FOUR SCOTTISH JOURNEYS

An Identity Rediscovered

ANDREW EAMES

Hodder & Stoughton
LONDON SYDNEY AUCKLAND TORONTO

British Library Cataloguing in Publication Data

Eames, Andrew
  Four Scottish journeys: An identity rediscovered.
  I. Title
  914.11

  ISBN 0-340-54157-1

First published in Great Britain 1991

Published by Hodder and Stoughton,
a division of Hodder and Stoughton Ltd,
Mill Road, Dunton Green, Sevenoaks, Kent TN13 2YA
Editorial Office: 47 Bedford Square, London WC1B 3DP

Photoset by Hewer Text Composition Services, Edinburgh

Printed in Great Britain by T. J. Press (Padstow) Ltd, Padstow, Cornwall

I shook him well from side to side,
Until his face was blue:
"Come tell me how you live," I cried,
"And what is it you do!"

Lewis Carroll, "The White Knight's Song"

Contents

Acknowledgments

Thanks are particularly due to Margaret Body, Julian and Jacintha Alexander, Jonathon Brown, John and Marie Christine Ridgway, my parents and my aunt Josephine, Tim and Pat Baker, the Mackinnons of Heaste, Malcolm Potier, Christopher Rathbone, Roger Banks, Dorothy Fleming, Nigel Abbott and Total Oil Marine, all of whom helped in many ways they will be aware of and in some ways they won't.

These chapters would have been empty without all those people in Scotland who willingly helped me on my way and showed me a piece of their mind and their world, many of whom will never know they earned themselves a starring role unless they get hold of a copy of this book.

Finally, my thanks to Susanne, my best critic, who provided the welcome voice of home.

AE

Winter – the West Highlands

Jimmy Morgan looked like something that the wind had loosely assembled out of scraps of heather and bits of bog cotton. His face came in patches, his beard in tufts, and his clothes were piebald with repairs and oil spills, all of which were the telltale signs of maintenance. The simple act of existing at Corrour required his twenty-four-hour, round-the-clock attention.

"Aye, I was in London last year," he was saying.

"Did you like it?"

He released his speech in shreds that were whipped jealously away by the wind or the turn of his head: "I couldnae get anyone ti gi' me directions. Naebody wuid stop. 'Excuse me, Jum,' I'd say, awfi' polite like, and whoosh – whey-face is off like a rockid looking straight aheid. 'Excuse me,' – whoosh. Thair ye go. That's London."

A metal slug of a train struggled over the Corrour summit and Jimmy straightened up to watch it approach his station, a bleak little oasis twenty-five miles by forest track from the nearest road. Corrour itself is not a pretty place. The two railway platforms are parked on the bog on a wide treeless plateau of nothing; it has no electricity, no water, and its nearest neighbours are a youth hostel (a mile away, open only in the summer months) and a hunting lodge (five miles away), but it does have four trains a day. A wheezing, grunting, arthritic exhaust pipe pumps out smoke from the side of the generator shed; chickens and geese rootle around half-heartedly in muddy pens behind the Morgans' house, which itself is squat, flat-roofed, ugly, and was built to last twenty years, fifteen years ago. On the wall is a satellite dish: Jimmy Morgan is an unlikely fan of American wrestling.

1

"Lucky you wirdna here last month. They stopped." Jimmy wielded his screwdriver in the direction of the two-coach ScotRail Sprinter.

"What, because of the rain?"

"Flooding. Five days wi'out trains, we wair." The Morgans – he was the ex-stationmaster – were the only people living at Corrour, but they could last all right; they'd plenty of food in the deep-freeze, but his point was that the new trains were inadequate for the job. Some while ago the papers had reported the story of how midges had stopped the train at Achna-shellach, on the Inverness to Kyle of Lochalsh line, when the heat of the rail had attracted the pests in massive quantities, so that where the gradient was steep the metal became too slippery to grip.

"They shuidae kaipt the steamies oan," Jimmy muttered.

With the new-fangled trains came a radio signalling system that eternally fell foul of the bad weather and the terrain, and which had put him out of a job.

"They shuidae mid that higher." Jimmy jabbed his screw-driver in the direction of the radio mast that stood beyond the now defunct signal box. The train was shunting backwards to get better reception: somewhere out there, floating in the airwaves, was a green-light instruction, if only it could be caught; perhaps it was too late – perhaps it had already dashed itself into demi-semi quavers on the mountains to the south. A couple of minutes later, after one more manoeuvre, the train caught its wave and disappeared, screeching across Rannoch Moor in the direction of Glasgow, leaving two crop-headed young men behind on the platform.

Only in the last couple of centuries has man tried to cross Rannoch Moor; prior to that most communication in the western Highlands was effected by sea. Rannoch is not a place made for human beings: the A82 nips across the western corner and dives hastily down into Glen Coe, and the West Highland railway struggles gamely over the centre, following the old West Highland Way along which the cattle drovers used to drive their herds to market. The Morgans are one of only half a dozen households in sixty square miles; others have tried to live there in search of a greater purity in their lives, but have been routed. Rannoch is the sort of place which will measure

2

the depth of your soul and hold the unflattering result up to your face. The land itself is the dominant personality in life here, the inevitable third party in any conversation and the main factor in any plans. Those who live on its surface have learned to accept it.

I've crossed Rannoch Moor sometimes twice, sometimes four and sometimes six times a year on the way to the island of Skye. The weather is always a feature of those crossings. Often it rains, and over the years I have come to see the moor, one of the western world's last wildernesses, as a kind of soggy hand-kerchief of land spread between the mountains. It's a sea of land. The Atlantic weather, which has its throat tickled by the peaks around Glen Coe to the west, blows its nose endlessly in the bogs of Rannoch. The weather bowls across this water-logged and windblown wilderness from end to end and the seasons only effect minimal changes on the monochromatic colour scheme: dun is the bedrock of all colour on Rannoch, dun with a touch of purple heather, dun with a touch of green grass, dun with a touch of white snow and white with a touch of dun when the snow lies deep.

I have yet to see a photograph which has captured its strength. The simple features of this wilderness are too subtle for cameras and film, which cannot properly record the colours of dead heather and dying bog cotton, and omits the atmos-phere of old peat cuttings and the agony of sinking wet-footed into treacherous ground. The place is at its best when it scowls. They say that in winter, when the moorland freezes the soggy handkerchief solid, you can ice-skate from one end to the other. The winter daylight arrives slowly here, like the last squeezings out of an old tube, and there's not much of it when it comes. The weather changes hourly, sometimes sucking away the desiccated light quite suddenly, replacing it with filth. It's night at two o'clock, but morning again at three. The weather can readily make winter out of summer.

On every journey I've made back into Scotland a sense of arrival usually crops up somewhere en route. It is the equivalent of the lurch of recognition that the body makes when someone familiar but long unseen comes into the room; it is a physical sensation, not a rational one. The brain may not be able to recall that person's name or the circumstances of first meeting but the body knows fully well that the familiarity exists; in most social situations the brain rules, however, and it won't be until it has actually sorted out the circumstances of previous acquaintance, dusted them down, and given the person a name, that it will allow acknowledgment and conversation.

So it is with Scotland. A sense of familiarity exists between Scotland and me, but I've never searched out the circumstances and dusted them down. I hadn't examined my relationship with Scotland rationally and logically enough to be able to name it and define it. Family links – Scotland was my grandfather's country – are strong enough to allow me some claim to Scottish descent, but I have never lived anywhere but south, so why that constant sense of familiarity? Is a family background alone enough to explain that sense of arrival? As with the unidentified person in the crowded room, my mind has never really known what it was that I was feeling familiar with.

At the end of winter I began to ponder this unresolved acquaintance more deeply. International sport tests any displaced person's sense of allegiance, and the rugby internationals of England, Scotland, Wales, Ireland and France have a remarkable polarising effect. In years of swilling around in the stomach of England, Scottishness seemed to me to be a sense of identity worth hanging on to, like a strap in a swaying crowded Underground train, and this sense of identity emerged most strongly when Scotland played England, and I was forced to choose between the two. But wasn't my sense of allegiance a little absurd, I asked myself as the Piccadilly line thundered on, reading someone's sporting headlines through a thick crowd of commuters. Why should I feel elation that Scotland had just won the Grand Slam, when all I knew of Scotland was the familiar territory of the family pilgrimages to Skye?

Right at that very moment it didn't occur to me that I should actually go to Scotland and have a good look round in order to try to define why it was such a familiar piece of land. Instead, I turned to books. Several months later I was still dissatisfied, for although there were reams of published material about Scotland, it seemed that very few writers had reached the top of a Scottish hill, looked down on the other side and seen what was actually there. Most had seen a combination of what used to be there, together with what they thought the reader would like to see. Their landscape was of crofters wearing tartan, cooking grouse, drinking whisky and playing the bagpipes, in a perpetual atmosphere of hardy merriment spiced with courageous foolhardiness. What is worst, they didn't give the country a present – and when a country itself makes a business out of people who come to it for its romanticised past, it too begins to despair of its present.

Somewhere in the autumn I decided that the only thing for it was to go and have a look myself. I settled on the idea of four seasonal journeys to four different regions – to the west, to the Lowlands, to the east and to the islands – with an itinerary which would be guided entirely by circumstances. I suppose, in truth, it was guilt – and my grandfather – who packed my bags.

II

So it was that I ended up on Rannoch Moor in winter, gathering together my belongings in the signal box at Corrour, while outside the steamed-up windows the clouds were weeping gently in the interval between one rainstorm and another; I re-wiped a window, heavy with condensation, to peer out at the sombre landscape, blotched with white. The snow of a week ago was fast melting in unusually warm weather for the time of year. Spumes of peat-dark water were bounding down the hillside and Jimmy Morgan had started to wrestle with a split pipe to try to coax some of it to come out of the tap.

It has some international notoriety, this station, being probably the remotest in Europe. Its isolation has allowed the media to take some liberties with the truth to perpetuate the romantic image of the Highlands. A German film crew turned up one year, took some dreary footage and mixed it with pictures from the railway station at Dingwall, near Inverness, which is altogether prettier. The following year a constant stream of German tourists got off at Corrour looking for hanging flower-baskets and tea-rooms. As Jimmy Morgan no doubt told them, the closest Corrour gets to a tea-room is a tap of mountain water on the platform.

In the bunk-room – once the peewee or permanent-way men's tea-room under the signal box – a squad of German students were saddling up. Three out of four had been in Frankfurt only the previous morning and they looked as if they were feeling the culture shock. They weren't enthusiastic about the clemency of the weather or the quality of the accommodation; perhaps they too had seen the film with the flower-baskets and tea-rooms. Sharing a room with them had provided a new experience for me: it was the first time in a climbers' bunk-room that I'd seen people put on pyjamas before getting into their sleeping-bags.

For a couple of minutes that morning there was a rare small crowd on platform one, consisting of the four Germans, the two crop-headed young men who'd got off the earlier train and who were still there, tightening their boots and studying their maps, and me. We all milled around like a small herd of cattle, happy for a couple of moments of tacit companionship. Then we all left at much the same time: the Germans crunched off over the gravel towards Ben Nevis, a benevolent mountain which has nevertheless claimed more lives than the North Face of the Eiger. The crop-headed young men hit the track towards Loch Ossian, jingling hard.

Glasgow had been full of such striding men, striding up Sauchiehall Street and striding in and out of equipment shops, pounding the pavements and preparing to toughen their bodies up on the moors and mountains, like blades on a whetstone. That's what all those Skye holidays had been about for me; the clean air, the mountains and the sea worked together as a whetstone on the soul. Scotland had always been a purifier.

The twosome could have been SAS – Jimmy Morgan had said that SAS regularly trained on these hills, filling their packs with logs and jogging through the peat bogs. He wouldn't agree that they were fitter or stronger than him – only younger. Young in the body and young in the head. I drifted along slowly in their wake, painfully aware that with my small, bright blue pack, and with neither rope nor crampons, I had barely merited a grunt of recognition.

We weren't alone in the shallow valley. Deer come low in the winter, their hides the colour of old, cold tea, and two stags were grazing fifty yards from the path, too weak to run. I searched the grubby face of the moor for other signs of life, of health, but it looked as if the winter had won, had killed everything except us five: me, the two deer and the SAS. Waterfalls on the distant mountains towards Glencoe hung like old and fraying white rope. The increasingly popular sport of winter climbing had been taking its toll. A Scottish wag had described it as the nation's gradual revenge for Culloden, because so many Englishmen killed themselves on the winter mountains: an average year claims 150 casualties of whom around twenty-five die. There'd been a report of the death of an experienced climber in Glencoe's local paper that week. He'd reached a safe ledge and put down his pack, but the pack had toppled, and a trailing strap had tripped him. The 250-foot fall had "grazed off" half his face, said the newspaper. "Grazed" is an innocent word in most contexts, but having one's face grazed off while sliding down a mountain is a nasty way to go.

I stopped to listen for any sounds of life or death – perhaps even the shriek of a distant falling climber or the bellowing of the mountain rescue team. The drizzle had stopped and the moor was very still, but in the stillness the mountains were surprisingly noisy. The further ones shushed like a distant beach, the nearest murmuring loudly, like the traffic zooming around Piccadilly Circus heard from Hyde Park. Closer to hand a couple of birds were singing; bird-watching was more a question of bird-hearing on Rannoch. But the SAS took no notice of birds or deer, and by the time I had dawdled down to the shore of Loch Ossian the crop-headed striders were nearly at the top of their first mountain, a long, long way away.

The loch lies in the small of Rannoch's back between two shoulders of mountains. At the far end is the shooting lodge, once a grand three-storey granite residence with a staff of forty, including fourteen under-stalkers and six under-gardeners, in the era (still a reality for some) when the Highlands was regarded as a huge game larder covered in fences. The railway station was originally built to cater for the lodge's visitors, who were taken from the station to the lochside in a coach and horses and transferred to a forty-foot steamer which took them down to the lodge in comfort. Every Sunday the minister from Tulloch came up in the train to take the morning service for the gentry, and every day of the season the trains brought in new supplies and carried away the venison. Then everything changed with the war; all except the chapel burnt down in an accidental fire in 1942. The lodge was replaced by a modest building in the style of a Swiss chalet and the steamer was dismantled and moved elsewhere. The last of the jetty has finally fallen apart, but the wooden receiving house where the eminent visitors used to tranship from carriage to steamer is still on the water's edge.

In the winter it has one inhabitant; he was standing outside it emptying a teapot.

"Are you Tom Rigg?" I called when I'd got within hailing distance.

"Ay."

I realised, with momentary disappointment, that he had a Yorkshire accent, something I'd not appreciated when I'd spoken to him on the telephone. His was one of those calls that had left me tingling, and he had a dialling code which was twice the length of the rest of the number. Rigg had picked up the phone but there had been a pause before he'd said anything at all. It reminded me of a story of my mother's about how her Aunt Christina, who spoke more Gaelic than English, had dealt with the telephone on a rare visit to England. My mother, who knew that her parents were out, telephoned Christina from the station to say she was coming home. The phone had rung and rung and rung, until finally the receiver was lifted. After a very long pause, during which my mother repeated, "Aunt Christina – it's me," several times, a thin nervous voice spoke somewhere into the air by the mouthpiece. 'There's noo-body here chust now," it said, and the receiver was replaced.

"The hostel is closed," was what Rigg had said into the phone after his long pause, but I'd hastily explained that I didn't want to stay – I wanted to see him.

"Have you had a good winter?"

"Ay, not bad." Now that I'd identified it, his Yorkshire accent was so broad, landing with a crump on the last syllable of every other word, that I couldn't believe that I had missed it before. I followed him into the hostel, a wooden building which was described as "simple" in the Youth Hostels handbook.

"Windy, it's bin windy. Do you want some tea?"

He gave me a little tour: the men's dormitory, the women's dormitory, the washrooms and the living-room. He'd lived there all year round for eighteen years, in isolation rare for anyone anywhere in the world. Not that he was alone in his isolation: only six people lived on the eighty-one-square-mile Corrour estate. It wasn't the place for people who got lonely, said Rigg. A young couple had recently come and gone; he'd wanted to be a writer and she'd had plans to dig things out of the moor that she could sell as art. They'd lasted six weeks and no more.

The water drummed into the kettle, a distinctly urban sound. "The loneliness is nothing to do with the environment," explained Rigg, reaching for the matches. "It's more to do with the person. Someone in a town can be more lonely than here. I tell you what I do miss about this place, though, and that's the telly. The only times I've done relief work at other places I have enjoyed watching the telly more than I can say. I think it's just the laying back and being entertained that appeals."

Over tea I mentioned I'd just been on a poll tax march in Glasgow.

"I pay poll tax: £236 for no facilities at all." He studied my face. "No dustbin collection, no electricity, nothing. They generously let me off £20 because I get my own water in buckets from the lake." I noticed he didn't say loch.

"Doesn't it freeze?"

"Ay, certainly it does, ay. Certainly." It took me a while to get used to Rigg's pauses, learning to wait for some visual sign that all the thought had arrived and been expressed, laid out neatly like a dish in an hors d'oeuvre, and that I was clear to proceed to sample it. Rigg was preparing a whole buffet supper of thoughts.

"But for the last three winters it hasn't. When it freezes you can walk down it or ski down the centre of it." He paused again, this time for considerably longer. It was as if a third party was in the conversation, someone whose contribution I could not hear. It was as if he was leaving a silence for the land to speak.

"We had an accident here in one of those cold winters. Lad was down by the water, slipped and fell through the ice and was killed."

I said I was sorry, but Rigg was quite matter-of-fact about it; I remember thinking then that living by oneself on the edge of civilisation must mean that one became more hardened to these things, but I learned much later that he had been very, very upset.

"I heard that you run some sort of round the loch competition."

Rigg grinned. "Ay. Here." He showed me a list pinned to the wall. "If you can run round the loch in under an hour your name will be number 436. Six out of seven don't make it. It's not easy."

"Can you still do it?" At a guess I'd say he was approaching his sixties.

"I've injured my knee."

He'd started the club in 1977. At the time he was very fit from hill-walking and deerstalking, which he combined with his hostel responsibilities. Four young hostel guests had had a race around the loch one day, and it was their boasting that night that challenged him; the following day he ran round the loch in fifty-nine minutes, never having run before.

"There have bin others like me, ay," he said. "One of the other stalkers from the lodge went round it in fifty-six minutes in his hobnailed boots. In his hobnailed boots, mind. I was behind him, and I can tell you that sparks were flying from the stones."

I mentioned that someone had told me that Rigg had his own secret technique for the round-Ossian run. He knew where to put his every footstep so that it rested on solid ground.

"Whichever way you do it it's still 7.5 miles," he replied seriously, as if I'd accused him of cheating. "Ay, I suppose I know it better than anyone else. And I've painted discreet little numbers on the rocks so I can pace myself exactly. And that helps."

"Do you get the SAS doing the run?" My mind was with the crop-headed young men.

"Mebbe. Not that they'd normally let on they were SAS. We used to have a regular here, mind, the Major. He'd always arrive in full SAS gear." Rigg should have had a pipe to pull on between pauses. "Ay, he was a character. He'd take out the young Germans staying here and give 'em stabbing instruction. One day he took a hammer and chisel up into the hills and carved the names of his dead colleagues on a rock. Wouldn't tell me which rock, but said I'd come across it one day and only I would know what it meant. He was a bit like that, the Major."

From speculating quite where the engraved rock might be, his conversation wandered around the mountain tops and on to the supernatural. In his slow deliberate way he filled my head full of stories of a poltergeist that lifted packets of digestive biscuits, of the power of a rock called the Witch's Chair where the old laird would go to sit when his deerstalking was going badly, and of the witch herself, whom the head gamekeeper had once seen flying horizontally through the Land-Rover's headlights. The witch played games with the men who lived on Rannoch, he said. One wild day one of his own sheds had taken off, he said, and flown over his motorcycle; as it did so the door opened and a can of creosote fell out – and if I didn't believe it I should look out for his creosote-covered bike, which was up by the station.

I did, and it was, and I still don't believe it.

III

Oxford won the Boat Race while I was walking the five miles between Corrour Station and Ken Smith's place. I listened to the commentary on my small personal stereo, wondering why such an uninspiring event deserved so much coverage. The previous year I'd been on Mount Snowdon on Boat Race day, taking my place in the queue of walkers on the way up to the summit. It had started to snow at the top so we decided to descend via the Snowdon mountain railway. The railway was running, and there, in the top shed, three Welsh shepherds were watching the Boat Race on a little black and white portable TV that one of them had carried up the mountain for the occasion, discussing the race in Welsh. I can only think they must have had some money on the result.

This Boat Race day my route lay partly along the West Highland Way and for a while kept to a well-trodden track which seemed to hold straight towards the mountains festooned with frayed rope which surrounded Rannoch Moor. Where the path dived to the west towards Fort William I abandoned it to its own devices and held on to my own course, toiling sweatily alongside the railway line, my ankles suffering from the eternal gradient. We descended slowly, the railway line and I, to the shores of a loch on the northern edge of the moor which penetrated through the ring of mountains to the outside world. Wherever I looked, there was a view, 360 degrees' worth of view on a scale that would readily show up the inadequacy of any camera; in most landscapes the camera lens's ability to select a portion of a scene enhances the final picture. In Scotland, selection of a portion of the view simply means that some of the magnificence is lost. A camera cannot match Scotland's scale.

Smith lived in the midst of all this, in a log cabin in the middle of a small fir wood on the shore of the loch. Rigg had said he would be friendly, but as the wood came into sight I began to get nervous. A man could well be jealous of his privacy, five miles from anywhere, and there was no telling what he might do to unannounced intruders, any more than there was any telling what living out in that welter of moorland had done to him.

In fact Ken Smith had had more visitors that day than he'd had for a month, and he was delighted to see me, no matter that he'd no idea who I was. I only succeeded in finding his cabin, on the shores of the loch, because recent gales had turned the wood into a pile of mangled firs, making travel laboriously hard but at least allowing me to see what lay ahead. I clambered over the fallen giants down the slope above his log cabin, whistling anxiously and tunelessly to betray my presence and to avoid any nasty surprises. There were no surprises. He was just having a cup of tea with a friend, he said. It could have been a Saturday afternoon in Surbiton.

If he hadn't given off a distinctly human smell I might have been inclined to believe him to be one of those Rannoch manifestations that Tom Rigg had been going on about. His name sounded like a bad alias, for a start. He was slight, pigeon-toed, effusive, bearded and with bits of fern in his hair. And he was not Scottish, either, not by a long way. His accent was thick Derbyshire of a real ee-by-gum variety, and he'd built the cabin where he had, he said, because the fir wood in which it stood was in a "nice vast wilderness" which was "just like t' Yukon"; to him, the wilderness was intimate, even cosy.

"Mind your feet," he said. "Bluidy pine-marten's bin doin its business behind t' door."

Inside the cabin his wood-burning stove was as excited as its owner. The place looked and felt like a sauna, the log walls bulging with old coats and the hard earth floor covered in chippings. Hanging from the ceiling was a sack of two years' worth of Cadbury's Smash instant potato powder, the departing gift of a previous visitor.

Alec, a retired stalker with plus fours and no teeth, was showing Ken how to assemble a tilly lamp. "I use fat, you see," Ken explained, pointing to a couple of mutilated tin cans nailed strategically to the wall. "If I cooks sausages fer dinner I saves t' fat and puts t' fat in them cans, stick in a bit of cloth and that's enough light fer me. But smoky, like. This will be much better." He rattled the lamp.

Nailed to the wall were lists, calendars, pikes' jaws and a yellowed Vernons' pools coupon which had once won him £360 – probably the only bit of genuine luck in his life. The list titled "Mice so far" had reached corpse number 314 and he'd hauled a running total of 121.5 pounds of pike out of the loch. On the joke list his latest entry was "Red sky at night means the sheep are on fire."

"What about 'Red sky at night means the shepherd's cottage is on fire'?" I suggested, once Alec had pronounced the tilly lamp ready to go and shambled off down the hill towards Tulloch. I think he'd been rather embarrassed to meet a stranger without his teeth in, otherwise he'd have stayed longer.

"And red sky in the morning means no one's put it out yet."

"Oh ay, that's a good 'un." Ken added it carefully to his list. On the calendar he kept a brief account of the main events of every day. "I keep a diary, too, and I've written 2,316 pages in't since I left home." Statistics anchored his life: the hundredweights of gravel moved to make a suburban-style patio – without a doubt the only patio on Rannoch Moor – outside his front door, the tons of logs cut, the extra mice killed, the pages of diary filled, these were progress. Living as he did in isolation, the steady clocking up of more of this, that and the other was satisfying. His statistics connected his present actions with those of his past and his future. He knew exactly where he was: he was 314 mice, 121.5 pounds of pike and 2,316 pages of diary into his life. They told him he existed; this was the real importance of history.

13

He explained how he'd arrived in that lonely spot with little prompting. "I used to work in't building trade doing flooring, travelling all around the major cities. Bluidy murder, it were. So I went to't Yukon for two years, travelled 22,000 miles. While I were away, me parents died. Me brothers met me off't plane when I coom back; me parents had only lived in a council house in Derbyshire so I'd nowhere to live anyway. So I buggered off with a pack up here, living rough fer a couple of year."

I'd heard some of the rest of the story from other sources: Ken had squatted for two years in a bothy in the middle of nowhere, with nothing to occupy him other than the need for wood for the fire and food for his belly. For a while he'd been unpopular with the locals. He'd written to Lord Macdonald asking permission to build his own log cabin in a small fir wood on the lochside. Two years later Macdonald had given him that permission and he'd started to build the log cabin with techniques that he'd learned in the Yukon.

It had withstood a fair beating already. His entry on the calendar for 13th February read: "Fled cabin at 8 p.m. as falling tree hit roof in."

"Oh ay, it was that bad. Black Monday, I call it. Thirty-two trees within a fifty-foot radius of t' cabin coom down. I was awake for forty-two hours and more frightened than I've ever been in me life. There was nowhere to shelter, you see."

He took me outside. The wood had been completely skittled and he'd built little crutches for those trees which still stood, so that if they ever did fall, they would miss his cabin.

"This is me bath." The tub was upside down under the eaves. "When it's finished it'll be over there with t' fire underneath it. You fill the bath, light t' fire and hop in when it's ready. We used to do it like that in t' Yukon."

"What about the midges?"

"Bog myrtle. You rub it on."

"Where did you get the tub from?"

"Estate. Seven months in't year I work on t' estate at Ossian. Most of this stuff coom down from oop there. Ten mile it is. I walked ten mile carrying that cast-iron bedstead in t' back room. It's unbelievable how much I can walk. The shop and the post office is seventeen mile each way, although you hit t' road after six. That's why I started making my own wine. I got fed

14

oop with carrying bluidy cans and bottles backwards and forrards."

Behind the door in the main room he had plastic tubs covered with labels. Tea wine, coffee wine, nettle wine, oak leaf wine, heather wine, birch sap wine – he made wine from anything that was in bloom at the time, although the birch sap wine was best, he said.

For seven months he only visited his cabin at weekends, living for the rest of the time at the Loch Ossian estate. Up there he worked as a pony-man, a gillie, trailing around the hills with a pony a mile distant from the "toff" – he who pays to be manoeuvred into position to shoot an unsuspecting stag – and the stalker. Bringing home the dead carcass was a job that not many people wanted. You have to know the hills like the back of your hand, to sit alone for hours in the drizzle until called.

"Coom out t' rowan tree, they say. Or coom out t' witches chair. You have to know what they mean. But it's all right. I was glad to get a job. They want me oop there all year, but I've built me cabin and I want to live here, so I go back on t' dole when the season's finished. Pick up me moncy at the post office – there's no post oop here."

As I prepared to leave he became a bit more pensive, perhaps because of my questioning and perhaps because it would be a matter of weeks before the next visitor. He bashed his transistor radio against the wall – it was the only way of getting it to work. "I like to hear what's going on in t' world. Always buy a newspaper in town. It's a while since I watched the telly; they've got loads of channels now, and I haven't seen owt of them. Still, I never get bored here because there's so much to do. Of course I'm stuck now. I'll never get enough money to get out of this. Sometimes I sit looking out t' window and imagine someone like me in t' city watching the cars go by, and then I think to myself, "What's better than a pine marten knocking at your door?"

In the gloom of the late afternoon I stumbled northwards along the shore of the loch, fleeing through the outer walls of Rannoch Moor, pursued by the arrival of night, which I didn't want to face alone. Ken Smith had given me directions to Nancy's place, but I was upon it before I'd even realised. Suddenly the loch ended in a dam, the land dipped and I fell in

15

amongst a burst of fertility that seemed like paradise after the sterility of the moorland. The river that descended through this valley went past Nancy's back door, said Ken. He regarded it as civilisation, but although there were half a dozen houses connected by a track, the nearest road was still a matter of four or five miles, and the main neighbours were the lochs, the moor, the mountains and the weather.

Nancy lived in a clearing in a tangle of woodland in a wooden hut with hobo's chimneys that smeared heavy smoke over the wet air. Everything was dripping, even though it wasn't actually raining. Nancy's place is a hostel known only by connoisseurs of the remote; it has no sign, appears only rarely in hostel literature and is at the end of a difficult track. With Ken Smith's log cabin it makes a strange pair, the hostel's appearance being more suited to a Florida everglade than the damp of Fersit. Wherever you turned there was a notice; notices kept the place running. Notices about shutting the gates, about not digging for worms in the garden, about people sleeping in vans, about ferrying wood, about dogs, about trains and keeping off the line, about where to empty the Elsan, about not peeing in the woods, etc, etc. The hostel ran itself partly on these notices, particularly when Nancy, a quiet, composed woman in her sixties, disappeared off on her travels – she'd also been to the Yukon, twice – leaving the doors open. You couldn't run an isolated hostel that kept shutting down, she said, particularly when there's no phone to check beforehand. She'd once left a note in a hut on a Turkish mountain, announcing the existence of her hostel. When she got back to Fersit she found a new note waiting for her: "Saw your note on a Turkish mountain . . ." it began.

She was there that night, unalarmed by my staggering out of the bushes by the river. No, she said, mildly, she had nobody else in, but you never knew. Nancy was the sort of person who took nothing for granted and was never drawn to make generalisations about life. People arrived at all hours from all quarters, whatever the season, she said. Sometimes she went to bed at night with no one in, to wake up in the morning to find the place full and breakfast – in these places every meal is a close relative of breakfast – under way. Although she lived in her rooms in the main building, she slept in a hut on the other side of the small garden because she'd outgrown the midnight parties and the all-night guitar sessions that enthusiasts for lonely hostels indulge in. The only way of securing her sleep had been to move out at night. If I wanted her in the morning, she said, that was where she would be, and she emphasised that she wasn't all that keen on getting up early.

The building had originally been erected hastily as one of several temporary bunkhouses for the men working on the Loch Treig hydro-electric scheme, and had been much patched since then. It had probably never been anything more distinguished than simply ramshackle. Architecture hadn't featured in the minds of its builders; given enough nails, planks and doors I could probably come up with much the same result. Nevertheless it had stood for fifty or sixty years and with regular waterproofing still kept the rain out. A touch of colour had been added by strings of beer-can ring-pulls, strung together across the ceiling to make festive chains, and a wood-burning stove kept it cosy.

The original men who'd erected the hut had played a part in a massive feat of engineering which has since been almost entirely concealed by the forces of nature. There had once been seven main sheds in this lonely place capable of accommodating 650 men, a large yard and a railway terminus. Starting in 1924 the men had built fifteen miles of fourteen-foot-diameter underground tunnel from Loch Treig down to the aluminium smelter in Fort William, drilling through the hip of Ben Nevis, working a fifty-four-hour week at a pay rate of 12d per hour. Eight hundred and sixty million gallons of water move along this tunnel every day, emerging above Fort William at a sort of concrete belly-button in the mountain flank.

In order to complete the tunnel, the men had built twenty miles of light railway that zigzagged around the mountainside. A train that left Fort William on this narrow-gauge track in the morning took four to five hours to reach Fersit because it had to stop at all the various camps (the tunnel was dug from twenty-three separate working faces for extra speed) en route, with supplies and post. The construction stories were numerous: there'd been an illegal still down one of the shafts, the trains had been regularly derailed (one plunged into Loch Treig itself) and four men had been killed. The quality of the track-laying had been poor, and the bridges (many are still intact, with their rails) became so weak that the driver would send his mate to walk the bridge first, then set the train in motion in low gear and walk over himself in its wake. The railway remained in place and continued to be used for maintenance and for bringing down bodies of climbers in accidents on Ben Nevis until the 1950s; these days maintenance on the tunnel is carried out by Land-Rover and very little evidence remains of so many years of work.

My white skin gleamed in the dark as I stripped off on the banks of the river to wash – the alternative was a pump in the kitchen. Reflecting that I was fortunate that it was too early in the year for midges, I stood in the snowmelt water, so cold that it made my teeth ache, and washed myself down with Paco Rabanne skin care cream – I'd forgotten my soap. Back in the hostel, smelling expensive, I settled into my bunk with the guest book, which read like a comic with the exploits of Festering Dave, Atomic Heather and Mogadon Maclean ("the only man to go up Chno Dearg with a shit bucket for company – something went wrong with his navigation on the way to the dump"), who were regular visitors. "I'm glad I'm not here this weekend when both Fiona and Heather are here," Dave had written. (Nancy had apparently gone off hitch-hiking with her grandson.) Underneath, Fiona had added, "Thank God I missed the braying bothyman Festering Dave McFadzean. If I hear him sing 'lonely in the bothy' once more . . ."

IV

I caught the early train – a two-coach Sprinter – well before light the following morning. Judging by our unchecked progress the radio waves were obviously threading through the eye of the mountains more smoothly than usual.

The Sprinter screeched back over the gloomy face of Rannoch, a tube of light, heat, cigarette smoke, upholstery, perfume and instant coffee which passed by the still lives of Ken Smith adding to his tally of mice, Tom Rigg contemplating where the SAS Major's rock might be and Jimmy Morgan cursing his leaking pipes, each looking up for a moment to chart the progress of the distant eyebrow of light across the forehead of the moor. They none of them seemed lonely; all of them seemed to have an intimate relationship with the land.

Inside the train were not just a couple of dozen semi-awake bodies and their smells, a tube of instant civilisation, shuttling between the cities, shunning the more elemental world that lay between. If you were to take those passengers out of that tube and sprinkle them like sweets over the moor, their pride, their prejudices, their assumed personae and even their major motivations in life would count for nothing. Instead of measuring themselves off other people, they would have to rebuild themselves, reassessing their priorities in relation to trees, to water, to wildlife, and to the number of mice they could catch per week.

It was light by the time the train reached Tyndrum, but the drizzle had descended on the hills like a curtain. Tyndrum is a small cocktail of mismatched establishments lodged at various points around road and rail junctions: a petrol station, a couple of tour bus hotels, a couple of cafés, a small housing estate of bungalows, a handful of shops and two railway stations, all spread thinly as if to demarcate the outer limits of a planned town whose centre had never been built. The Little Chef was doing a steady breakfast trade and the windows of the Royal Hotel dining-room were steamed up with the tea-laden breath of three coach parties; tea that had been nurtured and picked in hot Indian hills was being consumed in great quantities in that brown and wet moorland.

The dingiest of the three roadside cafés had a sign that said Home Baking on the outside. Inside three local lorry drivers who looked as if they'd slept in their clothes were commiserating each other on the size of their hangovers. A boy at the counter, presumably filling his holidays with £1.50 per hour, stood poised with his pen on his order pad. Radio One echoed out of the kitchen behind him, drowning the skirl of bagpipes and the songs about lochs, laddies and long-lost ones playing on the café's sound system.

"I want some home baking," I said. "For breakfast."

"Weel, we've mince, or they wee yins wi' cherries in it." He pointed cautiously to two tired-looking pies sitting alone in a big perspex cabinet.

"I'll have some of the mince."

The boy carefully wrote 'Mice pie' on his pad and disappeared into the kitchen. Perhaps this was where Ken Smith found a market for his 314 executed mice so far.

The train to Oban was fuller, but not as full as someone had hoped: most of the seats were reserved, but only about twenty of the party had turned up. They were American journalists, mostly well-preened middle-aged ladies, hosted by a dour lady from the tourist board. They stared disbelievingly out of the window at the passing scenery; a dead sheep in a scuff of wool that had fallen off it like the peel of an overripe fruit, the bones of a shed blown apart by the wind and seven horses standing in a quagmire at the foot of a hill. This was not the Scotland of blue skies and dreamy castles they'd seen in the books. My newspaper reported that there had been eighty-nine consecutive days of rain at Loch Linnhe since 24th December, and that a forty-seven-year-old climber had died on Glen Coe the previous day; if the day had been still, I might have heard his dying cry on Rannoch.

As these dismal scenes unfolded, the Americans looked more and more depressed; what could they write for their readers? Why should people ever want to come *on holiday* to a desert which their forebears had obviously left for such good reasons? But the tourist board knew what was expected of it: a young bagpiper – I hadn't seen one since the previous summer in Leicester Square – met the train as it drew into the quayside station at Oban, his kilt whipping erotically around his thighs in the cold northerly wind. The well-preened ladies poured out excitedly on to the platform to surround him and the piper flirted vigorously between reels.

Next to the quay a middle-aged trawlerman with a nicotine-stained beard and an oily boiler suit was guiding winch cables down through the hatch to the fishboxes in the hold. He stopped to stare at the excited ladies, a splash of quite savage colour in an otherwise steel-grey townscape. "Lookit that, Hughie," he called over to the winch operator, who'd also stopped work to watch. "Ah dinna know aboot you. But when tha's bin four days at sea, ahm thinking ahm aboot ready for a gangbang mesel."

Oban is a bit like an overgrown Scottish version of a Cornish village, shoehorned into a small bay, with the fishing industry on the seafront backed by small Victorian hotels and narrow terraces that crawl up the hills. The seafront is an odd confection made up of the fishing industry, the car ferry harbour, the Oban distillery, the railway station, the promenade of a seaside resort and the facilities of a major shopping centre, all in one small bay. Being the first major town on the west coast and the easiest access point for the outer isles, it has the bustle of a frontier town. The people in Oban very rarely belong to Oban. Many are visitors from small and isolated island communities who wander, wide-eyed, down the lines of shops and listen furtively to the funny accents of the tourists. Frontier towns around the world are the same: the Sudanese, dark-skinned and shy in the Egyptian town of Aswan, stare at the tourists; the Burmese in the Northern Thai town of Chiang Mai riveted by their first shop-window glimpses of western technology. On that winter's day a large proportion of people in Oban town centre had rucksacks, and judging by the way in which they hovered around the Jobcentre window, not many of them were tourists.

The town is capped by an absurd crown, McCaig's Folly, an imitation of the Colosseum built in the 1890s to provide work for the locals, but never finished. Even today the work situation has not improved: the Jobcentre was full of advertisements for live-in maids and bar staff for a salary of around £60 per week, all to start at Easter. Until then there was little on offer apart from tree planting on Mull (around £40 a day, and very hard on the skin) or working in a mussel farm for £130 a week – but the mussel farm was in Sutherland, and who wanted to go to Sutherland, said the girl behind the desk. It was people from the outlying areas such as Sutherland and the islands who came to Oban, hoping to move into the mainstream, not the other way around.

I hung around with the men with rucksacks. The well-preened American ladies had disappeared into the grandest of the seafront hotels, for a lunch which was bound to involve haggis or oats or herring, and probably all three. A fishy smell was hovering around the Oban public conveniences. In the shed next door a man in wellington boots was packing prawns and scallops for France. I'd heard rumours about Oban and fishermen and drug-running. Customs and Excise recovered a shipment of eighteen tons of cannabis here in the 1980s. More recently, bales of marijuana had been washed up on the shores of Mull, and the islanders had fed it to their chickens for some weeks before someone realised that it wasn't the usual sort of grass and it was making their chickens forgetful of the need to lay eggs. Oban has its dubious side: rumours of rampant freemasonry, of aristocrats with a penchant for making swift money, of fishermen with outside interests, are common. Border towns attract such things. So not wanting to appear too inquisitive I asked the fisherman next to the gents where I could find the post office. From there we moved gracefully on to the subject of the fishing season.

"Diabolical, it's been so far," he said. "It's the weather. This is the first decent load we've had."

It had started to rain. With the full force of the wind behind them the raindrops were winging their way in over the bay and crashing into the shop-windows. Only a handful of fishing boats were banging against the quay. I ventured that Oban didn't seem to me a very sheltered port.

"Bloody useless. That's why there are no boats here any more," said the fisherman. "The fishermen's mission there. The missionary's gone and they're converting the building into a restaurant."

I said I'd noticed all the fish and chip shops and pizza places seemed to be owned by Italians.

"Oh yes, we've got Dante's and Luigi's up there, Mario's round the corner. And there's another place called Onorio's opened up. It's all the same family, but they don't all talk to each other." I added the mafia to my mental list of organisations operating in Oban.

Somewhere a phone rang. The man was already past me out of the door. Wiping his hands on his overalls, he reached inside a sparkling new black BMW parked outside and pulled out the car phone. Suddenly I felt somehow let down by all this talk of bad seasons and poor catches, but then I'd never met an optimistic fisherman.

I left Oban that afternoon in a bus littered with old cigarette ends which headed north along the coast. "I've got the wirld cup, but I'm no going tae swap it wi' you," declared an eight-year-old sitting in front of me. The bus emptied at the first housing estate out of town and I thumbed a lift north.

V

"Mrs Campbell takes in drivers," said a man washing an empty shop-window in Dingwall's High Street. It was a bright, sharp evening, the crisp air so completely still that a soft and odourless blanket of peat and coal smoke was descending gently into front gardens like a freezing fog. I was clearly not a driver, but Mrs Campbell didn't seem to mind. She was a professional bed and breakfast madam in the B&B uniform of lilac tracksuit and slippers. The house was immaculate and acrylic and there was a telly in the bedroom which was on from the moment I stepped in until the moment I went to sleep; a television in a bedroom demands to be watched. On the news England looked green; although none of the newscasters actually mentioned it, it was clear to me that the programme's main news was that English grass was emerging from winter in fine fettle. In Scotland the true state of the grass was not yet known.

The only other lodger was a lorry driver from Milton Keynes. At breakfast he started talking as soon as he heard my accent and decided that, although posh, I was definitely an ally. He'd never been this far north before, he said. He was doing a circuit of building society offices, picking up bagfuls of confidential documents for the Milton Keynes shredder, and he was supposed to go right up to Wick and Thurso that day.

"I was thinking last night of going back to Milton instead," he said, helping himself to more tea.

I asked him why.

"It's a long way north to these places and it's been snowing." He sounded plaintive, as if I had the power to allow him to turn back. "Anyway, I doubt they've got more than a couple of bags. There can't be that many people up there."

I agreed that it was not a highly populated place. It did seem quite a long foraging trip to find food for the Milton Keynes shredder; did the shredder really need it?

"Oh yes, it's very big," he said, his eyes lighting up with almost paternal affection for his monster with the insatiable mouth lurking down south, for which he was the hunter-gatherer.

"As big as this house – bigger," he exclaimed, excitedly. "And it's so quiet. We recently had to mince a million cameras; something to do with infringement of copyright. And Aerospace have asked us to mince paper even smaller. The lads reckon it's because the Ayatollah's got a team of students working on piecing shredded documents together."

It all sounded a bit like mincer gossip to me, but it created a happy picture of the Ayatollah's sidekicks writing incisive reports about the spending habits of the honest burghers of Thurso.

It is not easy to linger in a professional bed and breakfast. Banging doors and hoovering drove me out on to the streets, where Boots the chemist was deserted but for three shop assistants. I had time to waste before the market started, so I browsed. Within five minutes I was back on the street, routed by long hard stares from the staff, who obviously felt that I spent far too long looking at packets which were nothing to do with men.

I bought a two-pounder in Cockburn's prize haggis makers. Cockburn's turn out nine tons of haggis in January in preparation for Burns' night – enough to keep the Milton Keynes shredder chewing for ten minutes. Seeing the little fellows lying there in the chiller cabinet made me want to smile; somehow, the haggis, round, speckled and featureless, has acquired a personality without the help of TV advertising, without a haggis marketing board's backstage manoeuvring. I wouldn't spare half a sentence on a hard-boiled egg or a saveloy, but a haggis is a conversation piece. One of the best Scottish sayings is "Even a haggis can run doonhill", because its use can only be surreal. Remember it when you're told to clear your desk on a Friday afternoon and not to come back: "Ah well, even a haggis can run doonhill." Remember it when the clear favourite at Ascot comes last, and the longest odds comes first: "Even a haggis can run doonhill."

The man behind the counter at Cockburn's took his haggis seriously.

"Oh ay, there's a lot of rubbish about wi' the haggis," he agreed. "This annual throwing the haggis business is not in oor line at all, at all. Sacrilege, we think."

Winter – the West Highlands

The postcard I'd bought the previous day of a cheery young haggis yomping about on the moors dressed in a kilt began to burn a hole in my pocket. It didn't seem a good place to repeat one of my family's favourite myths about one of our holiday haggises which had remained unwanted for so long that it had walked to the edge of the cliff and thrown itself off in despair. I gave the man a London address and consigned my new haggis to the British postal system, blissfully unaware that it was about to run amok in the InterCity network and that I would eventually have to use all my telephone charm to prise it out of the arms of postmen, long after I myself had returned home.

Inverness has long eclipsed Dingwall as the administrative centre of the Highlands, even though Inverness itself is essentially a Lowland town in a Highland gateway situation, economically and architecturally more in sympathy with the towns of the east coast than the west, rich with oil, the whisky industry (two of the UK's top five industries) and administration.

Dingwall is far more Highland in character. In the 300 years until 1266, when much of the far north was in Scandinavian hands, it was the seat of a Norse 'Thing' or parliament and a very important administrative centre. While Inverness is occupied with the more rewarding and prestigious industries of oil and whisky, Dingwall has remained the agricultural focus of the western Highlands and islands and its market is the principal arena for livestock trading from the furthermost areas of Scotland.

The two auction halls are the source of much of the town's local employment. Farmers from outlying areas assemble here to buy and sell; a twinkly old gent with bandy legs and a stick told me that much of what was sold would be going to Stornoway in the Outer Hebrides; was I buying or selling? Watching, I said.

The auction was conducted in an indoor arena inside a massive wooden shed; the auctioneer on a raised pedestal behind the ring, the buyers in brogues, corduroy and deerstalkers, lounging around the metal fencing opposite him, their breath and the breath of the scared beasts mingling in a cloud of freezing vapour in the ring. A dozen onlookers – the professionals had thermoses and sandwiches – sat on a stairway of wooden benches around the back of the arena. Sunlight filtered through corrugated perspex in the roof, making the dust shimmer. "Store cattle and stirks, cast and breeding cows, simmental cross heifers with breeding potential" were on the agenda. In the pauses, it felt a bit like church.

The proceedings were conducted incomprehensibly and at great speed. I didn't see one gesture from a bidder, but I dared not try to follow the auctioneer too closely for fear of ending up with a stirk to take home.

Up behind me a couple of girls were talking. "He jumped offa the phone box ohn the stag night. Ended up in hospital, the lump."

"Noo! Not on the vairy night befoor?"

"Uh-ha, and the nurse said he'd be going up the aisle in a wheelchair, but in the end it was just bruising."

"Well there ye go. And where did ye go for your honeymoon?"

"Emboro. It's noo far, but we've got the rest of our lives fae holidays in the raist of the wurld."

An old man with a barrel chest decided I might be worth talking to.

"You a tourist?"

I agreed that I was. This seemed satisfactory to him; he introduced himself as Jimmy, sat down and unpacked his sandwiches.

"And what d'ye think of oor toun?" asked Jimmy.

I said that I thought it very nice.

"That's mince," growled Jimmy. "It's as corrupt as hell."

This came as a bit of a surprise. Dingwall had only struck me as a hotbed for haggis-making and stirk-selling, and I said so.

"Ay, well ye've not bin reading my letters tae the noose-papers, have ye? Thairteen I've had printed the year," said Jimmy.

I intercepted a look of sympathy from the two girls and began to fear I'd fallen into the company of the town's stirrer.

"Folk are frightened o' me right enough because I speak my mind, write the truth," he was saying. "Folk are frighted when ye write the truth."

"What about?"

Jimmy let me see his eyes for the first time; they were as small as nuts, hard, flat and empty.

"Militant. Polis harassment. You name it, we got it right heer in Dingwall. There's a fella in the polis is a pal of mine and he says I'm absolutely right, but ye canna dae anything aboot it wi' the government sae weak. That's the fella in the polis says that, not me. They've got nae pooer, nae pooer at all. They need guns. If ye ask me we need someone wi' balls fer oor MP."

Jimmy's oration reminded me of a friend's generalisation that the trouble with any countryside, anywhere, was that it was full of fascists. He was my best example so far. I kept my mouth shut for fear of revealing my true nature as a pinko-liberal leftie wet.

"They shuid bring back the birch and hanging, that's what they shuid dae right enough. And the aithnic minorities should nivver have bin allowed intae the country in the furst place."

As he munched deeply into a consolatory sandwich I took the opportunity to mumble my excuses, get up and go, leaving him to speak his mind to the stirks. The cattle auction wasn't worth much more of that.

VI

I headed west in the company of a fish-farmer from Lancashire who'd settled in Scotland. He talked fish all the way from Dingwall to Ullapool, a strange soundtrack for an increasingly pure landscape of rock, snow and river, its purity divided into shoulders by the ribbon of road. To tourists the west coast may reek of history, of battles and clan clashes, but this fish-farmer saw its landmarks entirely in terms of fish. He pointed out sharp corners where speeding lorries had spilled tank loads of flapping salmon on to the moor, he pointed to hatcheries through the trees and to roads from the south up which came lorries loaded with chemicals. Fish-farming had actually increased the number of semi-wild salmon, he said. He'd worked on a landbased farm which discharged unsellable smolts down a four-inch drain into the sea. A couple of years later the smolts had returned as thirty-pound fish and had tried to get back up the pipe to breed. And then there'd been the recent case of the fish-farmer who released a whole batch of smolts because they'd got an eye infection, only to find many of them came back the following year, fully recovered, and fought the mesh to get back into the cages. To him this was a quirk of business; to me it seemed very sad.

The clouds were down and the klondykers were in at Ullapool. As we descended into Loch Broom the fish-farmer told a story of how, when he was on a farm in Ullapool, he'd woken one morning to find that a klondyker ship had dragged its anchor in a storm during the night, had come right across the bay and smashed his farm, with 80,000 fish, to smithereens. His insurance company had slapped a writ on the foot of the mast, he said, and the Romanians had paid for it all in cash, without argument.

Ullapool, a name which suggests an Alaskan whaling station, is a small town laid out in an American-style grid on a sandy ledge of flat land that prods out into the long belly of Loch Broom. It's the only place of any size between Kyle of Lochalsh and Thurso, on the hundreds of miles of wild coastline of the western tip of the British Isles. In most people's opinion this western corner of Scotland is a crazy place to live, and were it not for the high-sided loch, Ullapool's site would have been a crazy place to build. On the open coast, the seas would have swept the houses off the ledge as in a game of Monopoly. But Ullapool exists only for the sea. It was purpose-built in 1788 as a fishing station for herring, and fishing station – neat, governmental-style housing, like the first of a whole regiment of suburbs planned for the West Highlands – it has remained ever since, with the more recent addition of a ferry service to Lewis, which attracts transiting tourists.

In winter Loch Broom fills steadily with Eastern bloc klondyker factory ships which drop anchor in the autumn and raise anchor again in the spring. At the height of the season up to fifteen factory ships shelter in the steep-sided loch, looking as if they are hiding from the scrap merchant. They buy fish direct from the Scottish trawlers and process it on board. The system works by the fishermen returning to the quay, making contact with the klondykers' representatives onshore, making the sale on paper, motoring out to the factory ships where the catch is winched away, and presenting a chit at the local bank where the klondykers have made their financial arrangements. The fishermen like the klondykers because of their prices and their constant demand. Moreover, fish sold to factory ships don't necessarily feature on a fishing boat's yearly quota.

As the tourists fade away in the autumn, Ullapool fills up with a migrant winter population of Romanians, Bulgarians and Russians, winter birds in huge black flapping coats, hopping in and out of boats, huddling in groups on the street corners, peering earnestly into shop windows, and wiping their noses with their thumbs. These Baltic heron, Lithuanian storks and Bulgarian crows come to Ullapool from places like Plovdiv, Riga and Murmansk. They know the answers to strange questions that would not occur to us to ask, such as how long does it take to get from Plovdiv to Ullapool? Or how many Bulgarians does it take to put a herring in a can? Many a stray tourist, late to depart south, has come across swarthy men on the quay at Ullapool and gone home mistakenly pleased to have overheard so much Gaelic being spoken in one place.

The factory ship workers come in relays, each shift spending six weeks or so in the loch. Then a new shift, with paper bags full of black market currency, flies in to replace the old. The shifts change frequently, but not because conditions on board are unpleasant, the life in the loch lonely and the work hard, which it is: crews want to come because of the shopping. To them, Ullapool is the Harrods of the north-west, a Harrods that reeks faintly of fish oil and sweat.

The Ullapool shops are full of cassette-players, cameras, irons, electric kettles, bulk soap and coffee. The shopkeepers do very well out of the klondykers, and every year they are made anxious by rumours that this year the factory boats will pass them by. This prosperous, neat little outpost is a strange place for a Bulgarian's first – and probably only – taste of the British Isles.

The girl in the fish and chip shop was a bit of an expert on the Eastern bloc. "It's the Bulgars are in today," she said. "And the soonest they gae the better. They smell and they have a way of looking at youse. It's not nice." She giggled, and slapped her other customer – who was ogling her – with a spatula. She added that she thought the Russians were nicer, especially to children.

The klondyker smell – fish oil and sweat – was particularly

noticeable in one of the smaller shops, where a group was crowding around a ghetto-blaster. I tried to buy a telephone card, but the shop only had denominations of £20: "For calling America and Russia, I suppose," shrugged the shop assistant. I made a long call to London from the phone box by the quay – probably that call box's least exotic call of the day. As I talked to a very distant suburban office I could see the klondykers who had done their shopping waiting in the dinghy by the quay, hunched against the cold and thumbing their way tenderly through pornographic magazines as if they were valuable editions of old manuscripts. No doubt they were valuable; their future was probably to be resold, rethumbed, restudied and resold again; the glimpses of pictured pink flesh, tinsel and silk sheets looked incongruous against the austere and stark backdrop of the steep-sided and still loch.

Billy Macrae had reached the oratorical stage by the time I rubbed up alongside him in the bar that night. He was a tall prawn fisherman, with a flat Para Handy cap and a coat covered in rusty metal poppers and zips and he too smelt of fish oil and sweat, although the aroma of whisky and beer chasers was stronger. At his elbow was Alex, a sticky, grizzled man with glasses as thick as Fox's glacier mints who spent the evening staring into the mirror behind the optics.

I repeated what I'd heard from the prawn buyer in Oban, about the season being dreadful. Billy didn't need much more incentive. The life of a prawn fisherman was hard, he said, but it was getting harder every year.

"I'm already £5,000 behind wi' last year. It's survival of the fittest these days – the wairst invaistment anyone can make is a fushing boat of more than thairty feet. Isn't that right, Alex?"

Alex nodded at the optics.

"I have to make £400 in a week before I've paid my expainses," Billy complained. He had three houses and a Vauxhall Carlton; his boat was his, but he had three daughters and none of them would be wanting it. He had decided to give it to his crew-member when he retired. "He's a wirker that you couldn't ask for a better, right enough. Had a boot himself the once, but he just couldnae get the accounts correct and the bank took it awi."

I sympathised with the principle of a business failing because of the quality of the paperwork and not the lack of endeavour. "Even a haggis can run doonhill," I muttered.

Billy Macrae stared. "Eh?"

"Accounting is a dreadful business," I said lamely. "Although I always feel good when I've finished mine. It's like coming out of church." Billy Macrae frowned.

Fish-farming was a better and a safer subject. The scenic impact of the cages didn't concern him, but the quality of the fish did. "Thalidomide fush, I call them. They've no fins and no muscle. And the flesh, it chust falls off. It wouldn't be pink unless they fed it with pink chemicals. The chemicals they use to de-louse them kill off everything undern' they cages. Aye, but they've got some problems with the staff now, they have. Can't get the people, you see. We've a new mine up the road, see, which pays much better. But that mining business – if you ask me it's chust hole-making, so they've got somewhere for their nuclear waste."

Whether or not anyone had such a sinister plan I had no idea, but I could see that a deep mine-shaft in a particularly abandoned part of the western Highlands could be attractive to someone with a bit of N-waste on his hands and a few budgetary corners to cut. On the other hand, I could also see the danger of Billy Macrae getting a bit too morose.

"It seems like you're well off out there on your boat." To me, after a pint or two, it seemed ideal.

"Och well, God gives us fingers, hands, arms, legs, toes, a brain and a bit more besides and it's up to us to make the best of what God gives us, eh Alex?" Billy Macrae continued to look at me, but somewhere behind him Alex grunted his agreement.

"You're religious then?"

"Surely. I'd never go out on the sabbath. I'm not one of these fellers wanting to go swumming on a Sunday. It's the English as goes swumming on a Sunday."

This, I knew, was a reference to Ullapool's vote to open its leisure centre on a Sunday, which was on the front page of the local newspaper; Billy had been one of those in opposition but it was the incomers who had won the day, he said. "At this rate the west coast will be as bad as the east," he declared, darkly, swigging his whisky.

It was from Billy Macrae that I learned about Scoraig, the

incomers' township on the Loch Broom peninsula. Macrae's family had come from Scoraig and he himself had been one of the last to leave, but the township had since been refilled, I understood, with what was referred to darkly in Ullapool as a "community" of incomers. I took this to mean that the English were living out on the Loch Broom peninsula in a nest of sin.

With an incentive like that I was on the path to Scoraig the following morning, armed with directions. Scoraig was "Opposite the cluff that looks like wi' the queen. Alex knows it, don't you, Alex?"

"Ay."

"Doesn't that cluff look like wi' the face of Queen Victoria, Alex?"

Alex seemed happy to recall Queen Victoria's face, but his attention had never left the mirror behind the optics.

VII

The road on to the Scoraig peninsula – the bare, steep side of Loch Broom on the other side from Ullapool – died about four miles out, and from then on a track wound around the side of the cliff on the south side of the peninsula, a couple of hundred feet above a sea that rippled and heaved gently with the nearly exhausted effort of the Atlantic. At times the track was alarmingly narrow and near the edge, but it was all there was. The lack of road had killed the former community, not the poverty of the land, said Billy. He'd been off in the services – for many a Highlander the army, the navy or the air force provide an opportunity to see the world and gather together a bit of money – and he had returned to Scoraig, to "bugger all". He'd moved to Ullapool for the sake of his social life and his sanity. Isolation had literally killed many a similar community, and there was news in the local paper that week of a house fire on the Knoydart peninsula further south, opposite Skye. After nightfall the fire had been seen from Mallaig, on the other side of Loch Nevis, but by the time that the fire brigade had commandeered the lifeboat and completed the crossing, the house had been gutted and two bodies were found in the embers.

Macrae hadn't moved far from Scoraig, but many of the other

families had moved much further. Historians charting the agonies of Scotland invariably focus on the very emotive Clearances, when thousands of households were evicted by their landlords in order to make way for sheep and herded on to emigrant ships bound for the USA and Australia. In fact, the biggest surge of departing Scots came, not during the upheaval itself, but after the Clearances had been made illegal. The evictions helped trigger a depopulation that has continued steadily through the twentieth century. What once was a flood is now a dripping tap, but it nevertheless saps significant strength, particularly from the Highlands.

The process remains the same today as it was a hundred years ago. Uncles or cousins or brothers abroad set up the invitation; a bad winter, a legislative last straw from London, the death of a parent, all are enough to complete the move. My own existence in England is indirectly due to one of Scotland's best-known emigrants, Andrew Carnegie, who built up a massive business in the USA and used the profits to fund philanthropic enterprises back home. My grandfather, who was born and brought up on a croft on the Isle of Skye, won a Carnegie scholarship to a school on the mainland. When he stepped ashore at the railhead at Kyle he had two shirts in a paper bag and it was the first time in his life he had ever seen a train. Eventually he went to university in Glasgow to study to become a doctor and when the First World War ended he'd settled in England, attracted by better work opportunities.

He'd finally died on the Sussex coast, about as far away as he could get from Scotland without emigrating. He died while I was young, and I remember him little; the lingering impression, though, is of a rather dour man, saddened by the necessity of leaving his home – Skye was always "home". As a family we had attempted to holiday in other parts of the UK, but after a couple of days of rumbling discontent Grandfather would declare solemnly that there was nothing quite like home, the car would be re-packed and we would bowl northwards through pre-motorway Britain, ploughing unstoppably on through the night over dreadful roads.

After his death my grandmother maintained the tradition of the pilgrimages north, and the combination of a sense of belonging and deep sense of guilt for leaving is strong enough to have permeated down into his children and grandchildren. And so to me, struggling round a high path towards a village which had been abandoned by the Scots and refilled by the English.

Walking long distances provokes empty thoughts, and I was well into my third hour on the Scoraig path with my mind elsewhere. Ahead was the settlement, marked by a long patch of green on the end of the finger of land. Far below, a cormorant flapped off the water and skimmed along the surface. Momentarily distracted by the dizzying thought of flying so close to the water, I rounded the next corner and was almost run down by a woman and a horse coming up the hill at speed; the woman was not riding the horse, but flailing along behind, hanging on grimly to its tail.

She saw me at the same moment. "Hold it, Speedy," she panted and the horse stopped, looking positively relieved. We exchanged civilities. She was English, and looked and sounded like a cross between Boadicea and my granny; I could imagine her ensuring that I drank my prune juice before bed. She travelled the path every day, she said. On the flat bits she rode Speedy, and on the hills she got off and hung on to his tail. She confirmed that there was a place to stay in Scoraig; she even pointed it out in the distance. But was it, I wanted to ask, a nest of sin?

"Of course, if you don't want to stay there," the woman was saying, "you can always sleep in our barn." Then she and Speedy coupled up again, Speedy winced and they departed, leaving me thinking that perhaps it was.

Like many a Highland township, Scoraig is a scattering of croft-houses which sit in the midst of their land, although here most of the houses were unusually surrounded by trees, topped by the whirring blades of small power-generating windmills. The land glowed green like a healthy cheek on the peninsula; walking into it, I felt as if I were walking into a promised land, or on to a film set where the cameras had started to roll but no one had yet told me, the star, whether the film was documentary, tragedy or comedy.

It was a while before I met any of the other actors, but I read about them first. Halfway through the township was the new school with press cuttings pinned to a board. They told how the community had fought to set up their own school on the peninsula rather than ferry their children across to Ullapool; the implications of a couple of the articles were that the incomers didn't think the local schooling system good enough. The new school, said the cuttings, would teach the main curriculum "plus other things students might not learn elsewhere", which could mean anything and was doubtless intended to do so. There was also an article about a violin-maker at Scoraig who had taught himself from books and who now made among the best in the world; he described how he would play Hungarian folk music on his new violins in the converted croft looking over the water to An Teallach, the mountain on the other side of the loch.

Even so, I couldn't find any people. The crofts were spread out and surrounded by trees and the only sign of any activity was the whirring of the windmills. I moved along the peninsula in front of Billy Macrae's Queen Victoria. Her expression changed as I moved and I could imagine her enjoining me to do the right thing and not to let my morals slip, no matter what temptation should cross my path.

Nothing crossed my path until I reached the shed by the slipway. Topher, the boat-builder, had been commended to me by Billy Macrae, but he wasn't around and his shed was locked. I sat down on the ribs of a wreck and exchanged frowns with Queen Vic. Half an hour later I was idly watching the progress of a floating rag, when that rag picked itself out of the water and became an otter, hurrying into the rocks. I turned and left quietly, simultaneously exhilarated at having been so close to such a shy animal and disappointed at the implications of its presence: the residents of Scoraig could hardly be wife-swapping all-night ravers if they had otters nesting on their slipway.

At the tip of the peninsula, where the klondykers from Ullapool reputedly came ashore in the dead of night to snatch the occasional sheep when their diet of fish palled, the path curled around the point to a building which stood by itself, some distance apart from the rest of the community. This was the salmon bothy, and as I approached it looked oddly misshapen from the landward side. Writ in large on the door were the words BEWARE POLTERGEIST. I circled the building warily; the entire seaward face had been destroyed. It had burst outwards, as if some enormous hand had grabbed it like a rotten fruit and torn it apart, releasing a white-hot demon which had shot out over the Atlantic. An old Aga rested where the wall had once been, its temperature gauge frozen at 300 degrees Fahrenheit, like a clock that had stopped at the moment of disaster. It was not a place for human beings and I retreated, my heart thumping heavily with fear.

The first flesh and blood I met at Scoraig was Tom, planting a tree. Trees were essential to retain the topsoil and shelter the cattle, he said, in a quiet and unplaceable Scottish accent. The deforestation of Scotland had been its greatest natural disaster. He waved his spade in the direction of An Teallach. He'd planted all those trees, he declared solemnly.

"And I rebuilt Samadhan."

Something about the words and the resonance with which he uttered them reminded me of the Bible; I wouldn't have been surprised if Queen Vic, on the opposite shore, had opened her rocky mouth and echoed, "Lo Samadhan, the promised land." Tom too had his Biblical qualities. I could imagine reaching the pearly gates and finding the archangel planting a tree, steadily and purposefully, his wispy grey hair swaying just like Tom's.

"I've been talking to Queen Victoria," I said with what I considered to be an appropriate matching level of semi-mythology.

Tom obviously had no idea what I was talking about.

"I mean Billy Macrae's Queen Victoria," I explained hastily, not wanting to appear any more loopy than necessary. I told him what the fisherman had told me and pointed out the bluff; Tom agreed unconvincingly that it did look a bit like Queen Victoria, but you could see he still thought I was a bit of a nutter.

"Billy Macrae also said there was somewhere to stay in Scoraig."

Tom used his spade to point to a gate. "Samadhan." Again, that Biblical echo. I watched the gate, half expecting it to open on the command, and then realised that I was staring at a signboard. "Samadhan", it read. "Bed and Breakfast." Even a haggis can run doonhill.

Tom, the archangel at the gate, may have built the infrastructure, but Sundara ran Samadhan. Sundara was Tom's wife, an ex-actress some years younger than him who hadn't lost her sense of dramatic tension and her gift for summoning the spotlight to wherever she stood. In the midst of a small wood which positively hummed with the sound of things growing even in mid-winter, Sundara presided over workshops and retreats, breakfast, lunch and dinner. If there was any stage at Scoraig, Sundara was on it, and I was relegated to just another spear carrier as soon as I stepped through the door of her particular promised land.

Like the salmon bothy, the original croft-house of Samadhan had been exploded only to be meticulously rebuilt by Tom to twice the size. The hand-crafted interior had every appearance of springing out of a country living magazine. On the walls were pictures of Rajneesh Bhagwan, the guru who'd had a Rolls-Royce for every week of the year and unusual views on sexual relations. "You have the freedom to be yourself, your true self, here and now and nothing can stand in your way", said the sign at the foot of the stairs. Next door to it was a money box for donations. It was, said the brochure by my bedside, a place of spiritual healing; a retreat centre and an "unspoilt wilderness which is a delight to the wandering soul"; the land was to be the healer. I knew all about that, that was outside, but what about inside? It was hardly a wilderness, but was it a nest of sin?

I was not the only guest. The four others were upstairs, announced Sundara, skimming towards the door once she'd shown me my room. They were in the meditation room for an hour of Movement Ritual. Would I be joining them? I felt Queen Victoria's lurch of disapproval from the other side of the loch; "Don't get involved," she growled.

"No thanks," I mumbled. I didn't need any more movement. I had already done four hours of heavy-booted movement that day in order to get there, and I was already planning a swift retreat the following morning which would require an equal amount of effort. So I loitered into the kitchen, aware of a certain amount of shuffling going on somewhere upstairs.

There's something secure about kitchens that presumably hearkens back to childhood. You can be sure that in a party where no one knows anyone there'll be more of a crowd in the kitchen than in the party room, seeking security among the pots and pans. Not that there was much maternal about Alistair, a mop-headed and stringy Glaswegian who had started work as Samadhan's cook the previous day. His last job had been in the bowels of one of the London hotels.

"Quite a difference," I suggested.

"Och yes," he said. "The hairbs here are marvellous." We were to have scrambled egg and pasta for dinner.

A noise from upstairs which sounded like a groaning lavatory cistern became too persistent to ignore.

"What's that?" I asked.

Alistair threw open the kitchen door and the groan swelled into a monotone Gregorian chant. If they were having group sin then it didn't sound much fun.

"Intoning. They've funushed the Movement Rutual. Not long now. I'd better get on wi' the stairters."

By the time the others came bounding down the stairs enthusing about the light, the noise they'd been making, the food, the wildlife and anything there was to be enthusiastic about, insecurity combined with culture shock had driven me into a shell of brittle and uncommunicative Britishness, which involved speaking civilly when spoken to but not saying any more than necessary. The others had enough to say anyway: an American with a grindingly acute mind which pulverised every remark in a search for its wider implications, married to a Russian teacher of French with a penetrating voice; a gay and chubby Londoner with a wandering eye and hand; and a stone-faced man who said absolutely nothing at all but who pointed his silence like a loaded gun at anyone who spoke. If anybody had taken the words on the brochure literally and come for healing from the wilderness, it was him; the socialising passed him by.

Alistair had just begun to emerge from the kitchen with the first of the starters when someone announced that the sunset was beautiful and everyone bounded back upstairs to watch it. By the time we'd settled again it was dark; the electric light was so weak – there'd not been a lot of wind in the week and the storage capacity of the batteries was limited – that supper felt like a seance. Alistair produced his offerings from the kitchen in an unpredictable order. Tom, the archangel, sat quietly, listening benignly as each member of the dinner party took their turn to enthuse about the place, the food, the people, the air and anything in their heads.

Tom hadn't taken part in the Movement Ritual or the intoning; I don't think it was his sort of thing. He had waved his spade and created paradise, but what people did within it was their affair. He had a sort of romantic common sense nurtured in a community of dreamers which had been forced into practicality in order to survive. Knowledge hadn't killed romance: he loved sunsets despite knowing the scientific reasons for their colours; he knew why on a bright morning the islands beyond the loch mouth seemed to float on the water; and he'd spent the night on the top of An Teallach at midsummer, when the sun rolled around the world just out of sight before appearing again in the morning, despite knowing how many lives the mountain claimed in a year. He was suitably enthusiastic about the otter I'd seen; they get seals in the bay, he said, but he'd not seen any otters; the locals believe the seals to be the souls of the departed. Being the only true Scot amongst the group at table, he had nothing to prove; the sense of companionship with his surroundings was in his blood, and therefore was not something he felt a need to demonstrate. He looked up when the lights suddenly brightened after the pudding.

"Ah-hah. A touch of northerly wind. We may get more snow." While the others were chorusing about other, similar, healing centres that they had been to, Tom and I kicked the topic of Scotland's weather lazily back and forth. Was it really wild – any more wild than anywhere else? It had been a windy year, so windy that the Scottish fishing fleets had remained in port. While half of Scotland's reputation for being wild stems from simply being further north and thus more severe, the other half is the impression given by the fact that there is little or no shelter and no escaping whatever weather may be to hand. The same weather could pass over Birmingham or Paris, forcing shoppers to cling to bus-shelters, but they wouldn't call it wild. In Scotland there are not enough people or places to prevent the weather from becoming rampant in the minds of travellers. I asked him about the fate of the salmon bothy, which had been preying on my mind: had that been the weather?

It may have been a momentary lapse in the wind, but his face seemed to darken. "Probably," he said. "But if you met Billy Macrae you should have asked him. He was the salmon fisherman here for years. Where did you meet him anyway?"

"In the pub."

"Ah-hah."

"He told me how all the original families had left."

"Oh yes, we're all of us incomers here. There are not many Scots." Tom had been one of the first to come; at the time Scoraig had been virtually derelict.

"So why do you think you have stayed when the locals like Macrae have gone?"

He pondered a bit. "We haven't been here that long yet. I don't think you can really draw any conclusions."

It had occurred to me, wandering through the township that afternoon, that the bonding force between a community of incomers who'd resurrected a derelict community was their pioneering spirit and their sense of achievement. Without that, life would be more tedious. The scenery was beautiful for two weeks, but it never changed and even Queen Victoria didn't answer back. The Highlanders refer to something called the second winter syndrome, a complaint which causes many English settlers to flee. An incomer's first winter in Scotland is "*soo* stormy, gorgeous, strong, *soo* elemental". But when the second winter is equally gorgeously stormy, the incomer packs up and retreats back south.

Scoraig had mostly got beyond the second winter syndrome and seemed buoyed by its sense of achievement, but this sense of achievement belonged only to the pioneers; the new generations, the children attending the school, would grow up in a place which wasn't created by them, which didn't have any roads or mains electricity or water. Who were they going to marry? Would they ever go to a disco? Have a take-away on a Friday night? Scoraig could become the home of a shifting population of people who had taken their positive decisions to be there, but those decisions were not hereditary; their children had not made the same choice. The test would be whether the sense of the intrinsic value of clean air, a fine view and no traffic noise seemed as valuable to succeeding generations of the new Scoraig inhabitants. If they didn't burningly want to be at

Scoraig then there was bugger all to do, as Billy Macrae had pointed out. It even occurred to me, sitting in Samadhan with the echoes of enthusiasm from the rest of the party dying gently as the fire got lower, that at some time in the future this house too would have BEWARE POLTERGEIST written on the door, and that the seaward end would be open to the wind.

None of this I said. I already appeared churlish, I knew, and I didn't want to spoil the spirit of the occasion. And when I went to bed I fell asleep instantly and nothing, not a sin or a scream, woke me during the night.

VIII

The weather is a great purifier, cleaning and seeding and renewing with every change. It did snow that night, but not too deeply to make the return walk difficult. Away from the windmills, the Movement Rituals and the talk of the promised land, the ingredients of the landscape became simple and elemental again: earth, water, snow, ice, air, sunlight and metal fences – with me in the middle of it, a black shape hopping like an injured crow along a thin ribbon of brown path through the snow. The day was sickeningly beautiful and bright, but in the shadows the air was fiercely cold. The loch was deep, deep blue. An Teallach had been carved out of dazzling white sugar and Queen Victoria was wearing a nightcap. Without the interpretations of Samadhan to interfere with it the landscape had regained its own purity. Back out on the hill you kept your own counsel and relied on your own strength. The real Movement Ritual was the steady placing of each boot, one in front of the other, the real intoning the gentle shushing of the waves of a calm sea relaxing at last on to a beach after a long journey.

Self-reliance is the philosophy of the crop-headed, booted young men striding the streets of Glasgow, many of whom deliberately choose the winter to disappear into the mountains, when the face-to-face challenge with all that nature can throw at you is at its toughest. On a still January or February weekend there's a faint clinking coming from every mountain of note along the west Highland coast as men from Manchester get stuck in with ice-axes and crampons.

Doing the Munros – the 276 Scottish mountains above 3,000 feet – is a winter pastime for the country's tough nuts. The champion of them all is one Martin Moran, once a chartered accountant from Sheffield and now a mountain guide. Moran climbed all 276 mountains, in winter, in 83 days, averaging 3.325301 mountains a day – a strange number, but perhaps as a chartered accountant he liked strange numbers. While completing this feat Moran had sometimes run between his mountains, climbing many after dark. He is a tall, lean man, not one of society's natural communicators and I couldn't help wondering what he had thought about as he raced around the ice-capped roof of Scotland. Perhaps it was numbers. Perhaps he had deliberately wanted to achieve 3.325301 mountains a day.

It was Martin Moran, in his mountaineering centre in Strathcarron, who had advised me to go to Shenavall. Whilst in Glasgow I'd wanted to sidle up to the crop-headed young men and ask them what they thought about as they hacked their way up ice-faces, and whether the mountains or the activity or both made them into purer people. They seemed so compact and purposeful that I could only assume they had clear views about the world, which would be directly, probably brutally, expressed. But sidling up to crop-headed young men is not easy when they're striding out purposefully down Sauchiehall Street. In the mountaineering shops, where enthusiasts hovered among the ropes, boots and Gore-tex, fingering everything like dirty old men in a porn shop, they spoke a language I didn't understand. And so I decided to go where they couldn't miss me, to a mountaineering bothy in the middle of nowhere which is used as a kicking-off point for a popular peak and where they would gather like salmon in a pool about to attempt the waterfalls above. There, I thought, they would open up a bit in the hours before the last push. They would tell me that the exertion of going up a couple of mountains a day kept their bodies sharp like a kind of all-over dental floss, but what did it do to the mind? At the very least I thought they would tell some tales of narrow escapes.

As the crow flies, Shenavall is not much more than ten miles from Scoraig, round the back of An Teallach. Getting to it is not so easy, though.

Emerging from the Scoraig path on to the main road, I got a

short lift from an east coast builder with a carload of farting dogs; the work was on the west coast, doing up holiday houses of the rich English, he said, so he commuted coast to coast two or three times a week.

"Be careful," he warned, when I'd told him where I was going. "I hearrid on the radio that someone wiss killed on An Teallach a couple o' days ago. Sorry aboot that," he added, winding down his window as his cocker spaniel let rip yet again.

A Highland bothy is usually a shepherd's house or croft-house in the hills which has been abandoned and handed over to the Mountain Bothies' Association for their use and upkeep, although the building itself remains the property of the original owner. The list of bothies in Scotland runs into the hundreds but is not made public for fear that, once identified, the buildings may be colonised by squatters. Sometimes the bothies are used for hunting and poaching purposes, and walkers who arrive after dark to find the building unaccountably smelly may well wake in the morning to find themselves staring up at a rack of deer carcasses hanging from the rafters, their sleeping-bags covered in an overnight dew of blood and the floor covered in gore.

Shenavall is far too busy with climbers to be in danger of being squatted or used as a poacher's store. Besides, the bothy is a long two-hour trudge from the road, over a belly of brown heath that girdles the waist of An Teallach. It was a very pleasant two hours: the sun was turning the branches of the leafless birch and hazel trees into filigree as they subdivided themselves and the light; the air was so clean and bright that I could almost hear it squeaking against my ear. The light was so needle-sharp that if it could it would have shown me the grain on a tree's bark, the slow-worm on the hill opposite, or even a climber just below the peak of An Teallach, agonising over which step to take next. But my eyes told me none of this – actually they told me no more than usual, with the helpful footnote that it was a beautiful day.

Around the corner of the mountain the path dipped towards the strath. The snow on the moorland had disappeared quickly, exposing raw ground where the topsoil had stretched, slipped and peeled off the sandstone and quartzite like the skin burning off a face in a horror film. Ahead was a tapestry of mountains stretching benignly into the distance. This was the beginning of what climbers and walkers call the Great Wilderness of the Strathnasheallag, Fisherfield and Letterewe forests, a massive area of unbroken chains of mountains and lochs about twenty miles deep and thirty miles wide, so inaccessible that it forces the main road on a detour of seventy-four miles from the Braemar junction around to Achnasheen.

An empty building is frightening. An empty building in the middle of nowhere is even more frightening. Nevertheless, in the sharp winter sunlight of early afternoon I told myself there was nothing frightening about Shenavall, the last staging post to nowhere. The door was ajar, the floors echoingly empty but with the reassuring rubbish of climbers in the corners: a broken knife, a sock, a can-opener, candle-bottles covered in rivers of wax and half a Leon Uris novel whose missing pages had been used for firelighters. Shenavall had once been a substantial family house, complete with an upstairs reached by a ladder at one end and a steep wooden staircase at the other. It was silent as only an empty building can be; oppressively silent. The silence of a place built for people and then abandoned.

But someone had been there recently. Three old car seats were propped against the wall in the main room and a dirty sleeping-bag lay stretched across them. Alongside it, where the head had rested, was half a loaf of sliced bread, which, when I touched it, proved to be soft and reasonably fresh. I dismissed the sudden, horrible thought that these were the possessions of the man who'd been killed on the mountain a couple of days before. And that he'd spent his last day alive in his sleeping-bag, munching slowly through half a loaf of dry bread while it snowed steadily outside. I shivered with the morbid thought and the cold. While the sunlight lasted it was best to be outside, collecting firewood for when darkness came.

The Shenavall strath was full of deer; two that had been grazing close to the house trotted irritatedly away when I emerged, then turned to stare at me. "Sorry, deer," I said out loud. I hadn't heard my voice for some hours and it was reassuring to hear that it hadn't changed.

The river flowed down through the strath and into the loch at its lower end. Along the banks were occasional alder trees that got thicker up the valley, and it was towards these trees that I turned my steps.

The banks of the Abhainn Strath na Sealga had been picked clean by years of climbers overnighting at Shenavall, and I'd gone at least a mile before I'd got even a pocketful of twigs. Deer all the way up the valley kept me warily in sight but didn't show any great alarm; the winter drives them down the mountainsides and occupies their minds with simple survival, eclipsing their normal fear of humans. A grouse started up from under my feet, and a feral goat, black, shaggy and with horns that rose up and swept back like a sixties rock and roller, stood and watched my slow search.

At a place where the river looped in a wide D shape flood-waters had deposited the whole of the base of an alder on the bank. It was so twistened, whitened, smoothed and cleaned by the weather that it resembled nothing on earth, and therefore could only be art. If I'd had the energy to wrestle it all the way back to the road I had no doubt that I could have sold it at great profit in some city somewhere; meanwhile it served a useful purpose as a deer-scratcher.

About a mile and a half upriver was another house. The fence around it had broken and the gate hung open, but the grass was short-cropped as if it had been recently mown; grass of that quality must have been a delicacy to the deer. Big heavy stones were suspended above the ground, front and back, by long wires which looped over the roof, in an effort to keep the whole structure in place. I flattened my nose against a front window, expecting dereliction, and realised with a shock that the room was completely furnished, right down to photographs on the mantelshelf. The furniture was solid and serviceable. A tea-towel hung over the back of the only armchair, which had its back to the window. A small man could have been sitting in the armchair without being visible to my face at the window; a small, dead man could well have been sitting there as I looked. I shivered. As I did so I noticed a note on the inside window-sill which had been written for the benefit of people like me, but the ink had faded so much that it was now almost invisible unless you were looking directly at it. The handwriting was mature. "I understand that an open bothy in the hills is a tempting rest place," said the hand. "But this house is furnished and maintained by myself. Shenavall is two miles down the path. I would be grateful if you would . . ." The last words were too faded to be legible. It was unsigned, but according to the date on the top it had been lying in the window for two years, warding off idle wood-gathering walkers like me. Another two years and it would have faded altogether; without the quiet power of the note to protect it, the house would fall open to whoever walked in off the hill. Inside they would carefully examine the possessions of that quiet-spoken person with mature handwriting who'd hung boulders over the roof and left a drying-up cloth on the back of the armchair just before he or she had left. The message in the window was like the taped voice on the answerphone of someone who'd long since died. "This house is furnished and maintained by myself." Was it a masculine or feminine voice? Certainly well educated. It had a politeness and an air of resignation about it that suggested that the author was either old or old-fashioned. Perhaps someone who'd been forced to leave this white desert because of illness and age, but who had been sad to go. Respecting the wishes of the note-writer, and noting with a shiver that the sun had finally disappeared behind the mountains, I turned about and retraced my steps.

The shadows of night were quick in striding up the strath to meet me and by the time I got back to Shenavall with enough wood for the fire it was nearly dark – and terribly quiet. The inside of the bothy was like a fridge which was becoming perceptibly colder; the air temperature alone indicated that no one had arrived in my absence.

My fire burnt badly. The fireplace was piled high with ash and rubbish and even with the help of pages 252 to 301 of Leon Uris I had to keep blowing on it to get it to flame. I boiled a kettle, some soup, a pan of porridge and even toasted some of the bread that had been mysteriously left behind, but only my face and my belly were warm. I took the pans to the stream outside and listened: no voices, no birds, no lights, no wind. The stream was freezing cold, the porridge stuck under my fingernails, and when I warmed my hands up back in the house the oatmeal turned hard and crumbled. I clambered up the steep stairs, lit a candle and struggled fully clothed into my sleeping-bag. There I lay, listening for the slightest noise, until warmth came. In normal circumstances I would probably have gone to sleep then, but the note in the window and the loneliness of the empty bothy made me fear starting a long, long night so early. Above my head a gust of wind rattled over the loose tiles like a fingernail trailing down the keys of a mute piano. I lit another candle in order to read. Immediately a much wider area of the ceiling jumped into view; my eye was dragged into a far corner by a message written in spidery chalk. "I'm living here too," it said. "In the wee cupboard." Of course it was a joke, I knew it was a joke; it was merely the graffiti of a climber. Nevertheless it gave me a jolt and prevented me from concentrating on my book; my eyes would slip off the edge of the page, wander across the ceiling to the wavering writing, and wonder which wee cupboard was meant. Eventually I blew out the candles, picked up my radio headphones, and lay back in the dark. I spent some while searching the dial, but the only station that penetrated down into the strath was the World Service. It was *Test Match Special*, with live coverage of England against the West Indies in Barbados. The England bowlers were toiling away in the heat of the day, said the commentators. Visualising the scene was as soothing as counting sheep and not much more exciting; gradually the scores mounted, and gradually I fell asleep, dreaming that I'd rung up the commentary box and asked them if they could tell me who was living in my wee cupboard.

I spent the next day walking; I got up and walked into the Great Wilderness, up to the snow line and beyond, five hours out without a stop, with a crazy desire to break through the wilderness and emerge the other side on the shores of Loch Maree. The sun was warm, the air clear and the remainder of the snow melting fast. I was concerned about the level of the two rivers I'd crossed just south of the bothy. If the snow melted too fast they would become unfordable and I'd not be able to get back to Shenavall, so I moved as fast as I could. It was incentive travel: my legs and feet were wet and blistered and my knees hurt, but I kept myself going by promising myself rewards for reaching a peak or a loch or a track or a horizon; a lump of chocolate for the peak, half an apple for the loch, a handful of peanuts for the track and a cheese sandwich for the horizon. After five hours of struggling through crusts of snow and frozen bog I was deeper in the middle of nowhere than I think I've ever been in the British Isles, and still the benign tapestry of mountains rippled on and on as far as I could see. On a ridge to the south of Lochan Fada, surrounded by an audience of deer who were too weak and too surprised to see me to do more than totter a few steps away and then turn to stare, I called a halt. I stood contemplating it all; it was beautiful, the air breathtakingly sharp, but a Highlander had once said to me, scornfully, that scenery doesn't feed cows. Daniel Defoe's description of the Highlands as "frightful country full of hideous desert mountains" came to mind, and I realised that I was frightened, frightened because I'd got too far from what I was accustomed to.

Although I had a romantic instinct to go plunging into wildernesses, I didn't have the technique of the men of Rannoch like Tom Rigg or Ken Smith: I was barging in, hopelessly ill-equipped mentally and physically like some over-educated lemming, unprepared for a lemming's fate. So I turned and plotted my route back, plugging in the headphones and switching on my radio when the chocolate ran out.

The world hadn't ended while I'd been away. The empty mountains were suddenly peopled with invisible but familiar voices. There they all were, those radio people, talking about shops and Sunday lunches (I'd had no idea it was Sunday) and did I want a dedication? said a voice. Did I want to ring in and discuss education with the minister? said another. Borodin rolled around the valley, chased by the elegant voice of the Radio Three continuity man. A Radio One DJ shrieked and disappeared, giggling, over a peak. A Radio Two lady with a honey voice sank slowly into a bog at the bottom of the valley. A Radio Four presenter shambled absentmindedly along the shoulder of a mountain and disappeared from sight, still mumbling. They formed my escort, this crowd, they imprinted man's world on the face of the foreign land, and they shepherded me back down the track, round the loch, over the peak and to the horizon, muttering "facts are chiels that winna ding" and "even a haggis can run doonhill" as I went.

When I finally staggered across the strath back towards Shenavall, completely mullahed, my legs like haggis, and frozen to the marrow from my encounters with the two rising rivers, the shadows were already halfway up the mountainside and the sun was fast disappearing. There were socks hanging from the tree outside the bothy, boots on the doorstep and hearty voices booming around the hollow rooms. Something inside me groaned; I didn't want people. I was just getting used to being without them.

Three bearded men had colonised one of the rooms and their camping gaz was blazing away in the middle of the floor. I thumped past the open door. One of them waved his cooking fork in the direction of An Teallach. "Been up the top?"

I shook my head. "You?" I croaked. It was the first word I'd spoken since talking to the deer the previous day.

"Tomorrow. We want to go while there's still some ice," said another. "You'll be going up tomorrow as well, then?"

I shook my head again. "No. I'm just walking around a bit."

It was the wrong thing to say. They shut me out, shifting their attention back to the bubbling pan on the gas. I had excluded myself by not even attempting to conquer the mountain. I was not one of them. For all they knew I might have been a homosexual. And if I wasn't climbing An Teallach then what the hell was I doing at Shenavall?

With the help of Leon Uris I boiled the kettle, made myself some porridge, tea and toast. The climbers were in the next-door room so it wasn't hard to listen in to their conversation. At first they talked about food: the quality of the cheese sauce, the best packet foods they had known. Recipes they had tried. Restaurants they had eaten at. And then they talked about climbing routes and I realised why it was that I had totally failed to understand the talk in the Glasgow climbing shops: Gaelic mountain names spoken with a Manchester accent take some recognising. By the time I was in my sleeping-bag they'd got on to the subject of sex but perhaps out of respect for the deepening night their voices had settled and I could only distinguish certain words. Sadly, I concluded that there was no great wisdom in bothy talk after all and that *Test Match Special* would be more interesting. I settled back on the cold wooden floor and tuned in to Barbados to see how the bowlers were faring under the intense heat of the mid-day tropical sun.

IX

If you go far enough north in Sutherland you outstrip even history, and are left only in the company of strange people, a handful of odd apples who've floated up to the top of the barrel. The parish of Durness has a population of 2.4 people per square mile (the UK national average is 369 per square mile), so it was hardly surprising I barely saw a soul north of Kinlochbervie. The Durness craft village – a converted radar camp – was deserted except for a bookseller and his wife from Aylesbury who were busily writing their winter letters. On Faraid Head, Waggy and Geoff, a couple of lads from Newcastle, were gloomily thrusting their ferrets down rabbit holes and filling their van with ragged corpses.

Kinlochbervie had been quiet until Sunday evening, when it suddenly filled with fishermen who'd come across in fleets of vans from the east coast. I had got a lift back into town with an oil-worker, who'd explained the migration.

Kinlochbervie, he said, was the base of forty-odd deep sea trawlers, but boats and crews were not local. They came over from the east coast, four hours' drive away, driven off their own coast by fishing quota restrictions in the North Sea. It was a weekly invasion that brought the place alive, but which not everyone liked, least of all the minister. Some of the original crofters and fishermen had been swept up in the new trade, but only as lorry packers, fish porters or – if they were bright enough – representatives of fish-buying companies. Very few joined the crews of the east coast boats.

"East coast men are different," he explained. "We don't always get on well together, us and them. There's some that really likes the place, wi mistresses and the like over this side as well as their families back in the east, but there's others as think the best bit about Kinlochbervie is the road out, for sure."

I couldn't help but be drawn to the windscreen sticker on his car, which said "Kinlochbervie – God's handiwork".

I looked out of the window at what God had made. It all looked like raw material waiting for the making to begin. There was no snow up here, and every roadside crag had a deer nailed to it. Absence of light drained all detail from the ground itself, but daylight was lingering on the lochs, producing scenery like a photographic negative with light in all the wrong places. God's handiwork was still only a silhouette, a negative for a print, a rough model prepared for completion later.

That night the bar of the Kinlochbervie Hotel began to boom

with the voices of big men clutching little drinks. The oil-worker who'd given me a lift that afternoon introduced me to the skipper of the *Sparkling Star*, the east coasters' unofficial leader.

"If the local population wanted anyone to do well it'd be Big Al," he'd said. "Big Al lets the school use his van while he's out to sea and he wiss introduced to Prince Charles when Charlie came up to open the new port. I tell you, we were all a bit anxious what he might say because his language is not exactly the Queen's English."

Big Al wasn't just big, he was monumental. A black road-mender's jacket covered a boiler suit that went on and on until it finally tapered into his wellington boots. His popularity was easy to gauge by the number of rum and cokes that swum up on to the bar in front of him. He gathered them in like some fond father-fisherman drawing minnows into his net, and growled gently in my direction something about how interest rates were forcing him to work too hard, and how marvellous it was to be out at sea on a clear, still night under the stars. He spoke for three or four minutes more, but it might have been Norwegian for all I understood of it. All I picked out was the steady stream of blasphemies, though it was clear from his manner that his message was fundamentally gentle and maybe even poetic. Men, flashing tattoos on their arms, came and went around him and he mumbled a sentence for each. It was unclear to me what was directed to whom, but he'd get a reaction from somewhere along the bar for virtually everything he said.

Eventually the bar emptied. Big Al, trailing his crew like a bedraggled net, led the way down to the quay. The brand-new port – built with EC money – was yellow under sodium lights, and throbbing with the sound of diesels. Steaming lights were crisscrossing out in the deeper water as the earlier boats turned out into Loch Clash. The *Sparkling Star*, ugly, unappealing and livid with rust, was ready too. Big Al gave me a brief tour, switched on his computer and showed me where he'd had his catches the previous week – an honour, because all skippers are furiously secretive about their movements. Back on the quay, unsteady on my feet, I wished them all a good shot.

"Ach," Big Al bellowed over the engine noise, "there's maire tae li' then fuckin fush." At least, I think that's what he said.

It wasn't hard to get to Ardmore from Kinlochbervie. The post bus driver who dropped me off at the end of the track did so with the sort of pitying smile that the sadistic Greeks used to reserve for slaves about to be thrown to the lions. Ardmore was a "wee bittie walk doon there", he said. The man's a maniac, he implied.

I came upon John Ridgway at Ardmore at a rare moment of weakness, and I think I should be grateful for it. Ridgway is a towering, craggy ex-para with a broken nose and bushy eyebrows who made his name by rowing across the Atlantic with Chay Blyth in 1966, and he has continued to have an adventure once a year since then. In a sense he is the ultimate crop-headed youth, several years on, and far more interesting. In a sense, too, his centre at Ardmore is aiming to achieve the same purification and peace of mind as Samadhan had been, although the two couldn't have been more different: whereas Tom, the creator of Samadhan, appreciated the landscape in an almost subliminal, serene way, John Ridgway, creator of Ardmore, achieved his spiritual satisfaction by going at it like a battering ram.

John Ridgway's definition of a good man is someone who would pull on wet socks at 5.00 a.m. without a murmur of complaint, but fortunately I didn't have to prove my worth with this or any other test: he had a cold and his cold, which had rather taken the wind out of his sails, was prompting him to be open, frank, honest, self-questioning and self-doubting, and not at all the rather arrogant action-man I'd half expected. "I'm getting old and cranky," he said between sniffs. His age was patently a sore point with him; he was over fifty and his body was beginning to make hard work of the adventures his mind drove him to. For the last couple of winters he'd paddled up the Amazon into the thick of jungle terrorism, and next winter he was planning to canoe around Cape Horn.

It seemed to me that here was a man who needed a challenge, who needed to force himself up against that challenge, in order to feel his own existence. For most people, "I think, therefore I am," is enough; for him it had to be, "I row the Atlantic, therefore I am − for the time being." His exploits were made, not out of a sense of arrogance and the supremacy of his own self-reliance, but as a way of reassuring himself of his own existence and his own value.

As at Scoraig, Ardmore is an isolated peninsula sticking out into a loch, although the chances of growing anything here are far more limited than down by Ullapool. As at Scoraig, there had been no road and no electricity at Ardmore, and the locals had almost all abandoned it. I doubt that any coastal landscape in the UK could have been much more of a challenge to human life and provided a more severe beauty.

When he and his wife Marie Christine had come to Ardmore first in 1964, the community, which had once been a self-sufficient although scattered township, comprised just one remaining household. Ridgway's energy, aided and abetted by the force and enthusiasm of Marie Christine, had revitalised the old community and repopulated it. He'd started by opening the John Ridgway School of Adventure in 1969, almost too early for the fashion for healthy fitness-inducing holidays. In the winter he'd gone on his own adventures, generally writing a book about the better ones, and generally getting the book published. He had a bluff approach to literature and made no great claims for his writing, which covers what can be flashes of great insight. "I just write it all down as I feel like it. I let other people take care of things like punctuation and spelling." But the writing had an important purpose too: while he proved his own worth to himself through the adventure alone, it was only through a book that he could prove it to the outside world.

Over the years Ardmore had developed into a township again, moulded by his hands and nurtured on his breath. He had recently had a slightly ridiculous conning tower installed on the roof of his croft, protruding above a building which was already high on a slope above the loch, from which he could survey all that he had made, like a demi-god. The conning tower had been assembled elsewhere and brought in by helicopter as a whole unit, as had the telegraph poles which had brought in electricity in 1981. From it, Ridgway looked down over his little empire, hammered his books into his word processor, and talked to his various managers by walkie-talkie. In the bay beneath the house was a salmon farm he'd started in 1977, before the blossoming of the fish-farming industry. He'd never insured it because he couldn't bear the idea of other people getting fat on his premiums, and fortunately the farm had justified his decision by continuing to do well. A little further out were his fishing boat and his yacht, *English Rose VI*, in which he'd travelled around the world non-stop in 202 days two hours and fifteen minutes in 1984, departing from the mooring down below the house and returning to the mooring below the house, having only spied land for a handful of those 202 days, in an absurd experience that only someone in search of a sort of rigorous purity would ever envisage. "The boat is primed," said Ridgway, looking longingly at it. "Water, diesel, food, you name it. Always ready to just fuck off."

Two crofts to one side of his house and two to the other side were lived in again; at the foot of the slope by the water was the bunkhouse (for the School of Adventure's students) and the Wooden House, which usually accommodated the "instructors", young, physical, men who lead the students – adults and children – on expeditions around Sutherland's moors and shores in scenery which Ridgway describes as "inspirational". On the far shore, beyond Chadh-fi island, was the original School of Adventure, built in 1968.

All this Ridgway had created, but he displayed no overweening sense of self-satisfaction at what he had done. He doubted himself too much ever to let himself feel that. For him, standing still amounted to failure: there was only one way to move in life, and that was forward. I think he was also aware of the speed with which things can deteriorate. If no one of his energy and his motivation took over the centre, Ardmore would crumble away faster than he had created it.

"We could have built into a big company," he said, musingly, after discussing the movement of some smolts with the fish-farm manager on his walkie-talkie, the tiny oilskin-clad figure out on the distant cages who gesticulated wildly to illustrate his point. "We were asked for franchises in two or three other locations, but we weren't interested."

On the evening before my return south there were five of us at dinner, myself, Ridgway, Marie Christine, Rebecca (their daughter, in her twenties) and Lizbet, the Peruvian daughter of a dear friend whom Ridgway had saved from terrorists a couple of years before and brought back from the Amazon. Lizbet was clearly finding it hard to adapt to life in a foreign, unsophisticated culture, set in a desolation which was in its way just as complete as the Amazonian jungle. It must have been confusing, for what was she to adapt to? The images of her new world as seen on television or in magazines, or to what she could see in her immediate environment – a physical life on a loch in the middle of nowhere? Her shyness, her confusion, however, seemed only a matter of time. The Ridgways had built their lives – and Ardmore – on team effort and when on song they were unstoppable, harnessed to their task of her cultural acclimatisation and radiating family love of considerable power. If I'd been one of the young men in the Wooden House at the bottom of the hill I'd have found Rebecca and her mother enthralling: physically and intellectually strong, capable, accessible, and attractive to the extent of being rather overwhelming of a young man's fantasies.

The two of them, mother and daughter, turned out on the 6.00 a.m. run the following morning with the instructors. Someone from "the house" always participated. John Ridgway had excused himself from the run on the grounds of his cold, so I borrowed his gear and completed the bleak six miles to my own satisfaction, bobbing along the track behind one of the young instructors, who confided in me that he thought Ridgway was losing his grip and getting too old. I'm sure it was the presence of the instructors which reminded Ridgway, harshly, of his middle age, and while they were there he'd never allow himself to relent. How he was going to cope with finally being old it was difficult to see.

Spring – the Clyde to the Tweed

I

In 1724 Daniel Defoe described Glasgow as "the cleanest and beautifullest, and best built city in Britain, London excepted". In the years that followed came industrialisation, during which the city became additionally praised as the workshop of the world, and then the slump. In 1924, exactly 200 years after Defoe's words were first published, an MP described the city as the "earth's closest suburb to hell".

In the 1960s much of Glasgow was bulldozed; in the 1980s it suddenly became Miles Better, and today the Glasgow billboards have been repasted again, this time presenting the image of a place that is creative, fashionable, industrious and optimistic.

In the early days of spring I walked the streets looking for my own generalisations about Glasgow, but there were no glib answers. All worlds exist in the city – hell, heaven and all points between. There are far too many pulse points, each producing a different signal, for an overall diagnosis: Glasgow is alive and kicking, excited or comatose, striving for success or struggling for survival, depending on where you're standing and in which direction you're looking. Glasgow is Europe's enigmatic city of the 1990s, a city in the throes of exciting and passionate change which no doubt some social historian will give a convenient name to when it comes out the other side. Meanwhile, the best I can do is to say that it is the most un-glib place in the world.

There are several different Glasgows, several different sorts of Glaswegian and several versions of the success story of the 1980s, many of which don't even mention the word "success".

The city divides the country and divides opinion. Broadly speaking the west of Scotland feels allegiance to Glasgow, while the east prefers Edinburgh. This is as much a class division as anything else, with the east being more prosperous and rather posher than the west. All over Scotland, however, there are those who hold up Glasgow's revitalisation as evidence of the Scots' ability to get their act together, declaring that once the nation as a whole has – like Glasgow – overcome the trauma of the end of the era of heavy industry it too will feel a bit happier about its new identity.

Geographically, Glasgow sits in a broad bowl on the banks of the Clyde, hidden from most approaches until the final handful of miles. Once over the lip and into the bowl, there are no pretty approaches: from having started around two crossroads – the first up by the cathedral and the second around what is now Glasgow Cross – the city has been smeared messily all over the valley. Only a matter of minutes inland from Glasgow the Clyde is a beaming river tumbling down a leafy valley littered with garden centres and heritage trails; when it hits the city it broadens out into a sullen, putrid stretch of grey water, where suicides and sewage bob on the tide.

Glasgow itself has the air of having been partially dismantled, as if the city fathers had decided that the best thing would be to knock everything down and start again. In the recent past a monster combination of economic collapse and desperate planning has grabbed the city in its jaws and given it a thorough shaking, spreading bits far and wide and leaving great rending wounds in the centre. Vast areas of workland, some covered in warehouses and derelict factories, some cleared of all but piles of rubbish, encroach even upon the commercial centre, which has been christened the Merchant City by the council. The amount of disused stone is on a scale not often seen outside Egypt and much of the south bank of the river is like a despoiled tomb, plundered by banks looking for assets to liquidate and played in by children whose parents were casualties of those liquidations. These children are growing up with a redefinement of themselves, into a fashion and a style that is entirely Glaswegian and entirely fresh.

In a way the derelict spaces are still culturally important, because the bulk of the population still derives its sense of identity from the heavy industries which once stood there, and from the tenement housing nearby, where the factories' workforces lived. Work is the subject of an awful lot of the recent art – work that no longer exists.

Best-selling books in Glasgow are those which are filled with photographs of Gorbals slums, and the dominant political colour is still heavily socialist in what is now an old-fashioned way, even though the large unionised workforces no longer exist. Local politics are reflected in the composition of the regional council, Strathclyde, where eighty-seven per cent of seats are Labour-occupied.

With politics like these, Glasgow is not likely to endear itself to the establishment, and its modern creativity has been partly drawn from having been thrust into a role as Scotland's alternative, which it adopts almost unthinkingly.

Throughout its history Glasgow has been virtually monocultural: the tobacco industry was followed by the cotton industry which was in turn followed by shipbuilding and locomotive building. Everyone was employed in the same sort of jobs for the same sort of wages and lived in the same sort of accommodation, weaving a social fabric which still holds strong despite its physical dispersal through the satellite towns.

The cultural luggage of this lifestyle, rescued in part from the dereliction, is documented in the People's Palace, a "museum" that was once regarded as a depository for old rubbish – but Glasgow's social history lies in its rubbish, and the People's Palace is regarded as a shrine amongst Glaswegians. At the time of the big demolitions, when the council tried to clean up the slum image of the city, the People's Palace curator followed the demolition squads, salvaging shreds that together made up a picture of what was being erased.

Today even the Merchant City at Glasgow's heart is only half occupied. An active tourist within the city for a long weekend could be forgiven for thinking that he was trapped in the dwindling centre of a crumbling city, where only a matter of yards from the main shopping streets lurk dereliction and danger creeping in on the unwary shoppers.

Physically Glasgow feels like San Francisco, with a grid-like pattern of streets dropped on to swooping hills; dead straight vistas point unerringly at the setting sun, interrupted occasionally by motorways which have sliced up the city like a joint of meat and drained the centre of its residents. In the bloodletting of the 1960s and 1970s the middle class escaped to the hills and the working class were rehoused in satellite towns, leaving the centre as an island. The similarities with North American cities don't just stop at the road plan: Glasgow has a massive immigrant population (which includes a Jewish bagpipe band); it has chrome bars, a subway (here most definitely not an "Underground"), carry-outs and diners, all also reminiscent of North American cities, but then this is where American culture came from; this is no trendy young imitation, this is Grandad himself. The men who made the cities sailed out of the Clyde on ships that they had built themselves, on £2 tickets to Canada; their great-grandchildren return today to photograph the ruins.

Glasgow is a monument to sheer back-breaking physical work where the fundamental precept of life has always been to earn your bread, speak your piece and be content. This fundamental philosophy has survived in the modern city despite the lack of the work that was once at its core; in the 1990s, while the national tabloid newspapers were offering holidays in the sun and sizzling cash prizes for Bingo winners, one of the local Glasgow papers was giving away half a pound of mince to people who took out a regular order. A half-pound of mince, wrapped in last night's edition if you're lucky, is a meaningful lure in a city of no-frills survival. In the mid-nineteenth century, the worst days of the slums, the population density of the city centre was 583 persons per acre; now it stands at fourteen persons per acre. In the old slum centres of the 1850s, fifty per cent of children died of malnutrition or disease before they reached the age of ten.

Perhaps because everyone has got their hands dirty in the not-so-distant past, perhaps because of the immigrant nature of the city, class-consciousness in Glasgow is limited. After all, if eighty-seven per cent of the regional council's seats are Labour, it's fair to assume that the vast majority of the population have the same political outlook. There is a middle class, but it's a middle class which has levered, inched its way out of the working class and the dividing line between the two is so difficult to define that most people don't bother. Class-consciousness is pleasantly diluted in many parts of Scotland, and Glasgow is the most pleasant dilution of all.

In Glasgow, the sort of community spirit that pervades Scotland as a whole has become an institution, which partly explains the politics. Strong community spirit lends itself to socialism – everyone working for the good of the community, loath to break ranks – but that same spirit doesn't encourage private enterprise, which could help to explain why Glasgow has been so monocultural over the years. Especially in the rural communities in Scotland, there's a sense of distrust of ind-ividual achievement other than in academic circles, where success isn't aggressive; private enterprise usually entails the pursuit of individual ideals and individual wealth, and it doesn't sit well in communities used to unswerving adherence to tradition. In Glasgow, a burgeoning number of artists have thrived on this difficult situation, because they can use the strong sense of community as their subject matter while essentially pursuing entrepreneurial careers.

At the top end of Glaswegian society there is a small clique of rich people who glide up and down the escalators in the new shopping malls, particularly Princes Square, showing off mid-winter tans that certainly were not acquired locally. But they don't look classically rich in the way that they do elsewhere, with tweeds and pearls. They are not inherited rich: they are the new rich, who have made their money through flair, enterprise and initiative, and it shows in the gear they wear and the way they look. The landed gentry are present in small numbers, visible on occasional Saturday evenings when stag nights bring together the kilted young Hoorays in rowdy groups in the safer parts of the city. Most of them would probably rather be in Edinburgh.

Glasgow lacks that badge of mindless urban life for the sake of urban life – office girls in tight skirts teetering about in groups on white plastic stilettos, giggling and showing a predictable interest in flash men with fast cars. In Glasgow flat shoes, black clothes and self-confidence are the fashion. The women are composed, purposeful and individual. Time after time I felt subjected to a frank appraisal that made me feel simultaneously self-conscious and aroused. The city has an air of honest interest in sex that I've only really encountered in one other city, San Francisco, where the predominance of homo-sexual men means that single women have to assert themselves to find partners.

While Glasgow has gone through the mill of industrialisation and has experienced all its ups and downs, Edinburgh has travelled a smooth, level road unaffected by the vicissitudes of manufacturing. Edinburgh is where the trains from down south come in, unloading British legislation and lawyers, and generously tipping the Edinburgh porters; it is effectively a halfway point between England and Scotland, where English thinking is processed and made more palatable to Scottish tastes. Scotland is the child in a class of three who is ignored by the teacher; by rights, such a child should turn out to be delinquent. Edinburgh thinks that Glasgow is delinquent; Glasgow believes that Edinburgh is teacher's pet.

Edinburgh is full of "Piccadilly Scots" sitting on the fence and making a living out of interpreting, introducing, explaining, enforcing the thoughts of the south-east. Edinburgh confers with government through the right channels and is partly heeded by government; in Edinburgh, the top men speak out on behalf of the people while the people nod silently in the background. Glasgow shouts from the bar-room door to anyone who wants to hear, and when Glasgow's so-called top men try to do some speaking out on anyone's behalf they get shouted down by the babble from the bar, who disagree with every word. Everyone has their own opinion in Glasgow, and everyone believes that their own opinion is equally worth hearing. Glaswegians are natural, emotional and articulate, and they are endowed with a surfeit of a Scottish "problem" – an overdeveloped sense of natural justice.

In Glasgow's terms, the people of Edinburgh don't do any real work. The whole city has a sneaking suspicion that Edinburgh is filled with birthrighters, with people who know how to play the class game and therefore get on, with people who harvest money in stipends ("making" money is a Glaswegian concept) simply by being the right sort and saying the right thing. And there's a comfort and a complacency in Edinburgh life that makes the Glaswegians see red. Thus the competitiveness between the two cities, christened "Edin-buggering" by the Glaswegians. The Glaswegian novelist

William McIlvanney writes about the distinction in his novel *The Big Man*, describing Edinburgh as a "monument to a false sense of Scotland". On the other hand, he wrote, Glasgow "seemed to say without pretence: this is where we've really been, this is where we are." Today it is in the fields of literature, theatre, opera, music, painting and poetry that Scotland's capital is being truly Edinbuggered, say the Glaswegians. The upper class of Edinburgh have always considered the arts and their patronage to be their province, and so, while Glasgow's political insults can be safely ignored as the outpourings of a delinquent child, Glasgow's stealing of the artistic limelight hurts Edinburgh more deeply.

The press is fiercely partisan in this debate. The *Glasgow Herald* proclaimed, on the opening of Glasgow's new gallery, the McLellan, that "there are now two venues in Britain, the Royal Academy and the McLellan gallery." I went to the first show in the new McLellan and realised with a shock of surprise that I knew one of the subjects of a recent portrait by David Hockney. Jonathon Brown was a resident of Edinburgh; on the phone he laughed when I brought up the subject of the Hockney picture. Yes, it was him, he said. He was flattered, of course, but the main problem was that the burglars in his neighbourhood in Edinburgh all thought that he actually owned it and kept breaking in to try to steal it.

Despite Glasgow's media promotion, there's not yet been any attempt to paper over the cracks in its image. The city is proud of its faults, as a veteran is proud of his scars. Not far from the new and eye-opening sumptuous malls of St Enoch and Princes Square, towards Glasgow Cross, is shopping of a rather different style. The people of Paddy's Market, under the arches of the railway line, just to the west, are shoppers and stall-holders with no money at present, no money in the past and no prospect of any money in the future. One side of Paddy's Market are the cavernous railway arches and the other a tall, barbed-wire-topped fence; squeezed like cattle between the wire and the brick the vendors and shoppers look like refugees or prisoners of war, grasping on to fire-melted imitation furs and broken trowels as providers of hope. "All fresh stuff," said one crumpled gent to me, waving his yellow fingers at a pile of old track suits and a desert of old teasmades. What was fresh?

There was nothing that was not chipped, cracked, scorched or darned. Although in a perverse way I liked being seen as a potential customer because at least it meant I didn't stand out too much, I didn't risk saying anything in reply. I didn't dare open my mouth for fear that my accent would reveal me for the voyeur that I was. This is too raw a place for tourism, too real and too disturbing to become a living museum. Glasgow's history and Glasgow's tragedy are still too young to have left the streets.

Part of the appeal of the city lies in the co-existence of different styles side by side. The trendy Third Eye centre sits on Sauchiehall Street opposite a parade of excellent Indian restaurants manned by Sikhs with accents like Billy Connolly; trendy families toddle around the paintings in the Third Eye saying totally unpretentious things like, "I like the colours," and "Isn't that the Rangers ground?" Around the corner is the Follies disco in a converted church with pillars painted black, and further down Sauchiehall Street is the Pars Bakery, the sort of place where my granny would have taken me. The tables are primed with doughnuts to tide customers over that awkward gap between ordering and delivery; the heavy-footed thick-legged waitresses in black and with doilies on their heads sleepily pile one's plate with home baking with a conspiratorial smile; still a growing lad, and you thirty-two! Eat. And have some more.

Here you buy your breakfast by the pound and cake-eating is practised as a method of keeping out the cold. The tables are bulging with babies who look set for a lifetime devoid of health food, on the knees of old ladies swopping notes on the best places in town to buy scarves. And if it's not cakes then it's meat pies with chips and broon sauce from the carry-out just down the road. Most people, no matter what their income, eat the same.

The rich in Glasgow don't have the haughty *noblesse oblige* of the traditional English rich. Their only power is their money, and their instinct is to make more and to spend, but not to rule. Every city has to have a certain percentage of birthrighters, of people with an instinct to rule, in order to tug at the ear of the establishment. Without this ear-tugging ruling class, Glasgow is impotent; it has a very strong political will, but no political recognition. It has no acceptable messengers to deliver its thoughts into any inner sanctum. On a national level Glasgow's political punch "through the appropriate channels" is so weak that it is barely thrown. Passive resistance is the Glaswegian's best method of self-expression, and passive resistance has produced the highest percentage of non-payers of the poll tax in Scotland (34.6 per cent in the Strathclyde region in 1990). And yet, on an anti-poll tax march through the city the atmosphere was what the newspapers would describe as "fundamentally good-humoured". There was no confrontation; how could there be? The marchers were applauded like heroes all along the route, and if anyone had anything to say in favour of the poll tax, they did it discreetly, behind doors. I only heard one criticism. "They shuidnae pute they bairns on the street," said an old lady, but not because of any argument with the fundamental principle. "They're makin them wak fae nothing."

The march took place on the same day as a rally in London's Trafalgar Square which marked the start of poll tax in England. The English rally turned into a riot. In Glasgow a man with a loudhailer announced the news with a certain relish. "The English air having a bit rammy theirsel," he said. "The English thunk we're a nation ae beggars, whingeing awa' up here because ae the cauld wither. The English thunk their pain uz the genuine article, but iveryone else's uz character-building. Now they're squealing aboot the poll tax." Loud cheers from the audience.

Historically a country with a political will but no political representation is a good breeding-ground for anarchy. On the Glasgow march anarchy did emerge; but it didn't set fire to parked cars; it didn't break the windows of the shops en route or assault the police officers. It did arrive alongside the main auditorium in Queen's Park, where a somnolent group was playing cover versions of Pink Floyd and Billy Joel between speeches. It arrived in the form of a tarpaulin-sided beer lorry; the tarpaulins dropped away to reveal a kilted punk group tuning up. They were called "Fool-i-shite against the poll-tax", and the first number they belted out was "We're fool-i-shite against iverything".

II

Frustrated by the city I slept around a bit, changing bed and breakfasts nightly in order to change areas. The landladies were very varied. Mrs Ogilvie, a respectable, proper woman of the sort who was easily mortified, effectively confined me to my room with copies of the *Lady* and *Gardens of Scotland*. She wouldn't tell me how to get to Easterhouse or Drumchapel because they were "eh, not the sairt of place you shuid go. Eh, I'd be *mortified* if *my* son went there."

In a different part of the city I was woken in the middle of the night by a tempestuous argument between the two landladies, a mother and her daughter (the latter had recently had a baby; no sign of any father). When it came to breakfast time I ventured timidly down the stairs to find all the doors of the hallway shut and locked, but the front door standing open like the daylight at the end of a rifle barrel. I hadn't paid my bill, but the message was clear enough and I whistled through that corridor and out into the city.

Glasgow's modern literature has dwelt rather introvertedly and obsessively on its hardness, on the estates where the norm is to live "on the broo" (social security), where beer, fighting, football, women and work were a man's priority, and the struggle to hold the family together is the woman's problem. The city's performing arts dwell on similar themes. At the time of Mayfest, Glasgow's equivalent of the Edinburgh festival and the subject of occasional sniping comments in the Edinburgh press, a lot of the events are scattered around the city in community centres in deprived areas. Unlike in Edinburgh, where most of the festival theatre is performed by incomers for incoming audiences, the performances of Mayfest show the communities their own images on stage as part of the process of cultural consolidation, holding the mirror up to their own nature, as if their family albums and school photographs had come to life. For an incomer like me the adventure of finding the venues was as much of a cultural experience as the performances themselves.

One evening I ended up in Drumchapel (locally known as the Drum) as the shops pulled down their graffiti-covered shutters. The shopping centre benches were occupied by a young couple, both drunk, with two young children, and a couple of older alcoholics. But the thing that most struck me about this and any of the other estates was the almost total absence of cars parked on the streets; the kerbs were bare. Two-thirds of families in the Drum are on income support; thirty-seven per cent of sixteen- to nineteen-year-olds are out of work, and teenage gangs with names like the Young Hill Team, the Peel Glen Boys and the Young Boon Platoon work their small territories, giving opposition gang members a "doing" if they stray unaccompanied over their boundaries. Most of the talk of pitched battles between razor gangs – the image of Glasgow in the post-war years – is, apparently, a myth. The last good fights were in the 1970s, although Saturday nights in the Drum sometimes see a bit of a scrap on the border with the neighbouring housing scheme, Clydebank. Most of what little fighting there is takes place between rival gangs and for an outsider the housing scheme is not dangerous.

The Drumchapel pub had the decor of a betting shop and my feet scrunched over the dirty lino. Every pub, bar or diner in Glasgow is a community centre, and the community is surrounded by a light membrane of familiarity and a shared past. Outsiders, entering the pub, bar or diner, break that membrane and the resulting frisson is easily misinterpreted as hostility, when it's really just curiosity. In the bar in Drumchapel I wasn't so sure that the membrane – here an invisible unbreakable barrier – wasn't composed of rather more hostility than usual. I pointed at the McEwans tap. "A pint." I didn't dare say more than those two words. In the silence that had fallen on the other customers, everyone was listening for my accent.

"Are ye the polis?" said a man in a suit at the bar. He had a nice face. He was visiting the neighbourhood, he said. He used to live here, but he'd done well and moved out. It was best for people like me to stay away, he said, and not to provoke. He only came back because his family liked to see him because he'd done well. It seemed the natural thing to me for someone successful to be financially supportive of his or her parents, but when I suggested this he was indignant. They wouldn't want his money, he said. It was up to the state to provide for them.

No, their reward lay in the community agreeing that their son had done well, that was enough for them.

He wanted to know what I was doing there. A play in Drumchapel? Had anyone else heard of a play in performance in Drumchapel? he asked the regulars. No one had. Plainly he didn't believe me, I was "talking mince". Was I sure that I wasn't the police?

The play was an unsentimental series of sketches of how life used to be, written by local people, many of whom had never written before. Judging by the grunts of appreciation from two ladies behind me, it was accurate. The accents were precise and individual performances were excellent and the whole had a rare feeling of integrity. I couldn't help feeling, though, that such art didn't give Glasgow any future; it showed it its own face and its own past, but it didn't open its mind to the outside world. It only worked as a piece of art within the confines of the Glasgow estate; elsewhere it would become a piece of passionless social history. But its effects could be more disturbing, too. Art that confirmed and reconfirmed the city's own sense of its own identity and recent past is in danger of creating an inward-looking place with a doctrine of purity of blood, where outsiders are not welcome. Purity begins to be worrying where it slips into racism; in Glasgow prove your purity and you are eligible to be a councillor and an administrator; if your birth, accent and upbringing are all in place, then your future is more secure. Glaswegians who accuse Edinburgh of having birthrighters in governing circles are themselves creating their own birthrighters: there is a disturbing doctrine in the city of no power without purity, without the triumvirate of birth, upbringing and accent.

On a particularly warm spring Friday evening, after a week of finding no real evidence to support the image of the hard side of Glasgow before it became Miles Better, I opted to spend the night on the streets with the men with names like Shuggie and Boxcar Wullie whose favourite tipples were Thunderbird and Surge (surgical spirits). Everyone I met – and you can't help meeting people in Glasgow – advised me against it, and it was with a certain amount of trepidation that I clung to a bar in Byres Road until closing time. In the gents the notice above the urinals read "Please don't throw cigarette ends in the urinals".

Underneath someone had added: "It makes them soggy and hard to light". It seemed like a good place to be starting out from for a night on the streets.

Drinking stories are prolific in Glasgow, more so than drunks, who have mostly headed south to London. During a TV interview Glasgow comedian Billy Connolly was asked why he thought there were no IRA bombings in the city. Connolly replied, quick as a flash, that the IRA knew it was useless throwing a petrol bomb into a Glasgow pub because a punter would pick it up and drink it before it could go off.

I repeated this story to a man leaning against the Byres Road bar drinking cups of black coffee; he looked a bit like Connolly himself, but he was a carpenter and he had a phlegmatic, humourless approach to life. But I should have known better than to try to start up a lighthearted conversation about Glasgow with a Glaswegian. No, he said, the truth behind the IRA joke was far from funny. Both sides in the Irish dispute had strong support in the city, and they dared not alienate that support. That's what the Big Yin – Connolly – was referring to.

"Ah well remember queuing fae a job outside o' Harland and Woolf, the shipyard," said the carpenter, swallowing another coffee at one gulp. "They wur loyalist Protestant. Ahm an atheist masel', but ma schule wis Catholic. There must ha' bin thirty o' us. Ah had aw the right qualifications and experience, but ah wis the oanly ane who didnae get the job. The gatekoopor shooted efter me, 'We dinny want no bloody Tims in here.'"

"A Tim is a Catholic?"

"Ay. Billys and Tims. But they'll nae fight each ither. It's aw mouth. This buzness aboot fighting and gangs is shite, pure shite."

"This is the roughest bar on Byres Road," chipped in a small tubby man with a beard squeezing through. He didn't look as if he ought to be spoiling for a fight, but I hauled the conversation back to where it had started, just in case.

"Actually we were just talking about jokes." I grinned as sweetly as I could.

The new arrival grunted. "What's the difference between Rangers and a tea-bag?" he said.

We shook our heads.

"A tea-bag stays longer in the cup."

Given that jokes against Rangers were jokes against the Protestant majority in Glasgow and the fact that we were standing in the roughest bar in Byres Road, I thought this was a rather risky start to a conversation. I was ready to make my excuses, thinking the street would be a far safer place, when the newcomer put down a pile of books on the bar. On top was a volume of Glasgow's new writing. "Good stuff, that," he said, seeing my attention drawn to the cover. "My friend here has some of his poems in it." He was a painter and his friend was a poet, he explained, and they'd just been to a creative circle meeting. He turned and picked out another half-dozen faces in the bar – a composer and his wife, two novelists, another artist and a welder who was also a writer, all in "the roughest bar in Byres Road". Only the welder, who was wearing a white suit, looked as if he wanted to stand out from the crowd.

In such company I thought it was safe to admit that I was thinking of writing a book on Scotland. I was immediately hailed as a fellow artist and whisked away from the carpenter. "He's writing a book about Scotland," said the excited painter to each member of the circle he introduced me to. I was flattered and flummoxed by such instant celebrity; in the south, bar-room cynics would have waited until they'd seen the contract before believing any bar-room bullshit about being an author. Only the welder in the white suit wanted to know more. "Air ye jist," he said, perfectly politely. "And what exactly aboot Scotland wuid that be?" That had me stumped. The proper researching of any book seemed the business of hours in libraries and civic offices, not the product of propping up the bar in Byres Road and talking to anyone who'd spare a few slurred words. I hadn't really started on my book, I said, and it was only an idea, rather a simple one at that: I thought I'd go round asking the Scots what they did and what they thought of their own country.

I could hardly have said anything more provocative. Only the Americans have opinions that are as formed and decided as the Glaswegians, and when a Glaswegian is bevvied up he's almost as articulate as an American. The group gathered round and the conversation centred on politics and nationalism. It swiftly became a "we" and "you" affair. My accent allied me with

England, with the oppressors, the rulers and the aristocrats who only came north to knock hell out of the countryside, its animal life and its people. To them I seemed a representative of the ruling south sent like a messenger into their midst and they seized the opportunity to drum their views into me. I felt that it was my duty to listen. Glasgow had not become Miles Better, said the painter. In fact, Mrs Thatcher had made things a great deal worse in Scotland. The significant change of the last decade was that Glaswegians had realised that a lot of other cities were in a similarly bad – or even worse – state, and that had made things psychologically better for Glaswegians; united in self-defence, they'd come out of their shells and started to show the world their city and their creativity.

When it came to chucking-out time I announced my intention of spending the night on the street as part of my research. The poet and the painter were flabbergasted. The painter immediately volunteered a bed in his five-room flat. "Don't do it," he urged. "Why do you want to? They'll kill you. Folk out there are desperate. You'll get hurt. They've only got to hear your accent and they'll knife you for what you've got." He did a quick tour of the circle, telling them this latest news about the English writer. They all shook their heads sadly, as if he'd just announced my demise and they were preparing their quotes for the morning's papers, under the headline, "Tourist hacked to death for 50 pence".

The carpenter, who was still at the bar, seemed a little the worse for all the caffeine he'd drunk. "Dinna listen tae that load o' wummin," he said. "You'll be safe as hooses. In the wunter utz bad – ah usit tae wirk in the soop vans in George Square. At thus time o' yeer there's plenty wirk and iveryone's doon in London."

I thanked him. "How many coffees have you drunk tonight?" I was curious.

"Coffee? What wuid ah coom tae a bar tae drink coffee fer? The coffee's jist tae cover the taste. I canna abide whusky by itself."

All the talk of danger had increased my trepidation, so I headed for familiar places where the lights were still on. I loitered in the bus station until it closed. In the waiting-room was a handful of old ladies, wee, stocky and cheerful, enjoying their own company and the activity around them. If it wasn't impolite to even think of it, I'd have said they too had been drinking a bit more than just coffee.

"Mrs Elliot," said one, as another lady joined them.

"Kirsty."

"He's writin something." Kirsty was looking at me. She was right; I was dutifully trying to record something of what the group of artists had said to me.

"What time uz ut?" Someone told her. "Oh noo. Oh crumbs-and-eggie. Oh Crikey-Jane." She giggled. "Wullie says he's goin' tae get yow cards fer yower birthday."

"Oh ay – in here, hen." This was directed to a sliver of an Indian girl in a shimmering saree of silver and green who was looking for the toilets. "She canna open the door, the puir littel hen. Too skinny, puir wee thung. Gurels these days are too skinny."

"Going oot on Friday?"

Kirsty got up and retrieved a banana that had been left on a seat by another passenger. "Ah'll have it wi' ma breakfast in the morning. If ah laift it there someone else wuid come and pick it up."

Outside the glass window of the waiting-room a flustered woman was in earnest discussion with two bus station officials. "Ay, her purse is awa'. Doesn't she luik worrit?"

"They shuid have a luik in the toilet jist noo."

"They takes the munny and leaves the rest."

"What time uz ut? Oh noo, we've missed anither bus." Kirsty giggled.

They chorused "Cheerio" as I left, even though we'd exchanged no more than a smile.

George Square, a grey and lugubrious centre of the city that comes alive on civic occasions, Hogmanay and Saturday afternoons, was still throbbing at three o'clock in the morning. The night buses were parked around the sides of the square like a stockade, inside which were corralled the poorer clubbers and opera- and theatre-goers of the new young, all fashionably dressed in black. Weaving through them were the old drunks, leaving splodges of vomit like calling cards at the foot of Scotland's most famous men. These statues of the square, Walter Scott, James Watt *et al.*, all rather appropriately seemed to be trying to march out, away from such frivolity, an unfortunate reminder that an awful lot of Scotland's quality men and women have left the country, and continue to do so. The Glaswegians seem oblivious to this dourness in their civic monuments; at Hogmanay the square seethes with 20,000 delirious people, singing all the patriotic songs, dancing reels and offering policemen their chips. Just beyond the hour of the new year itself the self-important grandiose City Chambers explodes in sacrilegious fireworks, sending pigeons skeeting out over the square. Every year it feels like a new birth.

I was accosted by three abusively drunk Englishmen. They clung close together, emboldened by the fact that they'd been parading around the city abusing the Glaswegians and nobody had beaten them up yet. "What are you doing making notes," they jeered. "Write down that this is a shit city full of shits."

At that moment I was feeling particularly fond of Glasgow; I'd had a particularly good evening in the hands of people who wanted nothing except to invite me into their world. Incensed by the jeering louts, I waved my library card at them in the dark. I was police, I said, and if they didn't shut up and bugger off I'd make sure they had a criminal record by morning.

By half past three most of the night buses had gone and the remaining few were being gutted of their troublemakers by the police. A gang of a dozen young men started a running battle up and down the square, but it was far from being a serious fight; they'd end up in a motionless pile on the grass, grunting feebly, and someone at the bottom would scream: "Wha's farted?"

Eventually they too dispersed and only the dregs of the night were left, huddled on the benches and against the walls against the cold descent of the dew, the onset of sobriety or the contemplation of whatever it was that threatened to ruin their lives. Now that the square was quiet and still, it was easy to pick out the two or three middle-aged men who patrolled through it, like wolves hunting for the weak. They stopped occasionally by the huddled figures, holding brief conversations, sometimes squatting down to urge or to listen, or maybe even to hand over a note with an address or money. The same men were in the public toilets in St Vincent Street, a warm and welcoming hole in the ground at four o'clock in the morning, where the attendant was listening to opera on his cassette-player. They stood at the urinals, these men, their eyes sliding around the slippery tiled walls.

In the end it was too cold to try to sleep on the benches so I walked the empty streets, unaccosted. There was no one sleeping rough under the arches by the Clyde and no one under the Hielan' Man's Umbrella (Glasgow's nickname for the monstrous glass-sided railway bridge over Argyle Street). The nearby Dunkin' Donuts was open all night and I sat in the window and watched the dawn arrive in its deep blue coat. The morning shift was sweeping the place clear of a Friday night's litter. At the shop entrance a barefoot mentally retarded girl was swinging her black shiny plastic handbag repeatedly at an old drunk. A lad in a track suit with a sports bag sat down opposite me. I recognised him from one of the other benches in George Square; he hadn't been to bed either, he said. He had come over from Dunfermline the previous morning for a job interview. They'd asked him to start on Monday, so he didn't think it was worth going home. And he thought he might meet a lassie in the city.

"Did you?"

"Aye. I dud so. But I was tae tumid tae ask fer her telephone number." He bit gloomily into his doughnut, and I started telling him how I thought it was going to be a lovely day.

III

In Motherwell I booked into a boarding house at the same time as a musician who'd come to provide the live music for one of the town centre pubs. He wasn't looking forward to it. All week the newspapers had been full of British Steel's decision to close down the Ravenscraig steel mill at Motherwell with the loss of thousands of jobs.

In his survey of the nation in 1724 Daniel Defoe had criticised the Scots for wandering abroad. They needed "an industrious and diligent application to labour at home", he wrote. They had heeded his advice and settled down to create the workshop of the world, building monocultural industrial towns like Motherwell and getting down to the serious business of making things. But it had all gone wrong, and history was repeating itself at Motherwell, said the newspapers. First it had been the nineteenth-century Clearances of Highland townships by English landowners, and now it was the industrial towns which were being cleared by the English. Motherwell was the site of the latest, most emotive, of these Clearances by the remote control of a man sitting down in England – the chairman of British Steel. "We're bought and sold for English gold", Robert Burns had written in the 1790s; not much had changed. This was the result of the Doomsday Scenario, said the commentators: a scenario where the vast majority of Scots had voted overwhelmingly against the Conservative Party, but were still ruled by them. The result was, they said, a government that had an inbuilt prejudice against the Scots. No politician would lose their seat as the result of discontent in Motherwell.

To make matters worse, with so few Scottish members of parliament from the ruling party to choose from, the key positions in the Scottish Office were filled with people who, they said, in normal circumstances wouldn't be considered to have the ability to achieve high office at all. Had Scotland had a proportional representation within the party in power in Westminster, then Ravenscraig's fate would not have been allowed to pass so uncontested. The storm that raged north of the border on the announcement of its closure caused only ripples in a couple of sarcastic eyebrows in the south. The battle over Ravenscraig was not really to do with steel, it was the battle of an abandoned, ignored country trying to attract the government's attention.

In the event it only succeeded in attracting the attention of the hostile English media. A comment in the London *Evening Standard* condemned the Scots as "subsidy junkies" who were "wailing like a trampled bagpipe" over Ravenscraig. Mrs Thatcher was reported as saying, "We English, who are marvellous people, are really very generous to Scotland." Her press secretary was blunter: "The Scots are getting too much," he said. The newspaper even went on to suggest that North Sea oil revenue should be only to the benefit of the English, a theory that was based on the extension of the *angle* of the Scottish-English border out into the North Sea, which would place much of the oil-field in English waters. Scottish media outrage was tremendous.

In fact there was no evidence that Ravenscraig had been subsidised. British Steel had released no figures to justify the closure of the plant, and one of Scotland's Labour MPs pointed out the following day that the subsidy for British Rail South-East was several times the size of the subsidy for industry in Scotland. The *Evening Standard* piece struck home, however, perhaps because many Scots suspected that there might be some truth in their label of "dependency culture", and nobody likes to be dependent. The accusation was taken seriously, and some months later, after a period of research, the Scottish media produced their answer. They carefully avoided the plain fact that public expenditure is twenty-three per cent higher per person in Scotland than in England; Scotland receives some £14 billion of the total public spending of £130 billion, but then life is simply more expensive amongst all those mountains. Instead, the counter-attack was directed at the south-east, and the researchers rooted around in the £32 billion of public spending which is not attributed to any particular area. They concluded that most of this sum is spent in the south-east, including most of the defence budget of £19 billion, £4 billion on Docklands (equal to nearly half the Scottish Office budget), £6 billion on civil servants, and £6 billion on planned road spending. North Sea oil revenues of £100 billion had gone straight into London, they said, to subsidise the south-east.

The musician predicted heavy drinking, maybe even violence, in the pub that night. Normally he brought his girlfriend with him on the away gigs, he said, but this time he'd told her to stay home. He'd thought of cancelling, but he needed the money.

We both left the Motherwell guest house at the same time, parting in the town centre. It was unusually quiet for a Saturday evening. Although the mill was two or three miles away, the acrid smell of coal hung in the courtyards and streets and the screeching and shrieking of tortured metal advanced like an invisible spectre past the shop-windows.

"Mill" is such an innocent word for a nightmare of a place. Ravenscraig spreads along the horizon, totally devoid of people, like a photograph of a model projected on to the back wall of the sky to achieve a scale that was otherwise beyond the powers of man to create. In amongst the massive sheds and cooling towers were spurts of flame, dribbles of smoke and clouds of steam. With no other visible end result, Ravenscraig looked as if it had been made to pollute. Where they were turned towards the mill, the tenement walls of Motherwell had been blackened by the prevailing wind. I counted twenty-nine chimneys on the plant, each emitting a different-coloured stain on to the sky. As I watched, there was a massive release of smoke, totally without noise. Deep, deep down in that beast a living person had made a decision, pulled a lever or pushed a button, and the beast had performed a necessary bodily function, soiling the air in huge smudges. Standing in the lee of such a nightmare projection, I had to remember that inside Ravenscraig was a weekend shift of 1,500 people, working and wanting desperately to continue to work, in such surroundings. It was less to do with job satisfaction or pride, more a perverse tribute to the fear of unemployment.

In the jaws of the steelworks there was practically no activity. There was not much prospect of a guided tour on a Saturday evening, said the gatekeeper in the box in the middle of the approach road. He was a union man who'd been moved out of the mill itself. Despite the "fight for Ravenscraig" sticker on his box (they were plastered all over the town) he was surprisingly defeatist. The place was finished, he said. No one doubted that, and they'd known it was coming for a couple of years, but they'd fight the decision nevertheless. His phone bleeped; he leaned out of his box and called to a small, red-faced man who was shuffling past. Once the red faced man had continued, he returned to the phone. "Seems okay," he said. "He's oanly bin out ten minutes." The caller seemed satisfied.

"They wantit me tae see uf he was drunk," explained the gatekeeper after he'd put the phone down.

"Who did?"

"Security." The gatekeeper pointed to a darkened glass window on the roadside opposite. "They're in there."

"Was he drunk?"

"Nah, he wasna out lang enough. Takes a lot more than ten minutes tae get a steelworker properly bevvied up."

The following morning in the boarding house the musician took his breakfast early. He'd had a depressing night, he said, and he didn't mind if he never came back again. The pub had been half filled with morose drinkers who had paid him no attention at all; with hindsight he reckoned that a bit of violence might have been a good thing. "They looked as if they needed a good fight to shake them up a bit," he said.

IV

Glasgow's best-known industrial clearances of the post-war years have been along the banks of the Clyde. The shipbuilding industry effectively died on its feet in the 1970s when 170,000 jobs were lost, with a resultant massive loss of self-confidence amongst Glaswegians, who had staged a months-long work-in to save the last yard. "What is there to do in Glasgow on a Sunday?" a visiting tourism chief at the time had asked a hotel receptionist. "Go to Edinburgh," she replied.

That was then. As I travelled along the southern shore of the river by train I read in that day's paper how the last remaining big yard was once again having an argument with its workforce, asking them to take their tea-breaks on the job rather than in the canteen; the minutes saved, said the management, could save the company. It's been an unhappy end to an industry, and the shores of the Clyde will take a while to recover.

Greenock, once a shipbuilding town almost unequalled in the UK, had only two ships in its yards that day, both of them in dock for nothing more grand than routine repairs. Most of the craft in the grubby little fishermen's harbour were old motorised plastic pleasure boats, badly patched, but in amongst them were four or five prawn trawlers.

Because fishermen see the land from the water they sometimes have a wiser perspective on the affairs of men. Because they are pitting themselves against the elemental forces of wind and rock and sea, the articulate ones can achieve a mythical status locally. In Asia the fishermen are the drug-runners and the drug-users, beyond the reach of the law; on the Scottish coast they are the hard men, the poachers, the heavy drinkers, the men with hearts of gold, for whom the truth will never get in the way of a good story. "A travelled man has leave to lie," runs the Scottish proverb.

The Para Handy stories of Neil Munro, which centre on Captain Macfarlane and the crew of the *Vital Spark*, a Clyde puffer (a small steam-powered sea-going cargo boat with a very temperamental boiler), fit well into this tradition. Para Handy was a great and innocent fibber, in whose hands every event worth talking about acquired a mythical status. He had met "mudges" that were so big that you had to throw stones at them to keep them away. And work, although it was necessary, was not worth spending all one's energy on: "We went into Greenock for some marmalade, and did we no' stay three days." Para Handy was into quality and he enjoyed his fellow human beings; I wanted to find his modern equivalent because I couldn't think of a better antidote to take my mind off the spectre of a market economy that was about to steamroller the workers of Ravenscraig into the empty tarmac of Motherwell's deserted shopping centre.

But I couldn't find a Para Handy at Greenock. There were no skippers popping ashore for marmalade or sitting on their deck hatches ready to indulge in a bit of a blether: "And you'll be writing things for the papers? Cot bless me! . . . and do you tell me you can be makin' a living off that? I'm not asking you, mind, hoo mich you'll be makin', don't tell me; not a cheep! But I'll wudger it's more than Maclean the munister."

In the end Bernie said he'd take me out. I was grateful, even though Bernie hardly fitted the Para Handy mould. Dressed in bright yellow overalls with the word WATER stencilled on the back, he had been a builder until the building trade shrivelled as shipbuilding collapsed. He'd bought the Zephyr three years before, because someone had told him there was money to be made out of prawns. The Zephyr was a wooden boat with a ramshackle wheelhouse and gear so rusty that it could easily have put in a guest appearance on the deck of the Vital Spark. Bernie, middle-aged, lean and with thinning hair that he wore a cap to conceal, would not have won much of Para Handy's sympathy. He had no sense of the fishing tradition, no hankering for mythology and no affection for his boat; he wanted a metal boat which would mean less work, and a shorter one so he would have fewer restrictions and pay less tax. Bernie was no fisherman; he was a builder good at accounts who'd gone to sea. If he'd been a proper fisherman he would probably have been too superstitious to take passengers like me.

We steamed out of Greenock at 5.30 a.m. on a silent and still morning, accompanied by a pair of arguing seagulls. In the sky the white bone of an aircraft's vapour trail threaded through the clouds like a knitting needle on its way to America. Davey, the crew, was a shy, tubby man in his mid-thirties who settled down to do the crossword while we steamed towards Dunoon.

I was getting romantic feelings about travelling "doon the watter", a traditional weekend pastime for Glaswegians who travelled out on the Clyde to the seaside resorts and islands. Doon the wattering had effectively ended in the 1890s, but it still lived romantically in the minds of most true Glaswegians. Not Bernie. He was prosaic in what he pointed out through the wheelhouse window; the fishing grounds were at the junction of Loch Long, Gare Loch and Holy Loch, all of which had navy installations. Nuclear submarines were a daily hazard, he said, and the prawn nets sometimes brought up flatfish with sores as big as your hand when you worked close to the loch mouths. To make matters worse, they were building something "really big" up one of the lochs and dumping the dredged clay in the middle of the prawn grounds, and it was all too easy to snag and lose your whole gear, nets, cables, chains and all. And further out to sea was an explosives dump, where an unwary fisherman had recently found himself picking packets of Semtex out of his net. Bernie showed me the photocopied official warning; Semtex won't explode as long as it's wet, he said. He would make damn sure it went back overboard straight away. One or another of these hazards had caused the loss of a trawler with six crew only a matter of months before; only two bodies had been recovered. "We might get ane today oorsel," grunted Bernie.

The *Zephyr* was the second boat to reach the prawn grounds, shortly after six that morning. Once the gear had gone out over the stern and started scouring the bottom, we prowled up and down about half a mile offshore from Dunoon, watching the cars and buses beginning to move along the promenade as the town woke.

"That wis an awfy wile place once," said Bernie, gazing at Dunoon with his elbow on the wheel and rolling yet another cigarette. He had an open window by his shoulder through which he had a habit of chucking things without looking, particularly the dregs of his endless cups of tea. Holy Loch opened up, revealing a grey congealed lump of warships and floating docks in the middle of the basin; Dunoon is their shore base and their R and R. "The Americans oot ae Holy Loch crooded intae the Dunoon bars, and there'd be a rammy wi' the local lads because the Yankies'd pick up a' the spare. Wummin likes the Yankies. There wis a lot ae bairns born wi'oot their parents wantin'. Ah've two American brother-in-laws mesel. One o' them really loves the place, I've nae idea the why."

By nine in the morning we'd been joined by four or five other boats, steaming backwards and forwards on the same patch of sea like several tractors competing to plough a single field. As a rule the sense of rivalry between the boats was not unfriendly, but occasionally when one particular boat with a red hull threatened to cross his path and check his progress, Bernie would start to swear horribly in the wheelhouse, ejecting his tea dregs sharply at the seagulls. The red boat and he had crossed paths before and the art lay in how insulting they could be to each other in their boat handling without actually causing a dangerous situation.

Bernie was a builder and an outsider to the fishing world, and he felt his inexperience keenly. Jock, who also boated from Greenock and whose green boat had been the first on the patch that morning, was his friend, but Jock never said much on the radio and often switched it off altogether. So Bernie listened in to the others talking among themselves, laughing at them for being a bunch of wittering old women but alert to any mention of change of technique or quality of catch that might help his own trawl.

The first haul came up at about ten in the morning. The mouth of the net, hanging from the derrick, was tugged open, dumping a vomit of old beer cans, plastic buckets, weed, an old football, piles of hermit crabs and a smattering of prawns on the deck. Bernie groaned. It was not a good start.

The gear went down again, slightly adjusted so that it wouldn't scrape the bottom so much, and Bernie and Davey retreated into the wheelhouse. "Anither shot like that and we'll be greetin'. Two muir an' there's the dey wasted," Bernie muttered as the Zephyr started prowling up and down outside Dunoon again.

A submarine came in at speed from the open sea. Its police escort stopped to book one of the other prawn trawlers which had strayed out into the channel, forcing the submarine to alter course. Peter, the skipper of the boat being booked, was always getting into trouble, said Bernie. "He's a bitty abrupt wi' the polis. Seems like he disne care which is why they get him. I nivver talk tae him masel' but he's all right." Bernie didn't really talk to anyone; only he and Jock berthed and landed their catch at the same place. The other boats came from a variety of ports separated by a few miles of water, but up to seventy or eighty miles of road, and although they worked side by side, day by day, their skippers had never met face to face. Bernie didn't even know what the hated skipper of the red boat looked like.

The next shot came up at about midday; it was worse than the first. Silence settled on the wheelhouse. Out in the channel the navy came and went and the clay-dumping vessels did their business. Davey had started on the crossword of a second newspaper and Bernie listened in to the radio talk of the other skippers, taking some small consolation from the fact that they weren't doing all that well either. I sat in the bows, fearing that my presence on board had been a bad talisman. When I came back to the wheelhouse to pick up a cup of tea, Bernie seemed about to break an hour-long silence with a piece of true, contemplative wisdom, the product of that hour's contemplation. "The thing ye dinna want tae find in the net uz a wullie," he said. It sounded like a cue for a story worthy of Para Handy, but he didn't elaborate on it, relapsing into his somnolent pose, one arm on the wheel, roll-up in his mouth, gazing at the shoreline of Dunoon creeping past. He stayed like that until the last shot was completed, the net emptied of its poor selection of prawns, and Bernie and Davey had had enough. We were chased off the fishing grounds by a cloud of shrieking gulls diving for the guts that Davey threw overboard.

V

I'd never been to south-west Scotland before. In the tourist office in Largs I asked where I should go. "That's nice," said the lady, pointing to the map. "Oh and that's nice. And that's very nice. And you must go there, a lot of folk like that. And here is very nice. Do you want the brochure? It's full of nice pictures."

Largs seemed a bit like Bournemouth. A suburb by the sea, full of nice bungalows and nice old people, nice tea-shops and nice big sumptuous funeral parlours – so many of the latter that its detractors had subtitled the town "God's waiting-room". "We've got warm air," the lady in the tourist office had explained with pride, as if it was a commodity that Largs had bought in bulk as a tourist attraction. On a bright spring evening the benches on the grassy esplanade were lined with white-headed old ladies like human dandelions. A waterskier in the bay was being very vocal about his progress and his voice carried right across the water and up the promenade. "Holy shit . . . Wooooahhh . . . and again. Jesus. Ohhh . . . oohhh . . . ahh fuck." He overbalanced backwards, sitting down in a cloud of spray and the dandelion heads on the promenade nodded at each other sagely. Blasphemers deserve to get wet.

There was a time when two paddle-steamers a day came "doon the watter" and docked at Largs, releasing boatloads of Glaswegians on the resort. In those days the city's tobacco merchants maintained large houses in Largs which would be opened up in the spring to receive the merchant's family and its entourage, while the man himself remained in the city for the summer, visiting his family at weekends. The grand houses still exist, but many have been converted to hotels, old people's homes or boarding houses as Largs has slipped down-market and people go further afield for their holidays. Then, as now, Nardini's ice-cream and cake parlour dominated the esplanade, in 1930s cream-cake style, with 300 gilt chairs around circular wickerwork tables. "Danny Boy" was wafting out of the sound system while a dozen holidaymakers dutifully tackled knickerbocker glories and orangeade, looking as dazed as seagulls that had somehow got knocked off course and ended up on the wrong continent in the wrong climate.

For decades Nardini's had been a place of pilgrimage for evenings out of Glasgow. The family owned half the town, I'd heard. The patriarch himself had arrived as a refugee from Italy between the wars; the 20,000 Italian immigrants in Glasgow had all arrived at much the same time, mostly from the same small part of Tuscany. Nardini had intended to go to Liverpool but had caught the wrong train, ended up in Glasgow, and his recipe for ice-cream did the rest.

In the smiling, broad countryside just outside the town was the first of the coast's golf courses. Golf, in its present-day form, doesn't seem to me to sit happily with the rough, tough image of Scotland. One Colonel Thomas Thornton, who ransacked Scotland at the end of the eighteenth century for anything that could be stalked, trapped, hooked or shot, seemed to find it equally perplexing. "It is a wholesome exercise for those who do not think such gentle sports too trivial for men, being performed with light sticks and small balls," he wrote. This delicate piece of probably unintentional sarcasm comes from one whose writing style usually consisted of diary entries such as "Rose early, killed some small trout." Or "After firing a few more shots at different birds, we dined." Colonel Thornton, who described his night's sleep and his morning's sport in the same sentence, was no quiche-eater.

Golf courses line the coast of south-west Scotland and every small boy had pockets bulging with balls which presumably would be turned into pocket money; I was on the top floor of a school-bound double-decker in the outskirts of Ayr when one of those pockets burst and the balls flew around under our feet, pursued by the boy. At the time, the bus was passing yet another sumptuous house with a putting green outside the sitting-room. The owner was having a bit of practice on the green before breakfast; his wife was visible through the French windows sipping tea and flicking through endless piles of magazines, one of hundreds of golf widows waking up to another long day.

Some way south of Ayr I turned east and hitched my way along the Solway coast, blessing the weather, the sweetness of the air, the sound of the birds and the willing drivers who stopped to take me a couple of miles and chatted away comfortably without ever venturing on to contentious topics of conversation. I was half-heading for Kirkcudbright, if only because I was enjoying saying it; "Kirk-cooed-berry," I muttered, sitting in the hedgerow. "Kirk-cooed-berry, Kirckkk-cooooed-bury." The cows stared at me, unconvinced by my attempts at birdsong. It was one of those spring days when the year suddenly seems to accelerate so fast that it leaves you breathless. Bang – up comes the grass. Thump – out fall calves and lambs on to the springy turf. Tractors were hectoring up and down the hills cutting things as fast as they grew, wishing no doubt – as I too was wishing – that there was some sort of handbrake on spring that would hold it still so that it could be properly dealt with.

I walked a lot along the roadsides between lifts, sometimes not even bothering to stick my thumb out because it was so pleasant to walk. By the time that the day was creeping towards evening I'd only covered a handful of miles and Kirkcudbright (Kek-koo'ed-bry, I'd decided,) was still a long way away. I was beginning to contemplate where else to stop for the night, when the Video Man came by in his Video Van.

Man and van made a ramshackle pair. The van had probably started life as a travelling bakery, a laundry or a library, with a brief period of glorious respectability as a bank. It had then, belatedly, gone through its hippy phase, and now, re-carpeted inside and with the once-lurid covers of much-watched videos on the walls, it lurched slowly up and down the lanes of Galloway, dropping off little capsules of fantasy like the Tardis of the home delivery industry. The Video Man himself was long and languorous; coiled behind the wheel of the draughty old van, it was not immediately obvious quite how tall he was. His head was long and rectangular and his expressions came and went across his face like the thin clouds on a lazy summer's day. A key-ring on his belt tinkled gently like a bell on the neck of a pasturing alpine cow. He was completely calm, completely content, inestimably wise, and only interested in videos inasmuch as they allowed him to do what he wanted to do, wandering up and down the lanes of Galloway and making sure that everyone was okay. He didn't really care whether he rented more videos this month than last, whether his profits were ascending or descending.

Where was I going, he asked. When I said I wasn't sure he understood straight away. "Okay then, hop in," he said. "I've got a few calls tae make hereabouts and then we'll go tae Gatehouse. You'll like Gatehouse." And so that was settled.

The Video Man's passenger seat was fur-lined out of consideration for passenger comfort, and faced backwards into the van, so that passengers didn't have to confront the anxiety of road travel – although the sharp-eyed could find themselves staring at the rack of soft porn videos at the rear instead. The Video Man explained that he wasn't from hereabouts; he came down from near Ayr every other day, and had been doing for a couple of years. "I like this place," he said, tilting his chiselled face approvingly at the hedges, the birds and the blue sky. He knew pretty much everybody, he agreed, but not in a nosey sort of way; just as much as they wanted him to know was enough for him. "I'd like tae live here. But the wife isnae so keen tae move, and I don't blame her."

The van crunched up a gravel drive. The Video Man hooted his horn and switched off the ignition. "Jist listen tae those birrds," he said, gazing up into the trees out of his window once the van had stopped shuddering. "Hello, wee man. How are you today?"

A mother and two grubby-faced little boys had emerged from the house. One of the little boys handed him two videos: one was a cartoon and the other something to do with chainsaw massacres. "Did you like that one?" said the Video Man, as he checked off the chainsaw video.

"That's my mummy's."

"I bet yourrs was a lot better than herrs. What are you going tae have next?"

While their mother was deliberating in front of the racks of horror (the biggest section of the van), the Video Man gave the two boys a quick tour of the cartoon shelves. He knew what they had and hadn't seen, and if he wasn't sure he looked it up in his book.

"Everything all right, hen?" he said as he signed out *The Deep* and *Freddie's Revenge*. The question had an undercurrent of deep seriousness; he really wanted to know, and if everything wasn't all right, then the implication was that he'd do his best to do something about it.

"See you Friday, then." He waved out of the window as we scrunched away down the gravel drive. "Lovely little chaps. Their dad wis here last weekend. He's away in the army and she allus gets a bit fed up the week, the hen."

The next two calls were out, but at the cattle farm they were in the middle of the milking. The Video Man squeezed his klaxon.

"I didn't think farmers had time for videos," I said.

"They used tae watch them here," he said, leaning on his

wheel and smiling lopsidedly at the cows. "But now they've got satellite TV. I just drop by tae give young Peter a lift."

A young man in wellies came sprinting out of the cowshed waving at the gloom behind him. He clambered in.

"Hello," said the Video Man, starting up and bouncing back down the track. "This feller's going tae Gatehouse. Gatehouse is a nice place, isn't it, Peter?"

Peter, who was riding the bouncing van like a surfer with feet firmly apart between Horror and Westerns, nodded and grinned a chipped grin. He smelt strongly of cows and cowsheds. "Peter would prefer tae be on his motorcycle than in my slow old van," explained the Video Man, "but the polis have taken his licence intae safe-keeping."

Peter grinned his chipped grin again. "Ninety-two mile an 'our, an ut wuz oanly a 125." It was the only thing he said the whole journey.

"Poor lad. He has a few problems at home," said the Video Man, after we'd stopped to let Peter sprint off down a farm track. "His father's going through a bad patch and his stepmother's never taken a shine tae him. They've got a farm, but it's a mess. Peter canna get out tae work without transport. Transport is the key thing, you see. There's work here if you want it, but you have tae be able tae get tae it."

The Video Man knew a little about videos but a lot about people, that much was clear – but he was never indiscreet. From the fur-lined passenger's seat I speculated about each customer as they came and went. Their choice of video was as much of an insight as anything else: I thought that *Chariots of Fire* borrowed by the oldest son up at the big farm might mean a university place won; *Saturday Night Fever* borrowed for another week by the young waitress suggested that she was in love – a suggestion that was confirmed by her whisper in the ear of the Video Man. More difficult was the rather bruised and haggard face of the English artist – from London, the Video Man said. She looked older than she was and she selected *Last Exit to Brooklyn* for the third time in the month. "Not very talkative, that one," he said as we left. "Let's hope she doesna get any deeper into whatever it is she's into. Some days she's as happy as a skylark." He tilted his face at the sky. "We get these refugees from London. I went there once. How do folk survive there? The pressure you men must feel in the south of England is astonishing."

The van swayed into Gatehouse of Fleet. It was just as he had said: a ridiculously pretty place, ridiculously calm. Three old gents on a street corner waved. The Video Man explained that for centuries Gatehouse had had enlightened landowners who took a personal pride in the appearance of the town, hiding away the new buildings out of sight of anyone walking down the main street. Mrs Murray Usher had been the last of the line; she'd had her idiosyncrasies such as not allowing green paint on the main street, and she'd paid to have a house reroofed after it had been roofed in red. The village was waiting anxiously to see what would happen now that she'd gone and died; the solicitors were still debating the death duties.

He hauled up the van's handbrake in a side street. "Up there's the Angel. I understand they do a good line in bed and breakfast."

Somebody was playing the pipes in the house over the road as I descended into the street.

"That's Callum Kennedy. He's terribly good at funerals. They're voting in the new minister this weekend. No doubt there'll be a bit of piping there," said the Video Man. He squeezed his klaxon, cutting mercilessly across the piper's skirl and my thank-yous.

The klaxon sounded at intervals over the course of the next couple of hours; you could hear it even from the back bar of the Angel, where a couple of gentlemen were enjoying the pleasure of a pint or two after the satisfaction of catching a couple of nice trout in the Fleet. The bar girls dashed out, promising to be back in a minute. "It's that video van," said one of the fishermen, tut-tutting. "I don't know what's happened to the art of conversation."

VI

I crossed from one side of Scotland to the other, from the Clyde to the Tweed, in the company of Colonel Thomas Thornton, the bluff and honest meat-eating Yorkshire squire who was abrupt about most things except for the title of his book: *A sporting tour through the northern parts of England and great part of the highlands of Scotland.* Thornton had visited the Border country but had ignored the old castles and abbeys and had instead sought out the womenfolk in the woollen mills – although he didn't much like what he found. "As far as personal charms are in question, I confess I was never so much disappointed. Out of fifty there was scarcely one even tolerable." For the Colonel, everything was sport. He stopped his coach to watch girls fording rivers with the aside that there is nothing quite like a "healthy Highland lassie", preferably raising her skirts. For him, going to church (which he did with no sense of guilt at his own appetites) was an opportunity for looking at the women, and he was very disappointed when the incidence of beauty was low. "It appeared to me that the men came here to eat tobacco and the women to sleep. A tax on sleeping females would bring in, for this parish, a pretty revenue." Despite his red-blooded interest in women, his sport remained his overweening preference. When the fishing was bad he'd invite charming ladies to accompany him on the loch, but should the fishing improve, there was suddenly no place in the boat, and the ladies would be unceremoniously dumped on the bank.

The weather held fine as I dawdled down the banks of the Tweed, kicking pebbles and hoping to meet a few colonels like Thornton. The Tweedies were there, puffing away and flogging the water, but these were chubby businessmen with cigars who'd bought the tweeds for the occasion, not angular colonels with briar pipes and long memories. The Tweed has become too expensive for old money. A gillie in khaki digging his potatoes explained to me that his bank was £50 a day while the other side was £1,200 a week, and these were cheap beats.

Salmon are an emotive subject: they are the only fish that men build ladders for, and the only fish that make their own economy and their own black market, which can occasionally provoke violence and even death; the fish has four different sorts of people in pursuit of it – anglers, netsmen, farmers and poachers – and four different price structures when it's caught.

The cheapest Scottish salmon are the farmed fish, at roughly £4 per fish on the wholesale market. Next come the fish caught by poachers and netsmen which average £10–£15 each. But most valuable of all are wild fish caught by rod and line: if the current prices of fishing rights are related to the number of fish caught, Tweed salmon are worth something like £7,000 per fish and the best pool – Junction Pool near Kelso – costs a massive £19,000 per week at the height of the season. The Scottish Tourist Board has calculated that salmon fishing as a whole is worth £53 million a year in revenue for Scotland.

In the past bailiffs and the old school of landlords alike have shown a grudging respect for good poachers. But on the Tweed, the relationship between poacher and gamekeeper has deteriorated since fishing became so valuable. Not so long ago a landowner would ring up a poacher for a couple of fish for his dinner party, to be left in the back of the estate Land-Rover, no questions asked. Until half a dozen years ago the poachers and the bailiffs would swop Christmas cards, but now there are stories of vehicle tyres being slashed and fish-guts posted through the letterboxes of bailiffs' houses. The bailiffs' headquarters in Berwick-on-Tweed mysteriously burned to the ground.

At the height of the season a small Barbour-clad army of up to twenty-four bailiffs patrols the Tweed under the auspices of the Tweed Commissioners. It is an effective task-force. In a decade the estimated number of fish poached has been reduced from 30,000 to around 3,000. The bailiffs have the 1986 Salmon Act – the king of fish is protected by act of parliament – on their side. Once they had to catch poachers red-handed to get a conviction; now it is up to the poachers to prove that they caught the fish legally.

The riparian owners themselves have upped the value of the fish by clubbing together and buying – through the Atlantic Salmon Conservation Trust – twenty legal netting stations on the lower reaches of the river and closing all but two of them. Ostensibly this was done for reasons of conservation, but the increase in the flow of fish upriver is bound to have a marked effect on the value of the fishing; a fish in the river mouth or in the sea outside is worth only a fraction of its value upriver.

As I neared the mouth of the Tweed, learning what I could about the value of the salmon fishing and listening to the latest rumours about the poachers, one name emerged with remarkable consistency. He was a fisherman by profession, going to sea during daylight hours, poaching by night. When I reached the coast it wasn't hard to find him: everyone knew him and no one tried to hide him. It seemed better, though, to wait on the hillside some distance from the small harbour while his boat came in. From a safe distance I watched his catch unloaded straight into a minibus surrounded by a small crowd of well-built men.

Forty minutes later I came down from my hillside. He was in the back of a quayside coffee shop with his crew member and I approached him almost on tiptoe, hoping that I didn't look too much like a policeman. Would he talk to me, I asked timidly. I was interested in poaching. "And who are you then?" he said, his roll-up shaking between his fingers. He was a small, intense, ferrety man from whom sentences came in erratic spurts. I explained that I thought it was time a poacher's tale was told. His silence seemed favourable, so I took that as permission to sit down.

His sentences were not particularly coherent, but he felt passionately about his right to poach, that was clear, and the redoubling of the efforts of the Tweed Commissioners to catch him and others like him only served to increase his determination to carry on. He also resented being portrayed as a gang leader, a violent man and a criminal; the bailiffs had had all the publicity in recent years, he said, and their story was naturally biased. "Where wid they be wi'oot me?" he muttered. "Oot of a bloody job." His cunning was not restricted to an ability to move around by riverbanks undetected after dark; he knew that his court sentences depended partly on the public conception of poachers and poaching, and the more the bailiffs managed to persuade the public that armed and vicious gangs were brutally killing fish for cash, the more severe his own penalties would be.

He'd temporarily lost his driving licence, but if I was willing to drive the pick-up, he said, he'd take me to the river that night and show me what an innocent business it was.

If there was a crime known as provocative parking, I would have had to admit guilt, but it would have been my only crime; we had agreed in the coffee shop that morning that it would be dangerous for both of us if he actually caught fish. I could see that it was against his every instinct to park his infamous specially adapted pick-up ("If I bought a new van tonight they'd know aboot it be morning") in such an obvious place at such a time – shortly before midnight on a prime stretch of river at the height of the season; the bailiffs must have either thought he'd gone mad or finally made a stupid mistake. He's a well-known man, so well known that the Inland Revenue has billed him for £29,000 in back tax from poaching earnings.

If he'd been going poaching, he'd have been in place an hour before nightfall, watching the river from a safe distance to ensure that no traps had been set. "It wid be madness tae fish here," he said, sucking heavily on his roll-up which gleamed furiously in the dark (he chews gum when poaching). "It's far too accessible, they drive their jeeps doan the riverbank. Soon as ye become predictible you're catchible." He was taut and nervy, unused to being near the river for innocent purposes only. For him being caught was no longer an option. He'd spent two stretches of three months in prison and he didn't want to go inside again. He wasn't interested in theft, or any other sort of criminal activity. "My dad widn't speak tae me if I ivver did," he said, horror-struck at the idea of lifting something from a till, even though the penalties might well be less severe. Then he added, "The Tweed is my till."

The river gleamed dully like tarnished silver that night, a fat river of cash to some of the pairs of eyes, human and animal, watching it from the bank. It was particularly dark – no moon – and particularly silent, apart from the splash of the fresh-run salmon unsheathing themselves from the water in a bid to get rid of their sea lice.

It wasn't hard to see the bailiffs coming. Once they'd spotted his pick-up, they came charging down the riverbank in their jeep, the searchlight bounding off the riverbanks. It seems ludicrous now, but the poacher actually said "Hit the deck" as we flattened ourselves in a field and the searchlight swept over our heads.

"The best thin they ivver did was tae invest in these four-wheel drives," the poacher whispered, once we'd resumed our innocent walk and the searchlight wobbled its way down-stream. "They usit tae sit and wait in the darkness or wak in over the back. Now they come roaring doon wi' all their lights on. If I'da bin fishing I'da collicted my nets and the dinghy and got awi up thit hill there until they'd goane awi. The jeeps are gid though because they keep ivvery Tom, Dick and Harry awi."

The other piece of new technology in the bailiffs' armoury – the image intensifier – had recently proved his undoing, however. One night the bailiffs had raised the alarm but he and his partner had escaped by rowing over a weir and down amongst some islands. Seven weeks later he'd received a summons. In court several bailiffs swore blind they'd recognised him, even though he'd been wearing a balaclava; it was a fair deal, it had been him and he had been poaching, but the evidence was shaky, he thought.

The poacher is one of very few left on the river. During the season he's there five nights a week. "Once I had tae go sivven nights a week because I had sex months tae pay off a £4,600 fine." He poaches partly for a living (a good night produces forty fish, worth £400), partly because he sees himself fighting for his class ("The riparian owners air still in the feudal system, not in the 1990s. They expect us tae touch oor forelocks. To the Duke of Roxburghe I'm like a scritch thit he canna itch. He's thit wealthy I must drive him mad.") and partly because he believes that poaching is not theft because the fish are not the property of the riparian owners. "They own the right tae fish for them, but the fish air no theirs until they actually citch them. If crabs swum up rivers, nae doot we widna be allowed to citch them either."

The silhouette of Union Bridge loomed out of the dark. We had to sprint the last few metres to get underneath it as a jeep stopped on the span and prodded upstream with its searchlight. The bailiffs were talking on the radio above us, but we couldn't make out the words. "They reckon I'm fishing doon there," muttered the poacher. The searchlight of the first jeep was still visible downstream. "I reckon they'll be plannin tae come doon through the wids above where the net stands wid normally be."

When the jeep had gone we crossed the bridge to the Scottish side and continued up the bank, discussing the possibility of war in the Middle East. The air was warm and heavy. The poacher was wheezing from our fast walk over the bridge; he hated bridges because you could get trapped on them, he said. A heron shrieked and somewhere up the banks two dogs barked. "Black's dogs. He's a potato merchant." Out of sight of the bridge we sat and talked about the recent violence on the river. The stone-throwing and obscene phone calls were the work of unemployed lads ("toe-rags" he called them) in Berwick who were just after a couple of fish for pocket money, he said. They were not real poachers, any more than the gang from Dalkeith who'd assaulted a couple of bailiffs upriver, one of whom had died from a heart attack. The real poachers didn't get into fights and they didn't get caught.

I told him I'd been warned that he, too, was a dangerous man and carried three knives. He laughed. "They pute it roond that I'm dangerous coz it suits their purpose. I carry a knife tae cut myself free fro the net if I fall in. I can't swum, see." He was not a big man and physical aggression would be pointless. "I've hid gamekeepers and gillies outwith my door with shotguns. They're jist bad losers. I've had one blast awi at my back while I wis sitting in the middle o' the river. He knew fine well thit he wis so far awi the very wairst he'd do wis cost us a jacket."

We returned to the Union Bridge at about 2.00 a.m. and crossed back, only to be forced to dive into the bushes as two jeeps bounced across the river behind us, followed by a long, low-slung slow-moving Rover. "Shit. It's the polis," whispered the poacher. "They'll be setting up road blocks." The police car stopped on the other side of the bridge, turned, came slowly back and stopped again. A car door opened and again we heard the murmur of a radio. In the back of my mind I began to fear a possible court appearance.

A distinctive rattling sound echoed down the valley from where we'd been. "Boat trailer," whispered the poacher. Sure enough, soon afterwards, a couple of torchlights appeared on the water upriver as the crew of the launched boat searched for standing nets. "They'll be coming doon here soon," said the poacher. "More dangerous, coz we widdna be able to see or hear them." At which point we decided that things were getting out of hand and that it was time to go home by climbing out of the valley and finding the road.

Neither of us had expected to get back to the pick-up unchallenged. We stepped into a gateway to avoid a jeep's headlights, then walked the final nerve-tingling hundred metres with the bailiff's exhaust still hanging in the still air, expecting to be ambushed. Incredibly, there was no stake-out. The pick-up's tyres were intact but it was surrounded by the tyre-marks of other vehicles. Once we were inside and I'd switched on the engine the poacher leaned out of the window. "Nooo surely," he said in a loud voice. "Surely if there wis somebiddy underneath they wid have the sense tae show theirself by noo." There was no answer, so we left.

We sailed gently over the bridge which we had crossed so furtively on foot only an hour or so before; there was no road block. The poacher's relief was audible as we reached the Scottish side, and the Berwickshire lanes began to distance us from the river. "I hate being stopped in England," he said. "The English police ax sich stupid questions." Returning home was the most dangerous bit, he said. With the vehicle loaded with fish and gear, it was the worst time to meet the police. "Ye tairn the corner and there's the polis," he said. Whereupon we turned a corner and there was the police.

He didn't say much, PC Liddle from Duns. There was nothing in the vehicle. We didn't smell of fish and I didn't look or sound like a poacher. He gave me a ticket to show my licence at a police station of my choice; the poacher got one to show his MOT and insurance. PC Liddle knew him so well that he didn't even need to ask his date of birth. He politely enquired whether we'd seen anyone wandering around the river doing anything suspicious, and then let us go. Presumably, after we'd gone, he called off the search party on the river. They must have wondered what had been going on. What was the poacher doing parking so obviously? What was the other fellow doing in the car? And why did we go home so early and openly? If you're reading this, PC Liddle from Duns, now you know. It was just an innocent walk, but a pretty provocative piece of parking.

Summer – the Islands

It was tipping it down when the ferry dumped me on Arran, the holiday island Glaswegians had come doon the watter to; the watter itself was coming doon in such great quantities that I hightailed it to the nearest hotel, jumping the puddles, exhilarated by the strength latent in my legs, which had been idle throughout a day of travel.

From Arran it is possible to hopscotch all the way up to the Butt of Lewis, travelling up twenty-two islands and stepping from one culture to another. The difference between neighbouring islands is remarkable. The only other archipelago like it in my experience is Nusa Tenggara in Indonesia, a long chain of islands that almost connects south-east Asia with Australia.

Although the differences between the Scottish and the Asian archipelagos are enormous, the same general rules apply to both: in Nusa Tenggara some islands in the chain are Muslim and some Catholic; in the Scottish islands some are Catholic and some Protestant. In Nusa Tenggara people live off fish and drink strong *arak* or rice wine; in the Scottish islands they live off fish and drink *uisge-beatha* or whisky, the water of life. In Nusa Tenggara the islands have different dialects but Indonesian is widely understood; in the furthermost Scottish islands Gaelic is spoken but English is widely understood. Both have an offshore view of their mother culture: in Nusa Tenggara, politics are regarded as the province of the Javanese. The Scottish islands believe that politics are for the English. Celebrations in both island groups centre around music and dancing.

In Nusa Tenggara the Wallace line runs through the narrow

straits that divide Bali from Lombok; to the north of the heavily tidal straits the fauna and flora is tropical but to the south it is Australasian. There is no such single dividing line in the Scottish islands, although some of the straits are far more furious and would certainly prevent flora or fauna from making the crossing; north of the Isle of Jura the thundering Corryvreckan is designated as unnavigable by the Royal Navy. Hedgehogs were recently introduced by accident on the island of South Uist, causing some consternation amongst the islanders who feared that these new beasts – which they'd never seen before – had come to steal their peat. The only modern Wallace line of the Scottish islands is the Mull of Kintyre: beyond it the flora and fauna are increasingly Gaelic; before it the atmosphere is distinctly suburban.

In its structure Arran is a distillation of all the more remote western islands. Sociologists and archaeologists can do their studies here without the need to go further afield. Scotland in miniature say all the books and brochures, with mountains, moors, meadows, beaches, cliffs and more. Perhaps because of this wealth, Arran has been sacrificed to the tourist industry. It is as if the council of islands got together to debate the damaging impact of tourism and decided to create a single instant island which would provide a summary of the others for the benefit of coach parties, even down to the standing-stones and Norse remains. Having created Arran by shaving off little bits of themselves and throwing them into a cauldron of geological glue, they then produced the new island forward over the barrier of the Mull of Kintyre to a place where it would be easily reached. Then they retreated, leaving the buses to buzz around Arran, in the hope that they themselves would be left alone. It's a ploy which has largely worked and Arran takes it on the chin, the local population of 3,400 hosting an annual migration of 130,000 tourists – or nearly forty tourists for every resident.

Geologists, who find Arran a kind of nirvana, confirm that the island is a synopsis of all the others. Comparatively speaking it is a young piece of land, so young that it has exported sand to Saudi Arabia – a country that you might think had enough sand already. Arran sand, it seems, is so fresh and new that its edges are still jagged, while Arab sand has been blowing around for so long that its particles are smooth and rounded. For water filtration purposes, jagged sand is best, and thus Arran's export business.

Part of the charm of islands lies in being able to get to know them intimately in a matter of days. That's fine for holidaymakers, but for residents that "charm" can be a burden; an island can be so small that no secrets, no shame, can be hidden. Hebridean life is repetitive, claustrophobic and susceptible to the smallest winds of economic change: in the past the seaweed industry and the herring industry came and went, with fluctuations that destroyed whole townships. The islands' "sense of community" that so many visitors praise can equally justifiably be presented as a unifying sense of hopelessness and claustrophobia, but living alongside the sense of power of wind, sea, mountain, river and sky seems to keep the communities' sanity and sense of proportion; the raw beauty of the islands provides a spiritual companionship in an inhabited solitude. Scotland's landscape is particularly good at soul-washing for those who stand in the glens and on the peaks. There is a kinship between wild landscape and part of the human soul, a kinship which extends beyond mere appreciation of visual beauty, and this kinship produces a perpetual fundamental satisfaction, as opposed to the perpetual fundamental dissatisfaction experienced by people who live in housing estates. Urban men, surrounded by a complex urban ootting, become complex themselves. Islanders, surrounded by simplicity and nurtured on a diet of fresh air, seem to adopt a simplicity and therefore a clarity which is often confused with wisdom. Standing on the central hill of a small island and looking down on all sides to the shores it is very easy to conclude that islands were made by God for man to stand on. Standing in the middle of a housing estate on the mainland it's not God you curse, but the council; the islands are God's handiwork, but the council did the rest.

Visitors, seeing only what they want to see, assume that life on the islands is pure and good, and it's easy to gloss over the whingeing of the islanders as wistful reminiscences. History gives them plenty to complain about, and in a community which is a pale shadow of what it once was it is all too easy to dwell on the whittling away of island life. All too often Scotland produces a wistful beauty out of human misfortune, historical and contemporary, in the mind of the beholder. Conversations in island bars will cover the same subjects: the Highland Clearances, incomers, holiday homes and unemployment. Petty legislation worries away at the crofters; cynics say that the definition of a croft is a "small area of land surrounded by regulations". The complete guide to crofting law costs £50 and is a very unlikely purchase for hand-to-mouth crofters, of whom there are few left. On the islands a good education is still the key to life, and life begins on the mainland; significantly, twenty-five per cent of young Scots go into higher education compared to fifteen per cent of English.

The islands may be hard work, but they are nevertheless a highly valuable resource, appreciated by hundreds of thousands of people who regularly make long pilgrimages. Some are descendants of family who've left, like myself; some are complete outsiders who are so captivated that they decide to settle. A lot of these "white settlers" bring a new dynamism to their communities, becoming entrepreneurs, leaders, spokespersons and planners. A small number have bought estates and whole tracts of land, and a few have bought whole islands and all the people on them.

Islands worldwide have become the new acquisitions of the super-rich: Marlon Brando, John Wayne, Aristotle Onassis, Baron Rothschild and Richard Branson all own, or have owned, their own small worlds. The prices have been increasing steadily. Back in 1626 Manhattan Island sold for a mere $24; in 1989 the Scottish island of Gigha (six miles by three) sold for £5.4 million after furious competition (Mick Jagger was amongst the bidders) had doubled the asking price.

Lumps of land surrounded by water have a fascination that can turn even the property business on its head. Tow a chunk of land out to sea in an appealing part of the world and it is an instant lure for anyone with romance in the blood and gold in his pockets; its price ceases to relate in any rational way to its acreage or facilities. Paintings and islands seem to occupy similar emotional space in the minds of some of the new breed of island purchasers; Tony Curtis swapped three paintings for an island off Canada. There are island owners who never visit their islands, but keep framed photographs of them on their office walls as an image to provide solace in moments of stress. Some are like rich uncles to the native communities, their brains seduced by the messages produced by their hearts, ploughing money into their properties in a way that effectively subsidises the life of the islanders, perpetuating old attitudes and giving them employment but no freedom. These nouveaux riches (in island-ownership terms) are not normally locally liked on the basis that you don't make money without being a little bit of a bastard. Nice guys are usually poor.

Farhad Vladi, the world's premier island estate agent, lives in Hamburg. There are only a finite number of acceptable properties in the world, he believes; "acceptable" meaning that the island is within a stable country, a few miles from the mainland, and complete with a supply of fresh water and indigenous vegetation; only 10,000 such islands exist world-wide. Mr Vladi is a dapper, healthy-looking gent who spends his time roaming the world looking at dots in the ocean and going to all the right sort of cocktail parties. More seriously for the communities in the Scottish islands, he is opening doors for a new sort of ownership to replace the former lairds. One client wished to buy a Scottish island because he wanted to create his own stamps, another wanted to seal the island off with his own private army, and there are corporate buyers who want to use islands for waste disposal. The irony is that while an island owner may be king of all he can see at high tide, at low tide he is in most cases surrounded by the Crown, which owns the foreshore. This island shopping has rippled through the Scottish islands, playing havoc with prices and worrying the communities, because it is not only the land itself which is changing hands – it is also the ownership of the destinies (the jobs and the houses) of the people who live there. In the past these owners have traditionally been members of what used to be termed the ruling class: landed gentry who may have been absent for most of the time, but who valued traditional things and knew how to be properly gracious to their tenant farmers. These owners left things to run their own course, which is why the islands themselves have remained old-fashioned.

Increasingly, however, the property holdings and personal fortunes of old-fashioned landowning families have been diminished over the years by dispersal through children and grandchildren, opening the door to the new sort of owner, unknown to and feared by the islanders. He or she could be a pop star, a princess, an Arab, an American, or maybe just an Englishman who'd done well out of the Thatcher years. The likelihood is that, if a new island owner is a self-made man, he will have ideas and enterprise. The islanders, as a rule, enormously distrust ideas and enterprise.

The particularly wet night of my arrival on Arran also happened to be World Cup semi-final day. In the bar of the hotel the customers were glued to a small TV by the beer pumps on which England were playing West Germany. The voluble part of the audience were the Scots who supported West Germany. The English, despite being the majority in the bar, were keeping quiet, no doubt worried about the strength of Scottish nationalism when it was fortified by alcohol.

Edwin Muir wrote in *Scottish Journey* that the presence of the English created a suburban atmosphere wherever they gathered. There was certainly a sense of suburbia hanging over Brodick, Arran's main town, the following morning. In the hotels that lined the main street, breakfasts were being taken late behind misty glass in weed-fringed conservatories, from where fathers could see that their cars were all right. The sky was threatening; a couple of bold families were already out playing mini-golf on the prom. I fell into step with a road-sweeper who was wearing a bowler hat. "I ohanly wears ut whun ut rains, you knoah," he explained. "I got another new one, you knoah, in my trolly and I change ut every 'oor or sae. Why don't you come back?" I'd been invited to watch Brodick's equivalent of the changing of the guard.

"Is this all there is to do in Brodick?" I asked. "Play mini-golf and watch you change your hats?"

The roadsweeper peered at me suspiciously, off-balance for a moment. "Didye nae watch the fitba'? Was it noo beresk?"

I said I thought it was (Germany had won).

"Wull you luik at thus lot," he said, nodding at the tourists slouching along the puddle-spattered prom with too much breakfast sloshing around inside them. "See me, I've nivver seen such a soor bunch of people in my life as we've had thus yirr. A lot of glumphers they days. Soor faces, the lot of them, I'll tell you that fur nothin. You'd nivver thunk they wirr on they

102

holidays. I have tae wirr my hats tae cheer mysel'." He stopped and clutched his hat to his head, looking across the street. "Luik at the bazoukas ohn that one."

The baker's van lurched past on its first run of the day with the first infusion of cakes and pastries for the island's tea-rooms. Once the tea-rooms were opened then the island's circulation of tourists could really start. The tourist office at the Pier Head was already distributing the daytrippers off the first ferry; a coachload to the castle, two carloads to the King's Caves and the rest to do the island circuit, stopping at every museum and craft centre en route. I hitched around in their wake, trying a bit of everything, and enjoying the tea-rooms most of all.

The north/south divide that catalyses antagonism between Scots and English, and one half of the world for the other, even functioned on Arran. The people of the north, said a dustcart driver from the south who gave me a lift, eat their young. The north is physically and psychologically wilder, more deserted, more drunk and suicidal, less open-minded, less extrovert; it is a miniature Highlands, while the south is a miniature Lowlands. In the north-west corner the village of Lochranza sits in a steep-sided valley dominated by the sixteenth-century castle like a chesspiece in the middle of the bay, a landscape transplanted down from Sutherland. Like most Scottish castles this one looked puny in the bright sunlight of a summer's day, when the tide had retreated over furlongs of slack weed and dribbling rock, but it became gaunt and muscular in the evening when the water came back and the wind scoured round the crumbling corners, routing the chimney smoke from the village houses up the valley. In the heaving bar of the Lochranza Hotel the barmaid was dressed in a fringed and tasselled outfit that belonged to the early 1970s. She was pretty and half the customers – builders working on new cottages for the English – would have killed to do a round with her if they hadn't had too many rounds themselves already.

So I travelled south, to see what that was like, hitching a lift from two rough Geordies ("we only stopped out of bloody guilt") in a car held together by carpentry and string. They lived on the island but laughed at it. Bloody chaos, they said it was. And bloody nothing to do in the winter except get bloody pissed. We swung down into Kildonan and the island of Pladda came into view, not much more than an upturned dinner plate with a tall pimple on it – the lighthouse. I asked politely whether the island was still for sale. "Some bloody yuppie's bought it," muttered the driver. "Fuck knows what he's going to do with it. He can't fucking do anything with it. Fucking tax dodge I suppose"

Both the small islands off the coast of Arran had been on the property market. Pladda was being sold now that the lighthouse had been automated, and Holy Island, a humped lump off the east coast opposite the tourist town of Lamlash, was also for sale. Pladda had gone for £80,000 and Holy Island was on the market for £650,000, although it had started at £1 million. I had hoped to create a stir by wandering scruffily into the local property bureau in Brodick and asking interested and informed questions about both. Was I a pop star, an artist, an actor, a successful criminal, or the front man for any of them? Did I have the cash in my pocket there and then? I expected gossip, but the bureau wasn't in the least bit interested. The selling of islands is the business of posh agencies on the mainland, they said, and foreigners would probably buy Holy Island; it had been advertised in the *South China Morning Post*, Hong Kong's daily newspaper, and the Japanese had been showing an interest.

The Geordies dumped me unceremoniously outside the Kildonan Hotel. It stank of damp and dogs, the flock wallpaper and the pictures on the walls had faded and the nylon floral carpets had decayed underneath their cobwebby patterns. All the doors were scratched with claw marks but there wasn't a dog in sight; I imagined them being released at night-time to run howling and scratching up and down the corridors, terrifying guests who'd been enjoined by the one-eyed, limping hotelier never, never, to open their doors. In the hall a fish tank gurgled and glowed a luminous green; a dead Dublin Bay prawn lay on the gravel bed. I rang the bell until a stocky, elderly Yorkshireman appeared. Yes, they had a room. He showed it to me: it was small, threadbare and full of piping but the stink of mothballs covered up the smell of dogs. When I came back down the stairs I overheard his wife asking him anxiously whether the room had been all right, as if she'd expected the door to open on a pack of baying hounds who'd covered the counterpane in dog shit.

The quietly elegant, polished public bar was the sanctuary at the heart of chaos, the inner court of the hotel owner, who turned out to be the son of the man who'd shown me to my room. Maurice presided over the customers gathered in the bar as a music-hall compère presides over his tittering audience. He was a large man with an equally large voice and handlebar moustaches who was far more interested in boats and diving than he was in running the hotel, which explained the decor, the debris of failed projects and the excellent fish and shellfish on the bar meals menu. A girl came in from the kitchen with my baked potato and dropped the cutlery on the floor. "I get them through the job creation scheme – job cremation scheme more like," he confided loudly across the room. Everyone laughed.

I left for Mull of Kintyre early the following morning, pursued by a small cloud of midges which caught up whenever I stopped walking. It was one of those completely calm, completely grey days, where the water content of the air is so heavy that walking through the suspension makes the air drizzle on one's skin. A smirr, a truly murky smirr. Even the green of the fields seemed just another variation on slate grey. Feeling a bit gloomy myself, I elected to travel by bus rather than hitch-hike. Peering through the steamed-up windows I wrote on a postcard that there was something about Arran that was indescribably dead. "It's a drive-in island," I scrawled. Clearly the weather was getting me down.

II

There was some debate in the back of the *Bruernish*, the Gigha ferry, about whether we should wait or not. It was the last sailing of the day and the police had radioed the captain to say that there'd been a road accident further up the Mull of Kintyre which had blocked the roads, holding back two cars which wanted to cross to Gigha that night. The captain of the *Bruernish* was an affable, civil, gentle man with a nautical face creased in all the places which suggest a pleasant personality and a television advertisement for fish fingers, but he knew how to keep an appropriate distance between him and his crew. The *Bruernish* was small – capacity for ten cars only – and its passenger cabin doubled as crew quarters, carefully demarcated. The captain stayed alone on the bridge while Archie and

James, respectively relief captain and crew, occupied the four seats marked "crew only – ticket office" in the passenger cabin. James, who was responsible for tickets, apologised for not being able to let me on board until I'd sorted out somewhere to stay on Gigha. It was the captain's policy, not his, he said, and he lugubriously escorted me to a coin phone hidden in a farm outhouse near the slipway. I dialled two or three bed and breakfasts while James shouted out their telephone numbers from the other side of the door. The first two were full. "Ach," James shouted from the other side of the door. "It's they workingmen wi' the yella delvers. Uh-huh, they'll be building an airstrip, you see." His third number held good and I booked myself a room with a Mrs Fleming.

It had started to rain heavily, but back in the cabin of the *Bruernish* the debate was hotting up. The driver of the milk tanker wanted to get home to his supper – and he was the ferry's major customer, the only heavy goods vehicle to use it every day.

"We've decided that ten minutes' wait is possible but no moore", said Archie as we entered.

"Uh-huh. What about Mr McCoughlan?" asked the bear-footed James, padding over to his thermos. Mr McCoughlan was the captain. He hadn't been included in the council of war, said the milk driver. James nodded appreciatively; a good political move, not including the captain in decisions.

Twenty minutes later the ferry showed no signs of moving and Archie was getting fractious. "Once in every ten years you have a bad, bad day," he sighed.

"Every ten days moore like," said the milk driver, crisply. "Who said we should wait?" No one answered because every-one knew.

"What this island needs is a milk-pipe, not an airstrup," grumbled Archie.

The milk driver grunted, not over-excited at the prospect of being done out of his job. "What we need is a wee bittie more service on thus ferry," he said sarcastically. "Will ye be opening up fuir bed and breakfast, Archie?"

Archie turned to me. "Doan't you go listening to hum. This is the most reliable ferry in the isles," he hissed.

The milk driver pointedly unwrapped a boiled sweet as if

settling down to listen to a good sermon. Archie held out his hand for one. "Noo," said the milk driver. "You've been talking too much mince." He turned to me. "Want a sweetie? This island is crazy and it gets wairse in the night when they've tied up the ferry and you can't git off."

Unseen, the exchange would have come across as a convincing argument, but the body language in the cabin was that of old friends. Archie and the milk driver had their feet up on parallel padded seats and two of the island children were clambering around over them, involved in their own game and knowing the men too well to be convinced by the apparent show of impatience. By the time the second car had finally arrived and the ferry left, the topic was forgotten and island gossip had taken over.

Gigha is a quiet, fertile island mainly given over to cattle farming, all the more fragile for the lack of recent change. Mass tourism has passed it by. The island's one hotel is rather unsympathetic to scruffy land-based travellers, catering largely to the considerable numbers of wealthy summer yachtsmen cruising up into the Western Isles. The hotel had a radio-telephone so the yotties could ring it up and order their dinner before they'd picked up their moorings. In fine weather they came, had a good meal and a good sleep and left again, leaving Gigha unruffled and a bit wealthier. If the weather was bad the yotties stayed for longer, often frightened by the storms and only too glad to get off the heaving deck and stomp up and down the only road in their brightly coloured wellies, grateful for something solid underfoot.

It was uncompromisingly wet and windy my first day on Gigha and every mooring was occupied. Rapid squalls passed overhead, making enthusiastically for the mainland. The hotel restaurant was bulging at the seams. The milk lorry passed me twice as I walked the five miles of road that ran down to the east of the island's spine. To the west the Atlantic coast is wild and sparsely populated. Most of the houses are on the lee side, sheltered from the prevailing wind and clustered near the pier, but at either end Gigha is remote and virtually unpeopled. In a bay up on the northern tip I looked down on six seals playing in the rain. They were splashing and thumping on the surface, waving their tails lazily in the air like seaweed, pirouetting their heads at the sky and each other and sprinting around underwater like torpedoes. In the wild grey seas beyond the northern tip of the island the Islay ferry was bludgeoning its way into the hanging curtains of weather, trailing the dark threatening shadow of a submarine out from the Clyde on manoeuvres. A rainstorm scoured southwards on its own bombing raid as I returned to Ardminish, the only village, forcing me into the shop porch. "It's July, hay-making time. You wouldnae just believe it. A day fur snugglin' intae a grouthy bed," said an old man also sheltering in the porch. A thick-set young man with short-cropped hair brushed past us. "My God, you stink of fush, Seamus," said the old man. "But I suppose you are aware of that right enough."

"It's all they dead wee yins," said the man called Seamus as he foraged among the biscuits. The island's fish-farm had been having a problem with disease.

Ardminish, with church, pier, shop and hotel, is the centre of everything. From Ardminish you can watch the ferry crossing the sound, monitor the traffic travelling up and down the island's only road and the arrival of the yachts in the bay. Nothing goes on without Ardminish knowing about it, and the shop and post office, run by the McSporrans, is the centre of all knowledge. But even Ardminish, the shopkeeper and all, refused to commit themselves about a major factor of change: Gigha had just been sold, and the new owner was still an unknown quantity. Ardminish was a bit worried that where previous owners (notably Sir James Horlick of the bedtime drink) had treated the island with benevolence, the new owner wanted to make money out of it.

The airstrip was a symbol of this underlying tension on Gigha. The island had been bought for £5.4 million by a property developer from Kent who'd made all his money in the 1980s. He'd been to Gigha on shooting parties and had liked what he'd seen enough to enter the bidding when it came on to the market. Since then, aside from building the airstrip and pumping money into the fish-farm, he hadn't really shown his hand. The islanders were expectant. They didn't know what he was going to do with the land and therefore with them; like a puppeteer, he held the strings which ran the lives of the 160 people who lived on Gigha.

The tension was showing itself in the manners of one of the regular drinkers in the bar of the hotel. Every night he took his seat and talked loudly about sassenachs and the Clearances and rich yuppies, singing maudlin songs as he got increasingly drunk. He himself was not from the island and none of the locals would listen to him, so he was forced to collar embarrassed yotties who were trying to have a quiet drink in the bar before going through to the restaurant. He told them stories about islanders getting turfed out of their houses by the new, cold-blooded owner. "When he lands his plane, right, on his new airstrip, right, he might find an unexpected bump on the tarmac, he might just," he muttered.

The serious drinkers arrived already drunk. Tam, an old gent in a three-piece suit who looked as if he'd just come in from church, smiled and smiled and liked to meet tourists, particularly pretty young ones. His brother, whom he lived with, was a teetotaller who hugely disapproved of Tam's habits. Every night, after Tam had been in the bar for an hour or so, the brother pulled on his yellow wellington boots and walked his dog past the bar's open door, stalking stiffly through the stream of light. Every night someone would shout, "There goes your bro', Tam," and Tam smiled knowingly at the yellow wellies flashing in the gloaming as if he'd just seen a salmon turn in a spating river.

Sunday is a phenomenon of some reputation on the northernmost Islands, but on Gigha it was far from being a day of non-activity. The ferry started its duty rather later in the morning, but dozens of pairs of eyes watched its first trip across to the mainland. Its return was a catalyst for life, and when its ramp came grinding up the concrete slipway it was as if someone had arrived to turn on the lights. The island – which had been totally comatose until that moment – reverberated with the starter motors of cars and the crunch of boots on gravel. The Sunday newspapers came up from the pier and the island's shop opened for business.

I would have thought Sunday was the last day to choose to resurface the island's only road, but a wave of roadworkers came over with that first boat, spilling out like an invading force. They were working on the road as I emerged from church after the mid-morning service. The sight of the tarmac team hard at it on the sabbath was rather eclipsed by the discovery that the minister of Gigha was a German. I carried both nuggets of surprising information back to my bed and breakfast, where I discovered that at last I had something that triggered Mrs Fleming into a conversation.

I'd been impressed by my good fortune in finding a room with Mrs Fleming. She was one of only twenty born-and-bred islanders still on Gigha and she unwillingly crossed to the mainland only when she really had to. The house was bright, clean and unornamented, its garden busily growing vegetables in neat, orderly lines. The walls were three feet thick, the sheets were immaculate cotton, the milk jug covered in muslin, the best crockery was on the table for breakfast, and orderly piles of Reader's Digest sat in the deep window cavities behind the curtains. A leather-bound Bible was placed on the reading table by the fireside in the sitting room, next to the remote control for the television set. It wasn't a house for frivolity, either in thought, word or deed.

I never met either her or her husband in the hallway or at the door; the light spilling out of my door always fell into a darkened silent hall. Mr Fleming was a retired farmer who spent most of his time knocking about in the yard behind the house, where the centrepiece was an old but carefully preserved Land-Rover. Mrs Fleming was small, neat and rather formal. She shuttled quickly between the kitchen and the breakfast-room allowing no pause for small-talk. I tried various subjects: change on the islands, the new owner, the weather, but never got beyond a few futile spins, like a starter motor that turned but never quite got the engine to spark. Then, on the Sunday, she suddenly opened up when I mentioned that I had discovered the minister was a German.

"I used to have him here fur the weekend when he furst started coming," she said. "No one else would have him. In they days we had no Sunday ferry and the minister had to come over on the Saturday, take his servuce on Sunday, and stay until the Monday, and you had to cook meals fur him and entertain him. When the permanent job came up thus one was the only applicant, and nobody on the island could say noo even though a lot of people didn't want him. There are a lot of long memories on the island, you see. A lot of people were killed in the war, you see. My husband was in the services, too." She implied that they no longer went to church because of the minister's nationality, and that the same applied to several other Gigha households. "He knows I disapprove of him being there," she said. "He comes to see me sometimes. I know all about his family, you see, from the weekends when he used to stay here. He'd talk about them a lot. They're very nice people. Och yes, they've done well, they're all doctors and professional peeple. One of the gurrls has married a Skye man, I think it is, and she even speaks the Gaelic. Of course he still speaks German at home – his wife is German, you see."

The minister must have felt lonely and isolated on Gigha, but a remote island with a tight-knit community and a long tradition in the armed forces was hardly the ideal pastoral patch for a German.

I changed the subject. "You've got a daughter at university, I see," I said, looking at a photograph on the bookcase of a smiling girl in academic robes.

"Oh, that was yearres and yearres ago," said Mrs Fleming. "She's got four children now."

"On the island?"

"Och noo. In Manchester. There's nothing for her to do on the island, nae-thing at all. The island's terrible now. She's got a very nice house in Manchester. It's the ones who do well at school who get away." She said it with a degree of satisfaction, as if the nice house and presumably nice husband in Manchester were a vindication of their lives. Having shot their single bolt into the thick of the UK, they, the Flemings, were content to sit back and rest in peace.

Some months after I left Gigha I found myself in a sitting-room in Kent, opposite an aerial photograph of the island. In the intervening period I had remembered Gigha rather as one would remember leaving a subdued theatre before the curtain opened: the future held promise of something, but nobody knew whether it would be a comedy or a tragedy and I'd left before the action had started.

In the end my curiosity had led me to Malcolm Potier, property developer, who was sitting on the sofa below that photograph. Malcolm Potier was Gigha's new owner, the man the island had been talking about. He was candid and open. His had not been the highest bid for Gigha (an Arab offer outbid everything), he said, but he had been chosen by the vendor as the best and most responsible candidate for Gigha's future.

His was a success story worthy of the 1980s. At school he'd got two poor A levels, followed by eleven years of working as a chartered surveyor during which he became increasingly frustrated at clients who ignored his advice. He struck out alone with remarkable sure-footedness, buying, refurbishing, letting and selling office accommodation, particularly in Glasgow and Edinburgh, building up a business with assets of £40 million by the time he bought Gigha. His empire had been created from his home in Sevenoaks or from his car, by employing management consultants on contract, and dropping them at the first sign of intransigence or incompetence. Somewhere along the wayside he'd left his wife and children; the house in Sevenoaks was hollow, an office in homely guise, just as he was presumably a lion temporarily in the clothing of a lamb for my benefit.

With a gleam in his eye he acknowledged you don't make money by being nice. "The consultants will say I can be a hard, awkward bastard. It's business. I have a house style. But you can't go round giving islanders hard times like you can in business."

The airstrip was for nothing more sinister than a necessary addition to allow him to commute to London – which remained the centre of his business – with relative ease. He'd taught himself to fly and bought an aircraft in America which he planned personally to pilot back across the Atlantic once the paperwork on its purchase was done. But now that the airstrip was finished, he said, he'd not be making any more infrastructural changes to Gigha.

I mentioned the rather grumpy man in the bar who'd promised to make his first landing a bumpy one. "That'll be one of the Boys," said Mr Potier with a smile, adding that "the Boys" were nine bachelors between twenty-five and thirty-five years old who rather dominated the island's social life.

"We had an unfortunate incident with them in the summer. Presumably after you were there. The hotel manager banned one – perhaps even your friend – from the bar and all nine walked out in sympathy. These are youngsters bored out of their brains," explained Mr Potier, indulgently. "When the ferry stops at night there's nothing for them to do. We've got to try to solve the problem for them, so I thought I'd open the boathouse as a public bar in the evenings." Unfortunately this plan had seemed to misfire. The German minister called on him to protest at the prospect of a second drinking place, and wild rumours circulated amongst the islanders that they would eventually be banned from the hotel bar, which Mr Potier vehemently denied.

These were all problems of personnel management that Malcolm Potier admitted to never having dealt with before. "I don't consider myself skilled in 'come on, pull your socks up' management, but I'm not going to isolate myself from the islanders," he said from the sofa. "By rights I should close the hotel in the winter, but the staff wouldn't be able to get social security. There are things you just can't do when you're dealing with people."

He talked at length of the viability of the island as a project. As a businessman he obviously could not resist tackling Gigha's economy. "When I knew I'd been successful with my bid I sat down and wrote out headings of what I wanted to do," he said. "I've invested £1 million this year but I don't want to go on doing so. What we have is a loss-making situation. I believe we can break even without altering the existing infrastructure."

He went through the list. Goat's milk and goat's cheese would be added to the output of the dairy farms, whose cow's milk quotas are controlled by the EC and therefore unchangeable. In addition he was introducing deer farming for the high-value meat, marketing Achamore House as a conference centre, and bringing original ideas to bear on the fish-farm which had been plagued by endless disease. The fish-farm was an onshore installation which cost a fortune. "Other people would have looked at it and decided to close it," said Mr Potier. "But the fish-farm employs nine people. I analysed it to see what we'd got that an offshore farm hasn't. The answer is that our tanks have a smooth bottom, so I got in some bottom-feeding fish turbot of two or four grammes and sturgeon for caviar and flesh. If the winter temperatures don't kill them, we stand to make a lot of money."

The prospect of putting the economy of a small Scottish island on its feet filled the front room in Kent with excitement. "I want to make it break even. I will be in the top one per cent of

Scottish landowners if I do," said Mr Potier of what was presumably his biggest challenge in his business career. But Gigha, a microcosm of a far bigger island, is not just about sound economic management. If Malcolm Potier had a point to make to the islanders of Gigha – that he was a responsible, caring owner – he was going to make it the way he knew best, by improving the property as a business proposition, and hopefully by appealing to their hearts via their heads.

Getting the population on his side was important to him, that he admitted. He bought the island for peace, for walking, for shooting. "I bought the island to enjoy it – part of the enjoyment is in enjoying it with the islanders."

III

I had to go to Islay on my way to Colonsay. The weather was still bad, so it was a rough passage and the early ferry to Port Ellen had had to lie offshore, unable to get to her berth with safety. The Ileachs (Islay islanders) were a bit grumpy about this; their usual ferry would have been able to dock without any problem, but it had been temporarily moved to Skye to replace a breakdown there, which they thought was distinctly unfair. Islay had after all once been the meeting place of the Lords of the Isles, the rulers of the Hebridean island kingdom for 300 years until 1493, when their power was wrested away by the jealous mainland Scottish monarchy. But Skye, with the Cuillins and its Bonnie Prince Charlie tourism, had stolen Islay's thunder and its ferry.

Islay and neighbouring Jura have oddly industrial landscapes. The land is flat and barren except where it is suddenly interrupted by round-shouldered mountains which look like slag heaps. The straight-sided narrows of the Sound of Islay that runs between the two islands looks like a canal, although the tide courses through it at dangerous speed like the aftermath of heavy rain swirling down a drain. On Jura the pair of mountains – the Paps of Jura – supposedly look like breasts, although this seems to me the illusion of peat cutters who'd spent too long in the fresh air away from their women.

Once the notion of an industrial landscape was lodged in my

114

mind it was difficult to dislodge. Following the relaxation of protectionist barriers, particularly to Japan, Islay's distillery industry was booming. And despite the artisanal marketing ("brewed by hand on a lonely island") and the romantic isolated situations of the eight working distilleries, this is undoubtedly an industry of mass production. The distilleries are highly automated factories and warehouses turning out colourless spirit twenty-four hours a day, buying in fuel oil at 7.5 pence per litre and selling the whisky for much the same price. The enormous percentage increase to the final selling price is mostly due to taxation. Back in 1821 there were two million gallons of illegal whisky produced in Scotland and many of those gallons must have been the product of illegal stills on lonely sites such as Islay's.

The pagoda tops to the distillery drying towers inject a strangely oriental atmosphere into island life. These pagoda tops are about the only architectural interest on Islay: the central town of Bowmore looks like a dusty housing estate lopped off the edge of Glasgow or Dundee and spirited over the sea. Everywhere smelt of peat, even the grey boxes of Bowmore, which all had their own peat stacks by the back door; it's the peat, the quality of the water and – some say – the shape of the still that impart the flavour to the whisky during distillation, which is not otherwise a particularly skilled business. If there was anything more complex or subjective to the process then there wouldn't, presumably, be such extensive distillery tours for the general public. The more secretive flavour fine-tuning happens either in the maturing process in the sherry-soaked barrels or in the laboratory of the blender, who mixes various single malts together.

The smell of Bowmore and the flavour of the Islay malts was also the work of two men who spent their days struggling around Islay's flat lands. These were the contractors who had the task of providing the distilleries with enough peat to keep the malt drying furnaces burning with the right flavour. I'd come at the end of the peat-cutting season and although the weather had been good in June, it had been raining for a couple of weeks and the cut peats were still out on the moss waiting to dry enough to be worth collecting. Even at this point in the year – mid-summer – it was touch and go whether the ground would dry out enough for these late peats to be collected.

The state of the moss – peat lands – has been a hotly debated issue in Scotland's recent history. One-tenth of the world's peat deposits are in Scotland and are mostly condemned as useless by the people who live on them. The Forestry Commission has drained many blanket bogs and planted them with sitka spruce; local farms have drained what they can to try to improve the land for grazing, and peat from many of the more southern bogs has been extracted by the big horticultural companies and sold as potting composts. But while the locals see the key to their survival in improving the land and using the peat for fuel, the pressure from the outside has mounted for the preservation of the peat moss as it stands. Regeneration is a critically slow progress which depends on the anaerobic decomposition of a thin layer of spagnum moss; peat reproduces itself at a rate of about a metre every 1,000 years. It's a resource that we shouldn't be destroying, say environmental groups, who maintain that peat provides an unusual wildlife habitat and a unique biology. In the case of Islay, the Duich Moss is the wintering home for the rare Greenland white-fronted geese, and the naturalist David Bellamy staged a protest on the island which had stopped all cutting at Duich.

Tosh, who was one of Islay's two peat kings, had no time for conservationists. His waterproofs made expressive farting noises as he strode about his patch of boggy land, like a pocket battleship surging through the wet heather, prodding bits of spit defiantly into the wind. Conservationists were usually English, he said in the singing, shushing accent typical of the islanders, who seem to speak using only the front of their mouths. "Look at it chust." He gestured into the drizzle over the flat expanse. "This land isne useful for anything else. It's not even good for sheep, not even."

Tosh was a barrel-chested man with a handshake like soft toilet paper but with a reputation for enormous strength. During the season he concentrated on peat when the weather was good; when it was wet and during the winter he turned to fencing. No doubt he had only to bat a post playfully with his fist and it would disappear with alacrity head first into the ground, lest he should get angry with it and really thump it one.

He had built his empire on the soggy foundations of peat and sheer bloody hard work, and his best memories were of the days when he and the lads used to go over to Jura on contract jobs and stay out on the moss in caravans, taking their part payment in quantities of Islay malt in the evenings, talking and singing deep into the night. He still had the Jura contract but his peat machine had altered the job completely: where several days had to be spent by three or four men cutting by hand to fulfil the contract, seven hours with just him and the machine produced enough peat for his main client on Jura – a farm and three houses – for a year. When the weather was good he worked through the night, carving up the moss with the aid of floodlights on the tractor. The competition, the investment in the machine and the weather combined to make working nights and weekends a necessity, he said. But the distillery contracts still specified a certain proportion of hand-cut peats.

Only a knowing eye could distinguish where the moss had been harvested by the machine. It worked as a massive chainsaw dragged behind the tractor, biting into the ground and scooping up the peat and shovelling it through a processor which produced long black sausages. The incisions the machine made in the ground were narrow and the weight of the tractor quickly closed them up, leaving an almost unbroken surface. The only telltale signs of machine cutting were the thinner vegetation and a strange hollowness underfoot. The peat can never be hand cut again once it has been machined.

It rained the day Tosh took me to his moss. In bad weather the ground becomes too waterlogged to support the tractor, despite the extra wheels bolted on to the normal four. So we worked on the hand-cut peats, taking it in turns cutting and forking. The first stage was to remove the moss's live top with a turfer, cutting it off in rectangles and replacing it on the wounds of last year's cutting. Then came the actual peat cutting, using a peat spade like a long knife which slid down into the black slab with surprising ease. The arduous movement was not in the cutting but in the lifting of the peat, now balanced on the blade, and tossing it to the feet of the forker, who arranged it in rows. On each run we did two cuts, both about two feet deep; the top cut was more fibrous, with the roots of long dead plants and even some of the more deep-rooted live heather still holding it together, but as the moss deepened so the roots rotted away, producing a deep black peat with the smooth consistency of rich dark chocolate ice-cream. This second cut was the better one for fuel, said Tosh, but it was also the bottom. To demonstrate, he thrust the peat spade down a bit further and it crunched into a stony bed. Earlier in the year the strength of the growing roots would have made the first cut laborious work, but it was July and the moorland vegetation had already done its hard growing work and had lost enthusiasm for the year. The next growth wouldn't be until the spring.

Tosh cut peats like a machine, stopping only to change to the turfer or sniff the weather. He talked intermittently about the wildlife he'd seen, about Bowmore, and above all about peat. Occasionally we swapped positions – he did the forking and I did the cutting – but my slowness frustrated him and he wouldn't let me keep the peat spade for long. Towards the end of the day he got a bit tetchy, more because of the weather, which had deteriorated, than tiredness. The hand-cut peat needed three weeks to dry properly before it could be stacked and if the grass and the moss beneath it was soaked then it had little chance of drying out. Some seasons he'd had to abandon his whole year's work, leaving it lying out where it had been cut because it had been impossible to reach with the tractor and trailer over the waterlogged moss. The distilleries would only accept it once it was next to the road. The bulk of his contracts were satisfactorily completed, he said, but he hated to waste his day on peat that would never reach dry land.

The physical damage – blisters and a stiff back – of a day out on the moss was not as bad as I had feared, especially as I had been soaked most of the time. Tosh's pessimism about the weather seemed to be unjustified, because the following day was so confidently warm and calm it was as if no bad weather had ever existed. I took the post bus out to Pornahaven on the south-western tip and then walked the couple of miles into Lossit Bay. Some years before, a man from the University of Belfast must have walked the shoreline before me peering hard at the rock formations and the movements of the waves. He must have spent months, maybe years, with his pac-a-mac and sandwich box, walking the wild Atlantic coast of the western

islands searching for a suitable spot for his prototype
wavepower machine. In the end he had settled for Lossit Bay.
A farmer in a battered yellow Fiesta smiled up at me when I
mentioned the machine. It wasn't far, he said, I would see it
round the next corner. He was surprised I couldn't hear it – he
could hear it breathing when he lay in bed at night, and he lived
two miles away.

I'd expected an installation at least the size of a distillery, but
the wavepower machine was no larger than a bungalow. It sat
like a concrete conning tower on top of a sea inlet, its front lip
sloping down into the water. The Irish scientist had picked his
spot all right: out to sea a v-shaped rock formation funnelled in
what seemed at first a steady, calm roll of water. But as the
rocks chopped and sliced the water it became increasingly
furious and by the time they had forced it round the corner up
the skirt of the conning tower it was a seething, boiling mass of
foam. The conning tower responded by snorting and groaning
through its one nostril – a hole in the back to which the turbine
would eventually be linked – as the water level inside it moved
up and down, displacing the air. The turbine would eventually
be plugged into the island grid and the now-wasted snorting
would eventually produce heat and light. I wondered, as I sat
above the cauldron and munched my way through yesterday's
home baking, if the scientist himself had been too much of a
boffin to appreciate the sexual metaphor of his machine – the
water rising and falling rhythmically under the skirt and the
resulting groaning and snorting up above. It must have
occurred to the farmers and their wives as they lay in their
beds in the moments of wakefulness before sleep, and contemplating its emulation.

But if the machine was crudely reminiscent of love, it was
also about death. There was something tremendously alluring
about the increasing power of the water as it came cannoning
down the inlet, something hypnotic about the perpetual, violent
cycle. The cauldron of water was a place to commit suicide;
perhaps that too had occurred to the scientist with his pac-a-
mac. The suicide rate in the Highlands and Islands is higher
than in any other part of Scotland, particularly amongst the
younger generations, an increase that is attributed in part at
least to the effects of alcoholism. In the cauldron below my feet

a body would be whipped and rolled along the rocky walls and forced under the lip of the conning tower. Once inside, it would rise and fall with the water, making someone's light-bulb somewhere burn a little brighter.

The University of Belfast had a rickety old caravan on the hill above the machine. I would have asked the scientist if he'd considered his wave machine as a metaphor for sex, life and death, but there was no one at home.

IV

The journey north-west from Islay is one of the best in the Hebrides. On the mainland side of Islay the Atlantic is merely the tablecloth on which the islands sit, but beyond it begins to unfold with something like its accustomed majesty, in sweeps of blue. I once met a professional yachtsman at a wedding in England who had the kind of fidget which betrayed him as someone uncomfortable in polite circumstances on dry land. He stopped fidgeting when we got on to the subect of the outer islands and as the Colonsay ferry emerged from the narrow of the Sound of Islay on the conveyor belt of the tide, to be ambushed by strings and arrows of duck cutting across her bows, I remembered his words about his eternal surprise at how magnificent God's arrangement of land and sea had been among the Scottish islands, however often he'd sailed among them and whatever the weather.

I was also reminded how treacherous the seas were. The only two buildings on the shores of the Islay Sound north of Port Askaig are lonely whisky distilleries. Near the second of the two – Bunnahabhainn – an old puffer was perched on the point, speared by a rock. In the shelter of the narrows the weather had left it alone and it stood as complete as if the sea had placed it carefully on its own mantelshelf as a souvenir.

The shapes and arrangements of land and sea altered as the ferry progressed through this open room. In the brightness of the day the colours were like unmixed lumps of paint still in their box: a pure blue, a pure brown, a pure grey, a pure black, a pure white. These were oil paints when the sun shone, watercolours when the day became overcast, only to be finally intermingled and discoloured with the arrival of misty rain. The land, where it came near enough to be examined, was stitched here and there by dilapidated fencing and broken walls, patched with the colour of the occasional gable or a square of washing on a line, but its underlying features were of brown and black geology: every different light (and Scotland's range of lighting effects is enormous) picked out some new arrangement of rocks, another grain of strata breaking surface, another gleaming coating of moss or sheen of wet rock. Occasionally there were patches of a lighter green where centuries of sweat had managed to get the land to cooperate a bit; the shores were fringed with blonde weed. Above this landscape, different formations of clouds were having conversations in different parts of the sky: there was plenty of room for all of them and no need to do battle.

All in all it was a fine day for feeling fresh, for appreciating the penetration of beauty into the depths of the psyche – and for having a romantic encounter. As the ferry approached Colonsay I was unaware how ready for such an encounter I was.

Travel doesn't just reveal the world, it reveals the traveller, profiling him (or her) against new scenery. The experience of travel holds a mirror up to the traveller. Travel is also a sexually arousing business. Its intrinsic liberty releases single travellers to encounters which they wouldn't otherwise be able to have. In travelling you are no more than what you seem, judged only by voice, words and appearance, and your decisions taken on the road affect no more than your hand baggage. At home you are what you have created around you, and your decisions affect the whole edifice of your life and are liable to peer and parental judgement. On the road it is possible to suspend the morals and the inhibitions that are a fundamental part of that home structure, doing only what seems right at a particular time and particular place.

Honeymoons must have been partly conceived just for that very sensation of liberty from home morality. The guilt-free ending of chastity would be hard to achieve in the same surroundings that had enforced the idea of chastity originally; accordingly, sex is rarely as good at home as it is on holiday.

Scotland, with no scent of suntan oil and sangria to act as an aphrodisiac, is not necessarily the ideal venue for sexual encounters but sometimes the circumstances are unexpected and equally unavoidable. I once arrived at a lonely bed and breakfast in the Highlands in winter to be met at the door by an attractive Englishwoman who smiled at me in a way in which one wouldn't expect to be smiled at by a B&B landlady. It was one of those places where you look at the range of titles in the bookshelves and realise with a jolt that you are facing yourself; there was a sense of having arrived. I expected a husband in my image to walk in at any moment, so at first she and I talked practical arrangements – breakfast time, towels, hot water etc. But then, as the evening progressed, it became clear that husband had been long gone and the children were away on holiday. The decks, so to speak, were cleared and there was a heavy sense in the air of approaching a target neither of us was sure whether we really wanted to hit, but both were excited at the possibility. When I left after two days the atmosphere was so thick with the perspiration of two nights' talking about one thing and wondering about the other that I feared the pressure might force something foolish.

In the fresh air of Colonsay, at the end of the pier, there was no pressure. I only knew that the woman whom I'd started to quiz about bed and breakfast accommodation was pretty, very pretty in a quiet way, and was showing suitable concern about my lack of somewhere to sleep. The problem was that Colonsay, being a small island, had a very limited number of places to stay and all were full. I knew, because I'd phoned them all. The woman was not in the spring of youth, but neither was she old. She had gentle auburn-tinged hair that matched the slight teasing lilt of her voice. Her clothes were plain but small touches of colour – an earring, a bow on her shoes, a faint whiff of yesterday's expensive scent – were a glimpse of something. Something that had approached ripeness as near as it dared in the circumstances, and was ready to explode into a blaze of colour and light and sensation given the right climactic conditions. She was a fruit, now sweet and heavy on the tree, ready to drop like Sir Isaac Newton's apple, on to my head, into my hand and on to my pillow.

Of course this was all fantasy whipped up by a mere few moments' conversation. She was conscious of a need for decorum and I forced myself to be so too. I'd just stepped off the ferry with a rucksack on my back. She was presumably waiting for someone. From what she said, she knew the island well enough either to live there or be a very regular long-staying visitor. As such, she couldn't start getting picked up by the first smelly unshaven man who stepped off the thrice-weekly ferry.

To my mind, it was a glorious evening. Colonsay looked as if it had only recently been carved, and there was a perfection in the rows of cut grass, in the rills of the ridges, in the serrations of the roadside ferns. As the sun went down it was as if layer upon layer of web-thin silks dropped gently from the sky, gradually smothering the colour in luxury. Out to sea the gulls glittered like confetti in the wake of the departing ferry, watched sagely by the piermaster and the postmaster, who'd made haste to perform their duties while they had an audience, but now that the boat was gone were in no hurry to deal with the paperwork it had left behind.

"A grand pier," I said.

"Oh yes," she agreed. "It cost the council £1.5 million. Everyone thought at the time it was because they wanted to start dumping nuclear waste here."

I said I hoped they never did, and we both agreed that that would be a dreadful thing. "Well, I suppose I'd better make one more call," I sighed reluctantly.

"I'd offer you a coffee and a rest," she volunteered – and I had instant visions of myself catching rabbits with my bare hands, singing to potatoes to make them grow, and all for her – "but the house is a long way from here and it's not in the direction you want," she added quickly.

"What direction do I want? I was thinking maybe of settling down in that shed once everyone had gone." The bravado of sleeping rough was easy in her presence. If I wasn't to sing to her potatoes, perhaps she'd come back out of the gloaming and in through the creaking door of the shed to sing to me.

"You'd do best to go to the north of the island," she said, smiling at such transparent machismo. "Walter's got a barn and he likes people."

I went to make that last, fruitless telephone call and when I returned the woman was gone from the end of the pier. I was searching the thinning crowd of passengers for her auburn head and didn't notice the white car until it was level with me.

She tooted the horn in a gentle, quiet way and waved. From the back seat two fiftyish frumpy ladies glared out at me through the glass.

I trekked hurriedly across the island in the semi-darkness, spinning fantasies and sniffing the scent of fresh cut grass, until I found Walter. "They's a bugger, they's reelly a bugger," he said when I explained my predicament. "I canna reelly help. There's a few roofless hooses down the south, but a roofless hoose is no much use. I've only a byre which isn't reelly suitable, not reelly suitable at all." Having seen a few byres in my time, most of which were concrete floored and carpeted with wall-to-wall cowshit, I wasn't keen either.

Walter said that Nigel might have a better barn, so I trekked back to Kiloran Farm. Nigel stood in his yard and looked me up and down. The labourer's cottage was free, he said. The labourer had left last week. I could have it, provided I worked a couple of hours a day as payment. I told him I couldn't think of anything better, and instead of a tramp sleeping rough in the ferry sheds, my fantasies recast me as a muscled Lawrencian farm labourer in wellies, with a cottage door that creaked open in the gloaming to admit women with auburn hair.

Colonsay and Oronsay combine at low tide to produce a ten-mile island, but Colonsay is the principal land mass. In 1835 the population reached 839 but it had since declined to 115 at the present day. Oronsay, now barely populated, is the focal point for the historians. The Oronsay priory, the main feature of an otherwise featureless island, dates from 1380, and although it is in fine condition it would have been far better preserved if it hadn't been for the builders of the farm right next to it, who had "borrowed" many of the priory's stones. What remains is weatherbeaten. The crosses on the chapel walls have been licked into the shapes of bent old men like the souls of the Augustinian monks who once lived there; similarly the once-severe face of the figure on the Celtic cross on top of a small mound has become baby-faced with senility after centuries of erosion. But my most enduring memory of Oronsay was not the old stones: in the graveyard was a relatively recent gravestone on which was written, "A sailor of the 1939–45 war. Found 10th July 1940". The inscription was particularly striking not just because the sailor was nameless and stateless but also because I was standing there, contemplating his grave, on 10th July, 1990, on the fiftieth anniversary of his body's arrival, when it had been washed up after a violent death to lie alongside the ancient skeletons of Augustinian monks on a bleak, depopulated island. There I stood, a complete stranger, the only person to commemorate the half-century of the death of someone who had once belonged to a family of brothers and sisters and aunts and uncles, but who ended his life unidentified and a long way from his family.

Colonsay is a less gloomy prospect. Its west, north and south are wild and steep, but the Kiloran valley hidden inland at its centre is lush and green and Kiloran Bay on the north-west corner has one of the most beautiful stretches of yellow sand in northern Europe. Islay had had a touch too much unrelenting wasteland about it; Colonsay's land seemed cherished and cared for. Just occasionally in the Highlands the granite and the gneiss give way to bowls of limestone; suddenly the landforms are calming, soothing and balmy. In limestone country the fish grow fat in the lochs, calves munch their way rapidly into beefsteak. Moreover, the Colonsay holidaymaker was a touch above the usual category. On my way back over to the island's hotel for a drink on the evening of my arrival I passed two rather sleek cars in the passing space on the highest part of the road. Both their drivers were speaking into car telephones, calling home. One of them came into the bar shortly behind me to rejoin her husband. Her daughter had crashed the car, she told him. It was the other person's fault, wasn't it dreadful? And she'd have a Pimms and lemonade.

The hotelier, in bow tie and tweedy trousers, was partly responsible for cultivating the image for the island and particularly proud of his library of books that mentioned Colonsay. A new one by a Mr Norman Newton had just been published.

I walked back to the labourer's cottage with Mr Newton's book under my arm. Swinging along with the assistance of what the Glaswegians would call a "guid bucket", the journey seemed to take no time at all and the cottage seemed like luxury. To anyone other than me in my mood at that time the small house would have had few pretensions to romance. It reeked of the recently departed labourer, who'd smoked a lot, eaten Bovril crisps in bed and washed them down with McEwan's Export, read *Sunday Sport* and not bothered with the washing-up. All in all, the detritus of his presence sat strangely with the voice of the lugubrious American librarian, Mr Newton, who I doubt ever ate crisps and beer in bed. He had a way of giving something substance by describing it in detail, giving it its exact dates or its Latin or Gaelic name – or both – wherever he could: thus the house mouse, where mentioned, became the mighty "mus musculus". He had, however, allowed himself the luxury of dwelling briefly on the unusual, un-Scottish, breed of visitor that the island attracted; the Colonsay swimming club, formed by these visitors, had the surprising motto of "Only Death" – only death would stop them swimming at 8 a.m. – and many of the island's social events were organised by the YLF club, where YLF stands for You're Looking Fresh. It was clear that Mr Newton had felt his debt to the hotelier keenly. The hotel featured regularly in his account of the island; "mention must be made of the desserts" he wrote.

I put down the book and stood in the doorway to the cottage. The night was very still in the Kiloran bowl, so still that I could believe I heard the island's heart ticking. Somewhere in the distance over the hills was the laughter of the crowd dispersing from the bar; fishermen moving slowly down the loch side disturbed a sheep; a car came growling over the skyline and the driver stopped to light a cigarette. Somewhere to the south the tenant farmer was out in his tractor even though it was dark, making the most of the fine weather to pay the rent. History sat easily on the nightscape. Colonsay and Oronsay had been colonised by Mesolithic people as long ago as 4100 – 3400 BC, who then inexplicably went away again. Later the island was invaded by a Scandinavian chap called Magnus Barelegs whose exploits were written up by one Bjorn Cripplehand; standing in the door of the labourer's cottage looking out into the cold moonlight it was easy to image Magnus Barelegs striding fearlessly and floridly through the harvested fields in the Kiloran valley, whipping viciously at the tumbling stooks with a birch stick, Cripplehand limping and stumbling after him through the stubble, notebook in hand, asking for his comments and thoughts on his conquests so far. Somewhere behind

Cripplehand came mus musculus, squeaking hard and jumping through the cut corn.

It was silage time and my farming duties were simple: to labour in the silage pit, spreading the trailerloads of cut grass evenly so that layer upon layer could be easily placed on top. The weather was muggy and the flies unbearable; the grass was rotting fast, producing its own heat, and the compressive force of its own weight squeezed an increasingly full rivulet of stinking juice out along the concrete floor. The grass made me itch, the flies made me claw at the sky and the horseflies had me capering around the pit; thank God the midges weren't bad.

It wasn't a particularly sociable job. Nigel, the farmer, stayed in the fields. Angus the Boot – a neighbouring farmer with a muscular belly beyond the capability of any shirt to contain – shuttled between the fields and the pit with trailerloads of grass. Angus used his welly to fix everything – to open the back of the trailer, to change gear, and to fix the beams in the silage pit. At lunch-time he, Nigel and I tramped into the farm kitchen and munched our way through Mother's Pride and cheese, grunting agreement about the flies and the heat. In the mid-afternoon I knocked off, had a bath and explored the island along with the holidaymakers' children who were forming their childhood memories out of the freedom to roam. Out on Kiloran beach I sat on the soft machair and mused over the romantic legend of the young man of Colonsay who'd been betrothed to a mainland girl; on their journey out to the island to be married a storm had capsized the boat and she had been drowned. She became a mermaid and swam on to Colonsay; there her lover coaxed her ashore and hid her mermaid's skin. The couple were married, lived happily and even had children, until one day the mermaid had found her skin where her husband had hidden it, slipped it on and disappeared once more into the sea. Perhaps she had auburn hair.

The evening before I left the island the Colonsay young farmers organised a ceilidh in the village hall opposite the labourer's cottage. I watched the door from my window, partly waiting for enough people to arrive and partly looking out for the woman from the pier. In my explorations of Colonsay I had not been deliberately ransacking the island for her, but she floated across my thoughts as I sweated among the silage and when I'd finished work my feet did tend to take me south in the direction that her small white car had taken. I saw her once, guiding her white car tenderly around the island's circuit road, but I was too far from the road to make a cross-bog sprint worth the effort, standing instead on the highest rock I could find, in the hope that she'd recognise my silhouette and stop. Surely, I thought, she'd come to the ceilidh and we'd dance the night away in a fitting end to all fantasies.

The Colonsay ceilidh was perhaps the closest to the dictionary definition of a ceilidh as an "informal gathering with music, dancing, singing and story-telling" that I have been to. Ceilidhs are generally a combination of a formal recital and singalong which starts mid-evening, followed by a less formal dance which starts shortly before midnight and continues until the band can play no more. On Colonsay, the two parts were merged into one. Most of the population, temporary and permanent, were seated around the hall's walls. On the makeshift stage several of the children did their party pieces, playing the bagpipes, the fiddle, singing and reciting odd snatches of comic poetry. A very large woman sang Gaelic songs with much emotion, with a technique which seemed to involve pinning her upper lip to her teeth and letting her jaw do the work. She spluttered on the high notes like a piper who'd been too much on the bottle. Charlie, the bus driver who looked like a barber, neat and small and clean, told shaggy dog stories and anti-English jokes. "The bad news? The English have landed on the moon. The good news? All of them!" Charlie's jokes pulled in some of the crowd gathered in the dark roadway outside. These were the drinkers; as in many of the island communities, alcohol was not allowed in the village hall so anyone who wanted a dram or two had either to do so in his own car or book a seat in someone else's. By the end of the evening the cars closest to the hall entrance looked like bars, with collections of cans and bottles arranged on the bonnet, the boot and the roof, and clusters of drinkers marked by groups of glowing cigarettes and the murmur of conversation.

Charlie the bus's jokes were followed by the raffle and a couple of children's games, then tea in big kettles and sandwiches (Mother's Pride without crusts for the special occasion) were passed around the hall. When the plates and cups had been cleared the gramophone was switched on and the dance music began. At first no one stirred, so Charlie the bus and Nigel's wife from the farm set about a scottishe that had them skittering across the much-heeled floor. After that, everyone was up and dancing.

I'd arrived during one of the bagpipe recitals, at a time when few seats were left. To my great disappointment the woman from the pier was nowhere to be seen, so I sat on the floor near the door. When the dancing began quite a few of the families with small children left and I took advantage of a nearby vacant seat. Thus it was, quite accidentally, that I found myself next to the most striking girl in the hall, one of two Canadians who were working in the island's hotel. She was nice, I'll grant her that, but everyone else in the hall thought she was nicer than I did and I got knowing looks from the men from the farm. I was interested in who should come in through the door, not whom I was sitting next to. But the Canadian girl talked intelligently and it was rude to not talk back; and when the time came, it was rude to refuse to dance. As we twirled, I remarked on the stateliness of the dancing of a dignified old gent paired with a prim fat old lady. The Canadian girl was indignant. "That woman called me and my friend a pair of tramps," she said. The fat old lady had even rung up someone with whom the Canadians were going to stay to warn him against the immoral pair. "Oh yes, there's a lot of malicious gossip on the island," hissed the Canadian. I was just saying that it was perhaps fortunate that she was dancing with a temporary resident about whom there could be no gossip, when the woman from the pier appeared in the doorway. Did her eyes drop sadly when she saw me dancing, or was it just my guilt that imagined that? It must have looked bad; I was betrayed as a womaniser by everyone else's opinion – protesting that I preferred another would have been futile. Anyway the woman from the pier was a bit like a moth to the Canadian gazelle; I was dancing with the gazelle, but it was the moth I was interested in. She settled at the other end of the hall with one of the two frumpy ladies I'd seen in the back of the car, and suddenly the dance floor which had seemed so cosy before became a yawning gulf. I sat out the next couple of dances on the excuse of tired legs from too much silage and contemplated the massive expanse of floor that separated me and her. The dances went on, faster and faster and more and more exhilarating; the floor began to bound, the hall's windows to streak with condensation and the couples to shriek with excitement. Inevitably, while I sat there, the woman from the pier was asked to dance. Sadly, my last romantic notion ebbed away. The Canadian gazelle was encouraging me to dance again, so I did. I danced hard, and down the other end of the hall she danced hard too, our eyes crossing swords but never exactly meeting. Only once the Canadian gazelle had gone – her hotel duties started early in the morning – was there any meaningful exchange. She was dancing with Charlie the bus, who twirled her so hard that her skirt rode up, making her blush and lower her eyes. I was near the door, on my way out into the cooler air. I turned just before I left to find her suddenly very close, smiling deeply and happily at me for a full rich ripe second before Charlie the bus swept her away.

V

On a summer Saturday Oban was crowded, tacky, and stifling psychologically and physically. Not only was it a culture shock compared with Colonsay, but it was a culture shock compared with the other Oban, the empty rainswept port that I'd visited in the winter. There was melting ice-cream on the pavement, litter, whingeing dogs, aggressive dads, soot, the smell of frying, of slipping clutches, braying accents and guttural accents, crying children, arguing adults, the churn of cash registers, queues at the bakers', queues at the bank machines, queues at the tourist office, and the biggest queue of all at the ferry terminal for Mull. I'd planned to go to Mull and Iona because everyone went to Mull and Iona from Oban, but the sight of everyone getting ready for it put me off entirely. Instead, I joined a small queue of shy people who were going considerably further afield.

Oban is in Argyll, a corruption of the Gaelic word Earraghàidheal, which means "border of the Gael". Although Gaelic is still spoken in isolated homes in the islands which are level with and south of Oban, most are anglicised. The outer islands to the north of Oban are in the Gàidhealtachd, the

Gaelic homeland, administered by the Comhairle nan Eilean from the town of Stornoway on Lewis. Gaelic is now the encouraged official language of the Gàidhealtachd and place names are in Gaelic first, English second (if English at all). Even in the Gàidhealtachd, though, there is a reluctance to speak Gaelic in the shops and buses, a reluctance that commentators ascribe to politeness on the part of the islanders when outsiders are present, but is more likely to be pure shyness; Gaelic was once outlawed as illegal, and during the pop culture of the 1960s most of the young people turned their backs on the language and the culture as irrelevant and out of touch. There is still a hesitancy in the language's public use. The Gàidhealtachd administration is wildly, fiercely pro-Gaelic – anything less would fail in the battle to keep the culture alive. But this does mean that there is a small but strong sinecure industry for Gaels with any political motivation, and the ideological gap between the Gàidhealtachd administrators and the islanders themselves is often a wide one.

After a six-hour journey from Oban I arrived on Barra, the first island of the Gàidhealtachd, on the dying day of the Barra Feis, a Gaelic festival which was much promoted through the pages of the local newspapers. I'd heard about it many islands away, largely because of the extensive newspaper reports and the legendary tales of great drinking. But Castlebay, on that hot Saturday – the hottest in the year, it transpired – was comatose, with no sign of a festival at all. Virtually the only movement in the township was the gentle rippling of the tarmac on the road up from the pier, which was melting in rivulets under the unaccustomed sun.

Barra is one of the most perfect of the islands. Physically and geologically it sets the theme for its neighbours to the north: a crueller, more beautiful land, based on glaciated gneiss rock which barely tolerates scrabby earth to sit on its shoulders. Its uniform colour changes through the year from brown to green to purple and back to brown, a natural traffic light for the crofters. A single circuit road travels around its uninhabited mountainous centre. The east coast is rocky, sheltered and dotted with working crofts. The west coast is fringed by the machair, soft and fragile but fertile turf which grows on top of a mixture of sand and crushed shell. At the right time of the year the machair explodes into colour with daisies, buttercups, dandelions, pink and white clover, blue speedwell, yellow bird's-foot trefoil, tiny delicate silverweed and many, many more, clustering around the ancient standing-stones. In several places the turf gives way to silver-white beaches, licked spotless by the sea without a footfall or a tide mark. It also hosts the island's cemeteries because this is the only ground soft enough to take a grave.

On the southern coast Kisimul Castle (now owned by the McNeil of McNeil of Detroit and Harvard) sits on a rocky outcrop in the middle of Castle Bay, adding a touch of man-made picture-book romance to the natural beauty of the island. To the south of Barra, where the sun fingers the sea in steep beams of bright grey, stretches a trail of similarly picturesque islands; Vatersay, Sandray, Pabbay, Mingulay, Berneray, all uninhabited except for Vatersay, which was about to be wedded to Barra with a causeway built by the European Community at a cost of £1.5 million.

The more fertile southern islands such as Colonsay are farming communities where the land is cared for because it is a source of income. Barra is a crofting community and although the population distribution is still based on croft ownership, the crofts themselves are barely worked; such a poor allowance of land – a croft cannot comprise more than seventy acres, and is usually a fraction of that – was never really a basis on which to make a living and most self-proclaimed crofters on Barra earn their principal incomes elsewhere, particularly as merchant seamen. A survey in 1978 pointed out that only five per cent of the 15,500 crofters in Scotland found full-time employment on their crofts. This is a telling blow for the communities as complete entities, for the strength of any island community lies in its ability to live within itself, self-supporting and self-financing. The more dependent the community becomes on outside agencies, the more damage those agencies are likely to do to the community structure and cohesion.

Nevertheless, despite its deficiencies the crofting system has been responsible for binding many island communities together for longer than they would otherwise have endured. The Crofter's Act of 1886 established security of tenure for crofters provided they paid their rent; it also provided for fair rents as fixed by the land court, it ruled that there should be compensation for any improvements made to the property when the crofter leaves, and it gave the crofter the right to bequeath the tenancy. Many landlords have been unable to raise their rents for the last hundred years. The Act was recently modified to allow crofters to own and sell their houses separate from the croft land, in recognition of the fact that crofting, these days, is more a system of accommodation than of agriculture.

Many of the new houses in Castlebay – one of very few expanding communities in the Western Islands – are the ugly rectangular kit houses common to remoter, poorer areas. These kit houses scandalise visitors who are interested in the aesthetics of Scotland but not its economy. I have come to appreciate them as an emblem of new life.

That Saturday night I stopped for a drink in a particularly bizarre piece of new architecture on the western coast, the Isle of Barra Hotel, which looks as if it was designed as a high-altitude alpine bunker by someone who'd never been to Scotland but who'd heard the weather was bad. In the bar were the veterans of the Feis squabbling drunkenly in Gaelic over their drinks. A man in blue overalls heard my accent and started to berate me about the poll tax. "We don't use any services," he said. I pointed out the poll tax was for simple existence, not for services. "We don't use any services," he repeated. He was a crofter, he said, but when pushed he admitted that he, like many of the others at the bar, was really a merchant seaman who'd just returned to the island for the festival. It transpired that we had a contact in common: he worked for the shipping company of which my uncle, a Macleod, used to be a manager and he claimed to remember meeting him on the quayside in Singapore. "I thank you," he said, every time I finished his stumbling sentences for him. After a round of drinks he'd relabelled me a Skeannach – a Skye man – which made me acceptable company despite my accent. They'd all had enough of it, he said.

"Of the festival?"

"I thank you. It's too long, chust." It was all but over. A fiddler imported from Oban was still playing in the bars but otherwise there was only tonight's dance left.

"Tonight?"

"I thank you. Tonight."

For a while he'd worked in England, in Yarmouth, he said. "There's not much call for Gaelic there," I said.

"Och, you'd be surprised. The girrels from Barra even use-it to come down there at the herring gutting."

I nodded at the crowd along the bar. "What are all these people talking about?"

"Half of them wull be wondering what I'm doing talking to you," he said. "And the others'll be talking about the oil." He explained that exploration in the Minch had found as yet unspecified oil deposits and although no production plans had been announced, he estimated that there would be offshore installations within sight of Barra within five years.

"Great," I said. "That means you'll all be rich and there'll be jobs for everyone."

He eyed me sourly. "I thank you. It'll be terrible, terrible chust."

The dance, which took place in a marquee on the machair, didn't start until the bars had closed. It was a blustery night and the tent was flapping on the sward like a big bird that wanted to take off, the lights flickering and surging as the generator choked and recovered. Providing the music was the fiddler from Oban and a local bagpiper with brawny forearms covered in tattoos from most of the world's ports; he was a ship's engineer accustomed to relying on the din of thumping diesels to cover up most of his mistakes. Without that cover he managed to turn 'Amazing Grace' into an amazing disgrace. It was a dance quite unlike that at Colonsay; in the dim and flickering light sweaty faces reeled and surged and drunken menfolk were held into the dances by their women, who'd long given up all hope of romance. The turf yielded and squirmed underfoot, the tent billowed, the music brayed and shirts began to wring with sweat. It looked like a desperadoes scene from *Mutiny on the Bounty*. If there'd been any sense of decorum about drinking at the beginning of the Feis, there certainly wasn't by the end. Some people hadn't even bothered getting out of their cars but were passing the bottle around the back seat. The dedicated festival-goers – and many of the crowd were exactly that – were determined that the last night of the Barra Feis would be one that they wouldn't remember.

In the weeks that followed the Barra Feis the whole island chain to the north erupted in a series of island festivals like rockets in a row in a wet firework display. The Barra Feis is the biggest of these festivals both because of the beauty of the island and because of its religion. Barra is Catholic. There is no sense of guilt about drinking here as there is in the more Presbyterian north; there is no creeping, furtive feeling about having fun. Barra's Catholic priests don't make schizophrenics out of their congregations as do the Wee Free ministers, who severely chastise their flocks on the seventh day for even thinking of enjoying themselves on the other six. On Barra the whole family, including the children, of my bed and breakfast landlady in Castlebay went to the local bar after mass on Sunday morning, and they'd all been at the dance the previous night.

It was both a good time and a bad time to be on the island. Post-festival depression settled on most of the gathering places, but Barra had lost many of its tourists and the beaches were empty and the machair deserted. The working crofters were gathering their sheep for shearing and the merchant seamen crofters on leave for the festival took advantage of a week's peace to patch the roof, scythe the grass, repaint the boat, fix the tractor and mend the fencing, wearing the floppy hats usually worn by faded aristocrats when gardening; it reminded me that someone had once described the Highlanders as "nature's perfect gentlemen". I circled the island slowly, hauling my rented bicycle off the road several times for the same coachload of German tourists, which lapped me at least three times. The bus and I coincided at the airport to watch the arrival of the flight from Glasgow, not because there was anyone important arriving – there were fewer than half a dozen passengers – but because on Barra the airport is the beach and the aircraft land on the sand, according to a timetable that is subject to tides. The airport terminal is a tea-room; in fact it is more of a tea-room than a terminal, a gathering place for the children from the north of the island who are too young for the bar at North Bay, and who walk out to the low tide mark when the aircraft has gone to rake over the sand for cockles which they can sell to the hotels. It is the grit from the shells which makes the sand of the beach, producing a particularly hard and flat surface capable of taking the weight of an aircraft in all weathers.

It was a peculiarly emotional moment, watching the plane land with a spurt of spray on the wet sand. Whether it would have been so charged if there hadn't been the hushed, expectant audience of Germans I don't know, but their excitement – they were led by a tall, prematurely grey young man who was such a fan of Scotland that his eyes shone with the pleasure of being there – was infectious even to the weatherbeaten baggage handlers, who self-consciously placed the three suitcases of the outward passengers carefully on the sand. Few baggage handlers around the world can be as often photographed.

After the flight and the coach party had gone I wandered out over the beach to find the aircraft's landing tyre tracks. It took some time to locate them, for at first they were a mere dribble in the hard sand. After some yards they became heavier and deeper and were joined by a third track where the nose wheel had touched down. All three wheels dug deep for fifty yards or so, lightening again when the brakes had been released and the aircraft had been allowed to roll. On another part of the beach the take-off tracks thinned and thinned, reduced from three to two, and then eerily vanished altogether.

I've never written graffiti on an airport runway before and am never likely to do so again, but the fact was that I had a stick in my hand while walking the aircraft tracks, and when you've a stick on a beach, doodling comes naturally. After a false start I started to write a stuttering, nonsensical story in large capital letters, a sentence at a time. "THE AVIATOR TURNED ON THE RADIO" I wrote, wondering whether it would be legible to a descending pilot and even to his passengers. "IT CRACKLED AND A VOICE CAME OVER THE AIRWAVES. 'A CUP OF TEA AND A CHEESE TOASTIE PLEASE'." (This had been my order in the terminal tea-room.) "THE AVIATOR FLICKED THE SWITCH. 'THERE MUST BE SOME MISTAKE,' HE SAID. 'NO, LOOK ABOVE YOU, ON THE CLOUD TO THE LEFT.' THE AVIATOR LOOKED. IT WAS GOD. SO HE CIRCLED QUICKLY AND MADE A FRESH POT. 'HOW DO I GET IT TO YOU?' HE ASKED. 'DON'T WORRY,' SAID THE RADIO. 'I DRINK TEA IN MYSTERIOUS WAYS.' AND THE AVIATOR LOOKED, AND THE POT WAS EMPTY. SO HE QUICKLY LANDED AT

HEATHROW TO TELL HIS FRIENDS. NO ONE BELIEVED HIM SO HE (I, THAT IS) STARTED TO WRITE IT ON LAVATORY WALLS, UNDERGROUND STATIONS AND HEBRIDEAN BEACHES. AND THEY CAME AND TOOK ME AWAY . . ." I dragged my feet and flailed about me with the stick so that it looked as if there had been a scuffle, then did a couple of forward somersaults to get away from the scene as cleanly as possible. In the distance, about a hundred yards away from the end of the story, one of the girls who'd been out raking for cockles had started to read the beginning. I walked hastily away, feeling embarrassed, guilty and just a little bit pleased with myself.

The evening ferry for Lochboisdale arrived while I was on the terrace of the Craigard Hotel, eating airport runway cockles which had been fried in garlic and oatmeal. I was anxious to get down to the boat but the hotelier said there was no hurry. His rum babas were very good, he said, and they were. I lingered long enough to get most of one in my mouth before plunging down the hill to the pier. In the event I would have had time for a dozen rum babas because it took a while to load the last vehicles on to the ferry. The second-to-last was a young scrap dealer's lorry which appeared to have no reverse gear; once it had been shouldered into place by the crew it was the turn of the last, an ice-cream van driven by a very fat-bottomed lady. When the van was finally – and only just – on board, there was no room for the fat-bottomed lady to squeeze between the vehicles. With the help of the crew pulling her and the scrap dealer pushing her, she was manhandled over the roof of her van and across the top of the Germans' coach while most of the passengers stood up on the deck above and applauded. She took it all in good spirits and I later heard her ask the purser if she'd get a discount on her ticket for having given a public performance. The scrap dealer was in the gents toilets, stripped to the waist and scrubbing himself down.

Fog was lying in wait for the ferry when it finally left the shelter of Castle Bay. We entered it pointing north, steaming hard but apparently going nowhere, bleating into the blanket like a lost sheep. Occasionally it lifted a bit and the islands revealed themselves, peeping out from underneath like frightened children hiding under a bed. For a while it disappeared as if someone had snorted in up through giant nostrils, only to roll back over like a carpet shortly afterwards. In the bar the ice-cream woman spread out her many plastic bags on a table and started doing her accounts.

VI

There was a certain amount of talk on South Uist about the *SS Politician*. The *Polly*, as she is locally known, is the ship whose fate inspired Compton Mackenzie – who lived on Barra – to write *Whisky Galore*, which in turn inspired the film of the same name. The *Polly* had gone off course while joining a Second World War Atlantic convoy which was assembling off the coast of Scotland in 1941; she ran aground off Eriskay, a small island between Barra and South Uist where, incidentally, Bonnie Prince Charlie had first set foot on Scottish soil. As far as the local population were concerned the *Polly* had a more valuable cargo than the boat which brought Charlie: 24,000 cases of whisky, together with silks, perfumes, bidets, cigarettes, fur coats and bicycle parts, were in the holds, apparently ultimately destined for the island of Jamaica, which was to be the bolthole for the British royal family should the Germans look to be getting the upper hand. The islanders were unable to resist the temptation of relieving the ship at high speed of its liquid cargo and Compton Mackenzie's book tells the story of how the whisky was concealed in roofs, down rabbit holes, in hay barns and farm machinery, lest Customs and Excise should discover it and take it back. Some tales he couldn't relate for the sake of good taste, including the one of the crofter whom everyone thought was daft because he kept his whisky in a potty under his bed; the crofter was more cunning than he seemed, though, dropping pickled sausages into it to complete the disguise. The Customs men were so disgusted they left the croft in haste.

The wreck of the *Polly* was a fine story and is often retold by the older islanders of South Uist, Barra and Eriskay, particularly for the benefit of tourists. But with the course of time the combined fictional strength of the film and the book has to some extent outstripped the real events; truth may be stranger than fiction, but sometimes fiction is more appealing and lasts longer. The truth was that a fair number of the islanders went to jail for helping themselves to the cargo, so an adventure that had had a sweet taste at the start had a sour finish. Today the whisky is to all intents and purposes gone – although many believe that their parents or grandparents were too drunk to remember where they hid their stashes, some of which may be still maturing in old badger sets – but the Jamaican money (the equivalent of £3 million) which was also on board is still in evidence here and there. There is an air of discreet prosperity around some of these homes which may not all be due to the wages directly earned by the seafaring breadwinners. At the time, Jamaican money became impossible to exchange on the open market in Scotland, but in the back pocket of a sailor coming ashore in Jamaica it retained its purchasing power.

As I arrived, the *Polly* was again a hot topic on South Uist. Politician plc, a private company which had bought the diving rights to the wreck, had launched a new diving initiative to search a hold that reputedly hadn't been opened since the ship went down, and hoped to find still more bottles. Most of the islanders shook their heads sagely. There were no more bottles, they said. They should know. Politician plc, its shore base on South Uist, sounded efficient on the telephone, and various souvenirs were on sale in the tourist office in Lochboisdale. The company offered tours of the diving site – for a healthy fee – but on the day I enquired this was not possible, both because the diving had become "sensitive" and because it was a holiday to mark the South Uist games, to which most of the population of the island intended going.

In the end I never got to Eriskay, or even to the Politician plc's shore base. Their press conference some time later announced that they'd found fourteen bottles, the contents of which were to be put into paperweights, being presumably undrinkable. Honour and investment were to some extent saved, moreover, by the signature of a deal with a whisky blender for the creation of a limited edition SS *Politician* commemorative whisky, which although it may not have fully covered the cost of the whole operation, at least saved a certain amount of face.

Although I'd tried to hitch south towards Eriskay and the *Politician*, it was plain that everyone was going north to the

South Uist games, so in the end I capitulated and went there too. I was not alone from the ferry of the previous evening. The ice-cream woman was already there, the coachload of Germans arrived shortly after me, and later in the afternoon I noticed the young scrap merchant struggling in the wrestling competition and running in the 440 metres: "Are ye allowed onc last cigarette?" he joked before the gun.

The games were held on the edge of the golf course on the machair on the west coast. Although South Uist is far more low-slung than Barra it has the same basic coastal qualities: a rocky inaccessible shore with deep inlets on the east coast and a long smooth flat blade of land on the west, based on the machair. This soft and fertile west coast has its own silver lining: twenty miles of almost unbroken white sand. Lochboisdale, the ferry port and principal town, takes advantage of a particularly deep inlet on the east coast, but most of the population is scattered up and down the fields of the west side. Here the land, littered with peewits, is of a quality to support its owners and obvious care is taken of it. The houses are relatively new, built in a post-Clearances era. Old black houses (*tigh dubh*) are also here in considerable quantities but are so overgrown and decayed as to be almost an organic part of the natural landscape.

Adding to local prosperity is the site of a missile launching and tracking station at the northern end of the island, from where European weaponry is tested every day. The flashes of the missiles leaving the shores of South Uist are clearly visible, but on the whole the islanders are very accustomed to the military activity. Space City, a small array of antennae and control rooms, perches on the shoulder of one of the inland hills, overlooking a thirty-foot statue of the Madonna, erected by South Uist's largely Catholic population. Occasionally a well-known battalion turns up for a month's duties and gets banned by the bar owners, but otherwise the co-existence of military and locals is largely peaceful. The missile station has been absorbed into local culture, particularly with the apochryphal 'Rocket Song,' the tale of how a rogue rocket was fired out to sea but turned back, came screaming over the heads of a few startled crofters and plunged into one of the inland lochs. The song is long and evidently very witty in Gaelic – reducing its singer and audience to tears of laughter –

but speaking as someone who has sat stony-faced through it while all around me collapsed in heaps, the humour doesn't translate.

At the South Uist games the highland dancing was the most serious corner of the arena. The judge sat in a little wooden bus shelter below the platform; above him prancing girls leaned heavily into the scouring wind and towards the piper in case they lost track of his fingering. The piping competition was well subscribed but less of a spectator sport than the dancing. The pipers themselves were practising at even spacings all over the golf course, on fairways, on greens and on tees into the middle distance, rock solid while their kilts whipped around them in the wind, undermining their stern faces with quick glimpses of goose-pimply thighs. Fortunately the wind created little funnels of sound around each piper, and the judge's ears were not confused by the practising of all the contenders. But without the volume provided by the bag, the chanter – the melody-pipe on its own – had no hope in the wind, and the young chanter players took it in turns to get into the judge's bus shelter, with the judge, to do their bit. Meanwhile, in the middle of the ring the heavies went through their parade of chucking, thrusting and heaving, scattering weights like shrapnel.

In the beer tent I bumped into the piping judge. "Eh, it's a dreadful wind, something dreadful right enough," he said, with a whisky in one hand and a beer in the other. "Eh, it keeps on blowing me into the tent here it does by Chove. Och yes, it's dreadful. Sex shows was all I hearred the morning."

Other than its propensity for propelling judges into the beer tent, we agreed that the weather had been kind. Normally, he said, the South Uist games and the North Uist games were held on succeeding days, but this year North Uist had moved theirs to the Saturday before. This move had unfortunately lowered the quality of the pipers because the better competitors from other islands no longer had the attraction of consecutive games to lure them across. But more importantly it had rained hard for the whole day of the North Uist games, which had served them right for changing their dates. North Uist was Presbyterian while South Uist was Catholic and each regarded the other with a mixture of condescension and rivalry. "Eh, they had a dreadful day. The weather can be chust dreadful," said the piping judge. "Did ye no hear the business with the polisman the other night?"

I said I hadn't.

"Eh, a dismal night it was, a real storm it was. The polisman heard this banging in the cells at the back of the station in the middle of the night. He was a wee bit feart, you see, by this, because he didn't have anyone in the cells at the time. Eh, so he went downstairs in his pyjamas to investigate, locking the door that connected with the cells to stop anyone getting through into the hoose. It was an old ram that had got in the back, had come in out of the rain. A foul night it was right enough. Of course having found his way into somewhair warrem and dry the old ram didn't want to go back out into it, so the polisman had to get down and give it a good pushing. Eh, it was only as the blessed thing finally disappeared back into the darkness that the polisman realised his, eh, great big bunch of keys had got hooked up on the animal's horns, and was also fast disappearing out into the night."

"What did he do?"

"What cuid he do? He was outwith the hoose and he cuidn't get back in – the ram had all his keys. So he chased it." The judge giggled tipsily. "Eh, have you ever tried to chase a sheep over boggy ground in a storm in the dark in your pyjamas? No? Well nor have I, and I don't want to. Poor auld Robbie. He got his keys back, of course, but only when daylight came and he cuid borrow a dog."

The following day was grey as only Scotland can be grey. The smirr had descended, obliterating everything and dousing any attempt at high spirits. The grey land and the grey sky seemed so naturally and invincibly welded that it was hard to believe in the blues and the greens of the previous day. I plodded along, sticking my thumb out half-heartedly at passing drivers who sensed my mood and sensibly ignored me. A couple of times I was sprayed by passing seaweed lorries, which didn't improve my spirits. A substantial amount of seaweed-gathering still takes place on South Uist, but kelp as a major industry died in the 1820s, prompting waves of emigration that preceded the more highly publicised Clearances. If the kelp industry had continued healthily, then the land would probably have been able to continue to support the high population and the

Clearances wouldn't have been so disastrous. Today's weed, which is rich in alkali for the glass and soap industries, is paid for by weight and the longer it takes in transit the more its water content drains away and the lighter it gets. Accordingly, the seaweed lorries plough up and down the main Uist road at considerable speed, spraying hitch-hikers.

The seaweed lorries may have ignored me, but the scrap dealer whom I'd seen on the Barra ferry and at the games didn't. I was standing in a lay-by trying to look like I was good company when he came over the brow of the hill. With him in the cab were three big and wet dogs lying on a sleeping-bag which was covered in sand and dog hair. He swept them on to the floor. "Sorry aboot the dogs. They're awfi' smelly. We've just bin fi a run along the beach," he said. But I was just glad to be in out of the rain, and I said so.

Thus it was that I first met Mick the scrappie, who turned out to be quite an exceptional person.

"I saw you on the ferry," I said. "What happened to your reverse gear?"

"Oh, I came offa the road a wee whiles back and it's nivver bin right since," grinned Mick. His hair was curly like a boy's and his eyes bright with a boy's enthusiasm. "I can get it eventually, but it's awfi' hard. I've only had the lorry since January, but I reckon I've had my money's wirth." The cab was littered with old sandwich wrappings, batteries, razors, orange peel, paper bags, notebooks, a comb and a couple of broken pens. Every piece of paper had an oily thumb mark and everything was coated with dog hair. Whenever he stopped the truck and wound down the window to assess a pile of debris in a back yard or even just to look at the view, seagulls would descend on the back and start picking at soggy pieces of bread lying amongst the scrap.

Although his home was in Dundee, Mick spent much of his time on the road, particularly in the western Highlands and islands, looking for scrap. It was not that these were particularly good areas for scrap, but that they suited his temperament. "I'm a hunter," he explained. "I jist love it here. I don't need money. Mebbe the dogs'll catch a rabbit and mebbe I'll catch a fush. I'll sleep oot on the hill. Sometimes the dogs and I leave the lorry and just walk oot there on tae the hill fae a few days. Take Daliburgh beach, where the dogs and I have jist bin fae a run. It's awfi' beautiful. I'd give an awfi' lot fae an hoor on Daliburgh beach. If I get lonely up here I can always gae and sut in a bar for a crack and a gless, although I'm not much of a drinker mysel'. Anyone'll talk to ye. They're awfi' friendly." His arm swept over the wet landscape, which was unravelling itself laboriously under the wheels of the lorry. "I was up here only a month or so ago wi' the bairn wi'me. Normally I wouldn't come again sae soon, but it's the games you see. I love the games."

I said I'd seen him wrestling. Mick was made of india-rubber, bouncing back automatically whatever was thrown at him.

"Did ye think I wus okay?"

I had to admit that I didn't know much about it.

"Ay, well, nae mair do I, but I didn't think I did too bad fae the furst time. The fella that won was awfi' guid. He is the Bruttish champion. An awfi' nice chap. We had a guid session after. He taught the rest of us a trick or two."

Mick had the physique of a wrestler. "Do you do weight training?" I asked.

He grinned – he wasn't often not grinning. "I'm guid enough at judo and I scrap caravans wi' my axe. Do you want to buy an axe? I can gi' ye a real bargain."

As we passed a small roadside quarry he spotted a tent and a couple of trucks. "Looks like anither scrappie." He stopped the lorry. "Let's go and see how he's getting on."

Mick never walked when he could run, and he was across the quarry before I'd left the road, his broken trackshoes flailing the ground behind him. From the condensation on the windscreen it looked as if someone was sleeping in the cab of the smaller vehicle. As we approached, an alsatian came tearing out from under the low-loader to the full extent of its rope, snarling and barking. Mick steered away from it towards the tent. "Hell, pal. Hello. How are you," he was saying, as if whoever was in the tent was a long-lost friend.

Something in the tent moved and a man, still in oily overalls in his sleeping-bag, poked his torso out of the entrance, releasing a cloud of flies. He recognised Mick as a traveller like himself, but he looked suspiciously at me while the two of them then had a conversation about ferrous and non-ferrous that I

144

couldn't follow. The other man was a relative newcomer to the island and Mick made several suggestions as to where he might find something, which the man noted down on the corner of an envelope.

Back in the lorry, I said I was surprised that Mick had given away potential income sources to a competitor and had got nothing in return.

"I'm nae in it fae the money. It's spiritual. It suits me fine being here. He's in it fae the money, which is fine too. And there are some places where I can't go, where they've told me that they doon't want tae see my face again. He may get lucky there."

The lorry left Uist with no ceremony at all, crossed the perfunctory causeway on to the next island of Benbecula and turned left for the airport, just beyond the drab military city for army personnel. 'There was a time when ye cuid get an awfi' lot of copper here," continued Mick. "HIDB contracts, you get a lot of leftover scrap frae them. Mind you, there's too much competition on the islands now. I'm thinking of going tae Thailand."

This was such a surprising thing to say that it left me quite speechless, but Mick had stopped outside the airport and was disappearing at a jog amongst the outhouses before I could find my tongue. I was sitting there quietly with the dogs when a couple of smart, proper-looking military wives on horseback came past and smiled at me, in the glassy, frightened way that said that scrap dealers are rough, dangerous people not to be mixed with by colonels' wives. Mick came jogging back, pulled open the ashtray, which was stuffed with £10 notes, and took out a handful. "A nice bit of copper wire," he said, grinning like a Cheshire cat and disappearing almost as quickly. Once the wire was loaded he jogged off into the terminal building again, returning twenty minutes later, empty-handed but pleased. "They're doing a big rewire job next month. He'll let me have furst choice when I come back. Awfi' nice man. I saw him at the games yesterday and he told me tae come up."

Then we were back on the road again. "Where was it ye were wanting tae go tae?" he said, suddenly. It was the first time he'd asked me that since picking me up, and I must admit I couldn't really care. For the moment he was far more interesting than the rainsoaked islands.

"I'm happy to be going north, wherever you're going."

"Have you had anything t'eat? There's a guid bar at the junction here." So saying, he turned into the Black Isle Hotel car park, leaving his lorry so that there would be no need to reverse out. They knew him and liked him in the bar. "How d'you get on?" asked the barman.

"I was beaten by the Bruttish champion. Awfi' nice chap. Have the seafood platter, it's awfi' good," said Mick, handing on the menu.

Over lunch he decided he'd go to Berneray, a small island off the north of North Uist. I said I'd come along too, even though that meant sweeping through Benbecula and on across the causeway through North Uist as well. Before we set off again after lunch he called up the ferryman on the North Uist to Berneray run just to make sure that no other scrappie had been there for a while.

The lorry's windscreen wipers didn't do a particularly good job, so I saw little of Benbecula. The road lay across flat, wet land, sometimes on a causeway and sometimes on a narrow strip of dry land between two lochs. Mick stopped once to talk to someone else he'd seen at the games, returning to the cab empty-handed.

"The gear's not ready yet." The lorry lurched forward again.

"So you've got a couple of children in Dundee?"

"Uh-huh. They're not actually mine, the wee yins," said Mick. "They're June's. I live wi' June i'Dundee."

'But you'd rather be here?"

"There's an awfi' lot of drugs and stuff i'Dundee. June lives in a tenement wi' an unemployed wee man below, a prostitute above, a wee man who sells lorries on one side and a family doon the corridor who'll steal anything. June's had a rough time, beaten by her husband, that sort of thing. That's normal life in Dundee. And the bairns spend all day playing wi' computer games. Myself I canna stand the sight ae computers. They make me feel sick."

He seemed to lose half the colour from his cheeks, contemplating Dundee. "I'd nivver lived in one place before I moved in wi' June. Mother Earth – that's my home. I've been in Dundee sex years now and sometimes I think I'm going to have a nervous breakdown. She lives in a teacup, June does. Those foor walls – they squeeze the life outa ye. I can only stay there a couple ae days at a time."

"Can't you get them to move?"

"Move? They don't want to move. Somebody offered me a hoose on the island here but June and Lee and Clark were not interested."

The lorry slowed. "I'm no bothered whether Clark and Lee are mine or not. I love them as much as I can anyway – I wouldna love them any more if they were my ain. My friends say that I've given everything and got nothing back. Sometimes, when I come up here and stand on a hill, I think tae myself that I've jist wasted my life. They only seem pleased tae see me because I bring hame the munny."

As prepared for anything as I told myself I was, Mick came as a surprise. He was driving a lorry, perhaps the most stereotypical male profession ever, yet betrayed no stereotypical male characteristics whatsoever. It was as if he'd been created in a different, far purer, world before being let loose in this, and all the injustices and inadequacies of urban life hurt him deeply. It is rare to meet a man – and a scrap dealer at that – so open about his own emotions, and so trusting of another man. It is rare to start a conversation with another man with so little of the normal careful conversational rituals. I could see that, to the inner city tenement family, he was totally unfathomable. A scrap dealer who wanted to go to Thailand, who wrote poetry, who loved open spaces, didn't drink or smoke or eat chips. They called him "Daft Mick" at home; in their narrow ethos he may well be considered daft, but there was something great about him too. Although he'd had practically no education, he had a sure sense of the rightness of things which sometimes brought him next to tears. I, who'd had an expensive education and a protected, careful upbringing, could not bring myself up to his standard of openness. "They foor walls, they squeeze the life outa me," he kept saying, as we discussed the problems he faced at home. In a sense he was far too pure and therefore far too vulnerable for the household – and the society – that he'd got involved in, but was there any point in saying so? There was a purity in the islands that matched him fine, but if he moved to the islands he'd be abandoning his adopted family. There was nothing easy to say.

It was at this point that his truck broke down. We'd crossed most of North Uist in the direction of Lochmaddy when a rumble under the cab turned into the screeching of scraping broken metal. The engine ground to a halt and we rolled into a passing space.

"Sounds awfi' bad," he grinned. "What do you think? Piston rings?" We piled out into the pouring rain and he tipped the cab forward. The oil sump was full of water. Whatever it was that had gone wrong had also smashed a gasket. The engine would need stripping down and rebuilding.

My stomach sank to the level of the nearest loch. "What are you going to do?" I wailed.

But Mick looked to be positively enjoying himself. "Right, this is a problem I like. It's a concrete problem, and concrete problems are easy. I think I'll gi' up scrap fae a while. I'll leave the lorry here till September. Meanwhile I'll take June and the bairns on holiday tae somewhere wairm. Any ideas?"

Standing in the rain, by a lorry which ticked slowly as it cooled into a state of mechanical rigor mortis out of which it was unlikely ever to recover, we started to discuss which were the nicest and the cheapest of the Mediterranean islands. Mick's face was glistening, not with tears, but with rain. The breakdown seemed to have lifted a weight from his shoulders. He circled the lorry, assessing its value as scrap. "Two new batteries. And the back end must be wirth £500. No, no problem in selling it, even frae here. My problem is the scrap and the dogs – how am I going tae get them back tae Dundee? There's not exactly a lot of public transport and hitch-hiking wi' three dogs and a load ae scrap . . . where's Bessie?"

I said I'd seen her go into the heather on the other side of the road. "Bessie. Beeesssiiiieee. The auld gurl knows there's something wrong, that's why she's gone. Don't wait around, I'll go find her mysel'. You're getting wet. You'd best get yourself a lift. It's bin awfi' nice meeting ye."

I protested feebly, but I could be of no practical help whatsoever, and there was no reason for me to stay. I stood forlornly by the side of the road with my thumb out, not really wanting a lift at all, and when the first car stopped it was with some reluctance I clambered in. As we started off again, Mick was coming back down the slope with his dog at his heels. Both

I and the dog Bessie looked morose and miserable, but Mick the scrappie beamed and waved.

VII

I knew nothing about Berneray other than it was the birthplace of Giant MacAskill, a seven foot nine inch tower of a man who had been signed to Barnum and Bailey's circus, and even this gem I gleaned from a reproduction poster in the shed used as a ferry waiting-room, a couple of hours after leaving Mick. Underneath it was the note that Giant MacAskill had died at the age of thirty-eight while trying to lift a one-ton anchor which had fallen and pierced his chest.

I'd not particularly wanted to go to Berneray; I'd not have even thought of going there if it hadn't been for Mick, but I remain grateful to Mick both for the lift and for our ultimate destination, which I reached without him.

Over the years I have met a considerable number of people in Scotland whose lives struck me as being aesthetically complete. Unlike most modern careers, which are a combination of clever marketing of an imperfect product, these lives were almost a work of art, created and performed according to a few guiding principles, compact, self-contained, and working in harmony with other similar people in the community to create a single, humming canvas. Berneray was like that. I'm not saying that there was no dissent and no dissatisfaction in the community, because no doubt there was, but broadly everyone was there because they wanted to be, they were doing what they wanted to do and they were beholden to no one. In that sense, Berneray was a work of art.

Berneray is the largest of the multitude of islands in the Sound of Harris, the water that separates North Uist from Harris and Lewis. It's not especially pretty to look at: three miles long by a mile and a half wide, rising to a small hill in the centre, with no particular distinguishing features. It has the usual Outer Hebridean configuration of machair fringed by a long sandy beach on the west coast and rocky bays on the east. The machair was once cultivated for potatoes and corn, but the fishing business dominates nowadays, focused around the two main bays on the east coast, where most of the houses are strung out along the couple of miles of tarmac road. One hundred and fifty people live on this small island, a proportionately large population which is a tribute to its community strength, and Gaelic is the dominant language in a way that it will never be on its larger island neighbours. Berneray has a shop, a post office and a ferry. It has no hotel – a contentious subject amongst the islanders – but it does have a youth hostel operated by the Gatliff Trust. This trust was started by one Herbert Gatliff who visited the Hebrides in the 1940s and was dismayed to find very few places to stay other than the costly hunting-shooting-fishing hotels; he campaigned for the establishment of youth hostels where possible, and the resulting Gatliffe Trust hostels are the best located and the most interesting on the islands, if you can find them. On Berneray the hostel comprises two thatched black houses – now painted a shining white – on the tip of the promontory of the main bay; the front doors look out over the Sound of Harris into the thicket of islands crowding the narrows. Beyond is the Minch, a wide firth of flat sea, and beyond still are the distant purple towers of the Cuillins on the Isle of Skye. At one's feet the tide curls around the shore, bubbling over the rocks like a crystal-clear river in spate. The tides run through the gaps between these islands like water squirting out from between one's teeth.

The hostel, on whose bookshelves a Gaelic edition of the New Testament sat alongside the May issue of *Cycling Times*, is managed by identical twin sisters about whom there are plenty of anecdotes in the youth hostelling world. Most of these stories revolve around confusing the sisters and what was said by and to each of them. In fact, the sisters exchange so much information between themselves that I found the one who came in the evening would know what I had said to the one who came in the morning anyway. It was a peculiar sensation, though, completing a conversation in the evening with someone who may or may not have been the person whom I'd started it with in the morning, but who knew the essence of it anyway. The sisters, however, took it all in their stride and betrayed not the faintest sign of embarrassment as the hostellers stumbled over themselves to avoid having to admit that they didn't know which sister it was that they were talking to.

Although it is one of Berneray's proudest boasts that there are practically no incomers as permanent residents, there were plenty of visitors on the island. It was Berneray week, the time when those family offshoots who had done well elsewhere returned to contemplate their good fortune and the fortune of those who'd stayed behind. In the community hall – newly built by the islanders themselves, with their own money and their own hands – a slide show charted several decades. Every image of red-faced young men pausing in harvesting the hay or loading their boats with cattle was hailed with cries of "Who's that on the left?" or "Will ye look at Archie's ears!"; every picture of young girls on bicycles posing for the camera was greeted with gales of laughter, and the new generation of urban children looked on bemused as their mothers blushed, stunned at their former lack of sophistication. I was the only outsider, but even I knew one face. He was pictured doing the washing-up, having dinner and laughing uproariously: it was Prince Charles, and alongside him at the sink or around the kitchen table were two or three people in the audience. For that audience – who hushed suitably when Charles's image appeared on the screen – there was no need to explain what Prince Charles was doing looking so relaxed in their kitchens.

It wasn't until the middle of the following day, out in the middle of the Sound of Harris on the *Berneray Isle* with Angus and Roddy, that I learned the true story. It was a glorious, spotless day, but the two men were in bright yellow oilskins out of habit. They were fishing for velvet crabs; I was sitting in the bows trying not to get in the way, Roddy was preparing the hauler and Angus, whose boat it was, was in the wheelhouse assessing the landmarks. Roddy was probably in his mid-thirties, an islander with a nervous stammer and sticking-out ears (apparently a Berneray characteristic) who'd recently returned to the island after a period living on the mainland. He explained the Prince Charles episode rather furtively; it seemed that Charles had been out on the very boat that I was sitting on, with Angus who was Roddy's uncle, and Angus didn't like it talked about; he would never mention it himself. The whole episode, explained Roddy, had started when Charles and Diana had passed through Berneray for a couple of hours while on their honeymoon tour of the Western Isles. "You-you-you went to the s-s-slide show?" I said I did. "You'll have seen Splash then," said Roddy, enigmatically. It transpired that Splash was the man who'd hosted the slide show; "S-ss-ssp-lash will talk to a-a-n-nnyone," said Roddy. "He invited Prince Charles to come and stay with him whenever he wanted." A couple of years later Splash's phone had rung and Charles had invited himself, plus one bodyguard, back to Berneray. I remember it dimly as being the cause of a certain amount of newspaper speculation at the time. Prince Charles had disappeared, no one knew where. Had he had a nervous breakdown? wondered the papers.

On the island only Splash and his wife had known he was coming, but it wasn't long before the news was out. Someone met him walking on the island's road; someone else looked up from their washing-up to see him climbing the hill. Rumour flew round the island in minutes. And the Telecom man, who'd come over from the mainland to fix Splash's phone and who entered the sitting-room whistling, emerged from it white and silent. "Hey, pal, there's a chap sitting on your sofa who luiks helluva like Prince Charles," he whispered, uncertain whether he'd suddenly taken leave of his senses. The Prince had stayed a few days, told everyone to call him Charlie, planted a few potatoes and gone out fishing, after which he'd returned to his official life. Meanwhile a London hotel was offering exorbitant money for the potatoes and the media was using large cash incentives to lure an islander, any islander, to a microphone or into a newspaper to tell the story. But Berneray closed ranks behind its departing royal visitor, and barely a word was murmured on the subject for months afterwards. The community was united in a fierce pride that the beauty and the sanctity of their place – which had always seemed obvious to them – was also valued by the highest authority in the kingdom.

Angus came striding forward, saying something in Gaelic to Roddy which interrupted our gossip, and between them they started to jettison the fleet of creels they'd prepared the night before. "We'll be changing over to the lobster," he explained in English. "The velvet crab are finishing chust now." There was something naturally commanding about Angus. He had a broad, high-cheeked and kind face, lined by forty years of squinting at the sea. He worked efficiently but without a sense of hurry. There was an economy in his movements which was the result of a whole lifetime perfecting the things he did.

"Do you prefer lobster?"

"Och yes. No question." He opened the control box next to the hauler and gunned the *Berneray Isle* towards a distant buoy. "There's an excitement in catching lobster, right enough," he said after a moment's contemplation. "And they're sich an interesting shape. So well made. Catching velvets is like factory work for us, you see."

For the next couple of hours Angus and Roddy worked their production line, hauling in the fleets of creels, opening each one, tipping out the scuttling velvets, smashing up any other shellfish in the creels and rebaiting them with fresh whiting; crab prefer fresh bait, while lobster like it salted. Showers of crabs flew across the deck (it wasn't possible to hold on to them for more than a couple of seconds) with each creel. Sometimes the creels contained flatfish or dogfish, and one even contained a conger eel so big that its flesh sagged out between the mesh. The islanders would eat flatfish and maybe even the eel, said Angus, but never the crabs. No one ate velvet crabs in the UK; they were catching them for the Spanish. Years ago they smashed the velvets and kept the brown crabs; now it was the other way round, and it was all thanks to the Spanish.

The boxes filled steadily with angry velvets and even when the lids had been nailed down they continued to make a misleadingly pleasant bubbling sound, like a burn full with a suitable amount of water. At the end of the day the boxes would be dropped into the water on an inshore mooring so that the crabs would remain fresh for the buyer, who called on Saturdays.

In the wheelhouse Angus listened in to the radio chat of the other fishermen. "Will you listen to the Lewis accent," he chuckled, as a particularly singsong Gaelic voice was plucked out of the air by the radio. "They've got a very funny accent on Lewis," he said, as if Lewis was the other side of the country rather than the lump of land just over his shoulder. An English voice emerged from the radio and Angus looked at up me. "Now there's a sassenach for you," he murmured.

"I'll let the girls catch up, then come on," crackled the voice of a hearty yottie, booming with bonhomie. "If you get there before me, mine's large one. Over."

Angus turned down the volume. "What's the English like?" he asked, turning to me. "I'm wondering about this football hooligan business." I flannelled. Life was more confusing living in the south, I said, and people did silly things out of frustration more than anything else.

"An Englishman, a stockbroker at that, came up aboot fifteen years ago and bought Pabbay," he mused, nodding out through the wheelhouse windows at the small circular island whose sand-fringed shores we'd been skirting all morning. Englishmen were rare breeds in Angus's world. "Flew over it on a lovely day like today and said he'd buy it. He came back when the sale was completed and landed on the shoore at low tide. Of coorse when he got back to the plane the tide had come in and they had to push it up the shoore and wait for the sea to go down again before he cuid take off. He's not been back since, I'm thinking. It's a lovely island right enough, Pabbay."

It was a perfect day for fishing. Even out in the middle of the straits between Berneray and Pabbay, it was easy to see the bottom and to pick out the clusters of dark rock from the luminous white sand. The fleets of creels had to be laid on the rock and not on the sand, a task which was easy enough when the day was bright and the sea calm; on other days – the majority of the time – Angus had to lay his creels by memory, using his experience and the changing shapes of the surr-ounding islands to judge the position of the rocky undersea. The landmarks were all-important, he said; creels which were misplaced came up empty. To my eye there were no landmarks at all, only the changing shapes of the islands.

In the winter he and Roddy went out after prawns in the Minch, which was a far tougher proposition than muddling around Pabbay after lobster: winter prawning meant foul weather and long, dark steaming, setting out in the dark of the early morning and returning in the dark of the night.

Lobsters were far more pleasant – provided no one stole them, Roddy said darkly. One of the islanders had been lifting their pots for years, removing the lobsters, and it was only by setting a police trap that they'd caught him red-handed. It was a painful subject, that betrayal. "Ach, taking a lobster from my creel is like taking £15 from my pocket," said Angus. It was a major breach of island trust, of the island code of ethics, and it had been severely punished in the islanders' own way: since being caught the fisherman had had problems selling his own catch and had been heavily ostracised from social occasions. A strong community has to run itself and mete out its own punishment.

By mid-afternoon Angus and Roddy were well pleased. They'd returned to the fleets of pots they'd put down earlier and emptied them again; the fresh bait made all the difference, and the fishboxes filled steadily with bubbling crabs. If it hadn't been the day of the ceilidh they would probably have continued, but there was a concert and a dance to prepare for, so the *Berneray Isle* headed back. Roddy's young wife and son and Angus's dog Bob were waiting on the quay; Bob leapt while the boat was still some feet from the harbour wall, disappearing in a black blur into the wheelhouse to greet Angus.

The day after the ceilidh was a Saturday. It was to be one of the four occasions in the year when the crofters of specific townships on Berneray, who had the grazing rights on the offshore island of Hermetray, clubbed together to go out to visit their sheep. When I'd left the ceilidh at 2.00 a.m. that morning to walk back to the hostel I was prepared to predict the crofters who wouldn't make it to the boat at 11.00 a.m., but I'd have been wrong. Angus, who was to be the leader of the trip to Hermetray, had attended the concert part of the ceilidh in his suit but had slipped away once the dancing had really got going. Roddy had been there too, well drunk. In fact, very few of the men were anything approaching sober. By the time I'd left the celebration it was a question of who'd last the longest – the menfolk or the band.

On the quay Seanag was first. A great big, muscularly fat man with a quick tongue in any language.

"You'll be on for the shearing then," he said to me.

I nodded.

"It's a highly skilled business, I'll be telling you," he said, chucking his biscuit tin of egg sandwiches down on to the *Berneray Isle*. "Give me a gless of whusky and I cuid learren to be a doctor in five minutes, but to learn how to shear, that takes yearres."

Angus arrived with his dog and the red-eyed Roddy. The men gathered slowly on the quay, exchanging their views on the ceilidh in a grave, serious way that reflected their own state of health and the quality of the night before. It was almost a mark of respect: a ceilidh that creates an awesome hush of furred tongues the following day is a good one.

There was not a lot of English spoken on the journey, so I sat in the bows and watched the islands float by like driftwood. On the boat the crofters' dogs bickered amongst themselves – all but one particularly sleek beast that stayed between its master's legs, gazing up into his eyes. The two were like lovers. He sat by himself, his head hung over his dog, his hair slack peroxide blonde, his skin red and inflamed. Occasionally he would lean forward to vomit into the passing sea, and after every vomit he'd drink from the bottle of Lucozade by his side.

"Isn't it a dreadful shame just," said one of the crofters, who saw me looking at him. "He's been off it for days now and look at him. Think of the state of him inside."

I said it was hard to imagine him doing any work in that condition. "Ay, and when he's on the bottle he does nothing at all. You don't see him for days," said the crofter.

"Where does he get the money?"

"Ach, they'll always get the money from somewhere right enough, these people."

Angus piloted the *Berneray Isle* into a quiet lagoon on the west side of Hermetray and we all piled onshore, spreading out along both coasts to meet at the far side and drive the sheep back over the middle to the fank. Hermetray was smooth and largely circular, rising 150 feet to a little loch in a crater in the middle. I travelled around the western shore, disturbing a pair of duck, wing-drying cormorants, shrieking oyster-catchers and hosts of young gulls. About halfway round I met a ewe and her lamb who had slipped the main pack and I set about driving the pair of them towards the fank. Driving a pair of sheep single-handed is not easy; they were fit and fast and they knew every contour of the island. They zigzagged and I swore; I would have sworn in Gaelic if I could, but all I could think of was *slàinte mhòr*, cheers. Cheers, I bellowed as the blessed beasts once again outskirted me and seemed intent on getting right behind me. Cheers, you buggers, cheers. In the distance the main flock headed across the top towards the fank, the crofters bellowing at their over-eager dogs. One of them peeled off and came over to help, but his dog was deaf and the ewe was really difficult, so in the end we left her.

The fank was full, the dogs lying on the tops of the walls snapping at the heaving, bleating mass below them. "Roll me over in the clover," sang Seanag, wading into the middle of the sea of beasts, which parted in front of him. The clipping began, at first amidst high tension as several animals tried repeatedly to escape through the stone entrance. Each new one that was caught put up a panic attack of bleating, flailing hooves sending showers of dung flying through the air, and the rest of the flock rippled in waves of fear around the fank. I was elected to stand guard and my clothes were soon streaked with mud; the fank became a bath of mud, piss and bits of sodden wool and blood where the shears slipped or Angus's penknife had dealt savagely with foot rot. The men skittled their ewes on to their backs and slipped elastic bands around the testicles of the male lambs they'd not castrated earlier in the year. The alcoholic struggled through his work, walking away occasionally to be sick. Each crofter seemed to take it in turn to work alongside him, muttering what must have been advice, but he himself said very little. In the end, when the others had finished their sheep, they turned on his and finished those too, so by mid-afternoon the fank was empty and the sheep back on the hill, newly white and bleating confusedly.

The mood was surprisingly sombre as we returned to the boat. The sheep shear was an important ritual for the men; it was a time for reflection on island affairs. "The good old days of a singsong and a couple of drams of whusky every ten minute or so are over then," said Seanag wistfully.

"It's a pity if people can't meet each other without a dram," said Angus, who'd been quiet all day. The two of them lapsed into Gaelic, with the others chipping in to what became quite a heated discussion.

On the journey back Roddy explained. He no longer stuttered – a tribute either to the fact that he had got used to me, or that the alcohol of the night before had smoothed his tongue. "There's talk of building a hotel wiss a bar to make a social centre of the island and to stop people drinking at home," he said. "A lot of people don't want it. That's what that's all about." It was clearly an emotive issue. All of the crofters had withdrawn into the wheelhouse with Angus and they were arguing steadily and they continued to argue as they clambered back on shore.

After scrubbing off the stench of sheep I picked up my belongings from the hostel, which was suddenly bulging with people who were heading hurriedly south out of Harris and Lewis before the sabbath, like rats leaving a sinking ship. The men of Lewis are great people, but they are under the thumb of the minister, said a bicyclist. "You should see them all scramble for carry-outs in the bars on Saturday night. Stornoway on a Sunday." He grimaced. "I'd rather be in hell."

Half an hour later I was back on the water, on the small ferry that headed north to Harris and Lewis. It was one of those wistful, still evenings which has a natural grace and an undemonstrative beauty that one wants to remember for all time. It was so quiet that – as Mick the scrappie would have said – you could almost hear the trout farting. The low sun dug underneath the hillsides that floated past, picking out unusual shapes and colours. Close colours were crisp; distant colours were softened by a russet haze. A couple of days later such beauty may be forgotten by the conscious memory but only because it has gone deeper, adding to a store of sunlight somewhere deep in the soul.

VII

I was lucky to find somewhere to stay on South Harris. On that Saturday evening in Leverburgh most of the bed and breakfast signs had disappeared under sacking or been removed altogether, because the imminent sabbath could not be properly observed with a visitor in the house. On the sabbath you stay at home, you eat cold meats and cold potatoes prepared the day before, you do no work, you trap your chickens in baskets to stop them running around, you do not drive your car other than to the kirk, and then you spy out of the window to try to catch your neighbours breaking these rules. Guests are expected to stay quietly in their rooms. It is not easy running a B&B in these conditions, which is one of the main reasons why the tourist office has failed to persuade householders along the east coast road of South Harris to start providing accommodation. Fortunately for me there was an exception in Leverburgh – an English landlady on the road out to the west who took no account of Sundays and who no doubt was tongue-whipped behind her back by the local community for so doing. Her only other guest was a Jesuit priest called Jim.

In theory everybody is meant to remain at home for the sabbath, even if there is a war on. Wee Free ministers in Stornoway in the Second World War attempted to stop movement of convoys and battleships in Stornoway harbour on a Sunday, and Caledonian MacBrayne is still unable to run Sunday ferries into some ports. In my childhood holidays on Skye, Granny had tried to enforce the rules: "Read quietly," she'd say. "Now go to your room and read quietly." In those days a "busy" Sunday referred to the number of vapour trails of America-bound aircraft I had been able to count out of my bedroom skylight. Vapour trails over Scotland were – and are – symbolic to me of the gulf between Highland communities and the jet age and also reminiscent of those moments when I've stood on top of a 3,000 foot mountain after a day's solitary clambering to share its loneliness with a metallic tie-pin 32,000 feet further up. In the winter the vapour trails are all that many Highland and island communities see of the outside world.

Wee Free bashing is a popular activity, but wherever man is face to face with his own survival, beliefs – particularly the more superstitious ones – are strong. The Free Church of Scotland has provided a strong belief for the Outer Isles; without it the Gaelic culture would probably not have survived to this day. The original Free Church, from which the Wee Frees are derived, was formed in 1843 by 500 ministers who split away from the Church of Scotland. Their move was in final protest against the increasing patronage in the Church which was turning ministers into puppets of government. Under the patronage system ministers were appointed by the Crown and local gentry, who had their own self-interests in mind. The 1843 split was a bold and high-principled move, because in leaving the established Church and the patronage system the ministers were turning their backs on job security, home, servants and social kudos and throwing themselves on the charity of the people. For many years after the split Scotland's rulers, the landowners and gentry, were very hostile to the new Church, refusing to allow chapels to be built and forcing congregations to worship on public roadways or even on a floating barge in the middle of a loch. But the new Free Church (*the Free Kirk, the wee kirk, the kirk without a steeple*) was very successful, and its progress had the effect of gingering up radicalism within the conventional government-sponsored Church of Scotland (*the auld kirk, the cauld kirk, the kirk withoot a people*), which itself eventually overthrew the patronage system. By 1900 the Free Church had merged back into the mainstream, although a small rump movement – the Free Presbyterian Church or Wee Frees – kept their radicalism and their anti-establishment identity.

In the Wee Free creed are the important principles of the democratic election of the minister by the community and the lack of any ornamentation that could encourage idolatry. These are very clear principles, factors that are forgotten by those who condemn the Church as bigoted and narrow-minded. A strong faith tends to polarise opposition – as demonstrated by most wars of the modern era – and the Wee Frees have never compromised or attempted to gain the favour of the establishment. On the other hand, they are very severe.

Despite the noise that they make, the total contingent of Wee Free ministers in modern Scotland numbers less than twenty. While in the west Highlands in the winter I'd come across a community which was breathing a sigh of relief at just having lost its minister. He had distinguished himself by preaching hellfire and damnation at a funeral and offering not a crumb of comfort to the bereaved, and with a famous sermon on Christmas Day about how it had been Christ's hard luck to have been born a bastard. So it was that I went to the Wee Free service in Leverburgh that evening with some interest, expecting pyrotechnics.

The day hadn't been totally without activity. In Leverburgh itself the only thing that moved was the occasional salmon, unsheathing itself from the high tide in the bay, but it was a day for doing more than just counting vapour trails. The sky was blue to a degree only experienced over islands or snow; the drying sun meant the hay could be gathered by mid-morning;

washing on the line would dry within the hour, and the lovely beaches on the west coast waited for visitors. Jim the Jesuit had gone out on the hills in his shorts, bird-watching, and I'd set off around the coast. I'd walked for a couple of hours down the road before the first car passed me by, but I'd managed to hitch a couple of lifts in the day, one from a coastguard on patrol and the other from two English girls looking for a suitable beach.

Outside the church that evening the activity on the road was more than I'd seen all day. Most of the township was there, dressed in sober suits and hats, as many young people as old, filing into a modern building that was plainly elegant. The building had had a contentious birth, however, being built by a firm of Catholic builders from South Uist who'd delivered much of the stone to the Leverburgh pier on a Sunday. Inside it there were no images, no pictures, no altar, and no cross, but there was a clock. The young minister stayed in his raised balcony at the far end, with only his dour countenance appearing above the parapet to the congregation below until he was called upon to stand up and deliver his homily. Beneath him sat the church elders who'd shaken everyone by the hand at the door on arrival, and who dictated proceedings. It was both a judge and jury trial and a talent competition: on the one hand the ministers and elders being judge and jury on the sins of the congregation and on the other the minister having to do his best to the audience while the elders looked on from below and decided whether his best was good enough.

When it came to the time of the sermon the sound of sweetie-papers being unwrapped filled the hall. My next-door neighbour, whom I'd not even spoken to, silently passed me a raspberry-flavour pear-drop and we settled down for a good one. The minister's starting subject was the textual holiness of the Bible. Every single word of scripture was fact, he declared. Moreover, it was the only rock of permanence in this era of change. Others had tried to question bits of scripture, but look where it had got them, he said. Jim, who had accompanied me and was sitting by my side in the pew, was rigid. The minister rambled on. "You are all sinners," he boomed. "And there's nothing you can do about it. You can only understand God if He gives you a revelation, and you only get saved by His grace." After the first half-hour I stopped trying to identify concluding sentences; his whole homily was full of concluding sentences. And when the end finally came – after fifty minutes – it was not a logical conclusion at all. It was the result, as least so Jim claimed afterwards, of one of the elders looking at the clock and raising his arm, as if the minister had crossed the finishing line after the requisite number of laps.

The expected hellfire and damnation not having materialised, I felt like a naughty schoolboy reprieved at the last moment from stern punishment. According to the minister it didn't even matter whether I was well-behaved or not, I still stood the same chance of getting to heaven. The congregation sat passively, taking it all on the chin like seasoned sparring partners whose main concern was to limit the damage done to their physiognomy before they retired; it didn't sound as if the minister's punches, hard though they were thrown from his balcony, really hurt when they landed. His congregation knew the blows of old, they knew where they were coming from, where they would land, and how to take them. By contrast, their own contribution to the service was the soft and hypnotic cadences of the unaccompanied Gaelic singing of the psalms; there were no hymns – there was no organ. When the service was finally over my neighbour who'd passed me the pear-drop made some pleasant remarks about the weather and how lucky I was. His and the other smiles outside the church seemed to suggest that despite the deluge of blows from the balcony, the congregation had gained strength from being united under the hammer and this unity had enabled them to survive another Sunday.

Once we'd got out of earshot of the departing congregation Jim released his caged indignation. At first he'd felt guilty, he said, at trespassing into the service of a foreign camp, but as time progressed he'd become incensed at the stupidity of what the minister was saying and the length of time he took to say it. Although I'd not enquired about the strength of his own belief, I gathered that he had come to the island to reaffirm his spiritual convictions in which he was disarmingly unconfident, and the hare-brained sermonising of the Wee Free minister had interrupted his contemplation of purity, inner and outer, and thrown him off-balance. What made him so angry, he said, was that so many people were packed into a church to be fed such rubbish and on such a beautiful day.

My last and best memory of Jim is at the Leverburgh ceilidh later that week. The band in the school hall was the same couple who'd played at the Berneray ceilidh and they were looking as if the ceilidh season had already had the best of them. Jim, who'd had as many beers and whiskies as a ceilidh-player should, strode up on to the stage and volunteered to take over the guitar, which he then played for the rest of the evening. Little did the swirling, sweat-soaked bunch of drunks on the floor – many of whom had been in the kirk on Sunday – realise that the man belting out "Got myself a crying, walking, sleeping, talking . . . living doll. Got to do my best to please her just 'cos she's a . . . living doll," was actually a Jesuit priest.

I had to go to Lewis to appreciate fully the beauties of Harris. Travelling northwards, I'd come to expect each island to be more beautiful than the last, and accordingly I was rather bewildered to arrive finally in flat, drab Lewis to find it a bit of a disappointment both physically and emotionally. It wasn't until I'd got there that I understood the logic in calling what was effectively one island by two different names, and in dividing the landmass at what was effectively its widest point rather than its narrowest. If the dividing line had been at Tarbert, the narrow neck where South Harris meets North Harris, then it might have been understandable. But Harris and Lewis are symbolically separated along the line of a feeble burn which trickles into Loch Seaforth; I know it well, because I sat on the small bridge that lets it pass under the road, waiting for a lift. Crossing the burn doesn't feel much like crossing a frontier, but crossing the no-man's-land that precedes it does. The islanders refer to it as crossing the Clisham, and it is not unlike a ferry journey. Somewhere beyond Tarbert the road is suddenly picked up by the scruff of its neck by the mountains, which lift it to a giddy height and stretch it thin, gasping and thrashing, across their own backs, presenting it as a sacrifice to the sky. No one lives up on the Clisham. It only became navigable this century and prior to that visitors travelled between the two communities by boat, as they would between islands. Beyond the Clisham, Lewis is wide, flat and squidgy; before it, Harris is tall, bony, aristocratic and threadbare.

The Clisham is Harris's uncompromisingly savage side, and although today it would be physically possible to live up there,

163

it would be psychologically unpleasant, so nobody does. The ground is so poor throughout Harris that most of the island's 3,500 inhabitants live on the south or east coasts, looking to the sea for their livelihoods. Travelling along the "golden road" (so called because it cost so much to make) along the east coast is like travelling along a row of sloping molars with their cutting edges up in the mist above; the only occasional foliage seems to have got stuck in the toothy crevices like leftovers from a big meal, the last trace of the original vegetation which had been swallowed and digested by the rock, which had then excreted small droppings of peat for human beings to squabble over, to live on, to burn as fuel and to bury their dead in. The more fertile west coast, a sward of peaceful bays and gleaming beaches with flower-covered machair, is thinly populated because it was cleared by the island's landowners who forced the inhabitants over on to the impossible east.

Ironically it is the east side which has developed into the more self-sufficient of the two coasts despite its infertility, because once the hostile rock has tumbled into the turquoise sea, it instantly becomes fatherly and protective, providing endless sheltered hollows of water in which a small and healthy fish-farming industry has developed.

For many decades educational levels on South Harris were desperately low: in 1833 out of a parish of 3,067 only twelve could write, and even they were very confused between the English they were taught at school and the Gaelic they spoke outside the classroom. Attendance was very poor: besides corrupting their culture, education gave young people the wings with which to leave the islands, so their parents often encouraged truancy. Education was run by the English, who transcribed Gaelic names into their school registers with remarkable inaccuracy. Gaelic names are strings of five or six patronymics which connect several generations; under the English they were limited to two, anglicised versions. Even now the islanders have their official, anglicised names – Angus, Roderick, Donald, etc – and their unofficial, Gaelic ones – Padraig Seonag Dhomhnaill Phadraig, etc. Some of the older ones still have two birthdays, a hangover from the era when it was the duty of the man of the house to report all new births to the estate office; often, however, the man was away at the time of the birth and it would be days or even months before a child was registered. Because there were heavy penalties for late registration, most parents would pretend – on the father's return – that the child had just been born. With a new language, two names and two birthdays forced upon them it is unsurprising that the islanders resented the English, and they were not slow to express it, as two civil servants on bicycles visiting Harris at the turn of the century found out. They stopped to ask directions of an islander as they set off on their tour, and in order to ascertain whether all Harris men were really educationally subnormal they asked the islander to tell them how many people the two of them plus him totalled.

"One hundred," said the Harris man, gazing out to sea.

"How's that, my man?" said one of the civil servants, rather pleased with such astounding mathematical incompetence.

"Well, there's me, that's one." The Harris man spat. "And then there's you, and that's two complete nothings."

The road that crosses the Clisham is maintained partly with European money; a spur road off it to the five houses at Rhenigidale has also been built by the European Community at a cost of £500,000, and it was the EC who were behind the £1.5 million causeway between Vatersay and Barra. When I mentioned my surprise at such European activity in the islands to the men who'd given me a lift they nodded in agreement: "Aye, we've roofless hooses but new European roads up here now, God knows why."

The roads haven't served to make the two island communities feel less foreign to one another. I left my wallet in the back seat of that same car; at the police station in Stornoway the desk officer who turned it over to me made a point of saying that it was Harris men who'd handed it in. There was a police presence on Lewis: they'd had a murder on the island in 1969, the only murder that any of the Outer Hebrides would admit to.

The Harris men had been quiet for those last few miles over the threatening terrain of Lewis. We all looked out of the window at a foreign land and a primeval landscape of work and no beauty, minimal but big, slit and scarred with black wounds after centuries of peat cutting. The weather had closed down and a low ceiling of cloud hung facing the flat land, the two surfaces like matching faces that were preparing to glue themselves together in a wet kiss. Lewis, which has a substantial population of 24,000, was crawling with people like something out of a medieval painting by Brueghel. It was the peat season and whole families were out on the cuttings, laboriously lugging bags of peat across the mutilated landface to the roadside. At one time there was an industry on Lewis for the distillation of oil from peat, but today's uses are largely for domestic sale in Stornoway.

Ask anyone, even the Lewismen, whether they like Stornoway and the answer will almost invariably be "no". Stornoway is not particularly likeable, and it is also the foothold of foreigners on the island and the stronghold of Gaelic politicians and civil servants. It is not unpleasant to look at, but as the largest town in the island it attracts all the problems that such towns usually do. There is something virginal about the islands as a whole, but at Stornoway they definitely lose their virginity. You could tow Stornoway away from Lewis and reattach it almost anywhere on the UK's coastline and it wouldn't really be a misfit; it has teetering office girls on stilettos, whistling leather jacketed lads drumming their heels on the car park walls, Pakistani grocers' shops, modern street toilet units that play music and hose themselves down, one way systems, pedestrian zones, seaside guest houses, radio controlled cabs, German girls on the pier and a lot of fish and chip shops. The harbour is magnificent − but empty of everything except the visiting ferry from Ullapool and rows of small fishing boats in herringbone formation in the inner basin. Big-time fishing out of Stornoway has failed, and the oil industry (either rig construction or support ships) has largely passed it by. The islands are dominated by old-fashioned faces, old-fashioned clothes and old-fashioned lives, but not Stornoway. People, wages and lifestyles here have been borrowed from overseas.

Approached directly from the mainland, Stornoway (which has a population twice that of the island of Harris) presumably provides an introduction of sorts to the islands. Approached from the islands it provides a crash course in urban living which is so foreign to the Hebridean rural communities it might as well be intergalactic living.

I hired a car to escape from Stornoway on what was to be my

last night on the islands, which I had resolved to spend on the Butt of Lewis, the most northerly point of the Hebrides, and watch the fishing boats steam around it heading home from deep Atlantic waters. It was while passing along the ribbon development of the bizarre assortment of houses along the western coast of Lewis that I passed Kenneth Burns Stephen's workshop, marked by a glorious technicolor sign: "L for Leather". Something about the colour and the pun told me that this was no dainty English-run craft shop.

It was still a warm evening but Kenny the Leatherman's converted *tigh dubh* was decidedly chilly. The man himself, who looked like an underdressed hell's angel, was energetically rubbing a moss dye into a piece of goatskin when I poked my head through his open door. He was in shorts and a T-shirt but he kept his body heat up by lots of coffee, whisky and movement. The electricity supply had been cut off for the six months since he'd got back from a winter working in the construction business in Iceland, he explained. He used candles for light and cooked with a coal-fired Aga, and he would continue to do so until the days got shorter and colder.

The phone, too, was dead – he could no longer afford to pay the bill. "I fell madly in love wiss someone from San Francisco last year. She walkit in here one day, a beautiful dame, absolute pairfection. 'Greetings, greetings,' I said. I had to feel hair breast to see if she was real or not. Then she went back to San Francisco and we had these three-hour telephone conversations. Gerchevel." Kenny littered his conversation with bits of language picked up from his travels. "Gerchevel" was his word of the moment and his version of the Icelandic for "there you are".

I told him that I was pleased to find his place, having become rather fed up with arts and crafts shops run by the English which could equally well be in Tunbridge Wells.

"Ay, 200 years o' Calvinism killed the arts," said Kenny. "The munister's a very very bad influence on the community. There's barely a bit of music and poetry left to us. We've Walter in the village who's excellent at spontaneous music and stories. My uncle's a painter and my brother's a poet."

"What about Harris tweed?"

"What about it? The industry's dead at the moment. No wirk,

no shekel. No one's got any orders. The skill factor is high, but they're doing mass production." It was his opinion that the problem with the tweed industry was a fundamental one of the method of working: the factories are supplied with the basic tweed by home-workers, who have long since given up trying to market their own tweeds individually and settled for providing tweed to factory specifications. Without its own originality, the tweed industry has to wait for the old-fashioned look to return to popularity before it thrives.

Other than his workbench and the Aga, where a coffee pot bubbled most of the day, Kenny's workshop's main features were a dentist's chair that he got from a chiropodist, a set of old wooden golf clubs, and bits of a motorcycle that he had never assembled. The narrow, small-paned windows deep-set into the black house's massive walls were crowded with flies trying to get out. Along the back wall were the results of his work: belts, shoes and bags, but mainly bags, in all shapes, sizes and designs.

Kenny bellowed something in Gaelic at Socks, his sheepdog, who had sidled up to the dentist's chair and was discreetly licking my fingers. "My grandfather was a stonemason and a socialist," he went on. "He was always being blacklisted from wirk because he was always campaigning fae better rights, and in his time the only employers of stonemasons were the gentry. The system here on Lewis is feudal. The estate owners expect us to tug our forelocks at them." He enlarged upon the topic of the socialist Gaelic mafioso, as he described them, who dominated island social and political life, creaming off the money that came to the islands from Europe. Not that the islanders were poor, he said. They had food and clothing and light, but they didn't have anything extra. Half the problem lay in the society's own traditions, he said. It was an aural society which had no self-confidence in administration or marketing skills, especially because the imposition of the English language had kncked the self-confidence out of the older generations. The old people were shy and hesitant, and the young people saw entry into the Gaelic mafioso as the quickest and easiest way into a well-paid job.

I decided on a bag I wanted and returned from the car with my cheque book and a half-bottle of whisky that I'd been saving for the Butt of Lewis. Most of the bottle disappeared into Kenny's mug and I had to dissuade him from pouring the rest into mine. The Presbyterian nature of Lewis is stricter than Harris with the result that drinking places are few and far between. In the Ness area of the north of the island there are still a couple of *bochans* – drinking sheds in the fields operated on a co-operative basis. They offer no comfort, only relatively low-priced alcohol to be drunk in company. Kenny the Leatherman had no inhibitions about alcohol: he demolished my half-bottle virtually single-handed, but it didn't seem to impair him at all. If anything, his conversation became more frenetic and articulate. It was his luxury, a good drink, he said; intoxicants and a half-decent Sunday paper.

With the whisky inside him, Kenny related how he'd been turfed out of school at the age of fifteen for playing truant. "Anyway, I'd read more avidly than my teachers. I read Jung and Kafka when I was very young and found it very perplexing, I must say." For his own metamorphosis he used to change in the school toilets into a pinstripe suit and go out to be a mod in the town. Even at the age of fifteen he knew all the whorehouses in Stirling, he said. Later he moved to London and worked as a psychiatric nurse, as a cook, as a laundry washer and for a Jewish tailor in Finchley. He lived on the streets or in hostels and attended lectures at the London School of Economics. In the winter, if he earned enough money that season, he travelled, often to places like Morocco, Algeria and Pakistan where leatherworking is a speciality. But not every trip was planned. He is the sort of man who'll say he's just going out for a packet of Woodbines, and who then disappears for a month. He related how, recently, he'd only gone down to London for a weekend visit. He'd spent the evening – in his essential travelling gear of Harris herringbone tweed suit and brogues – in Ronnie Scott's Jazz Club, "skinning up a few numbers" with an American who was buying the champagne. Unfortunately he'd then timed his 4.00 a.m. stroll down a deserted Oxford Street to coincide with a bomb attack on one of the shops. "I'm afraid I have a low opinion of British justice." He imitated a radio announcer. "'Man with strange eastern European accent seen in vicinity wearing herringbone tweed suit.' So, gerchevel, I get the eff out of it abroad to the furst place I can."

In Amsterdam, he found himself an unorthodox room in the Sheraton. "I told myself, 'You're working on limited shekel, Kenny, so play it cool. Everyone thinks you're the bees knees in your herringbone tweed and brogues.' So I walked into the hotel at night, gerchevel, down the stairs and into the ladies toilets, gerchevel, and locked the door, gerchevel. Lovely room, brass taps and marble and thick carpets – I stayed there every night for a week. In the Sheraton ladies toilet. Gerchevel. During the day I painted with oils in central Amsterdam for this gaji who gave me a glass of wine and a wee bit of a blow in return."

We were sitting there digesting this story and our whisky when a boy of about ten or eleven dropped his bicycle on the ground outside and came in. This was Ian, said Kenny, Ian was a mad keen golfer. The boy set about trying to kill some of the flies on the window; had we been to the Barvas fair that day, he wanted to know. "You should've bin there, Kenny," he said. "There were a lot of ruch Americans, some of them gurls."

"Ian is going tae get a well-paid job when he grows up, not like me," said Kenny.

"Ay, I'm going tae wirk for the Highlands and Islands Development Board," said Ian.

"He's going to join the Gaelic mafioso," said Kenny to me. "And how was your golf? Were you any good? Ian was caddying for his HIDB dad on the Royal St Andrews coorse the other day."

"It beats fanny any day," said Ian.

Kenny and I looked at each other, stunned. "What did you say?"

'I'm better than fanny," said Ian. "Fanny. Fanny is Nick Faldo's caddy."

We both exhaled audibly.

I reached the Butt of Lewis after dark. The island stops without much fuss, the farmed land turning into a table of close-cropped sward that reaches out to where the lighthouse stands, and then stumbling steeply down through sharp rocks into the sea. That night the lighthouse at the end of the world, which is almost as visible from inland on the flat island as it is from the sea, was sweeping the water with its beams. The midges were out and the gulls on the rocks of the Butt were arguing endlessly. The lighthouse keeper on watch was in a

Portakabin by the gate of the lighthouse's small castled encampment. When he opened the door a wave of body odour squeezed out past him and almost knocked me over in its hurry to escape. He let me into the lighthouse, made me promise to touch nothing, and returned to his TV and to recharge his colour. At the top of the tower the giant chandelier was rotating gently and silently; a sign said "wear goggles – eyes cannot be replaced", but the light didn't seem dangerously strong. A trawler was steaming past quite close to the rocks, so close that I was sure I'd have heard its engines if it hadn't been for the gulls. I stood up for a moment in front of the rotating chandelier – I know that I shouldn't – but it gave me a strange satisfaction to know that anyone on the trawler watching the light might just have caught sight of my silhouette.

I returned the keys to the keeper on watch and moved my car out on to the sward, parking it pointing out to sea. There I settled for the night, winding back the front seat and counting off the trawlers heading around the Butt for the mainland. It was as effective as counting sheep, and I soon slept with the beams of the lighthouse swinging above my head, woken occasionally by the passing cars of the lighthouse keepers changing shift.

Autumn – the Eastern Seaboard

In almost every way Scotland's twin cities of Glasgow and Edinburgh contrive to be opposites. They are adopted twins who have grown up in the same family, but in totally different directions. They don't even share the same social class. Glasgow, the manufacturing city and centre of hard manual labour; Edinburgh, the professional town of service industries and bureaucracy. Glasgow, where an urban tenement background establishes street credibility; Edinburgh, where the right accent and quality of education is the key to a rewarding career in pensions or administration. Glasgow, modern, scarred, Scottish and European; Edinburgh, old-fashioned, unmarked, serene and British. On the banks of the Clyde it is impossible not to come face to face with fiercely patriotic Glaswegians at every turn. In Edinburgh the local men are hard to identify, and their ears will often bend towards what England thinks before they'll venture their own opinions. The Scottish Nationalists of Glasgow believe fiercely in partition and self-rule; the Scottish rationalists of Edinburgh know that partition is not a pragmatic line to take, particularly in their own careers. The nearest to modern fashion that Edinburgh has come is a distinct hippy culture which is accentuated at festival time; Glasgow has been so busy rifling through a whole catalogue of trends that it has forgotten what the hippy culture was like.

The people of Edinburgh run things: they are not part of the attraction as are the people of Glasgow. Edinburgh's guidebooks, which all proclaim the city the "Athens of the North", focus on the wealth of monumental buildings. As far as the tourist is concerned the Edinburghers may as well not exist, and the people themselves seem to concur in a conspiracy with the guidebooks to let the cold stone speak on behalf of the city. At festival time, the height of the Edinburgh tourist season, the city gives itself physically to the outside world, but it is like a prostitute surrendering her body to her customers while allowing no glimpse of her soul. Many Edinburghers freely admit to leaving the city during that three-week period for their country cottages or their summer holidays abroad; there were more Scots in the buses to London than there were on the streets of Edinburgh.

Edinburgh is no easier during the quiet periods of the year; the class system, which counts for so little in Glasgow, binds Edinburghers into tight boxes which are difficult to break into and to break out of. When you go to visit someone in Glasgow, the old adage goes, they put the frying pan on; in Edinburgh they put the gramophone on. "You'd be wanting something t'eat," say the Glaswegians; "Eh, you'll heve hed your tea, then," say the Edinburghers. Actually, the two cities are far more similar than the easy come contrasts would have us believe. Glasgow wears its social problems on its sleeve, while Edinburgh's veneer hides an underworld of poverty and drug-taking that focuses around suburban estates very similar to Glasgow's. In 1983 a boatload of Pakistani brown heroin was landed at Leith docks and hawked around the housing estates at £3 a bag, starting hundreds of habits and leading eventually to a very high incidence of AIDS, initially through needle sharing. In some estates, up to one in fourteen sexually active men has AIDS.

But this phenomenon rarely appears on the streets of the city centre. Physically the capital city looks terrific, every inch a commander. It is there to be looked at, and its visitors come to do just that. Edinburgh is a planned and preserved city in a planned self-preserving society, and nowhere does planning and preserving show itself better than in the New Town. The concept that modernisation is bad, largely accepted throughout Scotland, begins here. The newest things in the New Town are all the smart cars which line the magnificent streets. The New Town – a commanding area the size of a small town itself – was built between 1766 and 1840, and its inhabitants don't like anything newer than that. Everything here is locked: the cars, the doors, the jewel caskets, the safes, even the gardens in the many New Town squares. The New Club on the fringes of the New Town (founded in 1787 as a retreat for landed gentry and professionals) meets behind closed doors, with a strict code of etiquette about the decanting of the burgundy, and with a membership that includes on average twelve out of twenty of Scotland's top boardroom directors. In the New Town live the quiet hands on the tiller of Scotland. It is not a place where people loiter in the streets; pause too long to gaze in through the windows past creamy silk curtains at antiques and paintings and silverware and the police will arrive to move you on. The pavements here are smooth, not pitted by boots, crates, and falling steel as they are down the hill in Leith. I was aware as I walked through it that somewhere behind the Georgian frontages my pension was being salted away by wise men who sent me annual communications that I could not begin to understand.

It was in the crescents and squares of the New Town that I stayed during the Edinburgh festival. Some years before, I had attended my first festival as a performer in one of many hundreds of student plays on the fringe. I don't remember a great deal about it, apart from the fact that my line – "I'm done for" – which hadn't seemed the least bit funny in rehearsal suddenly turned out to be a great hit. I had a dreadful suspicion that the joke, which was invisible to me, must therefore be on me, but the rest of the cast seemed grateful for the extra laugh My aunt, who lives in Edinburgh, brought my cousins to see the show. I remember the stage lights vaguely illuminating their ominously still legs in the front row. All that my aunt would say afterwards was that there had been a lot of rushing around, and my Scottish accent had not been entirely convincing.

I returned to the venue of that former triumph: the room creaked and the acoustics were such that you could hear off-stage whispering as clearly as on-stage dialogue. The show was some sort of Raymond Chandler/invasion of the body-snatchers hybrid with ludicrous American accents and an immensely large devil-woman in stilettos called Lucy. There were more people in the cast than in the audience and most of the performance was taken up with the lighting, sound and props. Gradually the audience left – even the young man giggling in the front row, whom I had assumed must have been the author. My own patience was finally exhausted when the chief crook, who anyway had a very quiet voice, took to tapping the stage with his foot during his dialogue, completely drowning what he was saying.

Thinking that I'd been unfortunate with my first dip of my toe into this crucible of modern culture, I tried again. Not having any criteria other than a wish to avoid the twenty-seven performances of Shakespeare, a double bill of one-person shows seemed appealing, particularly as one seemed to be a satire on vicars performed by a vicar's daughter.

If anything these shows were worse than the first, but the audience of five were trapped in their seats. The structure of the venue meant that to have walked out would have been too insulting, so we all sat tight and clapped guiltily. Outside afterwards, the other man in the audience showed his appreciation. "Bollocks," he said, striding down the hill behind me. "Pretentious bollocks."

I slowed so that he could catch up.

"It's not as if it was cheap," he protested furiously. And then he added: "They could at least have shown us their breasts."

After this decidedly unsteady start I resolved to read some reviews and make some carefully judged choices. As a result the shows I attended over the next couple of days were better, slicker, but altogether less memorable. One or two things were very good by virtue of being complete surprises. The Hindu epic the *Mahabharata*, with a programme handwritten in crabby writing that looked like a Bridget Riley, performed by slightly dumpy women from south Wimbledon in leotards, was gripping. "Follow the sound of the words as they arise," said the narrator limpidly, and I did, and the story moved from darkness into light.

But the show which was causing the most debate and which had the most credibility as a fringe performance, beating even a world premiere of *Gary the Thief* in which a naked performer had accidentally found himself shitting on stage while being a human sculpture, was *Glad*, performed by actors and winos from the Grassmarket Mission at the foot of the castle rock.

In the media the debate was not about the message of the play at all, but whether the whole thing was just attention-seeking on the part of the director and whether theatre would be any help in solving the street-people's problems.

Glad was a portrait of a night in the Mission's dormitory and it was performed in the Mission's dormitory by men who'd spent more nights there than they could remember. It was certainly unique in Edinburgh for having half of its cast outside before curtain-up asking passers-by if they could spare a bit of change. The down-and-outs here have always been part of the street show, but actually putting them on stage for the festival was a novel idea.

The Grassmarket has long been an interface between respectable Edinburgh, hippy Edinburgh, sleazy Edinburgh and old-fashioned down-and-out Edinburgh. Two bars at its western end are crowded when the go-go dancers take the stage; at the opposite end the trendy Traverse Theatre does its own performances. The castle side of the square is lined with brasseries alongside the Grassmarket Mission, and the eastern end up Victoria Street has its share of art shops. Burke and Hare, a pair of Irish navvies who between them murdered fifteen victims and sold the corpses to a distinguished doctor for his anatomy lessons, operated here in the 1820s.

There was a certain amount of aggression on the door to the Mission. A large man, grinning dangerously, straddled the threshold. "No, ye canna come in, Jim. Not even uf you've got yoursel' they tuckets o' the kung," he said. "I'm jist the bouncer. Over thair, that brither is one o' the actors. He's brullian'." Over by the gents in the middle of the square a spiv drew heavily and self-consciously on a roll-up. "He's bluidy brullian'. Iverybiddy sez he's a bluidy guid actor," repeated the doorman, ignoring our attempts to squeeze past him.

"Danny," said a woman's voice from inside the dark corner. "Dannnyyy, ch let them in if they've got tickets."

The doorman frowned. "I wunt tae mek sure iverybiddy git the point, you pals who're meking so big munny," he said to the small crowd of ticket-holders who had gathered at the blocked entrance. It was his own big moment. "The point is, ye ken, that we are a' fuckin' hameless. And it's the government's fault. Wha's got ninety-eight legs but nae testicles at all? I'll tell ye, Scotland's Labour MPs." So saying, he drew aside and we all flowed in.

We waited in a small, dimly lit ante-chamber while the stage management assembled the cast and set about shaking them out of whatever they'd been into for most of the day. Then we filed into the dormitory and took refuge on a bank of seats erected on a scaffold at one end. The dormitory smelt of stale sweat, alcohol and smoke, and from their beds the cast watched us assemble sheepishly to look at them.

It was not much of a play in that it had no plot other than the passing of a night. It was a drama of characters rubbing up against one another and against the bank of the audience, like debris jostling at the high tide mark and trying with unco-ordinated effort to push it higher. They had different degrees of hope for a better life in proportion to their ages and it was the clashing of the different degrees of hope that produced the drama. The crudely conceived play within the play was the attempt of a director to get the dossers to perform a play, a clumsy device which at least provided an excuse, if not a framework. Mick the spiv – the man who'd been smoking outside – and Richard the young failed army recruit argued most of the time, and not always according to the script, judging by the alarmed expressions on the faces of some of the others. Arguments flared and turned into fights, the professional actor-members of the cast swarming around and separating the fighters lest they become too serious by force of habit.

The unguided missile of them all was Terry, a sixty-four-year-old building site worker who had a philosophical bent. In the set structure of the play he was useless, piping up from his bed when he disagreed with any of the content of the lines that the others spouted. "Alcohol is an illness," declared one of the actors, speaking from the script; "No ut uz noght, ut's sumthin tae look forrid tae," retorted Terry from the darkness, and the actor momentarily lost his footing, not prepared to be heckled from amongst his own cast. "Thus uz an underclass place," Terry said later to one of the front row in the audience. "Whit in the wurld are ye doin' here?" There was no guiding his incl-inations; a scene where the theatre director tried to prompt him into profound street philosophy ended with him repeating, "Guid heavens, mon, whit air ye axing me a' they big questions fower?" But left to himself, propelled to the front of the stage by one of the actors in the cast, he spouted Shakespeare, talked about the problems in the Middle East and he described the delight of alcohol on a winter's morning after a cold and miserable night on the streets. "I saw ane light come on, ane door open. Guid fowk, delight o' delights fae a chentleman like me. A licensed grocer. 'Guid morrow, my dearie,' I said un my maist unctuous manner. 'A quochter bottel o' Bells if ye please.' An' then I watched the dawn wi' my quochter bottel o' Bells by my side. An' ye know, guid fowk, nae maittur whit they say, life uz nae too bad."

It was Terry who ended the performance like a Shakespearean Puck: "Ye ha' seen whit we can be. We can be, at times, epsolutely charming. At times we air epsolutely dritful. We air whit we air, in here or oot there," he said, and the audience clapped, not quite sure what the relevance of the title was but glad themselves to have got through it all without being involved in any of the fights.

It was hard to reconcile the performance of *Glad* – where we the audience had been invited into the dossers' dormitory – with the picture story in the newspapers the following day of the Duke of Buccleuch welcoming the cast of the Bolshoi Ballet into his castle for lunch. In case I had forgotten it, this served as a timely manifestation of the official festival. Loyalties are quite firmly divided between official and fringe, and the cross-fertilisation between the two audiences – even the two cultures – is limited. The fringe is the pursuit of the young and multi-cultural; the official festival is supported by the good burghers of the city who feel that attending and sponsoring the arts is part of the duty of their social class.

In order to cross the border between fringe and festival I teamed up with Jonathon Brown. It was easy to single him out – a slightly portly figure with an outrageous dress sense – loitering on the pavement outside the Playhouse with the early evening opera crowd. His portrait-sitting with Hockney had been a casual affair, he explained, when I reminded him of the painting I'd seen in Glasgow. Hockney liked to have pictures of his friends; he had a whole wall of them. The great man had scratched his belly after a leisurely breakfast and suggested the portrait; three hours and two twenty-minute coffee breaks later it was finished.

As the music critic for *Scotland on Sunday* Jonathon had press seats for the Slovak National Opera's performance of

Prince Igor. The company was sponsored by the Royal Bank of Scotland, which had the slogan "Where people matter" under its logo. The people who mattered, the people from the top of the stationery (and even above that), were in the seats in front of us. A row of lords and ladies and captains of industry, seated according to a plan which was in the hand of an anxious-looking executive. These were the people of the New Town in the flesh, rarely seen and delicately scented. The rows of gleaming pates and glossy heads nodded politely and smiled as the introductions were completed. Where were they going for dinner afterwards? I wondered.

Jonathon, being a regular at such events, didn't find their presence surprising. He was thumbing through the programme in search of Eva, a soprano whom he'd seen earlier in the week in Slovak Opera's *Faust.* "Ohh, no, dammit," he wailed. "She's not on tonight." He then repeated again just how gorgeous and how excellent she'd been. The review that he wrote that Sunday was uncompromisingly adoring, the smitten critic. "She has everything – voice, movement, expression, looks. She can peel the paint off the ceiling and yet when required she can draw every ear in the house to within an inch of her bosom. In triumph she rides the orchestra like a ski slope, and in passion the music becomes a mattress." Perhaps she was locked in her hotel room and required rescuing, I suggested. "Not Eva," he said gloomily. "More likely she's out at the nearest disco having a bloody good time with half the backstage staff."

Needless to say without Eva on stage we didn't stay for longer than the first interval. The performance was wooden and slow and Jonathon's attention was wandering. As we left I felt a momentary sympathy for the row of semi-royalty from the bank's stationery; they were not in a position to exercise their own artistic judgment as we were: for them art, business and social duty had become so inextricably intertwined that they were effectively chained to their seats until the big Slovaks on stage had finished their last gasp.

Over a curry Jonathon talked. He is one of those people who function better as a talker than as a writer and the stories that he dictates to the newspaper's copytaker at the other end of the phone always turn out better than those he files on paper. The strange thing about writing for *Scotland on Sunday*, he said, was that although the paper comes from the same stable as the *Scotsman*, traditionally Edinburgh's paper, most of its circulation is in the Strathclyde region around Glasgow. The Edinburghers – the rows in front of us in the opera – saw themselves as British and were plugged in to the British Sundays, the *Sunday Times* and the *Observer*, ignoring the Scottish Sunday press.

I aired my theory that the quality of life in Scotland was somehow purer and better because of a closeness with a cathartic landscape.

"What a load of balls," said Jonathon, with his characteristic chortle. "This idea that a Hebridean islander is happy because he's got mountains out the window is nonsense. The idea exists because people like you and I go there expecting it. Anyway, cities are not unnatural environments: man made them, so they are natural to man. There may be an instinct which says, 'I want to go hunter-gathering over the hills,' but there's a stronger one which says, 'I want to live in a two-bedroom flat in the same street as an awful lot of other people like me.' If life is so good in Scotland, why are there something like fifteen million Scots overseas and only five here?"

In the next couple of days the fringe shows I saw were better. But perhaps the best show of all Edinburgh was free. It was the scene on the streets, in the Fringe Club, on the Mound outside the National Gallery. Jugglers, singers, bands, musicians, musicals, sketches, magicians, artists and Romanian dancers all did their bit to attract the crowds. After dark the streets were filled with shreds of audiences criss-crossing the town between venues, discussing performances, lines, themes and smelling of sweat, cigarettes and alcohol. From the castle at the top of the hill came the skirl of pipes from the Tattoo; an impromptu band thumped away at the other end of the Royal Mile, and the train announcer's voice floated up from Waverley station. At about 10.00 p.m. comedy bloomed like a dark, smoke-petalled flower. All over town venues which had been straight faced and strait-laced all day ripped into routines about contraception, drink problems, Eastern European cars and American stereotypes. In a city so full of life there was one dead patch: the New Town downhill. Rolling home full of beer late at night through the New Town was like entering a sullen country held hostage by annual invaders. Nobody stirred out of doors, nobody seemed to be participating in the sense of euphoria further up the hill. Only the torn-down posters from last week's shows tried to wrap themselves around my legs and get me to take them home.

II

In autumn the East Neuk of the Kingdom of Fife, across the Firth of Forth from Edinburgh, looks a bit like the *papier mâché* scenery of a model railway set. It has a judicious smattering of pretty cottages like thrown dice on a quilt of fields of shades of green to yellow, fields which are peopled with combine harvesters and straw bales and threaded by hand-brushed hedges and country lanes. The East Neuk, which stretches from Earlsferry around to St Andrews, is not the place for industry. It is one of those places where the only real gear to life is pottering about.

One of the prettiest of the line of ex-fishing and trading ports along the coast is Crail – the name itself sounds like an antique piece of fishing equipment. The port is distinguished by housing which is rather too grand ever to have been built or bought by fishermen. People of substance did and do live here. Other than the Dutch gable-ends and the trellises of flowers, the neat terraces had something else in common: none of the houses was alike. No developer had moved in to create rows of identical housing which had then been sold; every house was individual, with its own detailing and its own distinction. As a result Crail had a hand-made finish down to the last detail: every apple outside the greengrocer had been hand-polished, and every piece of fish in the take-away was individually fried to customers' orders.

Crail's harbourmaster, Roger Banks, was pottering about. It was Banks who'd written on the harbour lifebelt holder, "If you steal this it shows what value you put on human life" – a bit metaphysical for the average thief – and on the harbour notice-board he'd added a couple of notices about interesting natural features of Crail's shoreline. Banks himself looks as hand-made as the rest of Crail, a tubby and tufty Englishman, followed by a pair of snuffling, grunting and snorting ugly pugs wherever he went. He had the reputation of being the East Neuk's society eccentric, and lunch with Roger Banks meant eating snails from his garden while sharing the table with a couple of bantam chickens that lived in his sleeves – or so they said.

"Of course I've not got two sixpences to rub together," he said as he scurried around his harbourside house, which was littered with paintings and furniture. Many of the paintings sat on the floor, having been displaced from the walls by a new acquisition or a new creation. "The bank manager looks at me jolly seriously and asks what I have in mind. 'More pictures and champagne,' I say. You'll have to excuse the mess," he added, picking piles off the stairs in order to allow access to the bathroom. "The management is away. The management works part time in the National Trust office down the road with a friend who has this absolutely massive pile in St Andrews. You can hear the two of them laughing from the other end of the street. I always reckon they frighten people away."

I felt quite glad that the management was away, because I think she'd have frightened me too.

He started to prepare lunch. It was his task, he gave me to understand, to finish things up before the management returned. This meant devouring some rather unrecognisable cheese, artichokes which were beginning to turn black with age, a fresh salad and wizened fruit. "How did you get into East Fife society in the first place?" I asked when he emerged with this feast.

"I bought a house in Cupar for £3,000. I'd got fed up with England, and at the time Scottish property was dirt cheap. It was a massive Adam mansion with eighteen acres of garden; hadn't been repainted since 1848 and the garden was chest-high with weeds in bloom. Paradise for me, and it levered us straight into the right society. In this part of the world you are known by your property or the name of your estate. Have another artichoke." We sucked and grunted like the pugs until the bowl was empty.

"We got invited to our first posh dinner that winter," he continued. "In those days these dinners were all black tie. It was a rather trying experience; it was snowing, you see, and we arrived late in rather a hurry in our little car. We'd not been to the house before and the snow had covered everything. My wife pointed to a gap in the hedge so I turned into it." He giggled. "Everything was all right for a moment or two and then we started hearing a lot of scratching and bumping from under the car, then ornamental pots and sundials came sailing past like ships out of the blizzard. We were travelling over the rose beds, you see, and our wheels were picking up all the bushes as we went. By the time that we arrived outside the front door, with the butler looking on – of course he didn't say a word, no good butler would – the Mini looked like a paddle-steamer with flapping frozen floribunda wrapped around its wheels.

"So we gave him our coats and went in. Of course everybody was already sitting down to dinner and all those heads in rows on six-inch necks swivelled to stare at us like a lot of frightened geese, pausing for a moment in their honking. Please have another piece of cheese. We've got to finish it up."

I approve of finishing things up, so I did my best with the cheese.

"Of course we were introduced as the new owners of the house in Cupar. I remember a particularly sniffy snotty chap with a voice like a sheep – you know, baa, baaaaa – who came up to us during coffee. I think he suspected us of not really being good enough and he was going to submit us to a bit of interrogation. 'Who do you know?' he said. Anyway, my wife's the equal of a stuffed arse like that, so she said, 'You tell me where you're from and I'll tell you who we know around you.' He said where he came from, I forget where. 'Oh, we know a terribly nice man. Mr Carter-Brown,' said my wife. This snotty chap said he'd never heard of anyone called Carter-Brown in his neighbourhood, and he knew everyone, so there couldn't have been anyone called Carter-Brown living there. We must be mistaken. 'You see him everywhere, at all the auctions,' insisted my wife. At that time we'd had to go to a lot of auctions to buy our furniture because we couldn't afford to buy it any other way, you see. Anyway, quite a little crowd had gathered by this time, and my wife of course couldn't in the end pretend that Carter-Brown was anyone grander than the carter whose name was Brown who'd delivered all the furniture we'd bought at auctions ourselves. The snotty man hasn't spoken to us ever since, but everyone else thought it was a very funny story and we started to get invited to lots more dinners. Of course we have to sing for our supper a bit, which is why we're invited really. They expect us to be a little bit eccentric. Anyway I'd rather talk about what I want to talk about; they talk about the three Fs – fishing, farming and pheasant shooting – and of course fucking, but that comes after the port."

He started to clear up what we hadn't finished, always with an eye for miscellaneous things that might have got on to the floor, which would definitely disturb the management, he said. He talked as he moved about with the short-stepped, shuffling walk of someone who would really like to be able to spend more of the day in his slippers. For the finale to lunch he produced samphire collected from the Tay estuary. While we were grunting away over how good it was with the dogs snuffling a descant, he explained that the local shops found it hard to accept his rather unorthodox approach to shopping. At the greengrocers he tried to bargain for fruit and vegetables that were going off; the butcher knew that he would gladly accept organs or cuts that most people would never eat, and the fishmonger was amazed when Banks relieved him of whole trays of food which he considered inedible.

We were finishing lunch when three large elderly Scottish ladies – farmers' wives – knocked on the door. Besides being a part-time harbourmaster, Banks makes a steady but small income from writing about and painting plants, usually weeds rather than flowers. The ladies had bought a painting before and this time they decided on a watercolour of a corner of hedgerow, which they recognised as an authentic piece of their world. Roger Banks was pleased. I left him humming with the pleasure of the sale and preparing anxiously for the return of the management, and headed for St Andrews.

I've never been a great fan of the game of golf or the people who play it, which is perhaps why I didn't like St Andrews. The features of the Royal and Ancient golf course applied equally to the town and to the greens: groomed, well presented and well preserved. All, that is, except for the truly ancient buildings, the cathedral and the castle (which functioned as the bishop's palace). At one time when religious argument fermented most of the world's wars St Andrews must have been a miniature Beirut, and both cathedral and castle had been reduced to rubble by successive disputes and the disrespectful plundering of building materials.

Four Scottish Journeys

There was no disputing the elegance of St Andrews' location
– on a small promontory alongside a luxurious stretch of sand –
and the elegance of the unplundered buildings, particularly of
the university, which was established in 1410 and is the oldest
in Scotland. But, rather like Edinburgh at festival time, St
Andrews didn't seem to have its own life; its exports are
education and golf, and its imports are golfers, who stay a
matter of days, and students, who stay a few years. By dint of
having a Savile Row label St Andrews University has never
served its own hinterland, and overseas students (now 800 out
of a total of 3,400) have become a sort of cash crop. St Andrews
itself is a planted colony, not an indigenous growth.

One thing that St Andrews does amply illustrate is the scale
of the golf industry. The shops, tea-rooms and guest houses
were called Caddies, Fairways, The 19th Tea and The First Tea.
In the papers was news of the fate of the propeller from the
QEII cruise liner, which was moving from one Scottish-built
industry into another: it was to be cut up into 50,000 golf
putters, to be sold at a premium. In order to meet the demand
from the growing interest in the game, 700 new courses would
have to be created in the UK by the year 2000, said the voice-
over in the golf museum. I could only hope that there'd be some
fields left for crops.

Somehow there seems to me to be a mismatch between
Scotland and the very nature of golf. It is a game played by
squashy people with squashy faces on squashy ground which
is a sort of halfway house between the drawing-room and the
great outdoors. Sportsmen are usually bores about their sports,
but with golfers the potential to be boring seems to strike
deeper. In England golf courses harmonise adequately with the
man-tailored scenery, but in Scotland golf is played on turf that
feels as unnatural to one's feet as a clipped poodle to the hand
or white sliced bread to the tongue, in a landscape where
usually the great outdoors threatens to leap into the drawing-
room and grab the residents by the scruff of their necks.
Somewhere in golf's evolution, a wrong turning had been taken;
once the game had been a cross-country affair where the players
used their sticks to wallop balls at impromptu targets in the
trees, which sounds much more the Scottish sort of thing.

The Royal and Ancient course departs from and arrives into

186

the centre of town, and the terminus is surrounded by hotels. Departures from the small platform of the first tee are frequent and regular, announced by a man in a small box with a loudspeaker, his voice carried off down the links by the onshore wind. A party leaves the platform every four or five minutes, and most of them seem to be Americans or Japanese. It is said that no Scottish-Japanese trade agreement is signed without a round on the Royal and Ancient.

Non-members wishing to play on the course have to put their names and their credentials – no novices are allowed on this turf – into a ballot box and the results of the draw are posted in the tourist office window. Contenders are usually deliriously happy to get a slot, even if it means teeing off at six o'clock in the morning, as it often does. I stuck my nose to the window of the front room of the Royal and Ancient clubhouse; a pair of binoculars lay on top of a copy of *Who's Who* on the table by the window, suggesting that members gathered here, like twitchers, to watch the famous do their putting.

III

Dundonians have had a bad run of luck with their bridges: the first railway bridge collapsed in a storm in 1879, hurling a train into the Tay and killing all passengers. The current road bridge is bumpy, lumpy, constantly under repair and its lane closures and toll charges are as common a cause for complaint among Dundonians as is the weather. Nevertheless, crossing the bridge presents a wide panorama of the city and from a distance Dundee, with a magnificent beast of an oil-rig by the quay (if oil-rigs were Gothic we'd adore them), looks promising; close up things don't look quite so good. Dundee and St Andrews, so close geographically, could not be more different. The pairing is not unlike Glasgow and Edinburgh, with St Andrews playing the role of Edinburgh and Dundee a pale shadow of Glasgow – but without the Glaswegian humour, the arts, the creative sense of identity.

Dundee's most famous – infamous – citizen is probably William McGonagall, the dreadful poet, who wrote, "The most startling incident in my life was the time I discovered myself to be a poet, which was in the year 1877." People have been startled to discover he was a poet ever since. In an exhaustive series of poems McGonagall charted the history of Dundee's river bridges, particularly of the collapse of the railway bridge in a storm:

> Beautiful Railway Bridge of the Silv'ry Tay!
> Alas! I am very sorry to say
> That ninety lives have been taken away
> On the last Sabbath day of 1879,
> Which will be remember'd for a very long time.

Mick the Scrappie had told me so much that was bad about Dundee, its drugs, thieves, unemployment, bad health etc. that I had no enthusiasm for stopping. Mick himself was away and without his vigour and his enthusiasm I knew his tenement would have depressed me. I'd seen him again since his lorry blew up underneath us on North Uist: he'd turned up in London in a battered and smoke-spouting Ford Cortina estate, with June and the two boys. He'd not been able to fix the lorry since the disaster so he'd left it on Uist, bought the Cortina and struggled back to Dundee with his dogs and as much of the load of scrap as the Cortina could carry.

It was difficult to imagine that somewhere in the rather grim city were the creators of the *Bunty*, the *Twinkler*, the *Beezer* and the *Topper*, the *People's Friend*, *My Weekly*, *Annabelle*, *Jackie* and *Blue Jeans*, not to mention the *Beano*, *Dandy* and *Victor*. What would the offices be like where all these editors and artists and writers gathered together? Colourful, cheeky, chirpy and chatty, like starlings on a wire or songbirds in a cage? Playing pranks with farting cushions and giving each other sisterly advice? From the outside Dundee didn't strike me as being full of caged songbirds, but even though the publishing giant D. C. Thomson – whose creation all these titles are – had seen more influential days, the company's men still churn out characters and tales worth burrowing under the sheets with a torch for. The *Hotspur*, which had always been my favourite, had long since been merged with *Warlord*, which had in turn merged into the present-day *Victor*.

Sydney Scroggie, the valiant one-legged and blind

mountaineer, could so easily have been a character in the *Hotspur*'s pages, but instead he was sitting on the low wall outside his house on the hill behind Dundee sucking on a pipe that never seemed to stay alight, as real as real could be. Sydney Scroggie is a combination of most of the get-up-and-go *Hotspur* characters. At one stage he'd himself been in intimate contact with the pages of that comic, having been a sub-editor for D. C. Thomson, but that was before he stepped on a landmine in Italy two weeks before the end of the Second World War.

As a blind, one-legged mountaineer, poet, author, and Oxford man, Scroggie could have been in several of D. C. Thomson's comics and magazines all at once. I'd first heard of him from Tom Rigg, the solitary hostel-keeper on Rannoch Moor. The two recognised each other's credentials as having earned the respect of the land and of man. Rigg had told me Scroggie's story of the poltergeist at Ben Alder cottage, and how it had lifted up a packet of digestive biscuits and carried it across the room. Ken Smith, the ponyman in his log cabin down the railway from Tom Rigg, had also had a bad experience at Ben Alder: he'd been sitting close to the fire one lonely and still night, being pulled into the warm glow as the darkness seemed to get colder and colder, when suddenly there was a great banging in the chimney-breast and two heavy stones fell into the embers, terrifying him and covering him in red-hot ash. He'd left Ben Alder as soon as possible afterwards and had vowed never to go back.

Sydney Scroggie's experience of Ben Alder wasn't just limited to the levitating biscuits. Sitting there on his low wall, gazing at hills he couldn't see but knew intimately, he recalled the whole evening. "We got thair in darkness, lut a candle and the wee stove. It was when we whair brewing up that they tappings on the dooor stairted. High up, then low doon, they whair. Then we had trampings in the next-dooor room, big tackety boots, they whair, tramping up and doon. Then you had the noises o' heavy pieces o' furniture moving aroond followed by screeching and heart-rending human groans. Funny enough we whairn't awfi' feart, even though it was vairy fear-making. Of coorse nobody would gi inti the next-door room, which was anyway quite empty."

The match hovered above the bowl of his pipe; even after all those years of blindness, lighting his pipe was still a difficult task. "But we spent the night there all right. The vairy next dey it was lashing it doon wi' rain but no one wanted to stay, nae wunder. We were packing up. When we'd funushed there was a wee packit o' biscuits left over, ye ken. 'Leave them fi' the gods o' the bothy,' I said, and as I said it the wee packit rose up ti the ceiling, travelled across ti the ither side o' the rooom and then came doon ti land on its ither end. I can tell ye we left vairy soon efter that."

Sydney Scroggie's second wife, Margaret, produced crisp sausage rolls and we sat in the rather gloomy wood-panelled room while Scroggie puffed away, still wearing his woolly hat. Margaret agreed and disagreed when referred to, but Sydney didn't always wait for her verdict.

I muttered something about my origins.

"Margrit and I know that it's a tairrible ethnic tragedy, don't we, Margrit," Sydney said immediately, "when someone who in the ordinary run of events shuid have been born and brocht up in Scotland, gits his ehducation in England instaid." He shook his head. "If I had my way, Hadrian's Wall wuid be rebuilt, manned night and dey, and orders given that no toorists be allowed inti Scotland." He grinned. "Actually, some of them are not bad, especially the walkers."

"What is it about mountains?" I asked.

"Ah, now we ken a lot aboot mountains, don't we, Margrit?" The experience of being out in the Cairngorms was, he said, not one whit less valid, totally blind, than when he could see.

"I can remember the hills aroond Glen Clova vairy well, but prowling aroond the mountains is a psychological, spiritual pairformance. It isnae a visual thung and it isnae getting away from it all, that's a mistake peepel make, isn't it, Margrit. It's solving a problem, achieving something. You sets yoursel' a task ti accomplish and in getting ti the top you accomplish it. It helps ti restore self-confidence, and it's also ti do wi' being in touch wi' your origins, ken. The hills are subservient ti the laws o' nature. They're shapit by the processes o' nature, still in a state of obedience. Oot there, yu're in a microcosm of the cosmos." He waved the stem of his pipe in the direction of the window behind him. "It's a religion in itself. The hills are nae jist fi walking aroond in. They're fi sitting aroond in. You jist have ti go a long way ti find a guid place ti sit. Away from the English."

With an apology for generalising – "there's a place fi a cholly guid cheneralisation" – he explained that he believed the Scots to be more philosophical than the English. "The Scots are metaphysical. They take in metaphysics wi' their mither's milk. My feyther usit ti say that you cuid only study mathematics in a hard chair – ken, you can only philosophise wi' the rain running doon the back o' yoor neck. The Scots sit in bothies wi' broken windies enjoying the wind and the rain. Then the English come along and fix they broken windies and form an association fi bothy repairs. They miss the point, don't they, Margrit?"

IV

The Braemar Gathering took place a week after the final curtain of the Edinburgh festival, in a crook in the elbow of the road that ascends Royal Deeside into the Grampian Mountains, turns the corner at Braemar in a Highland wilderness and heads south rapidly down towards Perth, where Lowland respectability begins again. The Grampians sit like a great dark-browed brooding mass in the middle of the country, hatching silvery rivers which start their lives by snaking away like panicking elvers down the rocky slopes. In the heart of the brooding mass virtually nothing lives, but some sort of gathering has taken place at Braemar, where three passes meet, since the eighth century. Early games were supposed to be for the testing of the mettle of various clan warriors in order to select the king's own army, but it wasn't until 1848 that the gathering was attended by royalty. Queen Victoria and Prince Albert, who'd been to view a prospective estate at Loch Laggan the previous year but who had been put off by horrendous midges and excessive rain, leased Balmoral (nine miles down the Dee valley from Braemar) on the grounds that it was further to the east and therefore likely to be drier. That year they attended the games with a crowd of "70 or 80", and by so doing helped to accelerate the rolling stone of Scottish romanticism which had been started by George IV and Sir Walter Scott. The Queen's presence at such a pocket-sized occasion still suggests a sense of intimacy, even at today's gatherings, which attract about 20,000 people, many of whom are American and Canadian. The royal holiday at Balmoral and attendance of the gathering has become an institution, although Victoria's love for the place has never quite been matched by any of her successors except perhaps by Prince Charles, whose children's book *The Old Man of Lochnagar* gets its title from the mountain to the south of the castle. Victoria wrote of leaving Balmoral: "I wished that we might be snowed up and unable to move. How happy I would have been!"

Queen Victoria – and her outpourings in her journals – have been held responsible for the birth of Balmorality, a Scots kitsch, which is still very much an accepted image of the country and makes a substantial contribution to the Scottish economy. To some people Scotland is only worth noticing when royalty visits: the *Faber Book of Reportage* published in 1987 had only one item from Scotland in 700, and that was a description of Queen Victoria and Prince Albert deerstalking in the Highlands.

There is surprisingly little Scottish kitsch at Braemar. Perhaps the gathering's elders, who lean on their sticks at strategic points around the ring gazing up into the peaks behind, banned it, or perhaps Braemar is just too inaccessible for the lorryloads of woolly haggises and pipe-major dollies. The ground for the gathering is a pudding plate of green in a savage landscape. The natural amphitheatre provides its own viewpoints which are supplemented by grandstands raised by the committee. On the edges are the marquees and the picnickers, the associations, the band caravans, the tea tents and practising pipe-majors. Two major grandstands sit on either side of the main entrance, continuing on one side through ground-level seating into the private enclosure and so to the Royal Pavilion, which is little more than a freshly painted cricket club scoring-hut, decorated with flowers.

It was still a gathering in the old sense of the word, reuniting people who knew each other indirectly or distantly. After circling the arena a couple of times I accosted a bearded, red-faced man in Jacobite Highland gear, complete with a sword, expecting him to be an American, a little loose in the head and a few sandwiches short of a picnic. He wasn't – he was a local aristocrat whose family dated back to long before Bonnie Prince Charlie's time and he was dressed as he was because he belonged to a historic re-enactment society. Scotland's history had been a series of spectacular failures, he said, but that was no less a reason for Scots to try to understand it.

"Lawrence, is that you? You probably don't know me, it's Mary-Lou," cried an attractive middle-aged woman, crossing the trickle of passers-by and intercepting our conversation with all the grace of someone who knew that her social ranking and her looks gave her permission to interrupt.

"Of course I remember you, you were an extremely pretty girl," said the woolly Highlander, and I was left to enjoy my own company.

The competitors in the particularly arduous hill race were just returning to the ring as I took my seat alongside the private enclosure, which was full of rather wistful-looking, terribly well-bred women in tweed miniskirts. Some of the hill-racers were covered in mud, dripping blood from falling on rock; some were clean and composed. It was as if they'd been selected by the gathering to go and fight their battles elsewhere which some had won and some lost, and their composure and sense of self-confidence were more important, as they re-entered the ring, than their position in the race; the main battle in Scotland ever since man has been there has been as much against the landscape as against each other and these men couldn't let the hills reduce them to shreds of their former selves. When she'd first attended the games, Queen Victoria had been so horrified to see her ghillies coming down from the mountain coughing blood that she had asked for the hill race to be abandoned and it has only recently been reintroduced.

In those days the ghillies, many of whom were still smarting from English repression of the Jacobite rebellion, were not averse to seeing the English kill themselves in the Scottish mountains. An apocryphal ghillie story of the early twentieth century relates how a ghillie had returned with his toff from a successful day's shooting in the hills to learn that two gentlemen had died that day, one in the river and one on the hill. "This ha' bin a greet day," he announced with satisfaction. "Ten hinds and twa Englishmen." Local mythology still believes that the:

Bloodthirsty Dee
every year needs three
but Bonny Don
she needs more.

By early afternoon the Braemar games were in full swing. In the middle of the ring was a mêlée of activities – dancing, piping, running, jumping, tug-of-war – above which rose hammers, weights on chains, shot and cabers in a series of small, rather pathetic arcs – pathetic until you realised that the sound of distant thumping like heavy artillery was actually the weights returning to ground. Other than the heavies, most of the competitors in the field events were from different army regiments; many of the dancers were from America or Australia; the most massive man in the heavy eventers, pulling up his kilt to reveal tight lycra shorts before heaving the weight over the bar, was a twenty-five-stoner from the Netherlands; the smallest came from California. Sixteen different pipe bands (seven from Canada) took turns to parade around the edges of the ring. It was not a local competition as the games on South Uist had been, where Mick the scrappie had gone to join in the wrestling, it was an international Scottish show.

When the big moment came, the policemen's chests seemed to swell and someone in the Royal Pavilion was frantically swotting wasps. Picnics were abandoned and all of the 20,000 spectators crowded to the ring to watch the royal limousine draw up. "Fergie and the Queen and Philip," said a woman behind me, identifying the silhouettes. The anthem played, the contraltos within the audience quavered, and the royal party settled down into its wasp-free pavilion.

"They dinna make they menfolk like they used ti," moaned the woman behind me who'd been so quick to identify the royals. She had produced a half-bottle of whisky from her bag. Out on the field the men she was referring to were struggling to toss the caber, eighteen feet three inches of wood that weighed 120 pounds, and failing. The idea was not to achieve distance, but to get the caber to cartwheel through 270 degrees. Most of the heavies didn't even get it to ninety degrees. "When I was a young thing they usit ti soak the cabers in watter ti make them moor heavy, ken, but nae wee mannie can throw them any moor," the whisky-drinking woman lamented loudly.

Only Brian Robin, a local man, finally succeeded in cartwheeling the caber, to much applause from the crowd. I overheard him explaining to the Dutchman later: "You have tae use your hips. Thrust your pelvis forward." The Dutchman thrust his pelvis forward and the drinking woman behind me sighed with pleasure. A picture of Brian Robin shaking hands with the Queen was in the local paper the following day; she was laughing, perhaps at the pelvis secret. He had thought of retiring, he told the reporter, but without him no one would be able to toss the caber at Braemar and that would be a sad reflection on the state of Scotland, so he had promised to return the following year.

When the royal party left the ring it was as if a cork had left a bottle. The arena emptied leaving only the dregs – the competitors, who continued flinging, chucking, prancing, piping, hurling, pulling and panting to an empty house. If they'd ever thought themselves the stars, they had been swiftly disillusioned. I descended the Dee valley some hours later in a slow queue of traffic, leaving Braemar in the hands of hundreds of pissed, kilted pipe-majors and vansful of police.

The upper middle class have reclaimed this part of Scotland and given it a touch of the suburban atmosphere of the south. Simply being in the same narrowing valley as the royal family produces a feeling of intimacy. I loitered hopefully with a few enthusiasts outside the gates to Balmoral itself, which is hidden from the public behind woodlands. What were they doing in there, I wondered. Playing patience or other solitary card games in their own suites? Watching Grampian television and complaining that the advertising wasn't as interesting as it was down south? Discussing their year's crop of speeding fines? Practising the Highland Fling? I hoped they were having a good time.

I'd been there more than ten minutes when a tall, well-educated man in a Barbour with a cigar in one hand and a walkie-talkie in the other questioned me easily, just to make sure I was all right. I suspected that he might have done a few rounds of Trivial Pursuit with the royals in his time, but he claimed not to know whether the Queen was at home. And anyway it was none of my business.

There's an alpine atmosphere about the small town of Ballater, which is Balmoral's nearest centre. Hemmed in by fir-covered mountains, the town has a selection of buildings which are far too grand for its own economy. The station where the royal train disembarked Victoria and Albert after their long journeys north is amongst the most elegant. Old posters still in the building gave timetables so that Victoria's loyal subjects knew when to line the embankments and wave as she headed north. "A Prince indeed, above all titles a household word, hereafter through all time Albert the Good" read the inscription on the monumental building on the other side of the station square. The good people of Ballater had been enthusiastic in order to please their Queen; Albert may have been almost erased from history books, but we've forgiven him the fact he was a foreigner.

Several of Ballater's shops are decorated with royal crests that mark where the household does its shopping. A clothier with a fine handful of crests had its flag flying but the lady inside wouldn't give anything away when I asked her who had bought what this year. "We are not allowed to divulge," she pronounced grandly. "You might be a reporter." I suppose a new pair of socks for Prince Harry might make a paragraph in some newspapers; a jockstrap would be better still. I approved of the Queen Mother's (according to the crest) choice of bakers, which had some good cakes; the household's (three crests) choice of butcher had its window full of haggis, puddings, rolled venison, salmon, and little black corpses that were once grouse. A Range-Rover of the royal type arrived in the High Street, and the driver – tweed trousers and a green quilted sleeveless coat – chose two of the royal crested shops for his errands; he bought a bottle of aspirin and the *Aberdeen Press and Journal*. Perhaps the Queen had a headache and wanted to bone up on the local news.

I left the Dee valley with some haste, because although I'd not managed to inveigle my way into any royally connected households in Royal Deeside at deerhunting time, I'd persuaded an estate on the west coast to let me go out on a stalk, and it so happened that the head stalker suddenly had a couple of days free between lettings.

En route around the edge of the Grampians – there's no direct way east to west through the centre of the broody, river-hatching mountains – I made a quick stop at the schoolhouse in the Aberdeenshire village of Monymusk to meet a poet who'd leafleted the Braemar Gathering for commissions. At lunch-time on a Tuesday he seemed to be the only person awake in Monymusk.

I'd been secretly hoping to discover a second McGonagall in Munro Gillespie, who was the headmaster of Monymusk school. He was small, neat, meticulous, and he smelt strongly of eau-de-cologne. He was only the fifth headmaster at Monymusk in a century; his predecessor had been in the job thirty-one years. Munro Gillespie had already done twenty-three years himself, and he obviously had every intention of beating the record. His main interest was not poetry, he explained, but cricket, which struck me as rare for an Aberdonian. "Oh no," said Munro Gillespie. "There's mair cricket played per heid of population in Scotland than in England." During the off-season for cricket he'd taken up writing poetry in Scots, which harmonised with his school policy of retaining the Scottishness of local culture. Burns was on the curriculum, he said, to the disgust of several of the parents of English children – Monymusk is within commuting distance of Aberdeen and the oil industry – who came to him with complaints. Realising that this was a rather nationalistic and sensitive area, Munro Gillespie picked his word order and his sentences carefully, as if deciding which particular idea to send to the boundary for four runs. "They say they don't want their children to lairn this rubbish. I tell them ti go away. Burns is not fit technically ti lick Shakespeare's boots, but he spoke fi the people. He captured in simple terms whit a nation felt. It's a pity that he is now lauded fi his vices and not fi his verses."

I left the headmaster poet with a commission: to write me a personalised poem commemorating my journeys around Scotland. A couple of weeks later it arrived in the post:

> Whaur's yer Scotland noo?
> Wi independent step I cam',
> Auld Scotland fields tae view,
> An' weel I ken yer history,
> But whaur's yer Scotland noo?

Braw Border lands in growin' spring,
West Highland ways in snaw,
Fair Hebrides in simmer sun,
In autumn, east awa'.

Wi' ilka step, my hairt cried oot,
"Auld Scotland – are ye deid?
Are ye richer? Are ye puirer?
Are ye ta'en wi' foreign greed?"

V

It's difficult to feel sympathy towards landowners, especially when they have played a rather villainous part in a nation's past. Many of today's Scottish lairds are descended from the landowners who were imposed upon Scotland by the English in order to keep the unruly natives under control; they are also descendants of the men responsible for the Clearances, perhaps the worst of the landowning crimes. Today's Scottish landowners are often English, or American or even Danish, Japanese and Arab, and even if they are Scottish they are Piccadilly Scots. The old landowning barons who bought lumps of Scotland with cash because they loved the place have since had their land divided and subdivided amongst their grandchildren and great-great-grandchildren, who no longer have the money or the interest to sustain the estates. And so the thinly spread wealthy aristocracy has devolved into a more populous but penurious upper middle class. A large proportion don't live on their land for more than a couple of months every year; a large proportion regard their property as their own mini-kingdom, a source of recreation, a larder full of gamey products, a dramatic form of conspicuous consumption.

The Scottish Landowners' Federation claims that it is caught in a poverty trap, but it is true that very few of Scotland's estates in the Highland region do better than break even. Malcolm Potier, the owner of the island of Gigha, put the figure as low as one per cent. Patrick Gordon Duff-Pennington, convener of the Scottish Landowners' Federation, didn't disagree. Duff-Pennington's family owns the estate at Loch

Laggan which Victoria and Albert had decided against buying on account of the midges and the rain. He reckoned that it was his duty – and his association's duty – to try to keep the landowners and the general public talking to each other so that they'd understand each other's point of view. "What it's about is keeping that incredibly beautiful and wonderful land, incredibly beautiful and wonderful," he said when I met him in London. At the time, landowners were threatening to put up fences around their property, incensing ramblers, and the landowners' association had annoyed the tourist industry by suggesting that it was time that the landowners benefited financially from Scottish tourism in which tramping over their property was a principal feature. Moreover, one lord and the owner of property around the Glen Coe area had hit the headlines by threatening to sue a mountain rescue team for publishing a book which recommended walks over his ground, and he'd been very arrogant to any journalists who tried to ask him his reasons.

As far as Duff-Pennington and his association were concerned, the new breed of landowner was a particularly difficult specimen to deal with. "Our problems arise when a London owner thinks he's buying seclusion. The new owners are bringing in nasty urban ideals and ideas. They bring in the attitude that money is right. I think that the financial ethic in London is nasty." But not every new landowner has irresponsible ideas. A Dane – Count Adam Cnut – who bought the Ben Loyal estate in Sutherland wrote to Duff-Pennington when his purchase had been completed asking how he could be a good landowner, and how to keep employment in the area.

The sources of income for a typical Highland estate are limited to sheep farming, holiday homes, timber sales and grants for planting non-conifer trees, compensation from land designated as Sites of Special Scientific Interest and therefore unworkable for agricultural or other purposes, and hydro-electric power generation for sale to the national grid. But the main single and easiest source of income is the shooting of deer and birds.

Deerhunting has always been a classy thing to do, long before Queen Victoria popularised everything Scottish. Queen Elizabeth I used to practise her archery on deer which were corralled for her greater ease: the deer stampeded in terror around the compound while the Queen shot them down. In a hunting party of 1563 Queen Mary describes with excitement how a Highlander – one of the deer-trapping team – was trampled to death by stampeding beasts, as if it was all part of the sport.

I'm not a fan of bloodsports, and accordingly I approached deerstalking on the Fleming estate with prejudice. The Flemings and their offshoots own a large chunk of the western Highlands, maintained with money made by their banking interests. But they also had their creative streak. Ian Fleming, the James Bond creator, had been one of the family, as had Robert Fleming, the travel writer. Dorothy Fleming, to whom Ian and Robert had been uncles, had just demonstrated her own creative perversity by writing a book on mountain biking in the Highlands – an activity which incenses most Scottish land-owners, for whom the sight of a gaudily dressed biker streaking across their land is like a red rag to a bull. It was Dorothy, who lives on part of the estate on Glen Etive, who arranged my stalking, even though she too dislikes bloodsports.

The track into Glen Etive was almost underwater the day I arrived, and barred by four gates fastened with combination locks, supposedly to keep the poachers out. Dorothy Fleming came out to meet me with her JCB, the only vehicle capable of crossing the final ford before her house, which was spating furiously. "My dad was the best writer of them all," she said when I mentioned her writer-uncles. "But he had eight children so he wanted to make some money, which was very nice of him." Within the empty glen a small community functioned happily, she said: the head stalker and his wife, the under-stalker, herself, and whoever came to stay or shoot. The three households on the estate lived several miles apart, but they kept regular tabs on each other's well-being, often meeting up in the evenings. Until a couple of years before, the post had been delivered by the tourist boat which came up the loch from Taynuilt twice a week. Dorothy used to walk down to the shore to collect it, and the shutters of American-held cameras clattered furiously as they tried to capture this blonde, slightly shy woman who lived in the wilds. Privately she'd considered going down to collect the post in a deerskin loincloth, or something equally outrageous, but she was not the sort for public show. "People think I'm mad living here. I'm sure people think I'm going to grow a beard and smoke a pipe and spit and things. I suppose it would be nice in February to have a few more hands for Scrabble. My mother worries about who I'll marry."

Her mother and her aunt ran the estate together. By all accounts they were a formidable pair of women, energetic, quick up the hills and quick with their tongues. A visiting "gentleman" who had a reputation as a womaniser had apologised rather smugly that his flies had been open in the presence of the two ladies during drinks. "That's all right," said Dorothy's mother. "Dead birds don't fall out of their nests."

When the rain finally stopped we bumped along the track to the head stalker's place for supper, the glen's scenery unwrapping itself like a sweet. Glen Etive is one of those fairy-tale Scottish valleys with a massive swooping amphitheatre of unadulterated mountains around a long finger of loch like a long conference table at its centre, for the mountains to play patience on or to compete with each other's reflections on particularly balmy days. The head stalker's house sits in a commanding position on the lochside, with a clear view of 360 degrees of mountain peaks and several square miles of loch. This house, together with another on the opposite shore and a lodge at the top of the loch, are the only three houses in twenty-five miles of glen.

Sydney Scroggie had warned me about the effect of the shooting season on normally mild-mannered stalkers: they become crabby, difficult, and domineering to walkers, he said, perhaps because after a year of non-interference they were suddenly being pestered by their own lairds. Tim Healey exhibited none of those characteristics, but nor was he a particularly traditional sort of stalker. Tim was an ex-window dresser from Poole, probably in his late thirties, small, light and with a rather ratty face that grinned easily and regularly. He'd made a curry for supper and as we wolfed it down he related how he'd come to Scotland as a long-haired hippy, heading off into the hills for days at a time with his bed-roll. In those days he used to get invited in for a cup of tea at every lonely house he passed, he said, and people would ask him if he was one of those teddy boys from the south.

He had started his career by working for days at a time with the stalkers on Royal Deeside, an old-school world where the head stalker had traditionally found a sheltered spot for the toff to eat his lunch and the stalkers and gillies gathered round the exposed side of the hut or the rock in the driving rain to eat their "pieces". From there he'd graduated to doing whole seasons in Scotland and returning to Poole to do a bit of window-dressing in the winter.

Most of his stalking career was recorded in a photograph album full of pictures of dead deer, which made a rather morbid CV. One caught my eye, because the animals in it were alive; it was a blurred photograph of a herd running away and it was captioned in handwriting I could hardly read. I held it up. "Aha, yes," said Tim, with no hint of a smile. "That says 'After the fart'."

Apparently, at the climax of the stalk, once the gun is within a hundred yards of the target, the gentleman is often so excited and so nervous that he is alert to nothing but the target and the target's behaviour, Tim said. On this particular occasion the gentleman was a very polite, well-bred young chap recently married to an equally polite, well-bred girl who'd also come out on what was their first stalk. After a long and strenuous pursuit the party had reached a rocky outcrop from where Tim reckoned the shot could be made. He'd handed the gentleman the gun, and during the long, tense silence while the barrel settled, the gentleman had farted. "For him, this was a disaster. He was crippled with embarrassment, you see. I could feel him going red beside me. I could feel her going red behind me. So I summoned up my best efforts and farted too. The rock amplified the sound and the deer heard it. Then we all started giggling, and the deer were away." Tim sat back in his armchair. "The young wife sent me the picture as a souvenir."

He'd had some strange conversations at the moment before the shot. "Do you like sex in the bath?" one of the women guns had asked him. Her daughter, who was barely sixteen, had tried to seduce him every morning when he went in to tend to the lodge's boiler, one of his household duties when he had been under-stalker.

As a professional stalker he had a very low opinion of blood-hungry trophy hunters, of whom he'd seen a few. "I told one gentleman, 'Take the one on the left.' He said he wanted the one on the right because the antlers were better and the beast healthier. I'm not having that, so I stood up and the deer ran off."

Like most forms of culling, deerstalking is done for ecological reasons. Without the natural predators that man has long since hunted out, the deer would multiply by about twenty per cent a year until starvation or disease reduced their numbers again. Accordingly, estate owners are required by law to reduce their deer population by a percentage every year, a percentage which depends upon the census of deer on an estate. The census is carried out by men from the Red Deer Commission, who comb the ground counting everything that moves and their report of the quality and quantity of the animals is a source of pride to the keeper. That year, the Glen Etive estate was required to shoot seventy hinds and thirty-five stags. From a commercial point of view the estate charged £250 per beast shot, and £1,000 for the lodge for a week. Eight stags had to be shot in a week, and one of the conditions of the tenancy was that the stalkers and the tenants had tea together after the day's stalk.

There are far easier ways of shooting deer. During the rutting season the stags come down to the water's edge and bellow through the night, making simple targets for someone in a Land-Rover with a searchlight. Tim reckoned that a poacher working by this method could shoot up to twenty beasts a night, every one worth about £200. In the winter the deer become even easier targets, losing their strength and descending out of the frozen hills and moving as little as possible. However the stag stalking season coincides with the end of the summer, when the beasts are at their best and most athletic, and the idea is to cull the older, weaker animals out of the herd to maintain the quality. Correctly done, it is almost a form of enforced euthanasia; the beasts chosen for shooting by the stalker would have a good chance of dying anyway in the coming winter.

We went up the hill on Tim's free day between one tenancy and another, armed only with telescopes. The day couldn't have been more of a contrast with its predecessor, when the glen had been erupting with water. The sky was bright, the air razor-sharp, the wind a gentle south-westerly.

He had turned out in the whole gear: brogues, tweeds and plus fours.

"It's the best clothing for the job. The tweed is designed for this estate. The brown is the colour of the earth, the blue the colour of the heather and the grey the colour of the stone. If I wore this in the Cairngorms I'd stand out like a sore thumb. Here it blends perfectly."

As we climbed up the walls of Glen Etive he pointed out his nearest points of access to the outside world. The road from Oban to Tyndrum ran through the Pass of Brander five miles to the south, while to the north Glen Etive finally emerged at the top of Glen Coe, twenty miles away. Walkers sometimes entered the glen from the Glen Coe end, occasionally with unfortunate results. His under-stalker had found the body of a climber who'd fallen, broken his legs, smashed his glasses and dragged himself down into the empty glen before dying a long way away from the search area where he was last seen; if he'd stayed where he'd fallen he would have been found. Tim himself had saved the life of a Dutch walker he'd come across in a ravine which has since been re-christened the Dutchman's gully. The Dutchman had been a real tough nut; a solitary, long-distance walker whom no one had missed. He had waited for a couple of days for the bone in his hip, broken by his fall, to fuse together before attempting to move, and all his fingernails had been torn off with his attempts to haul himself out.

- The glen had also claimed the lives of two of Tim's predecessors, who'd been returning from Taynuilt by boat, in the days when Glen Etive was inaccessible by any other method. Both men had drowned, no one knew why. Tim suspected that they'd been drinking; that one – the non-swimmer – had been leaning over the engine and had fallen in, and the other, who could swim, had gone in after him. "There's a few stories. They say that pipe music on the loch means someone will die. We've got a couple of fairy places, too. Usually someone puts some sweets on one of them before we go out. It's a load of rubbish, of course, but it's surprising how often the sweets have disappeared by the end of the day."

The chill wind had razored the ground covering of heather, spagnum moss, and blueberry bushes. As we climbed, so the vegetation thinned like the headpiece of an ageing giant, and the mountain top loomed like a bald pate of rock. Scars in the valley below veined the slopes like the earth's stretch marks. In the winter, said Tim, he came up after hare, tramping across the roofs of the mountains so white with snow that the folds in the ascents and descents blended into one, through which the white hare bounded silently, like ghosts – until they bled.

When we'd got high enough he started spying – lying back on the slope to support his telescope, and scanning the corries for herds. He knew the identity of everything that moved up there; a female hen harrier, the silver male, a kestrel, a buzzard, people on the summit of Ben Cruachan three miles away. He started to point out the deer he would shoot: the grizzled fourteen- or fifteen-year-old stags, their antlers spiny and thin, their hindquarters sagging. They looked like the old men of the herds and they moved slowly and laboriously. "When they get to that age their teeth become worn and they can't chew the grass properly. When you gralloch a stag on the hill you can see the difference. In a healthy beast you get this bright-coloured purée in its stomach. In an unhealthy beast you get a rough mash. For a while I thought I'd never be able to do the gralloch, but I can tell you that on a chill day up here it can be a pleasure to stick your hands into the steaming belly of a beast."

We continued on up the shoulder of the hill for another hour, up to ptarmigan level above 2,500 feet. The snow suits the ptarmigan, said Tim, but it betrays the foxes. "I was dragging a beast down the hill one time and I saw this fox flatten itself against the snow and watch me like a collie watches a sheep. I thought, isn't that marvellous. What a sight. Normally, of course, I wouldn't have seen it, but it stood out against the snow. I continued a bit, pretending I hadn't seen it, then when it thought I'd gone I dropped on one knee and shot it."

As we reached the height of the peaks the view opened up over dozens of miles of hunchback mountains, blue and thickly veined with the cold; as far as the eye could see the land belonged to one arm or other of the Fleming family, broken up amongst great-grandchildren, but still basically in the family. Down on the loch a tourist boat from Taynuilt chugged slowly up the glen, gleaming like silver on velvet. Tim had had a running battle with the skipper who'd just retired, he said.

When he'd first arrived he'd been up the hill and he'd seen the boat drop off a dinghy with a man in it, do its circle of the loch, and return to pick up the man and dinghy later. Meanwhile through his telescope he'd seen the man picking silver things out of the water – salmon out of a net. So Tim, being a newcomer and wanting to do things cautiously and properly, had first called the policeman to warn him what was going on and then called the head stalker from the neighbouring estate, and the two of them lay in wait the following day. The boat came again but made no detour and when the two men went out to investigate the site of the nets, they found nothing. "They'd been warned off," said Tim. "The poaching and the police are all tied up with freemasonry round here.

"Freemasons are a load of rogues. I was asked to join and went to meetings for a couple of years. When I wanted out they wouldn't let me. They promised my land would be poached if I left; I did, and it probably is. They probably use a fellow who operates out of Fort William. He's a real wild man, a real mountain man. He knows exactly what he's doing up here and he's a bloody good deerstalker, but he's a violent bastard. A couple of years ago an estate up the road had a German tenant. The German and the stalker were walking up their loch when they came across a boat with a stag in it, so they staked it out. Sure enough, back comes our man with a stag around his neck. The stalker accosts him but our man threatens to shoot him, so the German comes out of hiding thinking that the man would give up if he knew he was outnumbered. But all that our man would say was "I really will shoot," and he meant it. It didn't seem worth killing each other over a stag, so they backed off and allowed him to row away. The stalker was a good shot, so he put three holes in the bows of the dinghy as it went, as a sort of marker. By the time he got to the police, though, our man had already reported having been shot at from the shore in a completely different location, and he now had five bullet-holes in his boat, two of which he'd put there himself, of course. Oh yes, he's clever all right."

"What would you have done?"

"I don't know. It's one thing to go out stalking with a gun but quite another to suddenly have to shoot human beings. I suppose I'd feel no compunction in shooting a rotten man, like an old deer. The only problem is what might happen to my family afterwards. Hold it."

We both froze. We'd been walking along the side of the hill too intent on our own conversation and had almost stumbled into a bowl full of deer. A hind and a calf trotted away, disturbed by something that they hadn't yet identified. We were approaching with the wind in our faces and none of the animals had scented us. Deer find scent like a brick wall, so intense that it is almost physical; they'll jump over an old human scent on a track rather than walk through it. Without scent of us or movement, they wouldn't yet run. Tim indicated that we should get down on our knees and crawl back whence we had come.

By the time we had reapproached the herd from a better angle the stags, although they'd been disturbed by the alarm of the hind and her calf, looked more settled. They stood, antlers erect, each staring in a different direction, watching and waiting. While we waited for them to resume grazing Tim produced his binoculars. The excitement he felt was infectious. "There's a royal," he whispered urgently, "a twelve-pointer. That's a nice one. And look at the bollocks on that one. Lovely." The herd was a good one and it filled him with an exhilaration which I could share, but not properly understand. He selected a possible target and handed the binoculars to me for me to confirm that the beast was grizzled and slouched. Then he pulled his flat cap low down over his eyes, as if he were expecting rain, and we started down the hill on our bellies.

It's an uncomfortable business following another man's legs down a boggy, stony hill. Tim's brogues dripped gently whenever he stopped. The landscape was only a couple of inches from my nose. It unrolled in lurches and slithers, sometimes producing a patch of shit, sometimes a bog, and sometimes a rock that disappeared painfully in the direction of my groin. I didn't feel that I was very good at stalking, barely containing urges both to grunt and yelp alternately, but Tim didn't seem too perturbed by my awkward progress. Occasionally he stopped and renegotiated an awkward lie of the land; occasionally this allowed twenty yards of half-crouching walking, a true pleasure, but mostly we were flat on our bellies. There were times when I thought it impossible to cover exposed pieces of slope undetected, but somehow we remained unseen. The deer were moving away from us, grazing at some speed, and it took a while and a certain amount of frenzied and rather comic squirming to get to a rock from which Tim was finally satisfied a safe shot could be made. "Don't move your head," he urged as I slithered on to the rock beside him. "Move your eyes only. There's your beast. A good shot right in the breadbasket and it'd go down without a fuss without disturbing the others." The animal he'd chosen was directly ahead of us, grazing peacefully. It would be an easy shot, hissed Tim. I had my doubts; the more I lay there, with my feet up the hill behind me and grasses sticking up my nostrils and in my eyes, the more the blood ran into my head, my forehead bulged, my face went purple, and the more I was inclined to say that I'd prefer to let nature take its course.

VI

I was lucky to get a bed in Aberdeen, said Mrs K. The bed and breakfasts were all full. It was the first time she'd had a room free in one and a half years; a contract had ended, and while they were waiting for a new one to be signed, her boys had gone back to Newcastle, but she was expecting them back any day.

"Ye ken, it's dreidful hard te unnerstan' fit they mean these Geordies, wi' a' their blether," said Mrs K, who wasn't particularly easy to understand herself. She couldn't remember a time now when Aberdeen hadn't lived and breathed oil, and she'd been running her bed and breakfast for nearly thirty years. "Ile, it's allus bin ile," she said. "Dinna gi' me the munny noo," she said. "I'll just gie oot and spend it."

For all the talk about the magnificence of the granite city, Aberdeen didn't strike me as being much other than a rather grim place. In the bright sunshine of autumn it looked like an urchin whose face had been viciously scrubbed spotlessly clean. The colour of sunlit granite is the colour of cold steel, uncompromising, gaunt, sharp-bladed and unwelcoming. The rain softens it metaphorically and literally – with all that industry in the neighbourhood the rain is probably corrosive – and every drop falls with a sort of grim deliberation.

Entertainment in Aberdeen is not spontaneous, it is Rest and

Recreation, the famous euphemism that turned many Asian cities into brothels and bars. Aberdeen is a Scottish Saigon or a Bangkok, filled with a transient alien population who bring plenty of money but who only care about the city inasmuch as it fulfils those needs which they can't fulfil offshore. The city is not loved by these visitors, so it gives little love in return. At the year end, despite having seen more prosperity than all the others, Aberdeen was the only one of the major Scottish cities not to organise a public Hogmanay party.

"Far too many bars," had been Mrs K's verdict on Union Street. Whenever a shop closes, the premises reopen as a bar, she said, and she never went there at night. Union Street is Aberdeen's broad back, conceived on a prophetic scale when oil was still undiscovered. As such it is rather like the Bay Bridge in San Francisco, which was built in the 1930s with five lanes in either direction at a time when the motor car was a privileged minority possession; Union Street was built in the nineteenth century, when Aberdeen had no real reason other than its own self-confidence to present itself with such a grand main boulevard.

Clustering around this boulevard are the shopping centres, little elaborate nuggets of luxury snuggling in amongst the austere granite, with exotic patisseries and foreign names. In a centre like the Bon Accord you could at least pretend you were somewhere else: it had nothing of Scotland and nothing of Aberdeen. Elsewhere in the country – particularly in the Highlands – shopping is an activity related to need; here it was related to boredom and spare money.

Despite Aberdeen's avowed self-confidence there's no avoiding the pervasive sensation that its prosperity is based on something going on somewhere else, for which the city is a transit-point, a shopping centre and a bank for a further town of 10,000 – 15,000 who live on 130 platforms in the middle of the sea. The business side of the industry is conducted either invisibly or in London; in Aberdeen the industry is made flesh in massive pieces of equipment and in talk of safety and survival. Aberdeen is like a war zone, a place of operations, an interface between man and a force he can barely control if something goes wrong. In the crowded harbour, drawing breath from the battle, are oil support boats whose very size and shape suggest inhuman purposes, whose loads are unrecognisable objects, and whose dents suggest inhuman forces. Somewhere out there, out to sea, man is using the biggest, most powerful and most expensive machinery he can make to fiddle with the works of the world. And, like anyone who sticks his hands in the works without fully knowing what he is doing, he occasionally loses his fingers.

From the evidence coming ashore the overwhelming message was that it was hell on those platforms in the middle of a hostile ocean. Costs of oil production in the Middle East average $2 a barrel; in the North Sea they vary between $10 and $15 a barrel. Every day several crew changes return from the front line and descend on the city to blow off steam. Before they are siphoned off like dangerous substances by the transport network, they make their presence felt in Aberdeen's streets and bars.

In late afternoon in a bar down by the harbour, a go-go girl started her set on a small platform surrounded by flashing lights. The bar was thick with men and the air a soupy mixture of body heat, cigarette smoke and alcohol fumes. When the girl stepped out on to the small stage it was as if her body-weight had suddenly made the ship roll, and the whole bar full of bodies slid to the port side. For the most part it was good-humoured enough: the men looked tired and pleased that their work was finished. Two or three were already far too drunk to remember much more of the day and one or two, hovering close to the stage and drinking steadily, looked dangerous. The girl had her bodyguards at the bar and once her set was over she retreated into the centre of a group of men where studded leather jackets closed in a secure ring around her, excluding hungry eyes. By six o'clock the bar was getting rowdy, and in another hour it was shut.

From bar-room talk I picked up what titbits I could about the industry. The money wasn't nearly as good as it had been ten years ago, said one. Another told me that the four meals a day on a rig all consisted of either steak or cereal, and depending on which shift you were on, you either had one or the other. Another said that one of the rigs had the largest collection of pornographic videos in the world, that drugs were relatively easily obtained and that oilies would rather give up their marriages than their work.

But trying to understand the operational side of the industry from Aberdeen was like trying to appreciate the finer points of a football match from interviews with the departing crowd. Accordingly, I was grateful for two things as the helicopter clawed out over the North Sea – grateful that Total, the French state-run oil company, had taken pity on me and agreed to take me out for a day, and grateful that the wind was a mere thirty knots, calm by North Sea standards.

I'd never been in a helicopter before; if travelling by aircraft is like cruising along an empty motorway in the best of cars, travelling by helicopter over the North Sea is like crossing a ploughed field on a tractor. Clambering into survival suits seemed to plunge the passengers into a coma almost instantly, despite the volume of the rock music soundtrack ("Wear your headphones," said the co-pilot. "They're the best way we've got of communicating with you"). On the ground I'd asked the pilot what chance there was of auto-rotating to the ground if the engines failed; none, he'd said. Without power, the helicopter would go down "like a greased wardrobe," he said.

After an hour or so the helicopter descended – more in the manner of a soaped bathroom shelf than a greased wardrobe – through the swirling cloud to a dinner-plate of sea, on which MCP-01 stood like a big pimple. One moment it was a pimple, and the next it was a whole concrete island on the roof of which the helicopter had perched, 200 feet above sea level, to be well clear of the 100-foot wave that ostensibly comes along only once a century, but which had already been around at least twice in the last decade.

MCP-01 (Manifold Compression Platform number one) is about as big a thing as man can make, a 150,000-ton structure with a massive hollow concrete stalk or a wellington boot that had its foot on the sea-bed, 300 feet below sea level, where its toes were weighed down with a further 50,000 tons of sand ballast. And yet in the heavy swell – as much the effect of the previous day's weather as that day's – it was just possible to feel MCP-01 move, a tribute to the pure power of the sea, a raw power that instantly begged the question: why drill up all that oil and gas for power, when there's so much spare power just lying around?

The platform was humming hoarsely, and the sea swilling

through the moonpool (the hollow inside of the boot) was never out of sight between our feet as we clambered around the catwalks. Although there were ice-coated pipes and blasts of heat, most of MCP-01's tangled masses of machinery had been mothballed. Sited midway on a crucial gas pipeline, the platform no longer had to compress the gas in transit; its task was principally to monitor and service the line, a task which could eventually be carried out without permanent resident staff (currently numbering fifty-five). Without people or purpose, sections of MCP-01 had already become rather forlorn.

On the platform the wild talk I'd heard in the onshore bars was almost totally contradicted. The month's accident history board that greeted new arrivals "from the beach" was blank. A typical year offshore in the North Sea as a whole sees something like three to four deaths and seventy to eighty serious injuries, and the injury level would be far higher on a drilling rig or a rig under construction and installation; rigs (which are usually floating) are more mobile, closer to the water and therefore wilder; platforms like MCP-01, which stand on the sea-bed, are more solid and safer.

Living conditions on MCP-01 were hardly wild and rough, and the men were hardly bull-necked or foul-mouthed. The accommodation block was startlingly clean; the floor shone, everything was neat and tidied away, and I saw no pin-ups on the walls. The nightly film show had nothing remotely pornographic about it; touchingly, the crew-member in the cabin opposite the radio room had two portraits of Princess Diana on his wall. On MCP-01, leisure time was not used for watching heavy sex, heavily stoned; nor was it dominated by homosexual lust for Filipino support staff; instead, it was devoted to computer games, to snooker, to workouts in the gym and to reading library books such as the *Joy of Decorating*. Drinking (at all) or smoking in the wrong place would result in instant dismissal "back to the beach". Presumably the remoteness and the isolation must have caused some stress, but the most visible problem was the temptation to eat too much of the excellent food. Veterans on two-week rotations had learned, they said, to stay away from the pudding, at least until the second week.

"Staying away from the pudding" was hardly one of the

hazards of the industry I'd been told about by the drinkers in the Aberdeen bars. Their talk had been of wild men, wild seas, huge hours and big money. The men on MCP-01 seemed calm, relaxed, content, and rather overweight; they'd been living offshore lives for so long they'd become institutionalised by the oil business, and they'd had too much offshore pudding. Many had been working offshore ever since the industry had started in the 1970s, and they were moving towards an age where they had started to think of retirement; an ageing workforce is a problem affecting the whole industry, which is not yet old enough to have made a ruling on whenabouts an oil-rigger should retire.

By the time I'd seen most of the platform my mixed feelings of fear, pity and admiration for the men who worked in the North Sea had begun to evaporate in the face of a crew who seemed thoroughly happy, well paid, fed, and provided for – although this may have been partly the result of relatively benign weather. I transferred my feelings of sympathy to the men on the stand-off vessel, a converted trawler which had to wallow around the rig for three weeks without once being allowed to anchor, whose eight crew spent their lives bucketing up and down on the North Sea waiting for something to happen.

The impression given by the men on the platform – of serenity, safety and security – was so contradictory to what I'd been told on land, that once the helicopter returned to Aberdeen that afternoon I headed straight for the bars to make sure that the wild tales I'd been told and the wild men I'd seen weren't figments of my imagination. They weren't; the bars were still full of drunk and abusive men, propagating the same message and telling the same stories. It was as if they'd had a personality change somewhere between the rig and the "beach", or as if they had a duty to themselves to present a rougher and tougher picture for the folks back home; either way, it provided a necessary excuse for drink on a big scale. When the institution delivered them back on to dry land and released its grip, the boundaries of possible behaviour suddenly stretched wider than the horizons of the North Sea.

Aberdeen is not what it was, and I left it feeling that I hadn't seen it. Lewis Grassic Gibbon, the north-east's most famous writer, suggested that "One detests Aberdeen with the detestation of a thwarted lover. It is the one hauntingly and exasperatingly lovable city in Scotland." Gibbon was essentially a ruralist, the north-east's Thomas Hardy, and the central character of his books was usually the north-east's sinewy, unwilling, recalcitrant landscape. He was writing well before the oil business; Aberdeen today is full of industrial estates, shopping centres and strangers, for whom money is a stronger power than love.

I got the bus north, away from the artificial warmth of oil money, through countryside that was shot through with the gleaming grey of granite. It was harvest time, but the land had given one last groan and given birth with a shudder to a poor crop and a few people were scratching around trying to make sure they picked up every last bit. The trees were giving up pale, drained and colourless leaves that were hard and wrinkled from sheer exhaustion and the land had a raw, scorched look – scorched by a searing chill wind, and not by heat. Unlike Angus, to the south, where fertility comes naturally, things grow here by hard graft alone – and sometimes they don't grow at all. After the bad harvests of 1987, five farmers in central Buchan had committed suicide. Unlike the west, this is still an abstemious society: a household buys a bottle of whisky, a bottle of brandy and a bottle of port for Hogmanay and expects to have something left for next year.

A fair old storm was driving shoppers off the Peterhead streets that afternoon, the gutters running with rivers of rain and oil. There's practically no unemployment in Peterhead, but job opportunity options are limited. For men the choice is threefold: the oil-supply industry, the high-security Peterhead jail, or the fishing. The options for the girls are simply to process fish or get married. The matter-of-fact men of Buchan will assert that Peterhead has been ruined by the arrival of the oil industry; Aberdeen has not been ruined, because Aberdeen was already a city and can take it. But Peterhead was a monoculture until the arrival of oil, which increased the town's population from 13,000 to 18,000 almost overnight, pushing the community up the league table of the richest towns in the UK, where it settled without ostentation near the top.

Fishermen in most parts of the world band together, and the community in the north-east of Scotland – the most flourishing in the country – has always been an impenetrable one. Despite the handful of fishing museums along the coast, nowhere was I to find an explanation of why fishermen won't go to sea wearing leather shoes, don't allow the mention of rabbits, pigs or ministers on board, why Swan Vesta matches are forbidden, and why they call salmon – which they despise – the red fish. The fishing season of the New Year must not be started without some blood having been shed – usually an animal shot – on land first. Boats must be launched on a Thursday, pointing mustn't be done with a finger but with a whole hand, and counting of people is considered very bad luck. Flat feet and red hair are regarded as a deadly combination in a man, and a fisherman must either speak to this harbinger of doom before all others or keep well out of his way. And woe betide the fisherman who gets a reputation for carrying bad luck with him: he'll never get a job again.

So closed are the fishing communities that their Jobcentres could as well be several miles inland. Near enough 10,000 fishermen go to sea on a regular basis, but jobs on boats are not advertised, ever. If you want a job, you either hang around the quay talking to skippers, or you know someone who knows someone. Other than when they're on or around their boats, it's very hard to meet the men who count; I found the Peterhead bars well nigh deserted.

The principle behind the industry and therefore behind the secrecy is self-employment. Most boats are at least half owned by the skipper, who usually has an onshore investor who takes a share in the profits in return for looking after sales and paperwork. Without self-employment few people would opt for a job away from home, with uncertain reward, anti-social hours, unpleasant conditions and a chance of instant death. Presumably it's this last feature that keeps them religious, but even that is impenetrable. The fishing towns are full of halls where fishermen and their families meet to worship in ways which are only known to them. The dominant group are Plymouth Brethren, but it's hard to find those words written anywhere outside any of the halls. "A church of Christ will meet here on Sunday", "If the Lord's will be done, His worship will be held in this hall", read two equally non-committal signs outside separate Peterhead buildings, with no indication of any denomination. At one time the fishermen's religion meant that no boats would leave the harbour before midnight on a Sunday, and while that tradition is no longer, there's still a strong anti-alcohol, anti-smoking, anti-fornication movement amongst the fishermen. A hotelier with a bar and a restaurant said that many of these "good living" (here used in an opposite sense to its interpretation down south) fishermen and their families always asked to be positioned in a room where they couldn't see the bar when they came out to dinner, and they'd always eat fish.

Peterhead is Europe's top fishing port, and by the look of the BMWs on the quayside on Saturday morning the industry was doing all right despite the political manoeuvring in the newspapers which suggested the fishermen were screaming under the constraint of fish quotas to protect the stocks. A hundred years ago the first steam drifter came to Peterhead with the revolutionary technique of trawling rather than the established technique of fishing with long baited lines of hooks; the fishermen drove the drifter off because they said it'd be destructive of stock. They were right, it has been, and today's problem is how to prevent the trawling industry hoovering up everything in the sea. Skippers who do well buy boats that are ready for the scrap heap, because in buying the boats they are also buying a licence for an engine of a certain size. By combining the licences they are allowed to combine engine sizes, and therefore build a new larger boat, which in turn allows a greater range and greater efficiency. Some of the trawlers in Peterhead are huge.

The combination of legislation and diminished stock means that today's catches are down but prices are up, although the economics of the trade in general are a mystery, as is the income of specific boats. A boat's annual catch is unlikely to be accurately recorded because the fish can be sold to klondykers – Eastern bloc factory ships – or in Scandinavian markets as easily as in Peterhead's own market. Avoiding quotas by landing "black" fish has become a necessary dodge for all skippers. An average boat achieves around £1 million in turnover in a year, but even that is a huge generalisation. The closest I got to a true figure for anything was from the same hotelier with the bar and the restaurant. He cashed the crews' cheques when the boats came in on a Saturday. A couple of years ago they'd be getting up to £1,500 for a ten-day voyage, he said. Now the average was £800.

The storm developed as Saturday night progressed in Peterhead. During the day the harbour, jammed with rusted, dented and dripping boats which gently oozed films of oil into the water, was relatively peaceful. In the late evening the wind was reaching over the wall, raking up the surface of the inner basin with its fingernails and chucking it into the air. The ranks of gear swayed and creaked, a thousand antennae moaning a thousand different complaints. Erratic billows of rain surged past the sodium street lighting. Nobody walked the quay except me; surely, I thought, one of those dining skippers with tandoori or chop suey half way to his lips would resolve to take his wife, strapped and straddled as she was in her tightest and finest Saturday night gear (for which she was far too plump, but he'd not had the nerve to tell her), down to the quay so that he could slip through the creaking hulls to check that his true home was OK. But no one came. The warehouses on the harbour side stood tall and eyeless, their windows long since bricked up against the tax and the weather. The puddles winked on their behalf as the wind brushed their reflections of the streetlights. The boats moaned and the narrow streets hummed with the wind as a car came lurching round the corner on to the main quay. Ah-ha, I thought, a skipper at last. But the car was being driven too fast, it tried to turn too quickly, it spun, spraying puddles like a garden sprinkler and came to rest having almost spun full circle facing the stern of the *Noble Star*. The yellow sodium street lighting fell full on the face of a young man which cracked into a wide grin when he saw me; it was a grin which meant "ye saw tha', dud ye. Tha' is nothing. Ye shud see fit we hae te face at sea, a hunner time wairs." I stood there for a while after he'd gone while my pulse steadied. As I stood, a boat slipped in from the pre-harbour, tied up against the market, and in the glare of their own decklights the crew started furiously derricking out their boxes of fish as if their lives depended on it, before the rising waters came over the bulwarks and floated everything away.

The weather had only moderately improved the following day, which was a Sunday. I walked out of town, through long housing estates of the matter-of-fact, ugly bungalows of some of the richest people in Scotland, furnished with the best fitted kitchens and carpets that money could buy. Most of the cars were full of people going to church, but I managed to hitch a lift from a man going stock-car racing in Crimond, where the Crimond psalm tune was composed by Jessie Seymour Irvine, a daughter of the local manse. In the bus shelter – the rain deterred me from further hitching – the graffiti was traditionally irreligious: "If you want a good night phone Smellie McGee".

Fraserburgh harbour, although smaller, was as full with boats as Peterhead's and equally deserted. Occasionally water flopped over the distant harbour wall like the forelock of a feckless aristocrat, belying the true state of the sea outside, which was still running high and hard. Fraserburgh lighthouse, the oldest in Scotland, sticks like a pimple on the forehead of the town, protruding out of the top of the pocket-sized Fraserburgh Castle. The lighthouse keepers here had recorded the highest winds in the country – 140 mph – in January 1989. The mechanism of the lighthouse works like a grandfather clock, driven by weights on pulleys that run down the centre of the tower; every half-hour throughout the night the weight reaches the bottom, and every half-hour it is the job of the lighthouse keeper to haul it up to the top again.

Fraserburgh had a sense of uniformity which Peterhead had lost; its business was unadulterated fishing, with one strange side-effect. On a Sunday night Fraserburgh town centre became a giant traffic island, its main street choked with cars going up to the main square, along the High Street, down to the leisure centre car park, turning and proceeding back up to the main street again like an endless carnival procession, every car leaving a stain of music on the air as it passed. Sometimes a delay opened up a gap in the procession, and a gap in the procession was an opportunity for machismo: it was swiftly closed with a spurt and a squeal from the vehicle behind.

The cars, which were fast and new, were full of young men. The pavements were lined with girls in groups, huddled around their chips or sitting on low church walls. The larger the group the longer the cars dawdled alongside them. Sometimes a couple of girls got into a car with a couple of guys; sometimes they merely exchanged a few tart remarks. To all intents and purposes it looked like kerb-crawling on a grand scale. The police had been asked to "dae something aboot it, nae wunder" several times, said my landlady, indignantly, but she was not concerned with the propriety of it all. "Ye'd think ye'd be ebble tae cross the rood quietly of a Sunday nicht," she said instead. "Sometimes it's impossible tae get oor car awa' oot 'a the garage. And that of a Sunday nicht," she emphasised. Despite a lot of local encouragement the police had not done anything about the parade, presumably because simply using the roads did not amount to breaking the law, and because Sunday nights are an important ritual amongst the young people of Fraserburgh. They were kerb-crawling, and their kerb-crawling was a sort of mating game, but they weren't kerb-crawling for prostitutes. This was their disco, youth centre and pub all in one. It was a meeting point and a starting point for romance for young men who were only on dry land for as little as a quarter of their lives and who had plenty of disposable income but nowhere to go. Their cars were their privacy.

VII

The east coast of the British Isles doesn't make a fuss about its meeting with the sea. The two elements, land and water, sidle up to each other and rub shoulders like old colleagues, without the clashing of cymbals or banging of drums that there is in the west, where the land takes the sea on its forehead in a frenzy of head-butting. The east coast gives way to the sea by agreement; the boundary is not disputed and the seaside villages are often largely unfortified against the water, which knows its place and stays there.

The north-east coast of Scotland is a far more sensible coast to live on than the west. The neep and tattie fields slope down to the sea in a long shirt, tucking in neatly to the trousers of the sea, fertile almost to the waist.

I loitered in and out of the coastal villages, hitching lifts and eating breakfast, lunch and tea out of cake shops. In Gardenstown, a substantial place that dribbles down a hirsute cliff on to a shore ledge, I discovered a particularly fine bakery just above the harbour. Walking down through the steep town to the sea was a bit like coming from backstage into a theatre for a play and seeing the actors lurking behind the scenery waiting to come on: the minister emptying his dustbin, the craft shop owner hanging out her washing, the boat repairer mixing up some toxic fibreglass mix in the open air behind his shed.

The bakery I discovered was piled full of bargain packs that knew exactly how a cake-eater's mind works: three fruit slices for the price of two; six for the price of four; ten for the price of seven; a hundred for the price of sixty. Thus the bakers of Gardenstown lured in their victims, quietly confident that the combination of a desire to eat more cake with the gratification of saving money would be deadly.

I felt quite ill as I walked up out of the village with ninety-four fruit slices to go. The fertiliser rep who gave me a lift must have thought me an unusually quiet chap. He showed me a sample of his fertiliser; it was mined in Tunisia and shipped in bulk to Ayr, he said. A soft furnishings fitter gave me a lift the rest of the way to Buckie.

Buckie was the town of Big Al of the *Sparkling Star*, the giant whom I'd met at Kinlochbervie in the winter. But Buckie too was big and I wasn't going to bump into Big Al in the street, particularly as it was Monday, and he'd be away at sea already. Even so, I felt confident that if I walked up to the woman in the newsagent's or the man in the butcher's and told them that I knew Big Al they would give me the freedom of the town.

It was the spirit of Big Al that lured me down to the waterfront, to see if by chance the *Sparkling Star* was at home.

Most of Buckie's fleet was marooned in harbour by the weather, but the *Sparkling Star* wasn't amongst them. Instead my attention was drawn by clouds of chaff and grain dust across the harbour to the *Ashvan*, a bashed and ancient 600-ton Panama-registered coaster. She was unloading grain from Antwerp for the whisky industry in the Spey valley, but every bucketload lifted from her hold was scoured by the howling wind as it cascaded into the waiting lorries. All the better for the whisky industry, which was having its grain cleaned free of charge; all the worse for the fishing boats, who were getting a free coating of cereal.

Where was she going next and when? I asked one of the

dockers. "Berwick," he said. "Tonight." It occurred to me, suddenly, that I'd very much like to go to Berwick, tonight, on the *Ashvan*, despite the fact that she looked horribly unseaworthy, and that the weather outside the harbour was obviously foul enough to keep all the fishermen tucked up in front of their tellies. So I hovered. I hung around. I looked interested. I renamed the *Ashvan* the *Ashcan* in honour of the flying dust. I tried to look nonchalant. I must have looked like a policeman. Eventually I plucked up enough courage to ask one of the dockers in my best BBC English where I might possibly find the captain.

"Ye jist gae inside and shout," he hollered into the wind.

Captain Renton was the first man I clamped eyes on in the warm, wood-panelled, lino-floored corridor under the bridge, a sanctuary where the wind didn't penetrate, but where the hum of the boat's generator made the brass fittings rattle gently. A quiet, plump man in his slippers, he let me speak my piece and then said he was content enough to have me on board, and he'd square it up with the owner. He passed me to Ron, the mate, who found me a berth in the cabin of George, the senior deckhand, a Portuguese-speaking Cape Verde islander. George was tall, thin, bespectacled and bookish. He looked more like a schoolmaster or a doctor than a seaman, but on the tiny Cape Verde islands (off the west tip of Africa) there are few jobs, and ninety per cent of men go to sea. George had been on English-speaking ships for some years and if he'd shown any aptitude for the seaman's life he would have progressed up through the ranks, but his intelligence only showed itself in his English, which was remarkably good. He took sharing his cabin with a stranger in his stride, pointing to the bunk I could use. The third bunk in his cabin had been wrecked the previous day by Customs and Excise, who had chosen to take his cabin apart in a methodical and thorough way. George was offended that they had chosen him. Quite what they'd seen as suspicious about the mild-mannered bookish deckhand I have no idea. His only vice seemed to be a liking for mild pornography, but this was hardly secretive: the stack of magazines was on his cabin table for all to consult – which they regularly did, with George looking on like a benign librarian.

The junior deckhand, Lindos, was also a Cape Verde

islander, but he spoke no English at all. He'd only been on the ship a matter of weeks and been given the responsibilities of the kitchen. He did his cooking in wellington boots and bright-coloured Bermuda shorts, chain-smoking all the while, but the end result of his efforts wasn't bad. He called us all to the mess shortly after I'd settled into my berth. Captain Renton groaned something about how someone should tell Lindos to read the clock; it was not yet 5.00 p.m. and he was already serving up liver for supper.

Apart from Captain Renton, Ron the mate and George and Lindos, the two Cape Verde islander deckhands, the fifth crew member was the engineer, who was also officer class, which qualified him to use the officers' toilet in the little warren of passageways. Santos was a fat, talkative, cheerful man who claimed to be from Portugal, although Ron the mate maintained that he was really also a Cape Verde islander who'd bettered himself by resettling in Lisbon. He'd spent that day changing a cylinder head on the engine and he was pleased with the result. "Ya, leetel sheep but beeg enchin," he said, slurping his liver and implying that the Ashvan, albeit battered and bruised, had a big heart. The chief docker poked his head round the door whilst we were sitting down to eat. "Hev ye ony bottels fi us?" he said. Ron the mate apologised. He'd got nothing left, he said. He'd make sure that they got something next time the Ashvan was in the area, which wouldn't be long, he promised. The docker looked at him disbelievingly. Ron, his eyes magnified by powerful glasses, had to bring his best personnel management tactics to bear. He was almost eloquent. Didn't he always remember them with a couple of bottles? And wasn't the Ashvan always in the area? Then the dockers shouldn't worry. He, Ron, would remember them, never mind. The docker went at last and we all breathed a sigh of relief. "It's tradition," explained Captain Renton. "The dockers know we get alcohol duty free and they expect a bottle or two after every job. If you don't give them a bottle in the English ports, you see, they can turn nasty."

A soiled grey linen tablecloth was tacked permanently on to the mess-room table, along with the ever-present loaf of white sliced bread and a block of semi-runny margarine (the mess-room, directly above the engine-room, was almost tropical in its heat). The visiting cards of a couple of seamen's missionaries who came aboard to try to interest the crew in churches and museums rather than brothels and bars were tucked into the wiring of the light switch. The ashtray was loaded with cigarette butts and a fishtail from a previous gastronomic experience, and the stuffing was coming out of the padded seats around the table. Broadly, though, the MS *Wester Till* (the *Ashvan*'s original name when launched, since which she'd been through several aliases) was in reasonable shape internally considering her thirty years. She'd been built for river trade in northern Europe, with a correspondingly flat bottom and a low-slung bridge area. She didn't carry much ballast, and although she could cope with most seas when running full, she banged in rough seas when empty, just as she was banging like an empty tin can against the quay in Buckie. Accordingly, after listening carefully to the shipping forecast and noting that none of the fishing boats seemed keen to move, Captain Renton decided that departure that evening would be too unpleasant, if not too dangerous, to attempt, and we all went ashore for a pint.

Captain Renton's habitual gesture was to smooth his long grey hair longitudinally across the top of his head with the flat of his hand. He was in his mid-fifties and had the ease of someone who was so familiar with his tasks and surroundings that he could preclude the need ever to move fast simply by thinking ahead. His clothes sat on him with a similar ease of years of familiarity, and one of his first modifications he had made to the bridge of the *Ashvan* – he was relief skipper and had only recently come aboard – had been to buy a comfortable armchair from a charity shop in Buckie. Professionally he'd come down a bit in the world for no fault of his own, a decline which he felt quite acutely. One of the first things he confided in me was that he'd gone to a public school but he'd done badly at his exams and had been too lazy for sports. He said it rather guiltily, as if expecting me to round on him for wasting his life. But education didn't count for a lot in shipping, he said in gravelly tones. "I know a couple of skippers and quite a few mates who could neither read or write."

"How do they get to be captains?"

He smoothed his hair with his hand. "With these foreign registries, Panama and Liberia etc, you can buy a mate's ticket and sometimes even a captain's, you see. You don't have to prove anything."

He himself had had a long and pretty distinguished career in shipping which was nearing its end rather too early for his own liking. For many years he had skippered round-the-world oil-tankers, in charge of a dozen uniformed officers, a crew of forty-eight and with his own personal steward running around after him. Every meal had been a five-course silver service affair, and his salary at the time had been the same as the Prime Minister's. Eventually he'd given that up to become a river pilot to be closer to his family, but the river had lost its trade and made the pilots redundant, so he went into port consultancy, working for Colonel Gadaffi in Libya establishing an offshore oil-terminal in a desert area. Sometimes while out in the desert he or one of his colleagues had come across grisly remains from the Second World War. Sandstorms would shift whole dunes, revealing tanks and planes full of bodies of soldiers and airmen.

As the conversation had continued, we'd had our glasses replenished by the three Cape Verdes, who were drinking at the bar. Dark skins are quite rare in Scotland and very rare in the fishing ports of the north-east, so the Cape Verdes had become the focus of a certain amount of quiet attention from the handful of morose drinkers at the bar, a couple of whom had been muttering to each other. At this point one of them said something aloud which Santos heard. "Ya, ya want tell mee that again, ya come heeer an I knock you on the cheen," said the engineer, angrily. The fisherman scowled but didn't move. Both men were pretty pissed and they wouldn't have done each other much damage, but Captain Renton wasn't going to wait around to see. Presumably years of seeing the insalubrious side of the world's ports and bars had taught him when it was time to leave, and that time had now come.

Back in the darkened bridge of the *Ashvan* we sat and sipped coffee, watching the road and listening to the thumping of the hull against the quay, and Captain Renton told the story of how, during his ship-owning days, he'd lost one of his own coasters in a night-time collision with one of a pair of Russian trawlers steaming south in the North Sea.

"The two of them were quite far apart and they weren't

showing any fishing lights. That means they were not towing any nets, so I set a course to pass between them." The *Ashvan* banged like an empty drum. The Captain's narration was surprisingly unemotional. "As I got closer, one of them suddenly changed course towards me. I changed course and he changed course some more as if to head me off. We were pretty close by this time so I stopped all engines. It looked as if he was going to pass my stern all right, then at the last moment he swung and rammed me. It took about an hour and a half for us to sink. Fortunately no one was hurt and the Russians picked us up, but only after I'd suggested they do so on the radio. It was all pretty peculiar, because when we got on board it turned out that the skipper was still in bed. I demanded that he be woken up. Anyway, he seemed willing to take us to the nearest port, but someone else on board, a sort of government minder or something, overruled that and in the end a helicopter had to come out to pick us up. I think they realised that if they went into port the vessel would be impounded."

"Presumably you were insured."

"Certainly. My insurance paid up very quickly if I recall, but I don't think they ever recovered the money from the Soviets. If you ask me, the two of them were pair trawling illegally, which was why they were showing no lights, and by going between them I was aiming straight into their gear, so they had to persuade me to change course."

"All the same, ramming you was a bit desperate."

"My guess is that it wasn't deliberate. Whoever was in charge on the bridge decided to let go his gear to let it sink away before I ran over it. It was still attached to the other boat, of course. But what he didn't account for was the effect of letting go your gear on your steering and speed. With all that weight and drag suddenly released, a boat's steering and speed changes completely. Ah-ha, here's our Santos, safe and sound."

The street light revealed the tubby engineer coming reeling down the road. He hovered indecisively by the edge of the quay, head down and riveted by the movement of the *Ashvan*'s deck up and down below him, as if involved in some deep calculations about how much of the movement was due to alcohol and how much due to the sea. Eventually he launched himself off the quay and landed on the planking with a dull thump that we could feel under our feet. The other two Cape Verdes appeared on the road in the distance, walking more steadily.

"All right? No problems?" Captain Renton called down the stairway from the bridge as the singing Santos clambered into the accommodation block. He was roaring drink.

"Nooo. Santos no fighting," he bellowed. "Stupeeed man. I fight heeem no problem but hee not want to fight. Anyway, we go anozzer bar."

For the first couple of hours the following morning Santos was a pale shadow of his usual cheery self. Captain Renton had made clear his intention of leaving early, provided the forecast was good. The forecast must have been acceptable, because the first sound I registered in the morning was Ron the mate banging on Santos's cabin door. "Engine please, Santos," he yelled. "Santos. Wake up. Engine please."

The wind had declined to Force 6, low enough to be no problem, announced Captain Renton over the greasy fry-up created by a sleepy Lindos, who looked as if he'd slept in his wellington boots and Bermudas, while a taciturn Santos was in the bowels of the engine-room, coaxing everything up to the correct pressure. After about forty-five minutes the engineer arrived on the bridge and declared himself satisfied, and as the *Ashvan* left Buckie, he started to apologise stiffly and formally to the Captain for being drunk the previous night; it didn't happen very often, he said, and he hoped he hadn't made a nuisance of himself.

The *Ashvan* loitered along the coast retracing the route which I had followed over the last couple of days. There were Banff and Macduff, there were Gardenstown's houses tacked to the cliff, presented like a target: had the *Ashvan* been a warship, knocking down the houses would be like squashing flies against the windowpane; an artillery man's dream, an architect's nightmare. If ever the world started to rotate the other way, with the prevailing winds and weather suddenly coming from the east and not the west, then the waves would pick Gardenstown's houses off the cliff like a gecko's tongue clearing up squashed flies.

Fraserburgh's lighthouse in the town castle looked like a bandaged thumb, but the most unnatural sight of all was the St

Fergus gas terminal, where forty per cent of the UK's natural gas comes ashore in miles of convoluted piping, valves and tanks amongst the sand dunes of Rattray Bay.

In the early afternoon we parted from the shoreline so as not to be drawn into the Firth of Forth, the sea began to run a bit more heavily and the *Ashvan* began to slam. Everyone took to their beds. The accommodation block became like a deserted village, doors banging and furniture creaking in empty rooms. I slept intermittently, ignoring the call to supper which Lindos had created earlier than ever at just after four o'clock.

I didn't emerge from George's cabin until an uneasy darkness had fallen and the land had become a dark sliver of liver in a grey sandwich. The sea had quieted and both Captain Renton and Ron the mate were on the bridge. In any other context these two men would have had very little in common, but they shared an exhaustive knowledge of boats and skippers, whose names and last locations they were swapping like train enthusiasts. The now calm sea was speckled with the lights of trawlers making up for lost time; the bridge windows rattled gently in their frames and the illuminated dials of the various instruments throbbed gently with the distant pulse of the generator.

"Wells next the Sea is the place," Ron was saying. "Everyone scrambles for the loader there. It takes the longest. You've got three girls in a warehouse on the discharge side, you see," he explained to me. "They've got their names on the doors and they just like sex. No money required."

It sounded a bit of a tall story to me and I said so. "The seaman does have a certain appeal to a certain sort of lady," said Captain Renton, defensively. "You've only got to land in southern Ireland and the boat gets flooded with women offering to do your linen and mend your socks," added Ron.

"Do you ever get women crew?"

"Sometimes. There's a mate around at the moment," said Captain Renton. "Julie."

"Her last boat she had a tussle with the skipper," chimed in Ron. "He wanted to have it away. She chased him off with a knife."

Somewhere at around about midnight the *Ashvan* crossed the border into England; at 1.00 a.m. we were a mile off the harbour at Berwick. The deck lights flooded the scene in front of the bridge and Ron, George and Lindos gathered around the bows to let the anchor go.

Ron woke everyone at six in the morning, but it wasn't until nine that the pilot finally came aboard. I'd got to know Captain Renton well enough to appreciate that extra quietness meant trouble, so I left the bridge and joined the mate on deck. The *Ashvan* bounced off the pier at the narrow entrance to the harbour and Ron fumed. "Fucking idiot's bloody useless," he muttered. "Pilot's a bit off-colour this morning," he bellowed to the dockers who were watching the *Ashvan* lurch unsteadily around the harbour walls and readying themselves for the warp that he was about to throw.

The *Ashvan* touched shore and settled against the wall like a grateful dog come home. She'd be off by nightfall, having loaded more grain, this time for the brewing industry in Bremen. But I was getting off. I gathered together my belongings, said goodbye to everyone, stepped off on to the English quayside and headed up the hill to catch the train to London.

New Year's Day – Epilogue

I've never lived on Skye but my name, written first in the blotchy, spidery writing of a nine-year-old struggling with ink, and henceforth with declining legibility, appears regularly in the visitor's book of the Schoolhouse, in the thirteen-croft township of Heaste. The book is a modern-day memorial tablet to family holidays, to old friendships and early relationships. Therein are names of distant cousins who haven't been seen for years; therein are names of girlfriends whom I've dragged over mountains and through bogs, through grey days, drizzle and downright downpours.

The Schoolhouse is at the end of the road, right on the loch shore. The big, draughty schoolroom where my grandfather learned his lessons is no longer; an ebb and flow of visitors and family plans have reshaped its interior, just as the tides have remodelled the sea-bed outside the front door and slowly taken the wrecked herring boats to pieces. My grandfather's family croft, Number Eleven, is now a ruin with a broken greenhouse resting in the nettles. One of the things you learn, as a child in Skye, is that broken crofts often house the remains of things which crawled in there to die in shelter.

Anyway, they were building again on the land of Number Eleven. They were building in two places in the village – not prettily, of course, but at least they were building. I understood, from what they'd said, that the year had been pretty good. There'd been a wedding; two of the houses that had been standing empty for years and years had been reoccupied, and Neil Mackinnon, who has hands like meatsafes, had got a girlfriend. For a while, a couple of years back, it had seemed as if the village might die on its feet, but – as someone I'd met during the year had said to me – a country with so much beauty in it is never going to be abandoned; Heaste was in the hands of people who loved it, even though they were not necessarily the Scots.

Neil's father, Lachlann, is the elder statesman of the village and was a very good friend of my grandfather's. They used to go poaching together. Not so long ago he would torment me with news of monster fish caught in Loch an Eilean, a mile up the hill behind the house, half an hour's walk from where the road loops in a thin ribbon of steel across the brown moorland. I have spent long, cold hours flogging those dark, silent waters in that most forlorn of places, scared to look over my shoulder lest a kelpie – a mythical child-eating water-horse – had emerged from the swirling cloud. The Loch an Eilean fish have always measured the depth of a fisherman's soul before allowing themselves to be caught: my grandfather was successful up there, says Lachlann. The bard of Heaste, John McGuinness, used to spend all day there with his pipe and he too caught fish, but he was a hard man, a veteran of polar expeditions and quite a poet, it seems, and he could take the isolation. The fish of Loch an Eilean allowed themselves to be caught by him, he'd earned it. I have yet to do so.

When I went to say goodbye to Lachlann up at Number One on the first day of the new year he was sitting in front of a roaring log fire, rather fatigued by the number of visitors he'd received over Hogmanay. A couple of years ago we were all worried that he was going to die; now his eyes were bright as an owl's. He reminded me of the rhyme: "A wise old owl sat in an oak/the more he heard the less he spoke". Ishbel had been the one who'd always ask when I was getting married; Lachlann had spoken less and less in the couple of years since she had died, content to let conversation ripple around him, like a rock in the middle of a stream, getting wiser and wiser from the flow of the waters.

Neil's terrier grabbed my trousers as I clambered into the car. "Are you going back to England now?" asked Neil's son, never separated from his bicycle. It was a question he'd been asking all week.